7

STEPS
TO
SEDUCING
YOUR
Fake Fiancé

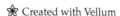 Created with Vellum

Also by Kelly Siskind

Bower Boys Series:

This Can't Be Goodbye

50 Ways to Win Back Your Lover

10 Signs You Need to Grovel

6 Clues Your Nemesis Loves You

4 Hints You Love Your Best Friend

7 Steps to Seducing Your Fake Fiancé

One Wild Wish Series:

He's Going Down

Off-Limits Crush

36 Hour Date

Showmen Series:

New Orleans Rush

Don't Go Stealing My Heart

The Beat Match

The Knockout Rule

Over the Top Series:

My Perfect Mistake, A Fine Mess, Hooked on Trouble

Stand-Alone: Chasing Crazy

Visit Kelly's website and join her newsletter for great giveaways and never miss an update! www.kellysiskind.com

"**Kelly Siskind nails down the "friends-to-lovers" storyline.** Jolene and Cal have a wonderful friendship that explodes with chemistry as they start to admit to themselves that there's more going on than just being BFFs." —Reads and Reviews on 4 Hints You Love Your Best Friend

7
STEPS
TO
SEDUCING
YOUR
Fake Fiancé

A Bower Boys Novel
Kelly Siskind

CHAPTER
One

(Appears as the epilogue at the end of 4 Hints You Love Your Best Friend)

Jake

Being the only sober person at a party blows. Cheers ring out from the beer-pong table, reminding me that tossing a ping-pong ball into a cup is only fun when you're three sheets to the wind. A chick bumps into me and laughs. Someone spills their drink on my boots without so much as a *sorry*, and if Katy Perry's "Firework" plays one more time, I might place an anonymous call to the cops. End this fucking misery.

"Isn't this party the *best*?" Jolene's words run into each other, her brown eyes glazed with happiness and beer. "I'm so glad we came."

"Yeah," I reply, annoyed with myself for my mood.

Even sober, I should be happy. I have a beautiful, sweet girlfriend at my side bopping to this awful song. Makers

Construction just gave me a raise, and I love the carpentry work I do. But I've felt out of sorts lately. Less in sync with Jolene. Distant from my brother Callahan, who's been acting weird. Or maybe I've been the weird one, edgy for reasons I can't explain.

Maybe I'm too old for house parties—twenty-five going on ninety.

Jolene leans her head back and laughs. "I can't believe they're playing this song again."

Yep. That call to the cops might be happening. "They should force prisoners to listen to this song on repeat. Guaranteed no one would break the law again."

"Such a grump," Jo teases.

I make a grumbly sound.

She nudges me with her elbow. "We should dance."

"Hard pass."

"You used to dance with me."

"Katy Perry and I don't mesh."

Jolene's shoulders slump, and I immediately feel like a dick.

I used to dance with her at parties. We'd people watch and laugh and make out in dark corners. At the drive-in, she'd drape herself over me. If we went for burgers—Jo's favorite food—our legs would always be twined together under the table. Tonight, the only times we've touched are when Jo has poked me with her elbow.

I fold my arms, trying to figure out what's wrong with me. Or with us.

Jo bounces her knee to the music and sips her beer. Abruptly, she says, "I'm gonna go chat with Tvisha." She kisses my cheek and heads over to her friend.

I mentally picture myself anywhere but here.

Callahan joins me and bobs his head to this painful song. "You're sober, right?"

Thanks to him, I am. "Since you told me I'm the DD before we left, I think you know the answer to that question."

"Right, cool." Cal twitches awkwardly and nearly drops his drink. Drunk *and* clumsy. "So, yeah, Larkin is a mess, and I told her you'd take her home."

I search out Jo first. She's laughing with Tvisha and another friend, looking way happier than she did standing next to me. "Jo's not ready to go, and I barely know Larkin."

"I don't think Larkin should be here any longer," Cal pushes, gesturing to the blonde sprawled on the couch.

I don't think I've exchanged more than a few words with Larkin, but I remember her from high school—two years below me and ostracized for hooking up with random guys. A double standard that's always bothered me. *Girls who like sex are sluts. Guys are high-fived.* I've seen her at the odd Windfall festival, usually with her much-younger brother, protectively holding his hand.

I look harder at her, notice a sheen in her eyes.

I may barely know Larkin, but I'd say that glassiness is only partly due to alcohol. She looks sad. Still, I don't answer Cal. I'm supposed to be here for Jo.

"Seriously," he says *again*. "You should take Larkin home before some guy decides to drag her upstairs. I'll walk Jo home later."

Imagining any woman being taken advantage of has my shoulders bunching. And he's right—guys are casting glances at Larkin. I don't know all of those dudes, but I know those predatory leers. Like Larkin is theirs to play with if they choose, all because she has some bullshit reputation.

"Tell Jo I'll call her later," I say, already walking over to Larkin. If something bad happened to her, I'd never forgive myself.

When I'm in front of Larkin, her sad eyes flick up to me. "What do you want?"

I crouch and force a smile. "I'm Jake Bower. I'm gonna take you home."

She blinks, that sadness morphing into something sharper. "Why would I get into a stranger's car?"

"I'm not a stranger. We went to school together."

"Right. Mr. Perfect Football Player. Too cool for the likes of me."

Sadly, she's not totally off the mark. I might not have trash-talked girls like Larkin, but I didn't go out of my way to befriend those deemed less cool. "I was a bit of a jerk in high school, but I like to think I've grown out of that bullshit, which we can discuss once you're in my truck. You're drunk and need someone to see you home."

"I'm not drunk," she says on a hiccup.

I raise my eyebrow.

"Fine, I'm *tipsy*. Still don't know why I should trust you."

"For one, I have a girlfriend. I'm not interested in hooking up."

"Having a girlfriend doesn't stop guys from being assholes."

Valid point. "Would it help if I told you my mother would have my hide if I didn't offer to help a woman who looked sad and drunk, while *actual* assholes eyed her like they had the God-given right to do as they pleased?"

I'm not sure why I feel so defensive. My voice has risen, and I've curled my hands into fists, like any guy who stepped close to Larkin would get a right hook to the jaw.

She stares at me for the duration of another agonizing "Firework" chorus, then rolls her eyes. "Fine. Lead me to your chariot."

Good thing she agreed. Tossing her over my shoulder was the next option.

I attempt to help her up, but she shrugs me off with a mumbled "So damn *chivalrous*."

I chuckle under my breath, thankful when we're out of that noisy house.

"I think my ears are bleeding," she says plaintively. "Fucking Katy Perry."

"I was seconds from waterboarding myself to end the misery."

She snorts. "A week of medieval rat torture would be better than listening to that song on repeat."

I glance at her profile, can't help noticing the cute slope of her nose. "What's medieval rat torture?"

She stops and faces me. Her blue-green eyes are no longer sad or sharp. *Villainous* is the only way to describe them. "They shoved rats in a cage and placed the cage over a victim's stomach. Then they agitated the rats by heating the cage until the rodents were frantic enough to gnaw through the person's stomach—anything to escape the fire. Death by rat gnawing," she adds with flair.

"You're disturbing," I say, twitching at the visual.

"But it's cool, right?"

"If you're a sadistic villain."

"Maybe *you* should be afraid of getting into a vehicle with *me*."

I laugh. "We should both text friends. Let them know our last known location."

I pull out my phone to take a picture of her. She sticks out her tongue and pulls a face, being adorably goofy.

"Now I'm really scared," I add and take the shot. I pretend to send the picture to someone, hoping it encourages her to actually tell a friend I'm taking her home. I want her to feel safe with me. "Your turn."

With a headshake, she pulls out her phone and takes her time lining up the shot. I watch while she fiddles with her phone, using the seconds to examine the greenish flecks in her blue eyes, the thick sweep of her mascara-lined eyelashes. Her blond hair falls in layered strands around her face. Her cheeks are pink from blush or alcohol. A one-inch scar beside her nose gives her feminine features an edge, and the word *sexy* pops into my mind.

There's no denying Larkin Gray's appeal. To *other* guys.

I raise my eyebrow, unsure what's taking her so long. The pink on her cheeks deepens, and she fumbles with her phone.

"Sent," she says quickly and pockets her cell. "My brother is at a friend's house on the other side of town. If you rat torture me, he now knows who you are, and you do *not* want my brother pissed at you."

"Isn't your brother, like, ten years younger than you?"

"Right, yeah." Her brow furrows and her nose twitches. "I just mean he's at a sleepover and he'll talk your ear off—worse than listening to Katy Perry."

I side-eye her as I unlock the passenger side of my truck. I'm not sure what Larkin is hiding, but it doesn't take a genius to notice the oddness of her reply.

I grab her elbow to help her step up into my truck, but she pauses. Larkin is a tall girl. Just under six feet, if I had to guess. The way we're standing, with her head tipped back as she gazes up at me, her lips are closer to mine than I'm used to.

"Thank you," she says softly. "Most guys I know aren't this nice."

"If guys aren't nice to you, you should tell them to fuck off."

Her answering smile is tight. "Easier said than done."

She glances down at her wrist. There's a faint bruise there I hadn't noticed, and anger has me seeing red. "Did someone hurt you, Larkin?"

She ducks her head and gets up into my truck, hiding her face from me. "It's nothing, and it's been handled."

I'm about to open my mouth and tell her any kind of bruise isn't nothing, but she grabs the door and slams it shut.

I don't know Larkin. We have zero relationship, but my mother made it a point to tell us often and forcefully that hurting a girl, even accidentally, was never acceptable—a too-firm grab, not listening if they said no for any reason at any moment, taking advantage when a girl was drunk and not of clear mind. Chelsea Bower has five sons, all of us tall and strong, and she drilled it into us that we have a responsibility to keep women safe and always treat them with respect. Or to step in if we see a girl in trouble.

To this day, the idea of a man hurting any woman has always infuriated me. How cruel and insecure does an asshole have to be to stoop that low?

And Larkin has a fucking bruise on her wrist.

By the time I'm in my front seat, my teeth hurt from clenching my jaw. Larkin is staring out her window. I shouldn't say anything more. She's not mine to look after or defend. Unfortunately, my mother did too good a job of baking in my protective gene.

"When you say the issue has been dealt with, what do you mean?"

"This isn't your concern, Jake."

"I'm making it my concern."

"So damn bossy," she mumbles, hunching farther away from me.

I stare out my windshield, debating my options. None of which are *let this go*. Larkin has no reason to trust me, unless I give her one.

"I broke in to my father's office last week."

She glances at me sharply. "Why?"

"There's something about him lately I don't trust. I mean, we've never been close, but he's been acting odd this year. More distant than usual. Traveling for work, when accountants like him don't normally leave their offices."

I have to support a client who's being audited, he told Mom.

I no longer live at home, but I'm there for family dinners. Mom didn't flinch when explaining why he hadn't been around much lately, but I sure as hell took notice. I'd recently caught him in a lie. I'd called him at home to discuss a time-sensitive birthday gift for Mom—concert tickets to Kenny Chesney that needed to be purchased the next morning. Mom said Dad was working late. I called him at his office and he didn't answer, so I went by. He wasn't there.

Assuming he'd stepped out for something to eat, I waited for a while, but he never showed. The next day, when I asked how late he worked the night prior, he said he was at his office all evening.

At which point, I got really fucking mad.

Mom's lectures to watch out for women may have been meant for younger girls we met and dated. As far as I'm concerned, I would also protect my mother with my last breath.

"I think he's having an affair," I tell Larkin—pissed-off words I've never spoken aloud. "I didn't find anything in his office, but I can't shake this feeling that he's going to break my mother's heart."

"Have you talked to your brothers about it? Are they also suspicious?"

"Haven't told them yet. We're all pretty protective of Mom. If I'm off base, I don't want to rile them up."

"And what does Jolene think?"

"Haven't told her either." Which feels odd at the moment. I've debated discussing my concerns with Jo. I just…never do. "You're the only person I've told."

She huffs out an incredulous breath. "Well, that's weird."

"Is it, though?" I'm angry about her bruise and my suspicions about my father, but I force gentleness into my tone. "Feels easier sharing this thing that scares me with a virtual stranger. Someone who won't judge me or my family. Someone who isn't emotionally involved. Honestly, saying it out loud felt pretty damn good."

Her eyes roam over my face, more emotion softening her features. Then she scoffs. "Save your psychobabble for someone with a lower IQ. I see what you're doing, sharing bullshit so I'll do the same. So fucking lame."

She returns to staring out her window, and I sigh. "I wasn't lying, Larkin. I'm upset about my parents and haven't told anyone, but I get that whatever you're going through is tough. If you need to talk to someone at any point, you can come find me."

She doesn't answer.

At a loss, I turn on my truck and start driving. I ask where she wants to be dropped, and she mumbles her address. I ask what she did during the day. She says, "Not much."

Her stonewalling is irritating, but telling someone about my dad *did* feel good. Those negative thoughts have been weighing me down for a while. Sooner rather than later, I'll need to confront my father or do more intense sleuthing. Head things off before they get worse. Maybe tell my brothers. Or just Callahan. He's the most level-headed.

"I have two half brothers," Larkin whispers suddenly.

We're a few blocks from her house, but I pull over and park at the curb, my heart knocking a faster beat. I don't say anything. Whatever she's sharing sounds personal. Pushing will only make her clam up.

She stares straight ahead and nibbles her lip. "My birth father is Otto Briggs."

That wakes me the fuck up. "*The* Otto Briggs who broke in to Malcolm Boyd's body shop and stole his cars?" The same lowlife who sold drugs to local kids.

"The one and only. Great DNA running through my veins."

"How come I've never heard that before?"

"He's not on my birth certificate and never lived with us. My brother Julian has a different dad, and my mother warned us no one in this town could know who mine was or I'd basically be crucified."

She's not wrong. As much as I love Windfall and wouldn't

want to live anywhere else, the gossip junkies here aren't always kind. Having links to a man who sold drugs to underage kids would have been brutal. But she's telling me.

"When you said you messaged your brother that you're getting a ride with me, you meant Otto's son?"

She nods. "Hunter and I are really close. He lives in Ruby Grove, but he's visiting a friend in town tonight. He's a good guy and super protective of me—hates Otto and all the shit that comes with sharing that man's last name."

"I'm glad you have someone who's got your back."

"Yeah, but like with your family, his reactions can be intense." She runs her fingers over the bruise on her delicate wrist. "I never told him things got scary with Derek. They used to be friends, but things went south when Derek stiffed Hunter on some cash he owed. Hunter *warned* me the guy was bad news." Her voice quiets. "I should have listened."

My fury threatens to rise again, but I force it to settle. I take a deep breath and say, "Will you tell *me* about Derek?"

Her next swallow stutters down her neck. "We started dating about five months ago, and he was nice enough. A bit of a bad boy, but not, like, a bad *guy*. Things got serious fast. I basically moved in to his house after a few months. Then a friend of his got out of jail, and they started hanging out more. Derek isn't a good drunk and was going on benders, during the day and stuff, staying out all hours. We fought way too often—verbally, not physically." Her exhale trembles. "Until Monday."

I don't say a thing. There's no way my tone will be kind or gentle. I grip the steering wheel and wait for her to go on.

"I decided to end things and went over to tell him and grab my stuff, which included my passport that I need for an upcoming road trip. He got mad and got...physical." She touches her neck, as though imagining his hands on her throat. "I kneed him in his nuts and told him to never contact me, but I didn't get my clothes or my passport, so I'm kind of screwed right now."

I look closer at her neck. The faintest bruise stains her smooth skin. "That fucking asshole."

"Isn't this supposed to be a safe space where you're not emotionally involved?"

She's right. It is. But there's no changing my nature. "Give me your phone."

"What?"

"Give me your phone. I'm putting my number in there. Your brother doesn't live close. If you ever hear from this prick again, or get caught in a bad situation with him, you're gonna call me."

"Why do you care? I'm the girl everyone calls a stupid slut."

This fucking town. "Your sexual history is nobody's business but your own. Anyone who makes you feel bad because of anything you've done isn't worth your time."

Her lips tip up into a sweet smile. "I hope Jolene knows how lucky she is to have you."

I blink at my lap, the same edginess I felt at the party returning tenfold. "Things are changing between us. I don't fully understand it. We have tons in common. She loves everything I love, even watching sports and going fishing. But things have been...strained lately."

"Have you talked with her about it?"

I shake my head, scrub my hand over my jaw. "Maybe we're just growing apart." Or I need to make more of an effort. Do something nice for her. Break us out of this rut.

"Whatever you do," Larkin says, "honor yourself. If you love her, fight for her. If your feelings have changed, don't string her along. Women aren't dumb. My bet is she knows something's up."

I nod. Jolene is far from dumb. She's smart and sassy, sweet and hot. Everything I should want. But I look at Larkin—this girl I barely know—and I feel strangely connected to her. I'm not sure why telling her my secrets has been so easy. Why the mix of green and blue in her eyes seems to suck me in.

Larkin holds out her phone. "If the offer still stands, I'd actually like your number. I'll feel safer if I have someone to call."

"Good," I say gruffly. I enter my digits into her phone and send myself a text. But I can do better than being a standby bouncer. "Is Derek home on Saturday nights?"

She curls her lip. "Doubtful. He's for sure wasted at that biker bar outside of town."

"How do you feel about a little breaking and entering?"

Her eyes spark. "What do you have in mind?"

"You need your passport and clothes, so we take back what's yours. If I'm with you, and he happens to come home, he won't be able to lay a finger on you." And I might get the chance to sink my fist into the asshole's face.

"Really?"

I turn my truck back on. "Consider me the Clyde to your Bonnie."

"Is that some crack because I'm the progeny of Otto Briggs?"

"You should be proud of the relation. Takes a strong woman to rise above her degenerate parent. Tell me where we're going."

I feel her attention on my profile as she explains that Derek lives in the house by the junkyard. After a beat, she says, "You, Jake Bower, weren't this kind and thoughtful during high school."

Busted. "I was an obnoxious jock."

"And brain-cell challenged. I remember something about you jumping off Amari Harper's roof into his pool, like you were an invincible superhero."

I smile at that wild memory. I honestly thought I had nine lives. "As idiotic as that was, it wasn't my fault. According to my mom, you can't grow balls and brains at the same time. That's why men take longer to mature."

She laughs, so hard tears leak from her eyes. "I like your mom."

"She's the best." Which has me angry with my father all over again.

I can't go to Mom about his possible affair until I have proof. And then what? I tell her and watch her fall apart? I don't tell her and live with the knowledge of his deceit? My stomach pitches and my palms turn damp. Maybe my instincts are off base. Maybe he really has been helping clients out of town. That office lie could have been a misunderstanding.

By the time I park outside a run-down bungalow near the junkyard, I'm freshly frustrated.

The lights in the house are off. There are no vehicles in the driveway. "Doesn't look like he's home."

"Based on his typical nights, he won't be home for another hour or so, and the neighbors on the other streets are super nice. I've always felt safe when walking to my mom's from here, but I wouldn't have had the guts to come on my own. So, thanks for doing this."

"Glad I could be here," I say, but I can't shake thoughts of my parents.

Larkin doesn't move to get out. She places her hand on my thigh. "You're worried about your mom."

"Am I that easy to read?"

"To me, you are. Which is kinda odd, considering we only officially met tonight."

Except I can somehow sense Larkin's troubles too. "If I'm right—if he's having an affair—it'll crush her."

She leans closer and squeezes my leg. "Only a strong woman could raise you five boys and live to tell the tale. And she has you to lean on. Whatever happens, you'll all get through it."

The pressure on my chest eases. "Thanks. I think I needed to hear that."

She smiles kindly, but her attention drops to my mouth.

Instantly, heat swells in my groin. More than appreciation spreads through my sternum. Larkin's bottom lip is fuller than her top—the kind of plump lip that makes a man feel thirsty.

Suddenly, the pressure of her hand on my thigh becomes unbearably intense.

Neither of us moves. The air seems to thicken with unspoken tension, our chests rising in tandem, until we both lean forward, like we're magnetized. Drawn toward each other. And the urge to kiss Larkin slams into me. So forcefully, I jerk back and bang my head into my headrest.

"Passport," she says as she uselessly pats her hair. "I'll just run in and grab my bag and passport. Then I'll be out, and you can drive me home."

"No," I bark, hating my harsh tone. How unraveled I suddenly feel.

I don't wait for her reply. I rev my engine and turn us around.

I feel fucking turned around.

I'm in a relationship. I love Jolene. At least, I used to. Maybe still do. And I was a millisecond away from kissing another woman.

What the hell is wrong with me?

Larkin braces her hand against the dash. "What do you mean, no? Why are we leaving?"

"This was a bad idea. You shouldn't be here. I'll take you to your mother's."

"But I want to get my stuff."

"And I said *no*." I need Larkin out of my truck. Away from me. Even now, I want to pull over, drag her into my lap, claim her mouth.

I press my foot on the gas, driving faster than I should.

Larkin's confusion is palpable, as is her anger as she says, "Stop."

"I'm taking you home."

"And I want out."

"Not until you're safe."

"Yeah, well, I don't feel safe with you anymore, so stop the fucking truck!"

Her words are a punch to my gut.

I instantly pull over, gripping my steering wheel so hard my knuckles whiten. I'm not surprised Larkin is uncomfortable. I'm shaking with barely contained self-hatred. I nearly kissed her a second ago, even though I told her I'm not the type of asshole who'd cheat on his girlfriend. Maybe I'm more like my father than I thought.

I should say something. Apologize, convince Larkin to let me drive her home.

I stare out the windshield and inwardly fume.

"Oh my God," she suddenly says.

Her tone sounds so shocked, I glance at her. "What?"

Fury burns a blotchy path up her neck. "Did someone dare you to drive me home and hook up with the town slut? Is that what's going on here? You thought you'd get in my pants but chickened out last minute?"

Hell no, is what I should say. Tell her the truth. I wanted to kiss her a minute ago. I want to devour her now. But I'm on a date with my girlfriend tonight—the only woman I should be devouring. I need to get back to that party. See Jolene. Kiss *her*. Make things right with *her*.

Feeling ill, I shrug. "Just let me drive you home, okay?"

Larkin's glassy eyes widen. "I am *such* an idiot."

She leans away from me like I'm contagious. Quickly, she shoves her door open and nearly falls while scrambling out. She slams the door so hard my truck rattles.

I roll down the window, thinking of ways to backpedal and erase the hurt from Larkin's face. "You sure you're okay to walk home from here?" is my genius retort.

She lifts her middle finger. "Have a nice fucking life, Jake Bower."

I know this area. It's safe. I'm the one who doesn't feel safe near Larkin Gray, but I don't like leaving her like this. Still, I pull my truck out and speed away from her.

———

Larkin

"Unbelievable," I mutter as I watch Jake's truck peel away.

My asshole radar is clearly on the fritz. I mean, how did I miss the signs? How didn't I see the creep under Jake's sweet-talking? I actually believed that shit about his parents. His stress over his relationship with Jolene. His care for *me*.

The jerk should be nominated for an Academy Award, and I need a reality check.

I was nothing but a joke to Jake Bower. The target of a cruel trick—make the slut feel safe and worthwhile for a minute, then take what you want.

My next exhale sounds like a growl.

Lampposts light the large trees and small bungalows on this part of Birch Street. A cat ambles on a front lawn, watching me—Lola, by the looks of her size and bushy tail. Hopefully she was out terrorizing the boys on the block.

"Men are such assholes," I tell her.

She mewls. I take that as an agreement, but I don't feel better.

I rub my eyes, barely resisting the urge to dig my nails into my cheeks. I am so *tired* of men using me. Of being physically weaker. Scared. Judged. A freaking damsel in distress, needing to be saved. It's time I find my backbone and take charge of my life.

What better time than the present?

Swallowing down tonight's humiliation, I turn and strut for Derek's home. I need my clothes and passport. Derek won't be home for ages, and I'm a strong, capable girl. The type of fierce woman who solves her own problems.

The last thing I need is Jake Bower to have my back.

CHAPTER
Two

L ARKIN

The second I step into Derek's bungalow, my bravery takes a
runner. The floorboards creak, and I flinch. Wind sends a branch
dragging against a window, and I shiver.

Technically, there's nothing scary about the stained brown
couch and lopsided curtains decorating this run-down house.
But decor doesn't create as much atmosphere as memories.

Mine catch me in a fierce hold—the strength of Derek's grip
on my wrist, his fingers digging down. Being shoved against the
wall, his hand on my neck while I struggled to breathe and
fought back, my knee finally slamming into his nuts.

Sweat gathers along my upper lip.

I debate leaving my passport and clothes, but giving up
means jerks like Derek and Jake win. I'm done letting them win.

I hurry to the bedroom, ignoring the sour stench and laundry
scattered on the floor. I find my duffel bag in the closet and
shove my clothes inside. My passport is still in the end-table

drawer, thank God. With everything gathered, I head for the living room, but I'm no calmer.

I'm breathing hard. Tearing up. I keep replaying Jake's stunt and my gullibility. I still can't believe he had the gall to try to take advantage of me, as though I'd ever let that happen.

Despite what this loudmouthing town thinks, I've never hooked up with a guy in a relationship. And I never would. Sure, I was mistakenly attracted to Jake. I felt instantly comfortable with him. We laughed easily together. I even shared the thing I never share, confessing I'm the daughter of Otto Briggs.

But I wouldn't have kissed him. Not while he was in a relationship.

Now I have to hope he doesn't blab about my father to his buddies. Ruin my life in this town.

I inhale deeply and try to silence my racing thoughts. I take one last glance at Derek's small house he inherited when his dad passed away. Dirty dishes are stacked on the counter. Open alcohol bottles and rolled joints litter most surfaces, along with more discarded clothing.

"Never again," I mutter.

Never again will I date a loser who treats me like shit. Never again will I trust a cruel man like Jake. My reputation with guys shouldn't matter. Who my father is doesn't determine my worth.

Those assholes should think twice before messing with me.

I'm not sure what comes over me then, but I grab one of Derek's dirty dinner plates and drop it on the floor. I jump when it breaks, but I feel a jolt of courage. "Who's in charge now, fucker?"

I grab a glass next and hurl it against the wall, followed by another and a half-full bottle of vodka. It explodes in a glorious mess. Nothing will undo Derek's abuse or Jake's humiliating joke, but I feel more in control than I've felt in ages.

Until I realize Derek will know it was me who trashed his place.

My clothes and passport will suddenly be gone. The shattered glass won't be considered a coincidence. Might as well hang a *guilty* sign around my neck.

Shit.

Rushing, I grab my stuff and get out quick as I can.

"I just have to make it a couple of blocks," I say out loud, attempting to calm my nerves.

Birch Street isn't too far ahead. Once I get back there, I'll be safe. More lampposts brighten the area, and actual houses are around. Even if Derek comes home early, he'll be driving from the opposite direction. He won't see me after that bend.

"I'm fine," I say as I hurry. "Totally fine. One foot in front of the other."

My pulse doesn't get the memo. My heart is hammering loud enough to wake the dead, and my hands are shaking.

Two steps later, a faint noise joins the cacophony in my head —the squeal of a loose drive belt. Forget a revving pulse. I hit full panic mode.

I know a piece-of-crap muscle car that makes a similar sound, and the noise is getting louder. I should run. Race away to find cover and hide. Everything in me atrophies.

When headlights whip around the corner, I bite my cheek and *move.*

Without any houses to hide behind, I run to a large hickory tree and huddle behind the trunk. Derek races by without pausing. He parks his Barracuda at his house as I hold my breath and plaster myself tighter to the tree. He steps from his car, sways a moment. Sits his ass on the trunk and lights a cigarette.

Not good.

Any minute, he'll go in and see the mess I made. If I run for Birch Street, he'll see *me.*

I fumble for my phone to call my brother, but I can't seem to press Call. Hunter warned me Derek was bad news. If I tell him why I'm here, he'll be mad and disappointed, get annoyed I was this dumb. The cops certainly aren't an option. Breaking and entering, property damage—I'm the only criminal here tonight.

Why the hell did I trash Derek's place?

I steal another glance at him. He's still smoking, watching the street.

I hover my thumb over Hunter's name but find it shifting to Jake's. I hate that he put his contact in my phone. He seemed genuine at the time. Caring and sweet. Like he'd help if I was in trouble, which makes his trick even more infuriating.

…Unless I was wrong about him.

Maybe he freaked out because we almost kissed and he actually liked me. Maybe if I call, he'll help me out of this mess.

Or he won't, and I'll feel worse.

Unfortunately, I'm low on friends and choices and find myself calling the last person I want to see right now.

Jake's line rings. I bite my lip and bounce my heel. For some unfathomable reason, hope builds in my chest. I picture Jake seeing my name. Worrying about me. Feeling like shit about driving away and hurrying back to make amends.

But he doesn't answer, and my hope crashes and burns.

Yep, I feel worse.

This was more proof I'm delusional and Jake doesn't have a caring bone in his body.

When his voice mail clicks on, I hiss out a quiet "Asshole. You told me to call if I'm scared and Derek's nearby. Well, I'm fucking *scared*, Jake. Guess you lied about that too."

I end the call and nearly smash my phone. Short on options, I stay huddled in my spot and pray Derek gets tired and passes out on the street, then I peek around the tree again.

Derek isn't there.

Muffled shouts come from his home—for sure rants about me

—and I don't wait around to see if he barrels out of there. I call my brother as I lift my bag and run toward Birch Street.

"Hey, Runt," Hunter says when he answers. That cute nickname doesn't dent my panic. "Thought you had a ride home."

"Hunter, I need help…" My shaky words trail off.

"Larkin." There's worry in his tone now. "I'm still in town, already in my truck. Tell me where you are. I'm coming."

Tears sting my eyes. No one knows how sweet and kind Hunter is. They see his stormy eyes and tattoos, and hear his last name, and they assume he's just as worthless as our degenerate dad. But he's never broken a law. He doesn't drink or mess around. He's taking night classes, on his way to earning an academic scholarship to study engineering and will prove how smart and capable he is.

He's a better human than me.

"I'm on Hickory Street by the junkyard. The guy who was supposed to be with me took off, and Derek just got home and—"

"Larkin!" a slurred voice bellows. "You fucking bitch! Where the fuck are you?"

"What the hell was that?" Hunter says, sounding less controlled.

I stop and glance over my shoulder. Derek is lit by his front porch light, scanning the area, practically frothing at the mouth. I see it the second he spots me—the same sneer when I told him our relationship was over. This grimace looks even more deranged.

"Fuck." I stumble and drop my bag.

Gripping my phone like it's a lifeline, I tear off to the side, heading for the fence surrounding the junkyard. If I can climb and hop over the barbed wire, I can maybe lose him. Long enough for Hunter to get here and drive us away.

"The fence," I tell Hunter, who's breathing hard in my ear.

"Derek's after me. I'm close to the Birch Street end of the junkyard. I'm gonna climb over, but I need to put the phone down."

"I'm a minute away. That asshole won't lay a hand on you. Not with me there. All you have to do is climb."

I nod, even though he can't see me. I want to cry at his instant loyalty.

I should have called him first.

Stashing my phone in my back pocket, I run, but the pound of footfalls gets closer, along with a shouted "You fucking bitch!"

I don't pause or look back. I run *hard*. Nearly fall over a metal pipe strewn across the grass. When I'm close enough, I launch myself at the chain-link fence like I'm some kind of Navy SEAL. But Navy SEALs don't quake with fear while tears sting their eyes.

The wire digs into my hand. My foot fumbles to get a hold. I finally get traction and haul myself up, but Derek's wheezy breaths are louder, his mumbled curses getting closer.

I scramble up, feel the bite of barbed wire as I reach the top. I don't quit. I press into the pain and haul myself upward, but a hand grabs my ankle and tugs.

My fall backward is both swift and slow. Like I've been shoved from an airplane and am falling into nothing...until my back *cracks* into the ground.

The wind whooshes out of my lungs.

I'm so stunned I don't react at first. I can't draw in enough air. Derek is over me, straddling me, holding me down with his hand around my neck. His eyes are crazed, glassy with alcohol and rage. Nowhere in that manic expression is the guy who gave me a tulip on our first date.

"Please," I manage before his fingers dig harder into my throat.

I flail. I try to kick up and grab him. He's too strong. Spots cloud my vision. Tears stream from my eyes. *Fight*, I think. My limbs barely respond. A distant shout registers, then there's slightly less pressure on my neck. Derek is miraculously off me.

I cough as I try to scramble away, only managing to curl onto my side.

"Larkin. It's okay. It's over. You're okay. Please tell me you're okay."

A gentle hand is on me, pulling me up. Huge arms cradle me against a warm chest.

Hunter.

Instantly, I bawl. Gasping sobs into his chest as he rocks me and tells me over and over I'm safe. At one point, I vaguely register him talking on his phone. Breathing hurts where Derek had my neck in his grip. My eyes are on fire from crying, but Hunter is on the ground with me, rubbing my back.

When I actually feel safer, I look around.

Derek is nearby, sprawled on the grass with a nasty gash on his head.

He's not moving.

The broken pipe I tripped over is beside him, and the end is bloody.

A new fear seizes me. "Is he alive?"

"He's just knocked out," Hunter says, but he sounds kind of wooden. Freaked out, if I didn't know better. "I've called the cops. Everything'll be fine, but you need to get out of here."

I shoot him a frantic look. "What?"

"You need to go, Runt. If the cops see you here, you'll have to explain why you called me. They'll figure out who your father is. It won't be pretty."

"No way. I'm not leaving you."

"Yes, *you fucking are.* Trust me when I say this won't end well for you. I can handle the backlash with the cops, been through it before. But I won't stand by and watch them drag you down. The second they know who your father is, they won't treat you fairly."

7 STEPS TO SEDUCING YOUR FAKE FIANCÉ   25

"But this is *my* fault. And it was self-defense. You're only here because I called you."

"Larkin." Hunter holds the back of my neck in a reassuring grip. "You are not to blame here. That fucker had no right to touch you. No man ever has the right to hurt a woman."

"Then come with me. Leave him here for the cops to find."

His jaw pulses. "It's not the right thing to do."

God. How could people assume this righteous man is a lowlife like our father?

"Hunter," I say, pleading now. "I get it. I really do, but Derek doesn't deserve your kindness."

"This isn't kindness. This is right versus wrong. If given the opportunity, I'd split his brainless head open again. That's how much I love you. But listen carefully, because I'll only say this once." He heaves out a rough breath. "If you stay here right now, we're done. I'll cut you out of my life."

"Wh-what?"

"I can't watch the cops come down on you because of scum like Derek and our father. I *won't*. You need to get the fuck away from here, and you need to do it now."

Distant sirens punctuate his ominous warning, but I don't move. I glance again at Derek, his limp body. The bloody pipe. He doesn't look like he's breathing.

"Hunter?" My voice trembles.

"It's okay, Runt." He helps me to my feet and squeezes my shoulder. "I can handle myself. Go home and clean those cuts on your hands. I'll call you later."

I flex my fingers, flinching at the sudden pain. I'd forgotten about the barbed wire, but the cuts sting now, along with my eyes.

The sirens get louder. My residual fear claws back to life. "You're sure?"

He winks, pretending like this is any other night, not a waking nightmare. "I've got this."

I'm not sure he does, but I don't ask again. I rush for my dropped bag and run, needing to get away from Derek's motionless body. My bad decisions. This horrible night. I keep to the shadows, struggling to breathe through my sore throat.

Hunter will be fine. He grew up with Otto Briggs. He's used to dealing with cops.

Unfortunately, I'm dead wrong.

CHAPTER

Three

TWELVE YEARS LATER

L<small>ARKIN</small>

I ease my foot off the gas, still awed I'm living back in Windfall. There was a time I never wanted to see my hometown again. Give me a match and light this sucker up.

Apparently, time does heal some wounds.

A crisp breeze blows through my lowered window as I drive down Main Street. Fall flower displays liven up the cobblestone sidewalks and cute patios. Brightly colored banners hang off the old-fashioned lampposts, each printed with pictures of adorable dogs and ponies for the upcoming Dog and Pony Show.

No word of a lie. Windfall is hosting an actual *Dog and Pony Show*.

I've been back here for six months, and this town still clearly loves its ridiculous festivals. And hopefully supporting locally owned businesses. Tonight is the grand reopening of the bar I now co-own. Anything less than a raging success is unacceptable.

Dave Tanaka pauses from sweeping outside his hardware store and waves to me. "Big night."

I check my rearview mirror and brake. "Do you have good news for me?"

"I'm offended you even asked."

"Sorry, let me rephrase. Since you, *of course*, have what I ordered, what time should our deal go down?"

"I can be ready in five minutes," he says, mimicking a mafia boss. "Bring the cash. And come alone."

I jut out my chin. "Don't you dare back out on me, Tanaka."

He scowls, and we share a laugh.

In addition to owning the town hardware store, Dave does gorgeous art and calligraphy. I gave him two mini puffy-jacket-shaped beer holders. On one side, he's painting the Barrel House's logo. On the other, it will say: *Touch my beer and die.*

Who wouldn't want to win that raffle prize at tonight's launch?

Unless the crowd I expect doesn't show. Unless people somehow learn who my father is and boycott the bar. Or they might decide the girl who had a *false* reputation for stealing boyfriends should be "canceled."

A rush of nerves hits me, but I force it down. My jitters are normal. Jolene is anxious too, but my new business partner and closest friend knew we'd make a good team. She let me buy in to the Barrel House because we had a solid vision and plan for its resurrection.

Our reopening will be a smashing success.

Focusing on the positive, I smile as I drive toward a parking spot on the street.

I continue smiling as I park close to Sugar and Sips, where I'll buy treats for our staff. That's the kind of boss I plan to be.

Tough but fun, empowering employees through positive reinforcement.

I smile as I hop out of my rust-flecked Toyota and lock my door, double-checking that the finicky handle is actually locked. My old girl gets temperamental.

I smile as I ready to cross the street, then I hear a woman call, "Jake!"

The edges of my lips plummet.

I stand stiffly, the ability to move whooshing out of me in a blink. It's just a moment. A millisecond of emotional paralysis, but it happens every time I'm in the vicinity of the Worst Person in the World.

I don't want to look at him. I *shouldn't* look.

My darn eyes have cut off communication with my brain.

And yep. There *he* is, chatting with Mrs. Jackson as though he's a congenial guy people should like and trust.

Liar.

His thick muscles are emphasized in his gray Henley. He's wearing a wool hat, as has been his habit of late, and he's recently grown a short beard. His wide stance is commanding and comfortable at the same time, which pisses me off, even though I should be used to seeing Jake.

Windfall is the size of a dehydrated pea. When I decided to move back, I already knew Jake and his family had returned. I'm aware his father was some kind of criminal accountant, who laundered money for a drug cartel. I know the Bower family spent ten years in witness protection. My first thought when I saw that tidbit on the news was *Karma is a bitch, and I like her*. But I remembered my one night with Jake, his suspicions that his father was acting weird, maybe cheating on his mother.

For the span of a galloped heartbeat, compassion throbbed behind my ribs. Jake knew something was off with his dad. I have no doubt the reality of the situation hit him like a sledgehammer.

Then I pictured the last time I saw my brother. The tension in Hunter's massive shoulders. The hard yet vacant look in his eyes.

If I had a sledgehammer, I'd aim for Jake's nuts.

He doesn't glance my way while he talks to Mrs. Jackson. Aside from the first handful of times I saw him after moving back, he never looks at me. Might have something to do with my death glares. Or more likely, I'm just a minor blip on his radar. That random girl he played a trick on twelve years ago.

Tearing my gaze away, I cross the street and march into Sugar and Sips. I breathe in the caramelized sugar and coffee smells, forcing my shoulders to drop. The owner, Delilah, is behind the counter, finishing up with a customer.

When I step up next, she gives a happy clap. "I can't believe it's tonight already."

"It's tonight," I confirm brightly, finding my inner Zen.

"Is everything ready?"

"It will be." *After* I get to the Barrel House, prep the last few cocktail garnishes, hang the final sign on the wall, and go over service with tonight's staff. "We're expecting a crowd."

"Is Jolene going out of her mind?"

"She's a minor stress case, but she's excited."

"The whole *town* is excited. And I was thinking about some cross-promo stuff we can do. Like, shared follows on social media to be entered into a draw, maybe feature each other on our menus. You know, help boost our female owned-and-operated businesses."

"Count me in for the girl power." Because I'm one of those women now. An actual business owner! Co-owner, but whatever. I'm an upstanding businesswoman, not the slut who supposedly slept around town. Not the girl who couldn't afford trendy clothes or new shoes.

I am Larkin Gray, upstanding woman who cross-promotes with her friends.

"We'll hash out some ideas soon," I say. "For now, I need a medium roast coffee and one of your addictive lemon pomegranate bars for me, and enough sugary treats to pump my staff full of energy for the entire night. Dealer's choice."

Delilah beams. "My favorite kind of customer."

I wander to the side and notice a bookshelf I haven't seen before. It's painted a soft pink with delicately stenciled flowers along the sides. The shelves are partly full, and the sign at the top reads, Free Library: Take One, Leave One.

I drag my hand down the smooth edge. "Delilah, this is such a great idea."

"Thanks, but it wasn't mine. Oh!" she says, kind of screaming the word. "Hi, *Jake*. It's so nice of you to stop by, *Jake*. What brings you by, *Jake*?"

Jesus. *Again?*

My body hits its usual locked-and-loaded pose, like I'm simultaneously frozen and ready to launch a grenade. Delilah isn't helping. She dates Jake's youngest brother, E, and the whole family is nauseatingly close. None of them knows why I despise Jake. I'm not sure why he didn't tell them, and it's just as well. I can't have people learning about my lineage. The early stages of a new business are too fragile to unleash Windfall's gossip hounds.

Unfortunately, Jake's brothers are irritatingly nosy. They won't quit prodding for the dirt on *why* Jake is Enemy Number One. The women in their lives, however, like Delilah and Jolene, make their love of Jake known, while still having my back.

I adore Delilah for warning me Jake is in my vicinity, but she's as horrible at subtlety as a circus clown.

I don't turn, but I hear Jake clear his throat. "I got a few more books for the shelves. My mom had some lying around."

"Oh, sure," Delilah says. "That's great. And thanks again for the library idea and building the case. The flowers you stenciled are perfect. Customers are loving the whole vibe."

"Glad it's been well received." His tone is low and gruff. Quiet, when I don't think of Jake as quiet.

I move to the side of the shelves and sneak a look over my shoulder. He's focused on the bookcase he apparently built for Delilah, which I'm no longer sure is such a great idea. He doesn't glance my way. Just ignores me like I'm not standing beside the furniture they're discussing.

"You're all set," Delilah calls to me. "You got my last lemon pomegranate bar."

I inhale deeply and try to resuscitate my good mood. "Must be my lucky day. Thanks for being an amazing baker. And a kind *friend*," I add. It's nice to know those actually exist.

I blow past Jake and take my coffee and treats, talking myself down from dumping the hot liquid on his head. Instead, I stop at the milk counter and dump two packets of sugar into the cup, so forcefully, some spills over the side.

He does not affect me, I tell myself. *The past does not affect my present.*

Channeling my inner yogi, I clean the counter methodically. I stir my coffee, then leave without glancing at Jake's stupidly handsome face.

I hurry to my car and deposit my goodies on the passenger seat. My last errand is to fetch the beer-holder "jackets" Dave painted for me, so I power walk there.

The bell on the door jingles. Dave spots me, holds up a finger, and disappears into his back room. As I wait, I wander past dryer vents and vacuums.

A couple of minutes later, the door jingles again and someone says, "Hey, Jake."

Un-freaking-believable.

Forget dehydrated pea. Windfall is the size of a malnourished sandfly.

Before returning to my hometown, I debated choosing somewhere different to live. I've bounced around a lot over the years. Bartended in bigger cities, followed help-wanted ads to small towns from Virginia to Arkansas. For some reason, I couldn't shake thoughts of this town.

Sure, I have bad memories here. I'll never forget the hell my family and I went through—or forgive certain people for the part they played in that mess. But there's a serenity to Windfall I never forgot. The mountains, the quaint charm, the sweeping forests.

I kept picturing a different version of myself walking these streets—an optimistic alternate Larkin, not beaten down by life, able to thrive personally and professionally. Strong, like the trees that bend in the wind but don't break.

Or maybe I wanted to prove I had overcome my past.

Either way, I didn't overanalyze my decision to return to Windfall. I wasn't about to let Jake Bower's existence alter my life again.

But dammit, why does he have to be everywhere?

"Larkin." Dave, *thankfully*, waves me over to the counter. The sooner I'm away from here, the better.

I march stiffly toward him, refusing to look for Jake.

Dave holds up the puffy jackets that will act as cozy coolers for beer bottles, and I almost kiss him. "These are *perfect*. So cute. The raffle will for sure be a success. And is that…" I look closer at the floral design he added around the slogan *Touch my beer and die* and press my hand to my chest. "How'd you know sunflowers are my favorite flower?"

Dave scratches his ear. He glances over my shoulder and frowns, then he looks at the ceiling for a prolonged beat. "Delilah was in and saw me working on the design. She mentioned you loved sunflowers."

A reasonable explanation, but Dave Tanaka is acting weird, and he never acts weird. If I had to guess, I'd say Jake is behind me, because this whole damn town knows he's my mortal enemy, even if they don't know why.

"That was sweet of Delilah," I say brightly. "And kind of you to include the personal touch. Will I see you at the opening?"

"Try to keep me away."

I pay him and turn, prepared to see Jake. Except I'm never really *prepared* for the thickness of his shoulders, the broody smudges under his dark eyes, that beard covering his strong jaw. I hate that I find him both attractive and loathsome at the same time.

His focus is cemented to his work boots. Of course. God forbid he look at me.

Not that I care.

Tonight is all that matters, along with my plans for the bar's growth. Starting tomorrow, Jolene and I will be implementing some of our new ideas—Wednesday dice-rolling to get discounts on lunch bills, kids entering contests to be a sous chef for a day, special cocktails, where purchases include a donation to specific charities.

Already, buzz is increasing. I've upped our social media presence, counting down to tonight's big relaunch. I've never been this excited about work.

I lift my chin and saunter past Jake, crossing my fingers as I go.

Please, dear God, do not let him show up at the bar tonight.

CHAPTER
Four

Jake

I drive closer to the Barrel House, feeling the way I always do when I'm near this place. *Angsty*, with a side of self-hatred. The parking lot is jammed, which is great to see, at least. I spot Callahan parking on the street and pull up next to my brother's truck.

"Looks like the relaunch is already a success," I call through my window.

He smiles. "I had no doubt."

Such a liar. "You were nervous as shit."

"Maybe. Just want tonight to go well."

He's not the only one. Jolene may be my ex from over a decade ago, but she's together with Cal now and is still a close friend. I only want the best for her...and her new business partner, who hates my guts.

I park my truck and join Cal, the two of us heading toward the busy bar. "Did you get the kitchen shelves installed in time?" I ask.

He nods. "Barely, but it's done."

"And the countertops—you got the company to fix the sizing issue?"

"All sorted." He side-eyes me with a knowing look I've seen too often lately. "If you have other concerns, you can ask Larkin directly. See if she needs anything extra done around the place."

"You know very fucking well I'm not welcome to work on the Barrel." Not that Larkin's hatred has kept me from covertly helping her and Jolene.

Unbeknownst to them, I sourced a lot of their materials at cheaper prices. I found Callahan extra workers when they needed more hands on-site. Fact is, I owe Larkin more than money and favors. I owe her my hide, probably my soul. I'm not sure even that would make amends for the hurt and devastation I caused.

Coming tonight is pushing my limits with her, but this is a big night for Jolene. Larkin can't kick me out for supporting my friend.

"She might have warmed toward you," Cal says. "I told her your connection got us that deal on the new kitchen flooring."

I glance at him. "Yeah?"

"She did say, 'Then tear the fucking floor out,' but she didn't follow through on the demand." He slaps my shoulder. "I'd say that's progress."

I grumble under my breath. There will never be progress with Larkin. I deserve every ounce of her hatred.

Cal slows his stride. "Care to telling me why Larkin thinks you're the devil incarnate?"

"Nope." It's the same answer my meddling family always gets. The idea of my brothers knowing what I did that fateful night, of the damage my actions caused, makes me physically ill.

I pick up my speed, like I need momentum to shove the bar doors open.

One step inside, I relax a fraction. At least the place is packed.

Country music plays as happy voices fight to be heard. Our brothers are easy to spot. The big men are standing by the railing around the dance floor, towering over most people in here.

They all look happy and tipsy, with their better halves tucked into their sides. After spending ten years in witness protection, I still find their happiness a shock to my system. There was a time I thought we were all destined to live unfulfilled, bleak lives.

On instinct, my attention strays toward the bar area. I don't see Larkin, but the newly renovated open kitchen beside it is a standout. The space is bright and airy, adding a modern vibe to the classic wood tables and booths around the bar. Makes me proud of Callahan that he did this on his own, even if I resented not being able to lend a hand.

A flash of blond hair catches my eyes, and my insides do an unnerving spin and pitch. Larkin's straight hair is in a braid down her back, swishing as she moves. Those cute dimples of hers show because she's actually smiling—an expression I haven't seen aimed my way for twelve years. She's glowing and laughing and charming the heck out of every person at the bar, and I hate the hit of longing that careens into me.

The only emotion I should feel around Larkin is *shame*.

Jaw locked, I march toward my family, but Tvisha Shaw stops me. She was friends with Jolene back in the day. She's outgoing and sweet, but I don't like the pity in her expression. "So nice to see you out."

"I'm out plenty."

"Sure," she says and pats my arm, like I'm some kind of pet.

I fight to keep my expression neutral. I get that I don't socialize much. I've had trouble reconnecting with friends since I've been home. I hit the gym when not at work and hunker down at home most nights. But people like Tvisha are partly to blame—well-meaning folk who treat me like my past has made me fragile. None of it is anyone's concern but mine.

Annoyed for a whole slew of reasons, I nod to her, then join my family.

Desmond passes me his partly finished beer. "You look like you need this more than me."

I grunt.

Lennon smirks. "He looks like a death-row inmate about to face the chair. And by *the chair*, I mean *Larkin*," he adds, like the interfering troublemaker he is.

I'm usually good at ignoring Lennon's taunts. Of all my brothers, he hides himself the most, covering his stress and insecurities with jokes and banter. Tonight, I'm not in the mood.

"Fuck off," I tell him as I take the beer from Des, with a quieter "Thanks" to him.

I knock back a healthy swallow, trying to unwind and shake off my angst.

Lennon turns his smirk on E. "As I was saying, the only reason you're such a great artist is because of how much we tormented you. You relied on art to channel your misery. You should thank us."

"Thank you?" Delilah rolls her eyes, tucking in tighter to E. The two of them are so in love, my mood lifts. "You told him he couldn't do sports because he was adopted, and he believed you."

"He can't do sports because he has no coordination," Des says. He takes Sadie's wineglass and helps himself to a sip of his fiancé's wine. "Right, babe?"

Sadie steals her wineglass back. "Don't stick me in the middle of your family pile-on. I'd go nuclear if someone teased Max like that."

"I would fucking *end* a kid for hurting Max." Desmond's dark eyes cloud over.

I would laugh if he weren't half serious. I'm amazed with how he's turned his life around, building Lennon's outdoor adventure programs with him and stepping up to be a dad to the son he learned about last year, but I have no doubt he'd risk jail time to defend my nephew.

"You Neanderthals can bust my balls all you want," E says with a vague wave of his hand. "The reason I didn't get into sports is because I have actual brain cells and don't love ramming my body into other bodies, like you nitwits. And being adopted would've actually been a plus. It's a shame that was a lie."

"True." Lennon nods. "You wouldn't be related to our sperm donor."

"I don't fully hate your father," Maggie says to Lennon.

"Do we need to oust your girlfriend from the family?" E asks, mock glaring at her.

Lennon sneers at E, then grazes his nose against Maggie's cheek. "Explain yourself."

"Don't get me wrong. I'd happily light the man on fire today, but if he never existed, I wouldn't have you."

Lennon beams down at her and gives her a filthy kiss. E makes a disgusted sound and shades his eyes, as the rest of them tease the hell out of one another. It's a normal family gathering these days. Good-natured taunts. My brothers paired off with the women they love. Even Callahan is with Jolene now, the two of them probably making out in the back somewhere.

As odd as it was seeing Cal and Jo together at first, they make a hell of a lot more sense than Jo and I ever did. I'm pleased as shit for them, but I feel a bit like the odd man out these days. The one single guy left in my family. Maybe that's why I'm hanging back, barely interacting with them.

Shattering glass has me whipping my attention to the bar.

Larkin's face is flushed, and she's frozen stiff, focused on the floor behind the bar.

I tense.

I see Larkin around town plenty and do my best to be respectful, saving her the displeasure of having to look at my face. If I frequented the Barrel House before they closed for renovations, I asked other people to order my drinks and sat with my back to the bar. If I'm running errands and our paths cross, like three damn times today, I avert my attention, hoping the lack of eye contact frustrates her less.

But I still find my attention drawn to her.

Thanks to those stolen glances, I know she takes her coffee black and dumps in two packets of sugar. When she locks her car door on the street, she tests the handle before walking away. She favors her right leg when she's standing. She loves sunflowers— a fact I happened to overhear at Sugar and Sips and mentioned to Dave Tanaka when he was working on her raffle prizes at the hardware store. Thankfully, he lied and said Delilah was his intel.

Guilt is why I'm attuned to Larkin. Why my throat tightens in her presence and all of me feels on high alert. Like if I learn enough about her from a safe distance, I'll be able to help her in some way and offset the horrible thing I did.

All this to say, I'm well acquainted with Larkin's glares, her effortless confidence, how easily she smiles at people who aren't me.

Right now, she looks rattled, and I don't like it.

She glances at a guy farther down the bar, who seems intent on her. He says something to her. She says something back. Abruptly, she drops out of sight, presumably cleaning up whatever glass she broke.

I suck on my teeth as laughter and music drift around me. That guy keeps glancing over the bar. At Larkin, no doubt. He's a polished type. Button-down shirt tucked in. Blond hair neatly styled. Innocent enough, but the look in his eye has an edge to it —superior and...proprietary.

Like he has some claim on her.

CHAPTER
Five

LARKIN

Lady Luck must have a bone—*or twenty*—to pick with me. First, Jake sauntered in here on *my* big night. Set up camp with his obnoxious brothers and faced his back to the bar. That's his usual stance in here. Like he's still in high school, shutting out everyone but those he deems worthy.

Seeing him for my fourth *awesome* time today was enough to have me fumbling the water glass in my hand. Seeing my ex had the glass slipping to the floor in an earsplitting crash.

Outside of my family, two people in this world know my father is the notorious criminal and all-around degenerate Otto Briggs. Car theft, drug dealing, burglary, conning innocent people out of cash—you name it, my father has sunk to that level. He caused damage to Windfall, leaving a wake of hurt and financial ruin when he skipped town.

Growing up, my mother coached me. She explained that no one could know whose DNA flowed through my veins. Windfall is a close-knit community that protects its own. One whiff of my lineage, and I'd be ostracized. I listened to her warnings. I knew gossip would spread through this town like a swarm of locusts. I didn't tell a soul about Otto Briggs, until the night Jake drove me home and I falsely trusted him.

To my knowledge, he hasn't shared my history with anyone, but he knows. And I know he's a liar. I should have learned my lesson. Realized people often have hidden agendas.

Sadly, I did not.

I trusted that my last ex, Drew, cared about me. He said he wanted to better understand what drove my sometimes-volatile moods. I thought telling him my secrets would bring us closer, help me shed the weight I couldn't seem to shake—my family history, that terrifying night with Derek, the horrible aftermath with Hunter.

Telling him was a huge mistake I won't soon forget.

Now, he's here. As is Jake—the two people who know the one thing that has the power to hurt my new business.

Staying crouched behind the bar seems like an excellent decision.

Jolene rushes over, stoops next to me, and eyes the broken glass. "Are you okay?"

"Physically, yes. Mentally is a question mark."

"Because Jake's here?"

I'd like to hire a bouncer to taser Jake on sight, but I say, "As long as he stays away from me, I don't care where he is. An ex of mine turned up."

She abruptly stands, grabs a cloth from the bar top, then drops back down. "The slick blond guy with the condescending face?"

"Nailed that one, but add passive-aggressive mansplainer." And trained psychiatrist who loves poking my weak spots.

Jolene glowers. "Want me to send him packing?"

Jo's brown hair is in a cute ponytail. She's wearing jean shorts, cowboy boots, and a button-up tank top tied at her waist.

She's the epitome of sweet country girl, but her expression reads, *Say the word, and I'll fuck him up.*

"I can handle Drew," I say. "I just needed a minute. I don't want to give him the satisfaction of knowing he gets under my skin." Or do anything that prompts him to mention Otto Briggs.

"Okay, but if you need him dealt with, I'll tell Cal and his brothers. They'll escort him out."

"Absolutely not," I whisper-hiss. "The last thing I want is Jake Bower up in my business."

The servers are walking around Jo and me, casting us curious glances. I flutter my fingers at Sue-Ann with a full-teeth smile. *Nothing to see here. Just a frazzled woman surrounded by the men who hurt her.*

Jolene presses her hand to my arm. "If you ever want to tell me why you hate Jake, I'm all ears."

"What you are is all nose. I know his obnoxious brothers asked you to poke that cute appendage into my business to sniff for dirt."

"What? No." She waves an erratic hand and compresses her lips.

"You suck at lying."

"Fine, they're all dying to know why the temperature drops to subzero when you two are near each other. I want to know too. I hate seeing you upset."

I *despise* that Jake still has the ability to affect my moods, but telling Jo about our history and that awful night means explaining who my father is. A fact I should have shared with her before we became business partners, when she still had the chance to turn me down. There's also the minor detail that Jake is her ex and he schemed to hook up with me while they were together. If she finds out, she might think I did something to invite his attention back then.

"I appreciate it, but I prefer not rehashing those days. And we have more important things to focus on than annoying men, like tonight's busy crowd."

"Right you are," she says as a shadow looms over us.

Another Bower is hovering above our crouched bodies, holding a broom—Jolene's boyfriend, Callahan. He studies me with a worried frown. "Did you cut yourself?"

I shake my head and gather the larger pieces of glass. "Just embarrassed myself, is all. An ex of mine showed up out of the blue."

His attention moves to the bar. He narrows his eyes. "Want me to have a word with the guy?"

"Definitely not," I say, firmer this time. "Like I told Jo, I can handle him. He just caught me by surprise."

Cal nods, helping us clean up, and I regret my hard tone with him. He's Jolene's best friend and now her live-in boyfriend—aka, the guy who makes her obscenely happy. I have issues with Cal, specifically with the rumors he spread about me when we were younger, but the extent of his love for Jo is potent enough to inebriate half the bar. Even with our intertwined past, I've grudgingly moved him to my Acceptable Human list.

His brother, however, is firmly on my I'd Rather Stick My Face in Raw Sewage Than Speak to Him list. If Jake says one word to me tonight, I'll slip laxatives into his drinks. If Drew says one thing about my family tree, he'll get arsenic.

CHAPTER
Six

Jake

Larkin finally stands back up from behind the bar, and I let out a relieved breath. She seems to be avoiding the slick guy, going about her work. But he says something to her again.

Her features pinch, and my lats bunch toward my ears.

Whoever that prick is, he's making Larkin uncomfortable. No woman should feel uncomfortable in her place of work.

Callahan pushes through the crowd toward our table. I'm up and in his face before he makes it there. "Is Larkin okay?"

He cocks his head, studying me so long I almost shake him. "For a guy who claims not to care about Larkin, you're awfully invested in her emotional well-being."

I am invested. Have been since I returned, because I can't shake my guilt. "Just answer the fucking question."

He glances back at her. She still looks stiff, but she's returned to mixing drinks. "An ex turned up," Cal says. "Seems to be making her uncomfortable, but she said—"

I move before he finishes. The idea of Larkin struggling with a guy again has me irrationally angry. I royally fucked up with her once. Broke her trust and let her fall. I no longer have my phone with her furious voice mail. The US Marshals confiscated all our modes of communication, but I remember her lashing word for word.

Asshole. You told me to call if I'm scared and Derek's nearby. Well, I'm fucking scared, Jake. Guess you lied about that too.

I replay the memory of it often. Usually during the quiet of night. Penance, I think. As are the times I remember the frantic call I made to her in the aftermath, the pain and anger in her voice as she told me how bad things actually went.

I'm not clearheaded enough to dwell on that mess now. All I know is I'm the reason everything went wrong that night. Larkin. Her brother. Derek. All because I worried I couldn't keep control of my dick.

Which must be why I'm risking my nuts by barging up to the bar. There are a multitude of sharp objects in Larkin's reach. I'm sure she'd love to castrate me with a twist of her lemon zester. She can mutilate me all she wants, *after* I make sure she's okay.

I shove past customers, ignoring the annoyed grunts from the people I bump. I settle at the bar, next to the guy fixated on her, and crowd his space. He shrinks his arms closer to his body. I dig my elbow into his side.

"Excuse me," he says.

They are apology words, but they're passive-aggressive in tone. Spoken to provoke me into moving. Except my stance is purely aggressive, minus the passive part. There's enough room for me to move over, but I don't speak or budge. I stand here unassumingly, elbow lodged against his ribs, hoping he gets irritated and leaves.

Larkin glances our way and startles. Hell, so do I.

I rarely come this close to her, and goddamn, her beauty still knocks me for a loop.

Like when she was younger, her features are strong yet

feminine. The scar by her nose is fainter but still edgy and hot, her braided blond hair adding cuteness to her sex appeal. Her heavy lower lip is doing strange things to my ability to swallow, but her eyes are a different story. Those blue-green beauties are attempting to explode my face.

She has a beer bottle in an unforgiving grip. The way she's using the bottle opener while glaring at me, I'm pretty sure she's imagining the popped-off cap as my severed head.

"Looks like you're still tending bar," Mr. Passive-Aggressive says. There's no missing the condescension in his tone.

A muscle in Larkin's jaw knots. "I actually co-own the bar. But yeah, I still bartend too, because I'm great at it and enjoy the work. I assume you're still rummaging through people's heads."

"Guilty as charged. I'd never have expected to see you here, though, back in your hometown when—"

"I'm here," Larkin barks, interrupting whatever he was about to say. "The guy I'm seeing asked me to move here with him."

Well, that's interesting. Larkin hasn't had a boyfriend since she moved here six months ago. I acquired that intel because I maybe prod about her a bit with Callahan. Subtly ask about her comings and goings, so I can covertly help her when possible.

"I'm surprised you're in a relationship," the guy says and sips his beer. "I assumed you'd stay unattached. Revel in your independence."

The venom in Larkin's expression shifts to unnatural calm. "That seems like a pretty *basic* assessment, Drew. Maybe I just hadn't met the right person yet. Real intimacy is all about connection, right?"

His answering grin drips with arrogance. "Absolutely. Just seems uncharacteristic, is all."

And he seems pretty fucking judgmental, even though she's neck-deep in her lie. Now I dislike this Drew guy even more. A woman only lies about her relationship status when she wants a man gone.

Larkin plunks the opened beer bottle down for another customer and snaps up her money. Nostrils flaring, she leans toward Drew. "Considering I haven't seen you in two years, I'm not sure you have the qualifications to know what is and isn't characteristic of me. I'm actually engaged to be married in a few months."

Larkin speaks with such authority *I* nearly believe she's engaged, when she most certainly is not. I stare harder at her, trying to figure out why this guy has her so rattled.

She ignores me.

For kicks, I dig my elbow deeper into her ex's ribs. He flinches but doesn't take his unnerving attention off Larkin.

Slowly, his gaze slides down her body and stops on her hand. "Did he not give you a ring?"

Larkin blinks and frowns, like she doesn't understand the question. Then her eyes widen. She looks at her traitorous hand, which has no ring to corroborate her lie.

I expect her to come up with a quick story. Larkin is witty and sassy, always fast to joust with my brothers. But her ringless hand shakes. Red climbs up her neck as her next swallow bumps down her throat.

Her growing anxiety is so palpable—*so painful*—I lose my mind and say, "I'm getting it sized."

"Excuse me?" Drew jerks backward, turning enough to dislodge my elbow from his side.

"Larkin's ring—I'm getting it sized. Right, babe?" I have no clue how I sound so calm.

Thankfully, Larkin's ex is focused on me. He misses the way Larkin's expression morphs into a vengeful Medusa glare. I think she mouths, *What the fuck?*

The same question is blaring in my brain.

"I'm Drew." Her ex tips his chin in greeting. "She may have mentioned me."

"Nope," I say and stare him down.

"We used to date."

I shrug and stay quiet. This guy wants some kind of validation. Watching him stew is a hell of a lot more pleasant than facing Larkin's lethal scowl.

Our section of the bar isn't as busy now, but I shift my stance and step on Drew's toe with the heel of my boot. He grimaces and yanks his foot away. I continue staring blandly at him.

"Funny," he says, sounding anything but amused. "Larkin didn't acknowledge you when you stepped up here."

I guess he's observant. "It's a game we play—pretending she doesn't know me. A little role-playing to keep things fun."

"Is that so?"

"You know how it is." I dial up my grin to cocky. "My girl's a firecracker. Keeps me on my toes."

He *humphs*. Barely audible with the surrounding chatter and music, but his air of superiority has me wanting to strike a match near his gelled hair.

"Guess you've really grown," he tells Larkin.

Grown? Is this guy for real?

"When it's right, it's right," she says and places her hand on my wrist. The move probably looks intimate, but she's digging her nails into my skin. "Right, *babe*?"

"Wild horses couldn't keep me away from you," I say, attempting not to wince from the pain in my wrist. At least the music and noise are too loud for nearby people to hear this shitshow of a conversation.

Drew taps his fingers on his beer bottle. His too-observant gaze darts between Larkin and me. "You two should come to my wedding."

"What?" I kind of shout. Larkin's nails sink deeper into my wrist.

"I'm getting married too," he goes on, an aggressive glint sharpening his features. "Natalia and I live in Raleigh, but she's from a neighboring town and wanted to celebrate close to home.

That's why I'm here—finalizing details at the Longleaf Inn. And I was thinking, you two should come to the wedding, maybe get some ideas for your own nuptials. Unless the whole role-playing thing extends to events and you don't acknowledge each other in public."

"We'd love to come," I say forcefully, because A) this prick is challenging me. I don't like how smug and patronizing he is. And B) I clearly don't value my life.

"Send Larkin the details," I add, planning my exit strategy. I need out of here before I offer to be this asshole's best man. "I also forgot something I need to take care of. I'll see you later." I risk a quick glance at Larkin to punctuate my farewell.

Bad idea.

She's not glaring at me. She's smiling in this slightly deranged way, attempting not to blow our cover story when she'd clearly rather rig me with dynamite.

If she does, I'll light the fuse myself.

The second she dislodges her nails from my wrist, I head for the exit, needing air and a slap across the face. Maybe a new town to live in.

I shove the front doors open and suck back a huge breath. I pace an agitated line as I tug at my hair.

Callahan appears out of nowhere and steps into my path. "What did you do?"

"The dumbest fucking thing I could've done."

During WITSEC, I obsessed over how selfish and cruel my behavior with Larkin had been. All I had to do that night was keep my word. Wait for her while she grabbed her clothes. Instead, I was rude and wound up leaving her on the side of the road. I let her think she'd been a pawn in some immature game, because it was easier than admitting I liked her too much and it scared the shit out of me.

I never even went back to the stupid party. I drove to the old quarry instead. Looked out at the vast crater. Tried to piece through my feelings for Jo, the intense connection I felt with Larkin. How badly I still wanted to taste Larkin's mouth, that tender spot below her ear, kiss the bruise on her wrist. Show her a real man could be gentle, even though my sudden attraction to her felt anything but.

At which point, her name flashed on my phone.

Nope, was my first panicked thought in that moment. If I spoke to her, I might drive back there. Tell her the truth of why I left. Kiss her like I was dying to. And she was no doubt pissed. I embarrassed her. If I answered, she'd tear me a new asshole.

So, I didn't answer.

I avoided listening to her message until a couple of days later. Way too goddamn late.

"Fuck!" I shout at the sky, wishing I'd made different choices.

"Jake." Callahan grips the back of my neck. He's always calm and easy with a smile. His worry right now has another wave of guilt washing over me. "Start talking," he says evenly, "before I go in there and ask Larkin what happened."

My fight drains out of me. The last thing I want is to add more stress to his or Larkin's lives. "I told her ex that I'm Larkin's fiancé."

"Why the hell would you do that?"

"Because I'm a moron."

"Clearly, but that explains nothing."

I slump and rub my jaw. "I went over there to make sure she was okay, and she was talking about a fiancé she has, which I know for a fact she doesn't, and her ex was being pushy. Asking why she doesn't have a ring. She started fumbling, getting anxious and"—I toss up my hands as though someone else is to blame for my idiocy—"I lost my ever-loving mind and said *I* was her fiancé."

Cal sputters out a half-choked laugh. "I'm guessing she didn't take that well."

"Depends if you consider Larkin digging her nails into my

wrist until she drew blood well." I hold up my arm to show off the red welts. "Then her ex invited us to his wedding."

"But you said no, right? Made an excuse about being busy?"

"I panicked, okay? He was pissing me off and asked in a challenging way, like he knew we were lying. I said yes before I could think straight."

Cal blinks at me. "Do you have a death wish?"

"Apparently," I mutter and curse the sky again.

"We could call our US Marshal handler," Cal says, sounding so amused I nearly deck him. "Ask him to reinstate you in WITSEC."

Growling, I jab at his chest. "This is your fault."

"How is this *my* fault?"

"You told me to drive Larkin home that night. *You* put this whole mess in motion."

Jealousy was the culprit—Callahan pining over his best friend, Jolene. He'd concocted an elaborate scheme to break up Jo and me. Made sure I drove Larkin home, then spread rumors afterward that we'd hooked up. In the end, Jo *did* break up with me. She said she didn't believe the rumors, but her feelings had changed. I was more relieved than upset. Then my family got shoved into witness protection for a decade.

None of it changed how sick I felt over what happened with Larkin.

"Care to tell me what exactly this mess is that I created?" Callahan says, trying to catch my eye. "Because I'm on pins and fucking needles over the mystery."

I debate finally admitting what I did—how despicably I behaved, the fallout with Derek and Larkin's brother—but shame engulfs me.

Not bothering to reply, I strut to my truck. It's a death march, really. Larkin must be sharpening her kitchen knives by now, deciding which of my appendages to carve off first.

CHAPTER
Seven

Lennon Bower, of the annoying Bower brothers, has been shaking the dice in his hand for at least two minutes.

"Just roll already," I say. "I have actual work to do."

"Don't rush me."

"By the time you roll, I'm gonna need hip-replacement surgery." Typical Bower, only thinking about himself. Does he not see how insanely busy we are?

Our first official lunch at the revamped Barrel House is exceeding expectations. Today is "Roll for a Discount" Wednesday—a weekly promotion we'd hoped would liven up the notoriously slow weekday. Every lunch bill delivered comes with a set of dice. If a customer rolls snake eyes, they get fifteen percent off their meal.

We've been so busy, I got stuck delivering Lennon's bill.

It's like I'm living in my own personal hell—all Bowers, all the time. But I will *not* think about one particular Bower who will get shanked if he walks in here. The only reason I haven't lit his home on fire since last night's fiasco is because no locals caught wind of his ludicrous fiancé stunt.

Fiancé. I'd sooner feed a bear honey using my face.

Lennon's girlfriend, Maggie, massages his shoulders. "You've got this, babe. Just keep your wrist loose."

"How about a good-luck blow before I roll?" He waggles his eyebrows suggestively.

Maggie's freckled cheeks flame red. "Inappropriate much?"

"On my hand, Mags. God." He looks at me with mock horror. "Her mind is always in the gutter. Not that I blame her, with what I'm packing."

I grab a cocktail napkin from my tray and hold it out for him. "There's a little bullshit on your lip. You might want to wipe it off."

Maggie tips her head back and cackles. "This is my new favorite lunch spot."

"That makes one of us," Lennon says, still shaking the dice. "If you come back here, you'll be coming on your own."

Maggie shrugs. "Fine by me. I recharged my vibrator last night."

My abrupt laugh surprises me. I'm not supposed to laugh around Bowers, but Lennon and Maggie are undeniably cute together, and Maggie is a smart, ballbusting woman. She wouldn't date an asshole.

I might have to grudgingly move Lennon to my Acceptable Human list, *if* he ever pays his bill. "Can you roll those dice before I reach menopause?"

"If I must." He holds out his hand to Maggie. She blows on it, followed by a soft kiss to his knuckles. Yep, they are sickeningly cute.

He mouths, *I love you,* then finally rolls. The dice turn up as a two and a five.

They groan but pay their bill with smiles.

I rush back to work, pouring beers, delivering checks,

cheering when the five construction workers at table seven actually roll snake eyes. They proceed to sing "We Are the Champions," and the whole bar joins in.

It's a fantastic lunch service. Until I pass a table and hear the word *Briggs*.

I freeze mid-stride, the beers on my tray teetering.

"Don't you remember that sweet Tully kid?" the woman goes on. "Otto Briggs sold him the drugs. Swear to God, if Briggs and his rotten kids hadn't left Windfall after that, this town would've burned them at the stake."

I grip the tray to keep the beers and my hands steady. This happens every so often. Gossip from the good old days relived. People raise their imaginary pitchforks to vilify my father and declare Windfall cleansed of his reign of terror—verbal attacks I applaud. Thinking about what happened to Xavier Tully makes me physically sick. What I can't have is them knowing I'm one of Otto's "rotten" kids.

Doing what I do best, I fit on a smile and deliver my beers. I get through the rest of the rush by absorbing the good vibes and energy around me. When the last customers leave, my adrenaline ebbs.

Normally, I'd fixate on that overheard conversation for a few hours, stew over what would actually happen if people knew Otto was my dad. Lucky for me, I have last night's catastrophe to subvert those negative thought spirals.

I'm not sure who I'm more furious with, Drew for his passive-aggressive posturing, or Jake for butting his egotistical head where it didn't belong.

The clear answer is *Jake*. Aside from my father, everything bad in my life always comes back to Jake.

I plunk a pineapple down on my cutting board and decapitate the crown in one blow. I attack the skin next. I hack off rough cuts, nearly nicking my fingers twice. I core the stupid fruit, then slam my knife through tender sections, shredding flesh that should be cleanly cut.

By the time I'm done prepping the garnish for tonight's special cocktail—pineapple bourbon lemonade—my cutting board looks like a crime scene.

"Did a Minion get murdered here?" Jolene asks from behind me. "Should I call the cops?"

At the mention of cops, my grip on my knife loosens. I hunch forward and almost rub my eyes, until I remember my hands are covered in murdered pineapple. "Sorry about the mess. I didn't sleep well."

Jo doesn't get annoyed that I wasted a perfectly good pineapple. She takes me by the shoulders and guides me to the sink. She tells me to wash up and reappears with a clean cloth. Once my hands are dry, she pulls me to one of the tables in the bar—I seem to have lost the ability to move on my own—and sits me down.

"I know what Jake did last night," she says. "That ridiculous fiancé move."

Of course she does. "Those Bowers like to blab their dirty laundry."

"The Bowers don't blab publicly. Cal followed him out of the bar, and Jake spilled the story. They lean on one another, because that's all they had for a decade."

I pick at a jag in my nail, pressing my finger into the rough edge. The tiniest part of me feels *bad*. Like, a ridiculously small part. The size of an undergrown gnat. I'd still like to high-five karma for doling out retribution to Jake Bower, but if I think too long about what it must have been like for those boys, torn from their lives in an instant, compassion weasels into my heart.

Then I remember that Jake is why my brother has been in jail for twelve years.

"I know I've asked this a million times," Jo says softly, "but I'm gonna ask again. And to be clear, I'm not asking because Cal wants to know or because I'm eager for gossip. I want to know what happened between Jake and you, because I think you need to talk about it."

I avert my eyes. There's too much worry under that sweet offer to look directly at Jo. I take in the refurbished pool tables instead, the new sayings we hung in the bar.

My favorite is:

I DISTRUST CAMELS & ANYONE ELSE
WHO CAN GO WITHOUT A DRINK FOR A WEEK.

That silly sign always makes me smile. Just a piece of hand-painted art on a wood wall in this bar I now partly own brings me *joy*. Because that's who I am now—Larkin Gray, bar owner and businesswoman. Born of an affair with a drug-dealing motorcycle gang member. Raised by a single mother who cared more about her next sugar daddy than cooking dinner for her kids.

But I still did this.

Today's lunch service and dice game was a hit. I have no doubt Wednesdays will be packed going forward. An outcome I manifested. Not through luck. Certainly not through nepotism. I worked my ass off to build my savings, learned how to be a great bartender, came up with ideas to grow this business and make customers smile.

I'm so damn *proud* of myself, but seeing Drew last night took some of that wind out of my sail. With a few choice words, he dusted off the low self-esteem I thought I'd buried. Hearing *again* today how much this town despises my father and his offspring didn't help.

I don't have the bandwidth to unearth it all with Jo right now.

"The Jake stuff is too complicated to unpack," I say, "but I'm all for trash-talking my ex, if you're up for that." Mocking Drew is much easier than confessing to Jo that her new business partner shares DNA with Windfall's most-hated man.

"Sign me up for trashing the ex. Should I ask Emmanuel to whip us up ice cream sundaes?"

I glance at our new chef, visible in the open kitchen. The tall Haitian man steps up to Sandy's cutting board and gestures to her work. I can't hear what he says, but he gives her an encouraging smile. Her body language stays relaxed.

"The staff totally respect him," I say. "He was a great find."

"Right? Working on menus with him has been effortless. But back to trash-talking your ex—yea or nay on inhaling ice-cold sugar?"

"Nay. Talking about Drew turns my stomach."

Jo makes a cute growly sound. "I hate him already. He seemed super arrogant last night."

And then some. "He's a psychiatrist and knows too much about my life. He enjoys making me feel small."

"Because he's small in the penis department?"

I snort. "He's not huge. Certainly not as big as his ego. I just don't get why he still affects me so much. I mean, I hadn't seen him for two years, and it was like no time had gone by. I was suddenly insecure and vulnerable again, lying about having a fiancé."

She brushes an errant crumb from the table. "All women love throwing their happiness in their ex's faces, even if it's an act. Giving off I'm-better-without-you energy is a breakup rite of passage."

"Sure, but it was more than that. Like, toward the end of our relationship, he kept finding ways to turn disagreements around and really tore down my self-esteem. He'd be late for dinner dates and blame my annoyance on trust issues. I'd get frustrated at the harsh tone he'd sometimes use, and he'd tell me I provoked him with *my* rude tone."

Jolene frowns. "Sounds like the type of asshole who gets off on feeling smarter and more self-aware than everyone."

"Pretty much, which isn't surprising, since his tycoon father is the same way. And last night, it was like I needed to prove I wasn't the problem in our relationship. That I could handle commitment."

A total joke, considering I've been avoiding men since we broke up. Every time I've trusted a man and have opened up, I've been hurt, physically or emotionally. All I want to focus on for the foreseeable future is me and my business.

"I'm guessing you ended things," she says, "and it didn't go well."

"Depends if you consider being told you're too cold and closed off to function maturely *well*." Gotta love dating a psychiatrist. At least when discussing my past with him, I never mentioned Jake's name. Drew would have had a field day last night, thinking the guy who tried to use me and fucked me over is now my fiancé. "He doesn't like to lose, in work or relationships. I think the breakup shocked him and pissed him off."

"Oh yeah," Jo says, "we definitely hate him."

"He's not awesome," I mutter, trying not to think too long about how deep his words cut.

Jo presses her hand over mine. "No part of you is cold and closed off, Lark." When I shrug, she puts more pressure on my hand. "You're not just my business partner. You're my closest friend. If I don't have time for errands, you always offer to do them. You brought me soup when I was sick last month and did extra work organizing the bar renos. Without you, I wouldn't have gotten through that mess with Callahan and have him in my life. I certainly wouldn't have had the courage to revamp the Barrel House. I absolutely love coming to work now, couldn't imagine not having the bar in my life, all because of you. What Drew said is plain wrong. You *are* caring and warm."

"That means more than you know." But I haven't told her the full truth about my past and my father, or about Jake's cruel behavior with me before they broke up. I'm pretty sure that's the definition of closed off.

"So…" Jo smacks her hand on the table, startling me out of my melancholy. "Drew is an asshole who we hope loses all his money in a bad stock deal. How do you plan to handle Jake and the wedding invitation coming your way?"

"Simple. If Jake ever tries to step in and 'help' me again, I will stick his face on my cutting board instead of a pineapple."

Calling me *babe*, like he had the goddamn right. Accepting a *wedding invitation* on my behalf to the last wedding I'd ever attend with the last man in this galaxy I'd attend with.

My fucking life.

"Drew should be out of town soon," I go on. "I'll decline whatever invitation he sends. The bar was too loud for anyone to hear Jake's asinine fiancé stunt, thank God. I'll just put the whole nightmare out of my head."

"Sounds like a solid plan." But Jo grimaces and rolls out her shoulder.

I wince in sympathy. "Is your back acting up again?"

"Seems to be my neck this time, but it'll right itself."

"If you need to book a chiro appointment, take whatever time they have. I'll cover for you." Otherwise, Jo will suck it up and work while hurt.

"You're the best," she says with a smile. "I'll book something today."

"Jolene." Emmanuel nods at her from the open kitchen. "I've made a sample of that vegan faux pork belly we talked about. It's ready to taste when you are."

"That's my cue." Jolene slips out from the table but casts another glance my way. "Unless you want to talk more?"

"I'm good. I'll steal the office while you're busy. Catch up on emails before I redo the pineapple prep." Make sure the monogrammed aprons I ordered are on time. Check that my Corona order was received. Send Delilah an email about cross-promotion.

Running a business means wearing more hats than just that of a bartender. I love every second of it.

After twenty minutes on the office computer, I open my personal email account and delete a ton of spam, but two emails stop me short.

Drew Carrington's name shouldn't be a surprise. He was here last night and said he'd send me a wedding invitation. This quick, aggressive move is totally on-brand for him. *When Larkin is at her most vulnerable, go in for the one-two punch.*

I don't click on the email. I gave him too much airtime with Jolene, and being forced to deal with this makes me want to hit Jake's house with a wrecking ball. He's the reason why Drew is messaging me. Neither of them deserves another second of my mental energy.

As frustrating as seeing Drew's name is, another email is the real reason my heart is thumping faster—Jesse Clark, attorney at law.

I'm not expecting news from my brother's attorney. The last time we connected was when Hunter's last appeal was denied. My brother has served twelve years of his twelve-to-fifteen-year prison sentence, but we know he'll be in for the full fifteen. I have no idea if an email from Jesse is good news or bad.

Holding my breath, I click on the email. Sections jump out at me as I read, each new line pushing my pulse into a gallop.

85% of the maximum sentence served.

Required time completed.

Post-release supervision under review.

I squeeze my eyes shut, then open them and check that this isn't a hoax.

I didn't dare believe Hunter would get early release, not after Derek eventually died in the hospital, twelve days after that horrible night. The prosecutor and judge were ruthless with my brother, as Hunter had predicted—victors bringing down the son of Otto Briggs.

The lawyer claimed Hunter was in town to get retribution against Derek and built his case by trashing Hunter's last name. The party Hunter had attended didn't matter. His clean record was brushed aside. Derek had owed Hunter cash for a Harley they'd rebuilt and sold, and, according to the cops, Hunter wanted what was his and killed Derek in a fit of rage.

Such utter bullshit.

Hunter still wouldn't let me speak up or testify, and the saddest part was I was *relieved*. I was terrified to get involved and be blamed, maybe get arrested too.

That's my shame to carry, and I'm scared to hope this nightmare might finally be coming to an end.

Praying this email is as good as I think it is, I call our lawyer.

"Jesse Clark here." His deep baritone sounds as sturdy as the large man himself.

"I just got your email," I say without preamble.

"Larkin Gray. Figured I'd be hearing from you."

"You said there was no way Hunter would get early release." God, wanting something this badly is terrifying.

"Most prisoners are released after serving eighty-five percent of their maximum sentence. Hunter is at that point, but yes. I warned you it was unlikely in his case."

"His last name," I say, repeating what we both sadly know. "His fights in jail too, and his time in solitary. You *said* he'd be stuck in there for the full fifteen years."

"Because I believed they'd keep him inside as long as possible. But there's a population issue. The Parole Commission is trying to free up cells. This isn't a guarantee. The Commission will review Hunter's files, talk to the prison psychologist, and confer with their team. If they feel he's sufficiently rehabilitated and not a risk to the community, they'll consider his time fully served and put in place conditions for his post-release supervision."

I used to dream of this moment, tried everything I could think of to fight his sentence. A few years after he'd been inside, I worked past my fears. I went to Jesse and confessed what really happened that night. Told him why Hunter had hit Derek with that pipe.

"I'm so sorry," Jesse said, gruff with compassion. "What you went through must have been devastating and, frankly, pisses me off. Abuse cases sit roughly with me. As for Hunter's situation, I can file for an appeal based on new eyewitness testimony, but there's no evidence beyond your word. Your bruises are healed. You'll be raked over the coals for not coming forward earlier. The prosecutor will claim the story is fabricated as a ruse to get your brother out, and your name will be dragged through the mud.

"As I said, I can do it, but you need to think about the implications, and Hunter will have to agree to the course of action."

Hunter, of course, said, "No fucking way."

I tried to locate the Bowers, who had mysteriously left town. Jake was the only one who'd seen my bruises. He knew why I was going to Derek's house. That asshole was the last person I wanted to contact, but if I found him, I thought I could convince Hunter to change his mind. But Jake's number didn't work. He had no social media accounts, no contact information listed anywhere.

Clueless to the fact that the Bowers had been whisked into witness protection to escape crazed drug lords, I was pissed off at him all over again.

Now Hunter might actually get out.

A twinge of excitement hits, but the past twelve years have been hell on Hunter. At my last weekly visit to him, he barely spoke. He picked at a cut on his dry cuticles while I blabbed about my plans for the bar, staffing highs and lows, advertising ideas. Like if I talked enough, I'd fill the emptiness in his soul, the vacant look in his eyes. So, I talked and talked and talked.

At the end of our time, he said, "I'm glad you're building the life you deserve." There was no warmth in his voice. Only resignation. He was ushered out, and I sat there, *furious*. I didn't deserve more than Hunter. *He* deserved love, success, freedom, happiness.

A full life to celebrate his kindness and loyalty.

"He's been down lately," I tell Jesse. "Withdrawn in ways that worry me. If we tell him he might get released, and they don't approve the decision, it could be the final straw that breaks him."

"He deserves to know, Larkin. It's his life in the balance."

I exhale twelve years of heartache. "Okay. I'll go see him. Tell him myself, if that's okay. Is there anything I can do on my end to improve his chances?"

"Not at this time. The Parole Commission will look at his files and do their interviews. The process usually takes six to eight weeks. As soon as I hear anything, I'll let you know. And Larkin?"

"Yeah?"

"This is good news. Stay positive."

We hang up, but I don't feel positive. I stare at my computer, eventually clicking back to my inbox. I stare at that for a while, trying to find some relief in this possibly amazing news, but I only feel more unsettled.

Drew's email is still unread. As annoying as reading it will be, I latch on to the distraction. I'll craft a well-worded decline. Take a page from Drew's confrontational book and tell him *Thanks for the lovely wedding invitation, but I'd rather attend a public hanging.*

I click on his message. His wording is as provoking as expected.

It was so nice to see you, Larkin. I never would have pictured you as a bar owner, but the business is clearly thriving. And I'm glad you found someone who has the same kind of values as you. I'm looking forward to getting to know Jake at the wedding. Unless your role-playing gets in the way of attending.

Knowing Drew the way I do, his message really reads:

It was so nice to see that I was right about you, Larkin. Bar owner is overreaching your potential, but you must have gotten lucky along the way. And I'm glad you found someone who is as emotionally stunted and closed off as you. I'm looking forward to proving as much at the wedding. Unless you were lying about him to save face.

My hand spasms. I look at my computer mouse and realize I'm nearly crushing the darn thing. God, how did I ever fall for Drew? How could I have been so naïve as to share my secrets with him, thinking it would bring us closer?

Not that it matters now.

I roll out my shoulders, ready to tell him where to shove his "values" in an equally snooty way, but my attention locks on his email's signature line. His private practice is listed with his website, but below that is another line. Five words. Just sitting there, like they haven't ripped the floor from under my feet.

North Carolina Parole Commission Adviser

I blink. The line doesn't change.

It's not shocking that Drew works with the Parole Commission. He was always broadening his psychiatric reach, taking extra courses, applying to mental health advisory boards —trying to prove to his tycoon father that being a psychiatrist came with status and influence, even if he didn't join the family business.

He loved boasting at parties, droning on about how in demand he was. But if he advises the Parole Commission, he'll be part of the committee deciding my brother's fate, examining Hunter's files, suggesting outcomes.

The same guy who told me I'd regret breaking up with him.

Shit.

Does Drew know Hunter's sentencing is coming under review? Did he show up at the Barrel House because he knew I owned the bar?

The possibility feels like a stretch. Either way, Drew will have the power to influence the next three years of my brother's life, and he has more reason to be cruel than kind.

I squeeze my eyes shut and breathe. This is bad. Like, really bad.

Or…is it?

Drew's wedding is in four weeks. Jesse said Hunter's decisions won't come down for six to eight weeks. If I make amends with Drew during that time, I might be able to soften him. Subtly influence his decision. Kiss ass like the greatest ass-kisser of all time and tip the scales in Hunter's favor.

Thinking about kowtowing to Drew has my insides revolting, but there's nothing I wouldn't do for Hunter.

Ignoring the queasiness in my gut, I reply to the wedding invitation.

It really was great to see you. I'm thrilled you've met your match and would love to celebrate with you.

I debate telling him my bar-owning success is due to his belief in me. Boost his inflated ego to smooth the path for my impending brownnosing. But he's too smart. He'll know I'm up to something. Subtlety will be the key to influencing Drew.

I send the message, feeling a bit more in control. Until I remember who will have to agree to this ruse: Jake "lying scum" Bower.

I'll have to speak with him. See his unnaturally handsome face, *if* he lowers himself long enough to spare me his attention when not sabotaging my life. I'll have to tell him he'll be attending the wedding with me and somehow pretend I don't want to electrocute him while cozying up to my fake fiancé.

CHAPTER
Eight

Jake

Callahan tosses me a water bottle from his truck. I catch it and chug half, then drag my forearm along my brow. The sun was hot today, unseasonably warm for early October. Not that I'm complaining. Cal and I have been working outside at our latest renovation job. Today, we measured and cut the wood for the Huertas' screened-in porch. Productive, physical work that normally relaxes me.

I'm still wound tight as a drum.

Cal lumbers up to me and tilts his head. "I'm guessing that face means Larkin has sent you death threats for the fiancé move."

I attempt to loosen my jaw. "What face?"

"The one attached to your neck. You didn't look this afraid during WITSEC."

Larkin is as intimidating as cartel hit men. "I'm fine."

"Good to hear." Callahan's tone is as placid as always, kind and sympathetic, but I know my brother. He's placating me.

"I *am* fine," I reinforce.

"I'm sure you're swell." He leans closer and squints one eye at me. "The etched lines by your puckered mouth aren't because you're terrified Larkin will show up any minute to stick your hand under the table saw."

I look at our equipment. There's no controlling the shiver that courses through me. She wouldn't hesitate to saw off my fingers. "Last night was stupid, but it's over. No one heard our conversation. She'll decline whatever invitation her ex sends and resume hating me from afar. All's well that ends well."

"Interesting," Cal says.

"What about this is remotely interesting?"

"I won't ask again what happened to make her hate you this much. I hope you confide in me eventually, but I've gotten to know Larkin over the past months. She sure as shit dislikes you. When your name comes up, she looks ready to spit nails."

"Do you have a point?"

He swallows the last of his water and wipes his mouth. "It takes effort to live with that level of hate so long. Simple animosity burns out over time. But this? How intensely she reacts to just hearing your name? That kind of unrelenting rage screams of deeper feelings she's trying to suppress."

I almost laugh at the absurdity of Larkin having feelings toward me that don't involve mutilation, but a jolt of...*something* tightens my chest.

After our family was forced into witness protection, I hit a massive low. I'd known our father had been lying. I'd been onto him for over a month and hadn't done a damn thing to confront him or loop in my brothers. I never guessed he was laundering money for a drug cartel, but I could have warned my family. Mom, at least. Distanced ourselves from him before he sucked us into his hell.

I was sick over my choices and lack of action. Never breathed a word to any of my family about my failure to protect them. I felt constantly ill and furious. Barely slept or ate. As far as I was concerned, I was responsible for E's breakdowns, Lennon's despondency, Desmond's vicious fury, Cal's quiet gloom, our mother's devastation.

My behavior with Larkin made it all worse.

I scoured the internet for news about Derek and Hunter, eventually learning that Derek died and Hunter was charged with second-degree murder. A bullshit charge, when all Hunter did was protect his sister. I had horrible nightmares during that time—imagined scenes of Larkin drowning or falling or being chased, and I could never save her. When Hunter got sentenced to twelve-to-fifteen years in prison, I went on a black-out bender.

I have no doubt their family tree played a massive part in that judgment, but my cowardly behavior was why he'd even been in that position. Because of me, one man lost his life and another lost his freedom.

It was a shit time, to say the least.

But there was something else I never forgot about that night. My draw to Larkin. How comfortable I felt with her. The intense pull to claim her mouth in a searing kiss.

Unfortunately, dwelling on her appeal only inflamed remorse, so I shoved those memories down. I ignored them. Locked them away and got on with taking care of my family.

Hearing Cal's talk of her harboring deeper feelings has a sliver of light slicing across those dark memories. I don't like it. I don't deserve to think about Larkin in any way except as a woman I owe.

"The only thing Larkin is trying to suppress," I say, "is the urge to murder me."

"Also a strong possibility." Cal shrugs, as though Larkin planning how to dismember me is of no consequence. "I've been known to be wrong."

"Like the time you interfered with Lennon's renovations and

he got slapped with a fine? Or the time you tried to get Jolene evicted from her bar because you thought she hated owning it?"

"Like I said, I've been known to be incorrect." His tone stays even. Typical Callahan presenting a neutral front, but a muscle by his eye ticks. At least he's vowed to quit meddling in people's lives. "The animosity between you and Larkin isn't blowing over," he says, pushing harder. "As far as I can tell, it's getting worse. And I know you well enough to know you feel something for her. If you don't make peace with whatever happened between you two, I'm concerned the tension will escalate and you'll get hurt."

The squeal of brakes has us both shooting our attention to the street.

The rusty white Toyota pulling up looks a lot like Larkin's ancient ride, but Larkin would never willingly come this close to me. Except...there's no misjudging the blond hair and that profile through the window. That's Larkin, looking as pissed off as ever, parking behind my truck.

I debate making a dash to the backyard and hiding out, but she's already out of her car, glaring at me while slamming her door shut.

I trade a wary look with Cal. "Not good," is all he says.

Whatever this is, it will be far from good.

She doesn't do her usual lock and recheck of her door handle. She marches forward so intensely, I step backward.

Callahan approaches her with his hands held up in surrender. "Look here, Larkin, I appreciate that last night—"

"Out of my way, Cal. *He*'s the one I'm here for."

The way she says it sounds more like, *He's the one I'm here to murder.*

She blows past Callahan.

I bow my head, always attempting deference when near Larkin. "I'm sorry about last night," I say quietly. "You seemed uncomfortable. I was trying to help, but I realize it wasn't my place."

"Not your place." She snorts. "That's an understatement." Face full of fury, she jerks her attention to Cal. "We need a minute."

Cal looks to me. I nod, hoping he leaves. I don't want him here for this dressing down. It's not like there's anything he can do to contain Larkin's fury.

Callahan sighs and walks to his truck. I listen as he drives off, but I don't speak to Larkin. I try not to breathe too loudly or make direct eye contact. The volatility rolling off her is hot enough to ignite, but she doesn't say a word. Unless fuming is considered a language. She's doing enough of that to write a tome titled: *Jake Bower is the Lowest Vermin on the Planet Who Deserves to Rot in Hell.*

When the silence drags uncomfortably, I slowly lift my gaze and flinch at her expression. Tightness brackets the edges of her full mouth. Anger is blowing through her eyes, but there's more below that glare—worry, if I'm not mistaken.

"Something happened," I say, nearly stepping forward.

She startles. "What?"

"Did that Drew guy come back?"

"No."

"Did he reach out to you? Send that invite and say something prickish?"

"Prickish?"

"Arrogant? Self-important? Condescending? The guy reeks of pretention."

Her cheekbones sharpen. "If you're saying I have awful taste in men, that's not a news flash."

And *hell*. I glance around, like I might find a rewind button to erase my uncalled-for words. Nothing magically appears.

I have no clue when I turned into a crass idiot around women. I don't date often. Haven't had any interest since returning to Windfall. I may be rusty in the female department, but I always try to be kind and thoughtful. I would never take a cheap shot at someone's past actions.

With Larkin, nothing comes out as it should.

"I'm sorry," I say.

"Seems you always have a reason to be sorry with me."

"Guess it's my default setting. But I am—sorry, that is. I overstepped."

She rolls her eyes. "Unfortunately, you're not wrong. Drew is prickish and all those other well-chosen adjectives. I'm guessing you picked up on that because all assholes excrete special scents to let each other know you're near."

My lips twitch. Goddamn, she's funny, even when she's pissed. Instead of smiling, which would no doubt annoy her, I lean down and sniff my armpit. "You're right," I confirm, wincing at my ripeness. I step farther back from her. "I definitely smell like an insecure loser."

A twinkle sparkles in her eyes, but it's gone in a flash. "At least we agree on that. And the fact that you and I are going to Drew's wedding together."

I freeze mid-swallow. "What?"

"Do you need me to write it out for you in large block letters?"

"Why would you go to his wedding?"

"It's not your concern."

She's right, but the worry I sensed could be vulnerability. Self-doubt. The kinds of qualities bullies inspire. "You don't have anything to prove to that jerk. You're smart and successful. Everyone in town loves you. Fuck him and his overgrown sense of self-importance."

Her eyes widen a fraction, and she touches her throat. She glances at the stacked wood beside the partially finished screened-in porch, blinking for several slow beats. "Like I said, why I'm going isn't your concern. I just am, and I need you there. I need us to sell our happy engagement and pretend to be"—a muscle in her cheek flexes—"in love. Do you think you can manage to show up for me this time?"

Those words are a direct hit to my gut. I lower my head. "Of course. Anything you need. All you ever have to do is ask."

She makes an impatient sound. "Save the chivalrous act for someone who hasn't witnessed your assholeness in action. The wedding is in four weeks. I'll get your number from Jolene and send you the details."

I nod.

She lifts her chin, huffs like she's royalty slumming it with the lower class, then swivels around. Two clipped steps away, her toe hits a small wedge of wood. She stumbles.

I lunge forward, have my arm around her in seconds. "You okay?"

"Fine." But she sways.

I tighten my forearm around her stomach. "If you're light-headed, take a sec. I've got you."

Her chest expands wider. Her hand comes to rest on my wrist. "I'm not normally clumsy and distracted. It's just hot out, and it's been a stressful day."

I don't know why her day has been stressful, beyond last night's shitshow. I don't know what's driving her to accept Drew's wedding invitation. I don't know why I'm not loosening my hold on her or why I'm about to suggest something really fucking dumb.

"I'm guessing Drew's smart," I say against her ear.

She shivers. Likely from annoyance at my proximity. "He is."

"And you hate me."

"I do."

The admission hurts more than it should. "If he's smart, he might realize we're faking. He'll ask us questions we'll stumble over, like how we met and what we love about each other. He seemed like the prying type."

Sensing where I'm going with this, she slumps and mutters, "Fuck."

I release her, and a hollow feeling settles in my chest. Like having Larkin close filled that void.

When she's steady on her feet, I step around so we're facing each other. "If we need to sell this story, we need to *have* a story. We have to spend time together and plan it out. Get to know each other." Maybe I'll finally have the chance to say all the things I haven't said. Explain why I behaved horribly with her.

Larkin's lip curls. "I know everything I need to know about you, Jake Bower."

"You don't know why I left you that night. You don't know—"

She holds up her hand before I can truly apologize and tell her that driving her home wasn't a cruel hoax. I didn't take a dare to hook up with a vulnerable girl. I want to shout that I liked her too damn much, and the strength of those sudden feelings freaked me out. But her caustic expression is clear—she doesn't want excuses.

There's no excusing my actions, period.

"Ground rule number one," she says. "You are never to speak to me about *that night*. Not one word. Ever."

"Got it," I say roughly.

"Rule two, no one knows who my father is or that I'm related to Hunter. I plan to keep it that way."

I nod.

"Rule three, and saying this pains me more than you know." She twitches her nose. "You're right. Drew will be up in my business. We'll need to agree on a past, including inconsequential details to prove we're in love. But we can't meet in town. I won't have the gossip hounds spreading rumors about us again. Which was awesome, by the way."

I wince and almost apologize again, but it's no use. The rumors Callahan started back then were vicious. One small comment—a subtle mention that I'd driven Larkin home and we'd been parked in my truck for a while—seeped across town like an oil spill, turning everything dark and ugly. Over the next week, I heard that I gave Larkin multiple orgasms. Someone said she was pregnant. The words *boyfriend stealer* were wielded unmercifully.

I denied it all. Groveled to Jolene. Told her none of it was true. She said she believed me but broke things off anyway. By then, I didn't have the energy to fight for us. I was still muddled over my feelings for Jo and wasn't sure what I wanted.

Two days later, I finally listened to Larkin's furious phone message telling me that Derek was near and she was scared. Sickness like I'd never known twisted my stomach. I hadn't seen Larkin around town since that night. Hadn't heard anything about her and Derek, but I'd been more than a little preoccupied with my breakup and denying the salacious rumors circulating about Larkin and me.

I called her quickly, unsure what to say. I just needed to hear she was all right.

She answered after four rings. Didn't say a damn thing, just breathed harshly in my ear.

At a loss, I finally said a timid "Hey."

Her hiss was pure venom. "You fucking *asshole*. Going to Derek's was your idea, and you took off and—"

"I know. I'm so sorry. I—"

"*No*, Jake. *You don't know.* I went there anyway, and Derek came home early. He came after me."

My breaths were so ragged, I barely forced out a panicked "What?"

"You fucking heard me, coward. And since you weren't there, I called my brother, who showed up for me, because that's what a kind, loyal guy does. And shit went bad. Now Derek is in ICU and Hunter has been arrested, and how do you think they'll treat the son of Otto Briggs in court?"

"Jesus Christ. Larkin, I'm so damn sorry." My room spun around me as my gut lurched. "Are you okay?"

"*Okay?* A man is in critical condition because of you, and my brother's life is fucked, never mind what happened to me. So do me a favor and don't pretend to be all chivalrous in the future. Save some other girl the trouble of having her life turned to shit."

Yeah. Remembering that call always feels like a nail gun through my sternum. I punched my wall afterward, nearly broke my hand. Still, to this day, I get sick to my stomach when I relive that domino of hell and the consequences afterward.

If I can help Larkin now, I'll turn myself inside out to oblige.

"I have a boat," I tell her. "I know a quiet lake where we won't see anyone." A beautiful lake where I fish and escape the world for a minute. The perfect location for Larkin to kill me and hide my body.

She watches a squirrel run up the nearby hickory tree, seeming to lose some of her anger and steam. Like life is weighing her down. Then she squares her shoulders. "I'll send you a time and day. You better come through this time."

One thing I know, I'll never not show up for Larkin again.

CHAPTER
Nine

Jake

Since leaving behind death threats and witness protection, I've adopted a slower way of life. I don't have to look over my shoulder constantly. My brothers are in love and happy, no longer needing me to hold them steady. Mom is back in Windfall too, sewing awful quilts and leading a fuller life with her old friends.

I've embraced this new beginning, working hard at my construction business, while allowing myself time to relax. Buying a good-size fishing boat with a cabin was a huge part of my newly acquired positivity, even if I had to use money earned from my father's tell-all book. It's become a place for peace and fresh air. Just me and the water and the odd egret or loon.

Today, there is no peace. All I am is agitated.

Larkin was supposed to meet me ten minutes ago, and she's not here.

I should feel relieved. Spending time with a woman who despises me will be as pleasant as hooking a crankbait lure in my neck. I barely slept last night and drove my boat to Lost Lake at the crack of dawn. I launched my girl off the small ramp, tied her to the dock. I've been doing busywork since then. I always leave my boat clean and organized, but I scrubbed the deck, tidied my lures and rods.

Now I'm standing on the dock, alternating between crossing my arms and tugging at my hair, worried something happened to Larkin on her drive along the unpaved road.

When I hear a distant rattle, I stand taller. A few unnerving seconds later, her Toyota bumps down the dirt road to this remote access point.

I strut toward her, ready to open her door and help her up the ramp, but she won't want any of that. I stop short instead, standing awkwardly with my hands stuffed into my front pockets.

She steps from her car, leans on the open door, and surveys the thick trees along the cove's shoreline. "Seems like a good place to hide a body. Yours, in particular."

I bite down on my smile at her predicted reaction to this outing. I have no clue why getting murdered by Larkin is amusing. Maybe it's how cute she looks with her hair tied in braids over each shoulder. "I'm sure you've thought of a number of ways to execute me."

"Five hundred and three," she says.

"That's specific."

"I have a vivid imagination."

I eye her trunk. "Are there piranha in there?"

She takes her phone from her back pocket, taps on it, then returns it, and smiles sweetly. "Five hundred and four."

"You have an actual list on your phone?"

"Number one is death by elephant trampling."

Of course she has a list. "I assumed it would be death by rat torture."

Something less vicious flashes in her eyes, too quick to decipher. She fiddles with a rip in the side of her worn jeans.

"Do you have a jacket?" I ask in the ensuing silence. "It can get cool on the water."

"I'm fine."

And stubborn. I tip my head to my boat. "I brought a saw, just in case the mood to dismember me strikes. And some lemon pomegranate bars to distract you while I escape."

Her shoulders stiffen. "I told you I didn't want anyone knowing we were spending time together."

"I'm aware. I haven't broken your rules." I turn, hoping she follows me.

Footsteps indicate she's not far behind. "Then who told you I like lemon pomegranate bars?"

"No one."

"Bullshit. How else would you know they're my favorite?"

I step onto my boat and hold out my hand to help her. "Same way I know you dump two packets of sugar into your coffee. You ready to board my girl?"

She doesn't give me her hand. A furrow sinks between her brows. She's wearing loose ripped jeans and a threadbare green T-shirt that reads *I dare you.* Her boots are scuffed. There's no makeup covering the freckles speckling her nose, dusted there like a sprinkling of spices.

Everything about her is casual and effortlessly cool. Or maybe she thought the old clothes would show she doesn't care about my opinion.

Unfortunately, women who prefer laid-back to primped, no makeup or airs, are my weakness. I have no place lusting after Larkin Gray.

"Chelsea doesn't like to be kept waiting," I prod.

That furrow sinks deeper. "Chelsea?"

I fan my hand to the name written on the side of my boat. "Named after the greatest woman I know."

She blinks at the carefully painted red lettering. "Your mom."

I nod and lift my hand higher.

Color suffuses her cheeks, but she doesn't take my hand. She steps over the side and moves to the opposite end of the boat. Probably best.

We don't talk as I get us going. She keeps her back to me and watches the water blur by. Wind whips her braids and flyaway hairs behind her, the air rushing past us with scents of silt and marine life. It's a calm and sunny day, but crisp. Larkin visibly shivers.

I don't ask her if she's okay, but I slow down, remove my plaid jacket, and call, "Larkin!"

The second she turns, I toss my coat at her. On instinct, she catches it and scowls at me, but I pay her no mind. I speed up enough to unbalance her—distraction so she doesn't give me shit for caring she's cold. She widens her stance and regains her equilibrium, but she doesn't put on the jacket. The headstrong woman just grips it while shivering.

Larkin would rather die of a snake bite than let me administer the antivenom. At least she doesn't toss my jacket overboard.

I mostly watch the water and the gulls overhead, darting an occasional glance her way. And yep, she's shaking like a scared Chihuahua. I debate cutting the power and demanding she put on my coat, but there's no forcing Larkin to do anything.

I navigate toward another cove and wave at an approaching boat before I realize it's Dave Tanaka, owner of Windfall's hardware store.

"Was that Tanaka?" Larkin shouts, probably to be heard over the motor, but definitely in horror.

"I don't think he recognized you!" I shout back.

She unleashes her signature fume. "*This area is dead in the fall,* you said. *We won't see anyone from town,* you said."

"Normally, it is. And honestly, I don't think he recognized you."

Her fume graduates to a vicious seethe, but she actually tugs on my jacket, easing some of my tension.

Smiling weakly, I head to the more secluded cove. It's a great area for sighting wildlife and catching bass—and avoiding other boaters while Larkin stares daggers at me. I take us in slow and steady, anchor us, and make sure we're secure. I feel Larkin's attention on me as I maneuver around the boat, my skin pebbling with awareness. Or I'm just chilled from the ride.

"The bars are in the cooler," I say as I settle on the bench seat and close my eyes. It's warmer here, protected from the wind, the sun bright and high in the sky. "There's water and gin coolers too. Help yourself to anything."

"Since when do you drink gin coolers?"

"I don't, but you do." I keep my eyes shut, enjoying the soft sway of the boat.

She makes too much noise as she stomps to my cooler. "How'd you know this is the brand I drink?"

I crack an eye open. "It's a small town, Larkin. I see you around a lot. Can't help noticing what I notice." Namely, everything about her.

She straightens, gesturing aggressively at the air. "You won't even look at me in town."

I bolt upright. "What the hell does that mean?"

"Exactly what it sounds like. When you've been in the Barrel House, before the renos, you'd sit with your back to the bar. If you have to speak to me, you stare at the floor. You walk right by me on the street without even glancing my way. You're the same obnoxious jock from high school, who's too cool for anyone outside of his inner circle."

Pissed off. That's the too-fast whir clouding my senses on this pristine day. "You honestly think I haven't changed the past twelve years? You think watching my brothers and mother fall apart and trying to protect them from death threats didn't have any effect on me? That I didn't spend the past decade desperately trying to keep everyone afloat? I'm sorry for my tone, but the guy I was in high school—he doesn't exist anymore. I don't know who I am now, but I'm not him. And no, I don't acknowledge you in public. I avert my attention when you're around. The last thing I want is to cause you more pain or discomfort, and I know seeing my face upsets you."

The boat sways. I don't know when I got to my feet. I don't recall stepping so close to Larkin that I'm hovering over her. She looks shell-shocked and flushed. Her attention darts to my straining neck muscles, which feel like they're about to snap. Her height is a surprise again—how close our faces are when we're standing nearly toe-to-toe—but my intense attraction to her is not shocking. Not with how soft and tempting her lips still are, no matter my haywire mood.

"I'm sorry," I say, stepping away. I rub the back of my neck until my shoulders lower. "I never lose it like that. Not sure what's up with me."

"You don't talk to anyone about what you've been through." It's a statement, not a question.

I don't like the way she's looking at me, like she can see through my toughened exterior to the darker places I keep hidden. "That shit from my past is over. There's nothing to talk about."

"Theoretically, sure. Witness protection is over. But emotionally? Experiences that heavy catch into you like burrs and stick."

"You don't know me, Larkin."

"You take the burden and don't share any of it with your family—that much I know from Callahan and Jolene. Same as when you were younger, trying to shield them from hurt."

This feels like that ride home all over again. This virtual stranger, understanding me in ways I barely admit to myself. "I didn't do such a great job of protecting my family, did I? Couldn't have fucked up with them worse if I tried. Never told anyone I suspected Dad was lying and hiding things, and look where that got us."

Her cheekbones are still sharp with frustration, but there's a softness to her eyes I'm not used to seeing. "You couldn't have known what your father was really doing, Jake. Even if you did, there was no protecting anyone at that point. That landslide was only ever going to flow in one direction."

I grunt but don't reply. She's not entirely wrong. Doesn't mean I couldn't have tried harder. Warned everyone.

If E had said a proper goodbye to Delilah, maybe my youngest brother wouldn't have wasted away in misery that first year. Delilah might not have been so devastated she hurt herself irreparably. Desmond might have found out about his son, had been motivated to stay in school, instead of wasting his days drinking and cursing.

But I didn't warn anyone that Dad was lying.

I scrub my hand down my face, attempting to shake off these bad memories. I watch a fish breach the water, then grab a lemon pomegranate bar from the cooler, sit my ass down, and take a bite. The second the tart sweetness hits my tongue, I groan. "Damn, these are good."

I devour the bar in three large bites, savoring as I swallow. By the time I look back up, Larkin is watching me with her lips parted. She's either fascinated with my mouth, or she's jealous of that fantastic bar. For sure the latter.

She follows suit. Grabs a bar and sits across from me, huddling in my jacket as she nibbles at her treat. "You better not start ordering these on the regular."

"I make no promises."

"If Delilah runs out because of you, my Kill Jake list will get longer."

I smirk. "Noted. Just don't add, Lock him in a room with Mrs. Cho. She can talk the salt from the sea, and my ears are sensitive."

She blinks innocently. "That's number three hundred and forty-nine. And how sensitive are those ears of yours?"

Nope. I don't like that question one bit. "Never you mind."

"Oh, I mind. I mind so much I might buy a Bluetooth speaker that will mysteriously show up at any table you occupy at the Barrel. It will be switched to high."

I shrug. "I'll bring earplugs."

"Smart, since I doubt anyone wants to actually converse with you."

I lean my elbows on my knees and tip my head. "You don't seem to mind, seeing as we haven't broached the reason you're in a secluded cove on this sunny Sunday with a man you despise."

She sits ramrod straight. "Right. Yeah. We need to do that—plan our cover story."

"How we met," I suggest, kicking back in my seat. "Let's start there."

She polishes off the last bite of her lemon pomegranate bar and licks her fingers. I follow the slide of her tongue, can't seem to look away.

Until she says, "Do you do anything for fun besides drive over puppies? Something where two people might connect?"

I raise an eyebrow. "If we have to be fake in love, maybe we should start by not bringing up dead puppies."

"I'll do my best. So…hobbies? Do you have any of those?"

"Vegetables."

"Like, people or the ones you eat?"

I chuckle under my breath. "I volunteer at a community farm

over in Ruby Grove. They supply lower-income families with food there and in Raleigh."

She pulls her head back. "Really?"

"Really."

"You thought it would be a good place to pick up chicks?"

"No." I try to give her a disapproving stare but probably look amused. "I enjoy feeling like I'm part of a community, helping out those who are struggling. I was isolated for a long time and never want to feel that way again."

Her next swallow is slow. She seems to be judging me and everything I say. I have no clue how I'm measuring up.

"Even if it wasn't a way to get lucky," she says, "I assume women are there."

I nod. "It's a good start to our fake story."

"How often do you go?"

"Every Sunday afternoon, until we shut down for the winter."

"You're not there today."

"No." I run my tongue over my teeth, realizing how much I like seeing Larkin in my plaid coat. Those wisps of blond hair framing her face are really pretty too. She's still strong and independent. Mouthy as all get-out. And yeah, I'm still intensely attracted to her, apparently. "Today," I say slowly, "I'm helping someone I care about."

Instantly, her full lips pinch. Her cheeks burn pink. "Don't say things like that. You don't get to fuck with my head like that ever again—make me feel special so you can hook up with me or, in this case, make yourself feel better."

"That's not what this is. And nothing about that night was a lie, Larkin. Nothing I said was—"

"Do *not* say another word." She stands, and the boat rocks. She looks around, like she can somehow get away from me in the middle of this lake. "We're not having this conversation. I told you that night is off-limits. All you want is to absolve yourself of guilt, and I'm not doing that for you. That's your cross to bear. I—" She blinks, moisture shining in her eyes. "Just take me home. This lie to Drew will sink faster than the *Titanic*. There's no point trying to fool him."

I sigh and hang my head, hating the slick of discomfort gumming up my throat. Yeah, I'm sick with guilt when it comes to Larkin. But I do care about her. A fact I should keep to myself.

CHAPTER
Ten

LARKIN

Whoever decorated Langmore Penitentiary's visitors room really nailed the hopeless theme. Between the stained cement floors, beige tables, and glaring fluorescent lights, no one walks into this room feeling cheerful. But every Monday since moving back to Windfall, I've made the three-hour drive here. I've waited with wives and girlfriends and kids, and some seriously intimidating men, while trying not to think too hard about what life was like on the other side of those oppressive walls.

The prisoners come in slowly as I wait at my table today. Some light up when they see their families. Most look like they've forgotten how to smile and sit morosely with their visitors. A couple of inmates cast curious glances my way, and I avert my attention.

I always dress conservatively when visiting Hunter. High neckline on my T-shirt. Nothing too fitted. Still, these men sometimes leer.

Hunter files in and takes his seat at my table. "Hey," he says quietly.

I smile, trying to make it look natural. "It's great to see you."

He nods, taps his thumb on the table, then bounces his knee and touches the front of his taupe shirt.

Hunter never used to be fidgety. He was calm, cool, collected. Confident in a way I totally admired. Now his nerves always seem raw. His gaze darts around the room, never holding anywhere long. He's a big guy. Thickly muscled from his workouts in here. Wide shoulders. Buzzed sandy hair. Deep-set eyes and severe cheekbones.

Inside, it's like the man he was has atrophied.

"How was the bar's reopening?" he asks. I love that he's interested, but the question is monotone.

"So good. Better than good," I add with even more enthusiasm. Enough for both of us. "The place was absolutely packed. Everyone loved the open kitchen and new menu. And we did this dice-rolling game on Wednesday."

I blabber on about the game and other promotions we have planned. I tell him about Delilah's offer to cross-promote and how much I love working with Jolene. He nods as I talk, never sitting completely still, but the longer I go on, the more his shoulders relax. I would talk to him forever if I could. Anything to offer him some reprieve from the monotony of his life.

What I don't do is ask him how he is. I used to. In the early days, I'd poke and prod, ask him if he was doing okay.

Eventually, he told me to quit asking. "Okay in prison isn't the same as okay out there, Runt. Please quit asking."

So, I did.

"Anyway," I say, noticing the time. I'm the fidgety one now, wringing my hands and biting the inside of my cheek. "There's something we need to discuss."

His brows pull tight. "What's wrong?"

"Nothing. Nothing bad. But Jesse contacted me about your sentence."

Hunter squints at me, everything about him suddenly more alert. "What about my sentence?"

I want to reach over and take his hand. Touch him and let him know I believe in him. Soon, he might be free. But touching isn't allowed. "You've served the minimum amount of your sentence, and the Parole Commission is considering you for early release."

He goes still. "Jesse said that wouldn't happen."

"I know. But things have changed." I explain about the overcrowded system. Even with his last name and the judge's harsh ruling, Hunter might soon be free.

He stares at his lap and blinks hard. "My record in here is shit."

"I know."

"They won't overlook that."

"They might."

"They *won't*," he says, forcefully enough to have a guard glaring our way. Hunter takes a deep breath and lowers his voice. "I have three more years. I'm doing *three more years*. Nothing and no one will change that, because what I can't have in here, Larkin, is hope. Hope kills souls. It's a fucking noose that tightens until we snap." He scrubs his eyes aggressively. When he removes his hands, his pupils are red-rimmed. "I can't see you again. Not anymore. If you care about me at all, quit visiting. And for the love of God, don't tell me shit like I might get out, when we both know I won't."

He gets up and stalks away from me, leaving without glancing back.

My eyes blur, but I refuse to cry in here. I knew telling him wouldn't go well. I *knew* he'd been off lately, down and withdrawn. I didn't trust my gut, and now he seems worse than ever.

I walk to my car, feeling helpless and so damn angry. I sit inside and stare at nothing for a while. I can't imagine not visiting Hunter anymore. Already, I feel sick for him. That kind of despair and loneliness will eat at him until the kind, sweet guy I knew no longer exists at all.

At least I didn't tell Hunter that Drew is on the Parole Commission. If hope is Hunter's greatest fear, knowing I might have an in with someone would have done more damage.

I start my car and head toward Windfall, spending the first half of the drive reliving Hunter's outburst and dismissal of me. I tell myself he's just protecting himself. I understand why he's pushing me away. My heart still hurts, but the awareness heightens my resolve to help him.

The rest of the drive is spent stewing over Jake.

I don't know what happened yesterday, why I kept bickering with him instead of working on our "engagement" backstory. Maybe he sprayed his plaid jacket with some kind of distraction potion. The soft material certainly smelled thick with masculinity—woodchips, leather, a hint of spice. The virile scents must have lulled me into that biting banter, which was a teeny bit *fun*.

Except I hate Jake Bower. Nothing about him is *fun*.

Watching his full mouth as he moaned over Delilah's sweets shouldn't have been sexy. I shouldn't have enjoyed the food and drinks he brought specially for me, when he's clearly just being nice out of guilt. Even worse was his outburst about his father and witness protection, stirring my compassion until the need to soothe him became too much.

Jake doesn't deserve soothing. His masculine smell and handsome face don't matter. The night we met, he planned to trick me into hooking up with him, and he ignored my call for help. He's the reason Hunter is in jail. He may feel remorse now, but there's no changing the past. Or my current predicament.

I was hoping I could tell Drew that Jake couldn't make the

wedding. I'd go myself and try to convince Drew my brother deserves his freedom, but Hunter is the worst I've ever seen him. I can't risk the Parole Commission denying his release. At the Barrel, Drew already suspected I was lying about being engaged. Showing up solo to the wedding will make him more suspicious. He might figure out I'm only being nice for my selfish gain.

Which means asking Jake for help *again*—the harder choice for me, but the better choice for Hunter.

On the outskirts of Windfall, I pull over and grab my phone to text Jake, but an email notification pops up. Probably bar business. I tap the icon, only to have Drew back in my inbox.

Normally, I'd be annoyed he felt a need to reply to *my* reply. He loves getting in the last word, but any communication with Drew right now is good.

I tap on his message. By the time I get to the end of it, my hope rises a notch.

> *I'm pleased you and Jake can make it. I'm looking forward to getting to know the man you deemed worthy. Also, Natalia and I had booked a dinner for our guests the Thursday before the wedding, but the venue had to cancel last minute. I was hoping I could rent out the Barrel House that night?*

For anyone else, my reply would be *No*. It's too early in our reopening to close for a busy Thursday night. Even worse, it would mean being fake engaged to Jake in Windfall. The staff would see us. There would be no hiding from their gossip-bright eyes.

Anything for Hunter, I remind myself.

I lay it on thick for Drew.

I'm so honored you'd want to host your party at my bar. Normally, we wouldn't be able to accommodate you. Thursdays are incredibly busy, and we're trying to be a bar locals can count on for their nights out. But since it's you asking, I'll make an exception. With our history, I'm happy to do you a favor. I'll even give you a discount.

And you better do me a solid back, I don't add. With that message sent, I pull up Jake's name and send him a text.

> Me: Where are you? We need to talk.

> Jake: Just leaving the hardware store. And yeah, we do need to talk. Tanaka saw you in my boat.

Yesterday, the prospect of Dave Tanaka recognizing me had me furious. Now, it's a good thing. If I'm hosting Drew's party, everyone there needs to believe we've been together for a while. We'll have to sell our relationship to the whole damn town.

> Me: I'll meet you at the mermaid fountain in ten.

CHAPTER
Eleven

Jake

I'm once again waiting on Larkin. I'm also, once again, fidgety and on edge. I haven't stopped thinking about her since yesterday. I caught myself smiling when reminiscing over our verbal jousting. I got stuck picturing that cute scowl of hers on repeat and nearly burned last night's pasta sauce, but each memory was swiftly followed by how the outing ended.

"Jake." Mrs. Jackson waves to me while walking over. She tucks her large purse close and leans toward my ear. "Don't you worry about that silly Larkin rumor."

This is definitely not good. I already saw Dave Tanaka at the hardware store this afternoon. He wasn't subtle when asking why I was out on a boat with Larkin. He seemed more worried about me than anything else. "What rumor?" I ask.

"That Larkin is blackmailing you."

"*What?*"

"Exactly." She tuts. "No one with any sense believes she caught you stealing books from Delilah's new bookshelf and is demanding you haul supplies for the bar in exchange for her silence. Utter nonsense."

"Why would I steal books from the bookshelf I made?"

"Exactly," she says again. "Those of us who know you two know there's enough animosity between you to fill the old quarry. And we're to blame. All those awful rumors this town spread years ago..." She shakes her head. "The only reason Larkin and you would spend time together is if Jolene needed some kind of help for the bar. So, no need to worry. I won't let this town drown you two in another flood of gossip." She pats my shoulder and walks toward Sugar and Sips.

I suck on my teeth, wondering how pissed Larkin will be about these new rumors.

Sandra walks up to me next. I don't know her well, but her outdated perm is impossible to forget. As was her role in Callahan's love life almost imploding.

Unbeknownst to me or our brothers, Cal had hired Sandra to spy on friends and loved ones while we were in WITSEC. Then, for some asinine reason, when we moved back to town, Cal believed Jolene hated the bar and was only keeping it out of respect for her late aunt, who'd willed it to her. So, what did my moron brother do? He schemed to have another purchaser acquire the building and evict Jolene, all orchestrated through Sandra.

Thankfully, Larkin was buying in to the business at the time, and her youngest brother bought the building instead.

Cal no longer meddles in people's lives and has since fired Sandra, but she pops up now and then, still intent on watching over my family.

"Sandra," I say in greeting.

She tips up her pointy chin. "Larkin is on her way here, presumably to see you, and she's upset."

At least Sandra is on-brand, knowing things she shouldn't know. But *I* already know Larkin's upset with me and the gossip circulating about us. It's the only reason she would have called and demanded we meet. "How do you know she's upset?"

"I have a friend who's a prison guard," is her reply.

I attempt to think through her riddle, but I get nowhere fast. "What does your prison-guard friend have to do with Larkin's mood?"

"You're smarter than this, Jake," she says and marches off.

I'm not sure I am, to be honest.

Larkin's white Toyota pulls into a parking spot on Main Street, not giving me time to think through Sandra's vague hints. Larkin gets out and checks her handle to make sure the car is locked. She abruptly lifts her attention, scans the grassy town square and mermaid fountain. The second she notices me, her lips flatten into an angry line.

Yep, she's pissed about the town rumors.

Her hair is in a ponytail today. She's wearing a simple high-necked T-shirt and non-ripped jeans. Still, for some goddamn reason, my body heats. Larkin could be wearing a potato sack, and I'd find her relentlessly sexy.

I dig my hands deeper into my jeans pockets as I wait for her. Water splashes happily into the fountain at my right. Townsfolk walk jauntily along the cobblestone sidewalk. Banners for the upcoming Dog and Pony Show hang off the old-fashioned lampposts, rustling in the light wind.

The town hosted the Scarecrow Scavenger Hunt earlier than usual this year, making room for this new festival. I'm not sure what the event entails, although I'd bet it has something to do with dogs and ponies. When I first saw the cute cartoon banners, I smiled at Windfall's love of oddball festivals. Nothing about me is smiling now.

Larkin marches straight for me. A few townsfolk notice and stop. Whispers are already happening. Whatever other strains of gossip are spreading about Larkin and me—maybe that she forced me onto my boat at gunpoint—we're about to fan the flames.

She stops a foot from me and crosses her arms. "We're back on for the wedding."

My mind stalls, taking a moment to get back on track. "Why?"

"Because I said so."

"Not good enough." Whatever's going on with her ex, it's rattling Larkin to the point of worry. I'm not sure if she's trying to make him jealous or win him back. Whatever the cause, I'm not about to stand by and let that guy hurt her.

Larkin hugs her waist tighter. "I thought you said you'd do anything to help me. That I only have to ask you."

"Pretty sure you didn't ask. You dictated."

Her nose twitches. "I guess those penis enlargement pills you took worked. You're twice the dick you were yesterday."

My laugh catches me off guard. I'm not sure why I like her feistiness so much. Maybe because other people around town treat me soft, like what I've been through has made me vulnerable and weak.

She huffs out a half-amused sound and glances to her left. Two women, one of whom is loudmouth Candace Sinclair, are watching us with rapt attention.

Larkin rolls her eyes and faces me. "I need you at the wedding because, thanks to you, Drew thinks we're engaged. Also thanks to you"—she steps closer and lowers her voice —"my brother is in jail, but he's up for early release. Drew is a psychiatrist on the Parole Commission. I need to convince him to go easy on Hunter and let him out. Is that a good enough reason for you?"

Everything in me turns leaden.

I should have known Larkin wasn't talking to her condescending ex to win him back. This, though? The burden of helping her brother, who should never have been locked up in the first place? Maybe that's what Sandra was hinting at. Larkin must have been visiting her brother today and left upset.

"Of course," I say quickly. "I'll do whatever it takes."

She's still leaning close and breathing hard. The urge to break eye contact strikes—shame heating me from my boots to my scalp—but Larkin admitted in the boat that my avoidance of her felt like a rude dismissal, like I thought I was too good for her.

I tilt my head instead, try to show her how sorry I am. How much I truly care, without saying the words. "Tell me what you need. Tell me, and we'll work our asses off to help Hunter. I swear, I won't make this about me. I'll never bring up that night again."

Her eyes glaze. She looks down sharply and chews her lip. I'm still intent on her. Won't let her think she's forgettable ever again. I won't let her down, period, no matter what happens.

When she finally lifts her head, she's composed. Her shoulders are soft, and her expression is kind. If I didn't know better, I might even guess she didn't hate me. "Pretending we're in love won't be easy."

I nod, even though I'm not so sure about that. Her biting humor hits me in a way I like. I had fun with her on my boat and haven't stopped thinking about her since. Then there's the undeniable attraction. "I'm sure we can act the part, but can I ask you something?"

"Only if it doesn't involve the past."

Instead of promising again I won't break that rule, I say, "Then forget it. I was going to ask what type of cage you envisioned when murdering me by rat torture."

The corner of her lips lifts. "Thick metal, and it hooks into your skin for extra pain."

I wince at the visual. "Maybe I'll put on some pounds. Loosen up my skin so it hurts less."

Her gaze slides down my torso. I'm wearing a blue Henley

and my work jeans. Nothing special. The way Larkin's attention lingers on my midsection has my abs flexing.

"I wasn't going to mention anything," she says, drawing her gaze back up, "but you look like you've put on a few pounds. Might want to lay off the lemon pomegranate bars."

I bark out a laugh. Fuck, she's funny, even though my body has been veering in the opposite direction. My appetite has been shit lately, and I've been at the gym when not at work. The former is one of my stressed-out symptoms, the latter my stress reliever. "You just want those lemon bars all to yourself."

She shrugs, looking like she's trying not to smile. I'm not even trying. I smile at her, wishing I could ask her out on a proper date, none of this fake nonsense. But there's no changing the past.

Rocking on my heels, I veer toward the more sensitive subject I wanted to broach. "Does it seem odd to you that Drew turned up when your brother's sentence is getting evaluated?"

"Yeah," she says slowly. "Drew has a history of being a bit… shady when he wants things."

"Shady how?"

"His father is a self-made man—mergers and acquisitions that earned him millions. From what I understand, Mr. Carrington did whatever was needed to build his empire and has no shame in bending the law. Drew didn't follow in his father's work footsteps, but he inherited the man's low scruples and drive."

"So you think he might be up to something? That he'd use Hunter's situation to gain something from you?"

Her brow wrinkles. "Drew doesn't understand the word no. I'm pretty sure he found a way to pass a course he should've failed while we dated, and I know he chased me initially because I wouldn't give him the time of day. He liked the challenge, but he definitely resented me after I broke up with him. I just don't see what he has to gain by fucking with me now. I mean, he's getting married. He's clearly over me. And he said he booked his wedding venue months ago, well before Hunter's parole review would have hit his inbox, if it's even there yet. I'm guessing his being in Windfall and at the bar was a coincidence."

I mull over her points, but I don't like coincidences. After the hell with my father, I prefer trusting my gut. "You're probably right, but I'd stay alert around him."

"You don't have to pretend to be concerned about me." She tips up her chin, challenge sharpening her eyes. "It's not part of the role."

Annoyance flares. I want to tell her—*again*—that I never pretended with her or schemed to get into her pants. I cared too much then and care too much now. Since any of that would upset her, I stay quiet, while trying not to stare at the tempting slope of her mouth.

A small dog jogs by with its owner. Someone tosses a penny into the mermaid fountain as we stand awkwardly together.

"Anyway," Larkin says in a huff, "Drew asked if he could host a special dinner at the Barrel. I agreed, while kissing his ass. Since it'll be in town, we'll have to sell our engagement publicly."

I cringe, thinking about Mrs. Jackson's wild rumor and Dave Tanaka's reaction to seeing Larkin and me together. "That might be an issue."

"Because being seen with me would ruin your studly reputation?"

The low growl emanating from my throat catches me off guard. Swallowing past my irritation, I say a softer "*No*. I have no issues being around you, but this town knows you hate me. When Tanaka mentioned he saw us in my boat, he asked if I needed to talk about anything and eyed me for damage. Mrs. Jackson said people think you're blackmailing me, because you caught me stealing books from Delilah's bookshelf."

"Why would you steal books from a bookshelf you made?"

"Because this town loves spreading nonsense as much as it loves ridiculous festivals. How do you propose we convince them we're in love, when we've spent the last six months avoiding each other?"

She blinks at me and seems to freeze. Her throat works reflexively, like she's got something stuck in there. Her blue-green eyes dart around my face, then to the stone at our feet, then back to my face. I attempt to read her mind but get nowhere fast.

Next thing I know, she kisses me.

Right there. Broad daylight. Townsfolk milling around.

Her lips are as soft as they look, but I'm so taken aback, I barely move.

She pulls away and lifts her forearm, as though to wipe her mouth, but she lowers it and plasters on a deranged-looking grin. "At least that answers that question."

"What question?" I say, addled. The faintest taste of her is in my mouth—warm and bitingly sweet. It's hard to focus on much except the word *more*.

"How you kiss."

"How do I kiss?"

"Like you're made of the same thing as your heart." When I raise my eyebrow, she says, "Stone."

This woman's goddamn nerve.

I have no doubt we have a captive audience, but all I see is Larkin's smug expression, those tiny freckles dotting her nose, that small scar I've always wondered about. I see her defiant nature and how vulnerable she is under her hard shell. She's terrified for anyone to know whose DNA runs through her veins, refuses to discuss that devastating night with me. She's not wrong thinking I want absolution, but I'd bet she's avoiding her own demons.

And she senses mine.

In a few minutes yesterday, she had my insecurities dissected like a brain surgeon.

You don't talk to anyone about what you've been through. You take the burden and don't share any of it with your family. Same as when you were younger, trying to shield them from hurt.

Yeah. Larkin sees me. Always has. Just like I see her. All that complexity wrapped up in a sexy-as-hell package, and there's no way I'll let her believe I kiss like a fucking statue.

Prepared this time, I grip the back of her neck and slant my mouth over hers.

A squeak of surprise escapes her, but she grabs my sides, like she maybe wants to tug me closer...or shove me farther away.

Hoping for the former, I kiss her bottom lip, tuck her into my body. Kiss her softly a few more times, and *Jesus*—she gasps on a quiet moan, like she's enjoying this as much as me.

I should stop. Step away after proving her wrong.

I kiss her deeper, unable to think clearly or give her an inch of space. I'm addicted already. High on her taste and feel, that small press of her hands into my lower back. I lick at the seam of her lips, coaxing her to open for me, and she *fucking does*. Our tongues slide as I explore the soft warmth of her mouth, her tiny sounds of pleasure driving me wild.

Until a high-pitched "Mommy, why is he sucking her face?" crashes into my consciousness.

I laugh against Larkin and feel her amused puff of air.

I loosen my hold on her, running my hand down her back as I move my mouth to her ear. "Care to amend that last statement?"

She doesn't reply. Her heavy breathing is answer enough.

"Text me when you want to meet again," I tell her. "We need to work on our backstory."

I pull back and wink. She looks slightly dazed, doesn't budge or blink, but her lips are red and puffy and perfectly kissed. I leave her standing there, feeling her attention on my back as I go, pleased with her state of paralysis. *Kiss like stone, my ass.*

The kid's mother gives me a dirty look, and Candace Sinclair is gaping at me with her jaw unhinged. Dave Tanaka is standing outside his hardware store, as though someone told him the show of the century was going on and he shouldn't miss it.

I wave at him, glad we at least don't have to hide our ruse in public. If the town had any question about why Larkin and I were in my boat together, the issue is now resolved.

The situation in my jeans might take longer to subside.

CHAPTER
Twelve

Jake

I pull down Elm Street and drive by the brightly painted Victorian homes, trying not to yawn. I barely slept last night. Went for a long run this morning, did some weights at home afterward. Anything to burn off thoughts of that unforgettable kiss. No damn luck.

With my early start, I expected to be the first one to arrive for work, but Callahan's truck is already parked by the Huertas' home. The Huerta family is on vacation this week. We're trying to get as much done as possible while they're gone. If Cal is here, he should be busy working on their screened-in porch. Instead, he's busy standing in their driveway, staring at me.

The second I park and step from my truck, he says, "Explain yourself."

He doesn't need to say more. News of that inappropriate kiss has no doubt traveled to Timbuktu. I certainly haven't been able to quit thinking about the hot slide of Larkin's tongue and her little sounds of surprised pleasure.

"Larkin and I are engaged," I tell Cal matter-of-factly. "Engaged couples kiss."

"You're engaged," he says with a hefty dose of sarcasm.

"Yep."

Cal lifts and lowers his baseball hat. He's the calmest and most level-headed of my brothers, but his resting congenial expression shifts to probing. "I assume this is the fake engagement you instigated at the Barrel House with her asshole ex?"

I nod. "Turns out we're attending his wedding. She needs him and the town to think we're madly in love and soon-to-be married, so don't say a thing to anyone about the fake part."

He rolls his tongue over his teeth the way I sometimes do. "Does Larkin still hate you?"

She didn't hate that kiss. That much I know. Pretty sure she found our bantering on the boat as fun as I did, but nothing with us is simple. "Mostly, yeah."

"And you? How do you feel about her?"

"It's complicated."

"Then uncomplicate it for me."

Instead of replying, I kick a stray stone on the driveway. Cal's brown hair curls out from under his baseball cap, like mine curls out from under my wool hat. His brown eyes are similar to mine too—dark and deep-set—but his are softer. Easier to face when I have secrets to keep.

"Here's the thing," he says, slow and calm. "I know you have feelings for Larkin. I see it every time she's near. It's more than guilt over whatever went down twelve years ago, and I won't stand by and watch her hurt you."

Her hurt *me.* That's a fucking laugh, when all I've ever done is let her down. "I can look after myself."

"No, you can't."

"Excuse me?" I say, stepping up into his space.

"For the past twelve years, your only focus has been taking

care of us. You got us busy when we were on the verge of breaking down. You worked tirelessly, making sure we all pulled through WITSEC and losing the people we loved—which is damn sure appreciated—but no one looked after you. So, this is me, looking after you for a change. If you pretend to be engaged to Larkin and get closer with her, you'll get hurt. I don't want you doing it."

"It's not up to me." My tone is rising, but he doesn't understand.

"She can tell her ex to take a hike. Screw the wedding."

"She *can't*."

"Then tell her to make up an excuse for why you can't be there." He waves an agitated hand, sounding more riled than usual. "She can go alone."

"My answer is the same, so just drop it already."

"Since when don't you have a backbone and a choice?"

"Since I let Larkin down twelve years ago and am responsible for one man's murder and another's prison sentence!"

Fucking hell.

Cal's eyes bug out.

I hold up my hands, like I'm surrendering to a sheriff. "I didn't say that. Please ignore whatever just came out of my mouth."

"Not happening in this lifetime." He takes a firm hold of my arm and drags me to the bench we put outside the Huertas' garage. A place for us to sit and eat during our workday. Right now, it feels like I'm being led to the gallows.

I sit with a heavy sigh. Plant my elbows on my knees and drop my head into my hands. "I promised her I wouldn't tell anyone."

"Good. I'm not anyone. I'm your favorite brother. And I won't breathe a word of what you say to a soul, including Jolene. We're not leaving here until you talk."

"You're not my favorite," I grumble.

He huffs out an irritated sound. "I'll excuse that because you're upset and emotional."

"Excuse whatever you want. My favorite is Desmond."

"Desmond barely spoke to us for ten years."

I turn my head just enough to catch his eye. "Exactly. He didn't do this." I gesture from Cal to me.

Cal does his best to give me a sharp look, but he only does a half-assed job of looking peeved. "As your second-favorite brother, I promise not to say a word to anyone."

I smirk. "You're not my sec—"

"Quit it with the diversions. I'm reinstating myself as first favorite, and I'm not budging until you tell me how you're responsible for a man's murder."

Sinking heavier onto the bench, I yank off my wool hat before I overheat from my building stress. If I admit what happened, Cal will look at me differently. He won't see the brother who helped him survive a harrowing time in his life. He'll see a coward who *ruined* lives.

"I can't," I force out.

His big hand rests on my back. "No matter what you did, I won't love you less. Come hell or high water, you're stuck with me."

I breathe deep, expand my back into the weight of his reassuring hand. Still, I keep my mouth shut. I don't want to say this awful thing and watch his expression shift to disbelief and outrage, but everything has been tougher since this fiancé mess. Not-sleeping tough. Distracted-all-day tough. So overwhelming that the urge to finally confess what I did grows so big and grave that the long-buried words scramble up.

"That night you told me to take Larkin home," I say thickly, "she'd recently broken up with an abusive ex."

I spew it all. My instant connection with Larkin. My confusion over Jolene that night. Larkin's criminal father. The half brother she loves. The almost-kiss that knocked me for a spin, and my cruel dismissal of her afterward.

Telling him about Derek has me digging my nails into my palms. "Larkin's never given me details on what happened. I only read that he died of a blow to the head twelve days after being struck. But for Hunter to hit him that hard, Larkin must've been in serious trouble. Hunter wasn't like their father, according to her. I don't think he'd get that violent unless her life was at risk. And if I'd answered her call, none of that would've happened. I might've gotten there sooner, before Derek did whatever he did. I might have shown more restraint."

"Or you might be the one in prison now. If Larkin was in trouble, you wouldn't have stood idly by. You would've done whatever was necessary to save her."

"Except my last name isn't Briggs. I would've been treated differently. At the very least, Larkin would've explained why I was there and what was happening with Derek. In all the articles I read about the case, I never once saw her name. As far as I can tell, no one knows she was there. Either her mother or brother, or both, told her not to speak up. Probably worried the courts would drag her down for being Otto Briggs's daughter, which is exactly what they did to Hunter.

"So, yeah, if I had been a decent fucking human and answered when she called—instead of freaking out over how much I liked her—a man might be alive, and her brother wouldn't be in jail."

I toss my hat on the ground and glare at the lawn. Cal's mirroring my pose, elbows on his knees, his broad shoulders tight. I want him to say something. Yell at me for being so damn selfish.

He fists and releases his hands. "I never should've asked you to take Larkin home that night."

"No, you shouldn't have. But everything that happened afterward is on me, not you." I feel his guilt already, though. I know my brother. He'll hold on to these regrets. "Don't go beating yourself up over the past."

He straightens and folds his thick arms over his chest. "If I don't get to feel like shit about it, neither do you."

Clearly, he's lost his mind. "What I did was way worse than what you did."

"No, it wasn't."

"So we're arguing over who's a worse person?"

He pulls off his ballcap and rubs his head. "Tell me this—if you'd known Larkin was in trouble, would you have answered her call?"

"Of course." There's no hesitation. Only vehemence and regret for not knowing.

"Exactly," Cal says, replacing his hat with a sharp yank. "Unlike you, I knew what I was doing when I orchestrated that shitshow of a night—wanting you to take Larkin home, the rumors I'd spread afterward, hoping you and Jo would break up and I'd swoop in and finally ask Jolene out. The consequences of your actions might have been worse, but you didn't know the facts. You assumed Larkin was still mad at you for bailing on her and reacted like a typical twentysomething, preferring to avoid a confrontation. I would've done the same."

He's simplifying my actions, but a sliver of his rationalization sinks in. Yeah, if I'd known Larkin was scared and in trouble, I would've answered in a heartbeat. I didn't ignore her call for help. I was trying to ignore my *feelings* for her.

Grudgingly, I sigh. Maybe Cal is my favorite brother after all. The one of us who sees the silver lining in a Category 5 hurricane. Not that it changes the outcome of that night.

"I appreciate your point and will think on it, as long as you do the same. You made a shitty plan that night, but everything that happened afterward had nothing to do with you. As far as Larkin is concerned, she'll never forgive me, regardless of why I did or didn't do anything. So, yeah, I'm interested in her. There's always been something about her that has"—pulled me in, been impossible to resist, made me oblivious to everything but her —"affected me," I settle on. "But she hates my guts."

"Doesn't sound like she was hating your mouth yesterday afternoon."

I drag my teeth over my bottom lip, like I can still taste her sharp sweetness.

Predictably, my body reacts.

I tense my thighs until they hurt. "It was just a kiss. She seemed to like it in the moment, but nothing will erase our history. She'll never see me as anyone except the guy who ignored her call for help and ruined her brother's life."

Two trucks stop on the street, and I groan. Desmond and Lennon are in one truck. E is in the other. Of course the rest of my family turned up, unable to resist needling me about that now-infamous kiss.

"Not a word to them," I hiss to Cal as they slam their doors and head our way.

He doesn't answer, and I glance at him. His features are pinched, his attention cemented on the ground, like he didn't hear me. "Cal," I say with more force.

He startles and glances at me. "Yeah?"

"Don't beat yourself up about this," I say again. "If you need to talk it out, call me. And please don't tell our brothers. I can't have this getting out."

He passes his hand over his mouth and nods.

Appeased, I stand to meet our annoying family on the driveway. Desmond crosses his arms and glares his usual glare. Lennon looks like the cat who ate the canary. He's no doubt busting to antagonize me for my public PDA. E has a soft frown denting his brow. Worried about me, no doubt, but there's mischief in his eyes I don't like.

Best to set the ground rules. "One rude word from any of you, and you get punched in the face."

Lennon screws his mouth to the side. "Does the fact that every woman near the town square yesterday is now pregnant from watching you maul your archenemy count as rude?"

I snarl at him. He snickers.

"What about the fact that you swallowed her tonsils?" E laughs while razzing me. Guy can never dish out jabs without cracking up. "Sounds like you need kissing lessons."

Lennon fans his hand to Desmond's resting Mad at the World Face. "Des agreed to teach you."

"Fuck you," Des says. "But you will be spilling the dirt on that kiss. I thought Larkin hated you."

I scowl and avert my attention. Mrs. Hadid is watering her lawn across the street. She waves. I wave back, attempting to offer a kind smile. Not easy with these interfering idiots in my face. Telling Cal was one thing. He'll keep his mouth shut. I don't trust the rest of my brothers not to share dirt with their girlfriends. If word gets out about who Larkin's father is because of me, any headway I've made with her will be toast.

Unfortunately, they know enough *not* to buy my engagement story.

"All you need to know," Cal says before I figure out how to get them to leave, "is Jake and Larkin have an agreement. She's still sore with him over something from their past, but they're pretending to be engaged. He would appreciate if you don't ask why and don't bug him about it. And don't breathe a word around town that their relationship is fake."

Their rapt attention darts from Cal's face to mine and back to Cal's.

"You know the full story?" Des asks him.

"I do."

"And you've got him covered?"

"I do."

Des grunts. That's as good as an agreement from him.

Lennon seems less mollified. "We know you're into her, Jake. This won't end well for you."

Based on how that kiss affected me, it'll end with me spending a lot of time with my right hand. "There's nothing to be done about any of that."

"Have you tried apologizing to her for this mysterious thing we're not allowed to know? Women love a man who owns his mistakes."

"Yes, moron, I've tried. She refuses to talk about what happened. Cuts me off every time I try."

E nudges Lennon. "Tell him about your windshield notes."

"Good thinking." Lennon brightens and punches my shoulder. "You should totally do a windshield note."

I run my tongue over my teeth. "What's a windshield note?"

"When I was wooing Maggie, I left her notes on her Jeep's windshield. Little things so she knew I was thinking about her. Except..." He taps his chin. "Random notes won't work for your situation, and I'm obviously wittier."

Desmond gives him a bland look. "Says the guy who failed English."

"Says the guy who flunked out of law school." Lennon steps back as he speaks, knowing Des won't let that dig lie.

Predictably, Des lunges at him, grabs his arm, and pulls him into a headlock. "Say that again, asshole."

Lennon laughs and punches at him, barely making a dent until he pinches the skin below Desmond's cargo shorts. Des growls and shoves him off, while the rest of us chuckle at Lennon's flushed face. Honestly, thank God for my idiot brothers. I could be on my deathbed, and they'd manage to make me laugh.

"If you nitwits could focus for a minute," Cal says, "Lennon's wrong about the wittier part, but not about the notes. A letter to Larkin might do the trick, something heartfelt and honest. She can't cut you off if it's written down and mailed."

I open my mouth to tell him it's a stupid idea. Any communication with Larkin about that night, verbal or written, will enrage her. She'll think I'm selfishly trying to absolve myself again, but I hate that she still thinks I was pulling a prank on her.

You don't get to fuck with my head like that ever again—make me feel special so you can hook up with me or, in this case, make yourself feel better.

Those words, as much as that unforgettable kiss, were partly to blame for last night's insomnia. Maybe there's a better way to word a letter so it's not focused on me and my regrets. A way to make Larkin understand no part of her has ever been a joke to me. Show her through my dead-honest truth that, to me, she's only ever been unforgettable.

CHAPTER
Thirteen

LARKIN

Wednesdays should come with an hourly shot of Red Bull. We've been packed since noon. Table after table filled, with a slight line at the door. The staff have been run off their feet. We've moved through today's featured beer. Emmanuel had to add a new sandwich special when the short-rib grilled cheese ran out. The kitchen was on point, though. No one had to wait too long for their food.

The only customer left now is Callahan, eating on his own, the way he sometimes does, just to be close to Jo. Except Jolene isn't here. She's working the night shift today, which I'm sure he knows. He could just be supporting our business, but he's been casting occasional glances my way, indecipherable, probing. Unnerving looks that have me on edge.

Or maybe it's the fact that every staff member and a few customers today have mentioned or asked about my kiss with Jake.

I had no idea you two were dating.

How long have you been together?
Did you need CPR? Is that why his mouth was on you?
Was it a dare?
Is he as good as he looks?
I always knew you two would be an item.

My nosiest waitress, Sue-Ann—*Is he as good as he looks?*—Hinkley, joins me by the cash register and half sprawls her upper body on the bar top. "That was exhausting, but awesome. Now we finally have time to discuss *that kiss.*"

I sigh inwardly while organizing the stack of receipts. "I was worried the POS system would freeze from all the orders going through."

Ignoring her kiss comment seems like the best move. I've already confirmed Jake and I are wildly, *madly* in love. Our ruse is in play. No more details are needed.

"This dice-rolling promo was a killer idea," Sue-Ann says, sticking to my topic change. "Even with the odd discount, my tips have gone up."

"It's your new purple hair. Purple is the color of royalty. Makes people want to spend more money."

"In that case, I'll wear a crown tomorrow. See if that takes things over the edge. Also…" She straightens and hums a flirty tune. "Three tables said Jake kissed you like a starving man devouring a meal."

I flash to the feel of Jake's firm body against mine. The sensual yet commanding way he moved. How perfectly our lips came together, like we'd kissed a thousand times before.

I bite my cheek until a metallic taste hits my tongue—today's distraction technic. Better to think of blood than kissing Jake Bower. I mean, the guy was only trying to prove a point. Dust off his ego after our first subpar lip lock. Typical man, unwilling to let a woman think he can't perform, even if he's not interested in her.

Not that I *want* him to be interested. Or to discuss that encounter ad nauseum.

"You've mentioned that kiss five times," I tell Sue-Ann. "Consider it discussed."

Jolene texted me about it too. I put her off with a quick *Too busy. We'll chat tomorrow.*

"Lame," Su-Ann says as she shimmies to the country tune playing. "As far as I heard it, Candace Sinclair said Jake was basically making love to you with his clothes on, and Aaron Rothman said that Shera Hadid said you fainted from the sheer force of his masterful kiss."

I sure as heck turned boneless, even if I didn't faint. "I don't kiss and tell. All you need to know is that Jake and I started dating recently and have been keeping it quiet. No need to grill me anymore."

"You're no fun. But I'm not surprised you two finally hooked up. The tension between you has been kind of evil, and evil gives good passion. Also, thanks for stocking the staff bathroom with painkillers and tampons. Both totally saved me yesterday."

She hurries off to clean and set the tables for dinner service. Sue-Ann may be nosy, but she's a sweet woman and a great waitress. I watch her, pleased staff appreciate the little extras I've done for them, even if her "passion" comment was off base. As far as I'm concerned, evil only begets more evil.

I turn to grab the stacked receipts and find Callahan standing at the bar, watching me.

"So," he says, "you're fake marrying my brother."

"Keep your voice down," I hiss and flick my head toward Sue-Ann. Thankfully the music is too loud for her to hear the word *fake*. "And mind your own business. This will be over as soon as possible."

He nods and drums his fingers on the bar. "I know I've apologized to you in the past for the rumors I spread about you and Jake, but I want you to know how sorry I am. I never should've asked Jake to take you home or let rumors start about you two hooking up."

I squint at him, unsure where this extra apology is coming from. I only learned about Cal's scheme to break up Jake and Jo this year. I was angry when he first confessed, but so much time had already passed. My resentment didn't have over a decade to dig deep. If I'd known from the start, I might have hated him as much as I hate Jake. Cal's stunt, asking Jake to drive me home, *did* put that whole night in motion. Or maybe my grudge would have mellowed.

Jake's actions had nothing to do with his brother's. Every choice Jake made—playing games to hook up with me, chickening out and leaving me on the side of the road, ignoring my call for help—felt like personal attacks.

Callahan's actions all revolved around Jolene.

"You shouldn't have done that stuff," I say, "but it's in the past, and Jolene loves you. If you've earned her love, you can't be all bad."

Cal dips his head, but his face remains drawn. "You're not working the dinner shift tonight, right?"

I pause at the odd segue. "Jolene is working tonight without me, which I'm pretty sure you know. Why?"

He taps his fingers on the bar some more. He aligns straws already sitting pretty in their stainless-steel container. "Just hoping you enjoy your evening. And you might want to check your mailbox at home. Jake said he left something for you."

He knocks his knuckles on the bar, gives me a pointed look I don't understand, then strides to the door.

I bounce my knee, unable to look away from his retreating back as he leaves. I'm aware Jake's brothers know our engagement is fake. They're too close to fool those men. The rest has me antsy. Why would Jake leave me something? Why did Cal feel a need to mention it? And why did my stomach just do a disconcerting spin?

Hunger. That's what this is. I didn't eat during my shift. Or I'm just nauseated from discussing Jake.

I finally deal with the lunch receipts. Clean up and prep the bar for dinner service, working faster than usual. I say a quick goodbye to Sue-Ann and the other staff and hurry to my car. I have a book to pick up at the Sandpiper's Nest in town—Amy Lea's latest romance I've been dying for. I was planning to do a small grocery shop too.

For some irritating reason, I find myself heading home.

That flipping in my stomach worsens as I drive. I feel a bit light-headed too. I better not be getting sick. Missing work isn't an option.

I turn down Spruce Street and drive a tad too fast, barely noticing the brightly painted Victorian homes. Growing up, I never imagined living in this part of town. Mom told me and my younger brother, Julian, these were the snobby people.

"They think they're better than us," she'd say as she smoked and sipped her vodka. "The only way to survive with them is to be invisible or have something they want."

For Mom, they wanted her looks. At least, the men did. Until smoking and drinking and living hard chipped away at her appearance. My brother followed her advice and attempted invisibility. He flew under the radar with his nose in his books. He lives in New York now. Works in a big building doing consulting work for massive companies.

He's happy, from what I can tell. We talk every few weeks about life and work and our future plans. He gave me advice on how to manage my money and buy in to Jolene's bar. I rag on him to work less and live more. Advice he flips back on me. And when Callahan stuck his stupid nose where it didn't belong and schemed to have someone buy the Barrel House's building earlier this year, Julian stepped in and bought it instead, allowing Jo and me to partner up and continue running the bar.

We have different absentee fathers, and neither of us sees our mother, but we're both good with that. We have each other, and I have Hunter.

Now I'm one of the "snobby" townsfolk, living in a cute coach house behind the light-blue Victorian in the middle of Spruce Street. No one calls me a boyfriend-stealing slut. People smile and wave when they see me. I feel accepted and successful.

Some days, though, it's as if I'm walking through life as an actress, playing a role, worried I'll be discovered as a fraud.

I park on the street and don't bother checking my car's door handle when I lock it. I'm too keyed up. And annoyed. Whatever Jake left for me, it's no doubt something selfish to ease his conscience. Or he's playing games with me again—kissing me the way he did, like he can't get enough of me, telling me he avoids me in town so I don't get upset, then probably writing a note to tell me he doesn't have the time or care to help with Drew.

Guilt. Games. A bit of both, maybe.

I don't know what Jake Bower is up to. Whatever it is, it can't be good.

My landlords, the Walkers, live in front of the coach house I rent and are incredibly kind. Mail is delivered to their box out front, but they sort mine and add it to the mailbox they installed outside my door. I march there and yank up the flap. Inside are a couple of flyers and one envelope with my name scrawled on it.

My stomach does another unnerving dip.

I'd love to blame my reaction on the start of an unpleasant bug, but there's no denying the source: Jake gets-under-my-skin Bower.

Why does one measly man have to affect me so much?

I debate tossing the envelope. Out of sight, out of mind. That plan lasts all of two seconds. I push into my home, dump my purse on the floor, and drop my butt onto a kitchen chair.

I tear open the envelope and pull out two neatly folded pages. A rough swallow later, I begin to read.

Larkin,

You're probably pissed off I wrote this letter. If you don't want to read it, I understand. But I'm not writing to ask for forgiveness. I don't want you to forgive me. I deserve to live with the consequences of my actions. Not answering your call that night was one of the worst choices I've ever made in my life. But that's on me, not you.

I'm writing because I let you believe I was using you the night we met, and that's not okay. I think you know now that Cal was in love with Jolene and schemed to spread a rumor that would break her and me up, starting by asking me to take you home. I'm also pretty sure you think I agreed to drive you because a friend dared me to hook up with you, even though I was dating Jo, and I chickened out last minute.

Most of that isn't true.

Callahan is why I asked to drive you home, but no one dared me to follow through. Cal isn't why I told you things I've still never shared with anyone. I wasn't hoping to hook up with you. I didn't want you to be a conquest I'd share with my buddies.

I let you believe that bullshit because I was shocked at the sudden connection I felt with you. I was attracted to you. I was dying to kiss you, but I was still with Jolene and was terrified if I spent another second with you, I'd do something dumb and hurt her.

I didn't answer your call because I thought you were calling to yell at me for being an asshole, and I was pretty sure I'd apologize and explain and would end up finding you and begging you for a kiss, because that was all I could think about in that moment.

Knowing my headspace that night might not change anything between us. It certainly doesn't change what happened to Derek and your brother.

I'm sorry I kissed you so intensely yesterday. I've been dreaming about doing that for twelve years, even though I had no right. My fantasies didn't hold a candle to the real thing, but I won't let myself get that out of hand again.

I know I'm the last guy you want helping you with your ex. I'm sure you'd rather be rat tortured than pretend to be married to me. I just want you to know that you're special. You're smart and gorgeous and witty as hell, and I never, not for one moment, felt differently or thought you were a joke. It's important to me that you know that.

I'll do anything in my power to help your brother get released early. Then I'll stay clear of you, so you don't have to deal with the reminders I bring.

Whenever you want to meet again to go over our backstory, send a text. I'll be there.

The paper shakes in my grip. I press my hand to my chest and close my eyes, attempting to calm my racing pulse. I try to sort through the ten thousand feelings fighting for dominance, but I can't. It's too much. This letter is too much. Our easy banter on the boat was too much.

That kiss was too much.

In the aftermath of my terrifying night with Derek, I didn't focus on Jake's treatment of me. I was furious he hadn't answered my call, but I was too panicked about Hunter's arrest and Derek's condition to think about Jake's motives for taking me home.

My crushed self-esteem hit later.

Jake the asshole. Jake the liar, pretending to be sweet so he could add a notch to his bedpost. Those mantras took hold. My confidence nose-dived. My sarcasm got pricklier.

I lumped Jake in with guys from my past who'd hurt me maliciously, stewed endlessly over why men treated me like shit. I didn't date for a few years afterward, mainly because of my experience with Derek, but also because of Jake and every other man who thought I was a plaything they could use for sex.

Now Jake is turning the tables, telling me he wasn't trying to hook up with me. He was *fighting* his feelings for me, shocked at how intense our connection had been.

Exactly how I felt at the time too.

I don't know if this absolves him of ditching me and not answering my call. I don't know if this changes anything between us, including the lingering hate I've nursed for so long. All I know is I'm more confused about him than ever.

CHAPTER
Fourteen

LARKIN

My hip twinges uncomfortably. I'm not sure how long I've been sitting in my car, staring out the windshield. Clearly long enough for my muscles to stage a protest. And for my mind to replay key points in Jake's letter eighty-seven times.

I'm sorry I kissed you so intensely yesterday. I've been dreaming about doing that for twelve years.

You're smart and gorgeous and witty as hell, and I never, not for one moment, felt differently or thought you were a joke.

Someone taps on my driver's side window, startling me.

Jolene waves with a concerned expression, probably wondering why I'm sitting here, immobile, instead of starting on cocktail prep and general bar work.

Time to get my shit together.

I get out. Lock and check my car handle, which didn't stay locked. Second time is the charm.

"Were you sleeping with your eyes open?" Jo asks when I face her. "If so, it's creepy."

I smirk. "That's just the tip of the iceberg. I'm not even awake during my shifts. I'm usually sleepwalking."

"Impressive multitasking," she deadpans.

We share a smile until I remember one of my errands before coming to work. I dig into my purse and pull out a small vial of arnica oil and a gift card.

"This"—I hold out the vial—"is for when that spot in your neck gets sore. It might help. And this"—I pass her the gift card for a massage—"is therapy, but also a treat."

"Oh my God, Lark." She accepts both items and wraps me in a hug. "That's so sweet. The massage is over the top, but hugely appreciated. And I'll definitely give the oil a try."

"Might not work, but it's worth a shot."

"Definitely. Thank you." She tucks the small tube and card in her purse, then knocks her elbow into mine. "Do we get to talk about the kiss heard 'round the world now?"

I groan. There was no avoiding this talk. Not with Drew's request to rent out our bar. I take a fortifying breath, parsing through which parts of this mess I'm comfortable sharing with Jo.

"Turns out my ex wants to host a party here on the Thursday before his wedding. I owe him for a favor he did, so I'd like to agree and offer him a deal." A massive favor he hasn't agreed to yet. "But I wanted to finalize the cost with him before talking to you about it. If the discount isn't okay, I'll kick in the rest of the cash myself. If you're not cool with renting the place out for the night, I'll figure out something else. Either way, since Drew thinks I'm engaged to Jake, we need to convince the town we're an item, hence the kiss."

She tilts her head and squints at me. "I thought you hated your ex."

"I do. But he emailed me, and I realized I'd rather help him out with this and cut ties afterward." When Hunter is finally out of jail.

Jo watches me for a few unnerving beats. "If it's important to you, I'm fine with the deal and renting out the bar...but why keep lying about having a fiancé? You don't have to prove anything to that guy."

Part of me wants to lay it all out for her. Explain what happened with Jake and with Derek. Confess that I visit my brother in jail every Monday. Admit who my father is. But each of those land mines could derail our relationship. Right now, I can't add more stress to the mountain I've acquired.

"There's more baggage with Drew than I mentioned," I say. "But it's nothing to worry about. I've got it under control."

A small furrow dents her brow. "Okay. Just remember I'm here if you need to talk."

I exhale, thankful Jo understands my need for boundaries. "I love you and will remember."

I'll do better than remember, though. I'll open up to Jo eventually. Find a way to conquer the fears I've lived with since I learned who my father was. Hope we're close enough to get through it.

"In other news," Jo says brightly, "our booth at the Dog and Pony Show is all set. Emmanuel is making pumpkin-peanut-butter treats for the dogs and salted-caramel-apple-hand-pie treats for the humans. All we need is to find a way to draw folks to our booth."

"I'd eat both of those, and I'll work on drawing a crowd."

She beams. "Perfect."

She turns to walk toward the bar and our never-ending to-do list, but she swivels back, looking hesitant. "Just so you know, Jake is like a brother to me."

"Okay," I say slowly, unsure where she's going with this, but hearing Jake's name has my pulse fluttering faster.

"What I mean is I still love Jake, but I have zero feelings for him beyond friendship. We dated over a decade ago, and I'm madly in love with his brother. So, if Jake dates someone else, I'll be beyond happy for him and for that person." She pauses, nibbling her lip. "Especially if that person is you."

"*Me?*" I jerk back, nearly stumbling over a rock in the gravel lot. "I barely tolerate Jake. I told you the engagement and that kiss were fake."

"I know. But I also know Jake and how charming he can be. And I think you two would make a great couple. If that's part of what you're dealing with—like, if you're worrying about me and my reaction—I want you to know I'd love to see you two together."

There goes Jolene, being the perfect friend, as usual. "I appreciate the sentiment behind what you said. Knowing you'd be happy for me, not mad, means the world. But I *won't* be dating Jake for real."

"Okay," she says lightly, like she only half believes me.

Honestly, I'm not sure I'd believe me and my defensiveness, but everything about Jake has me addled. This man, who knows more about me than anyone—my demons, my faults, my history —called me special and smart and gorgeous. He seems caring and *nice*. Attributes that are stressing me out more, not less. I'm scared to trust him again. Every time I debate letting go of my animosity, anxiety strikes.

But if Jake's letter *is* honest, then he was as shocked as I was by our mutual attraction, and nothing about our interaction that night was premeditated or cruel. Or he's lying to ease his guilt.

I attempt to start walking, shake these turbulent thoughts and get focused on today's work, but my mind is apparently stuck in a holding pattern, unable to communicate with my feet. I study the concern in Jolene's big brown eyes, needing a bit more from her. A better understanding of who Jake is at his core. "It's fine if you don't feel comfortable answering, but do you consider Jake to be an honest guy?"

"As loyal and honest as they come," she says instantly, then frowns. "Except…"

"Except?" I prod, expecting her to say, *he can be a player*. Or, *he'll lie to get what he wants.*

"He's changed a lot," she finally answers. "He was sort of oblivious when we dated. Focused on himself, not really on me or us. He wasn't dishonest, just a bit self-centered. But WITSEC and going through hell with his family changed him. He knows lying is unforgivable. You'd be hard-pressed to find a more upstanding guy."

I nod and drag my boot over the loose gravel. Jake got upset with me on his boat for claiming he hadn't changed. I felt badly in the moment, seeing the pain in his eyes, hearing how rough WITSEC had been on his family. I feel worse hearing Jo confirm how tough life has been on him.

She hikes her purse up her shoulder, her expression probing but kind. "I'm not sure if this is part of the drama between you two, but I *know* nothing happened between you and Jake the night he drove you home from that party. You've both told me as much, but since Jake's been back in town, we've talked about our past, hashed some things out. He told me he was into you that night. He said he didn't cheat, but he was tempted and felt like shit about betraying me, even in his mind."

My heart pounds faster. This conversation is getting too real, too fast. "I didn't have designs on him back then, Jo. I swear. Not before that night. I was tempted by him too, but I knew you two were together. I never would have cheated with him."

She gives my upper arm a squeeze. "I know, and it's okay. It was twelve years ago, and Jake and I weren't happy. I understand why he'd have been interested in someone else. If you recall, I was halfway in love with Jake's brother at the time."

My next exhale comes out shaky. Everything Jake wrote must be true, then. He wasn't playing games with me. He ignored my call because he was scared he liked me too much and felt guilty over Jo. He must really have been dreaming about kissing me for twelve years.

Some of the hate I've clung to seeps out. The idea of seeing Jake again doesn't have me wanting to slash his tires. I'm still unsettled—a swirling discomfort when I think about forgiving this man I've despised so long, but hopefully I'll sleep better tonight.

"Thanks," I tell Jo. "That did help."

"Excellent," she says, more upbeat. "When you two start officially dating, I can say I'm the matchmaker who made it happen."

I give her a playful shove. "I'm never dating Jake Bower."

She winks at me. "Never say never."

She walks ahead of me as I flash *again* to Jake's kiss, how hot it was. How *turned on* I was. Leave it to Jake to complicate everything.

Inside the bar, I get into my work groove, happy for the distraction. Cocktail prep. Email replies. One staff sick and another called in. A problem with an old fridge I need to handle, at which point Jolene says, "Thank God I have you and don't have to deal with the headaches on my own."

I actually don't mind tackling bar issues. I like problem-solving. I like that I can handle the parts of the job Jo dislikes.

In between the busy moments, my mind swings back to Jake. That man—always there, hovering close. After I read his letter, my plan was to avoid him and how off-kilter I felt. I'm less distraught now. Jolene's insights helped. Recalling how he'd thoughtfully stocked his boat with items he learned I liked showed more of his kindness, but there's an edginess I can't shake or figure out.

Maybe seeing him again, sooner rather than later, would be good. A chance to talk to him about his letter. Definitely *not* kiss him again, but airing my thoughts might kick this agitation. I could also put his handyman skills to use, since I have to be fake engaged to the guy.

I pull out my phone, ignoring the low-grade flutter in my belly, the strange nerves as I tap out my text.

> Me: Come to my place tomorrow at noon and bring your tools.

CHAPTER

Fifteen

Jake

I park my truck and check my phone for the hundredth time today. Larkin's text and my reply from yesterday are still there. No more messages have popped up.

> Larkin: Come to my place tomorrow at noon and bring your tools.
>
> Me: I'll be there.

She didn't mention the letter. The wedding. Any of it. Maybe she didn't get the envelope. Maybe she lit it on fire and cast a spell with the ashes, and that's why my gut has been in knots all day. Who the hell knows. Nothing to be done at this point but get on with whatever she has in store for me.

Dallas Humphrey, who's playing with her daughter on her

front lawn two doors over, waves to me. "Escaping for a quick...*lunch*?" she calls and winks.

Her innuendo almost has me tripping over the curb. Larkin no doubt brought me here to fan the gossip flames of our engagement. Not that much help is needed. This morning, Mrs. Santos asked me when Larkin was due—as in *pregnant*.

At least if Larkin did read my letter and has finally decided to kill me, my brothers will hear about where I am and find my body.

Hauling my toolbox from my truck, I walk to Larkin's door and knock. Footsteps approach, but the door doesn't open. A dog barks from a neighboring yard. A squirrel natters at me from the silverbell tree to my left. Unsure what happened to Larkin, I lift my hand to knock again just as the door swings wide.

My mouth dries at the sight of her—an affliction I can't kick around this woman. Ripped jeans hug her thighs. Her loose yellow T-shirt looks soft and thin, the wide neckline dipping past one shoulder, displaying a pretty flush on her chest and neck.

And those soft lips. *Fuck.*

The urge to kiss her again nearly bowls me over.

She briefly makes eye contact with me, then studies her bare feet—which are so fucking cute. She looks back at me with a more familiar fire in her eyes. "Seems you can follow simple instructions."

Okay. We're back to bantering. Better that than getting a verbal lashing. "When you said tools, I first grabbed my hair gel and blow-dryer, thinking you meant beauty tools and we were doing makeovers. But on second thought, I decided on this." I lift my toolbox. "Did I pass the test?"

"Depends." Her lips flatten. "Did you first think of makeovers because you think I'm ugly and need one?"

"Um," is all I say.

There is no right answer here. If I tell her she's the most

stunning woman in this town, she'll think I'm going overboard and lying. If I don't answer, she'll think I *do* see her as unattractive. And I still have no clue if she read my letter.

She rolls her eyes. "That non-answer was excellent for my ego." She turns her back to me and marches toward her open kitchen. "May as well come in. I'll see if I can find a mask to wear while you're here."

Hell no. There's only one thing I can say now. "You're drop-dead gorgeous, Larkin. So fucking stunning I can't think straight around you, hence the lack of vocabulary I just displayed. The only person in here who needs a makeover is me and my entire personality."

She freezes.

Unsure if I just made things worse, I focus on Larkin's home instead of my idiocy. She doesn't have a lot of furniture or decorative accents, but each piece is unique and interesting—a colorful patchwork couch with ornate arms, a coffee table made from an old door, a lampshade built from what looks like recycled glass. No two chairs at her small dining table are alike, as though everything in here has a distinct personality. I fucking love it.

I want to ask about each piece, where she bought them, if she finds them meaningful in some way, if she did any of the repurposing work herself.

Unfortunately, her back is still facing me, because I went with the overboard option and told her she's the prettiest thing I've ever seen.

Slowly, she turns around. The flush on her skin has deepened. Her intense gaze drops to my scuffed boots, travels up my worn jeans and gray T-shirt, finally settling on my face, which probably looks as overwhelmed as I feel. Sharing space with Larkin is both amazing and unsettling.

"Your personality definitely needs an overhaul," she says. "The rest of you isn't too bad."

Relief rushes through me. "Which part?"

"Fishing for compliments, are we?"

"I'm a fisherman, as you know. We're patient and willing to wait for what we want."

She touches the braid over her shoulder, playing with the frayed ends of her hair. "What do you want?"

To help Larkin and make her life easier, for starters. I want her to understand how much I've always respected her. How strong and competent I think she is, rising above her tough childhood. And yeah, I want to kiss her again, but that'll never happen.

I shift my grip on my toolbox and catch sight of a white envelope on her kitchen counter. Under it are folded papers. My letter. "You read it," I say, my voice suddenly rough.

She follows my line of sight. "I did."

She doesn't embellish, but she let me into her home. She doesn't seem more annoyed with me than before. Maybe she finally believes I didn't want to take advantage of her all those years ago. That I wasn't playing games with her. I want her to talk, tell me what she's thinking. Neither of us seems quick to unburden ourselves, and I haven't even answered her question.

What do you want?

Some things are better left unsaid.

"Do you need something fixed in here?" I ask into the silence. "Is that why I have my tools? Or did you just want to go over our backstory for our engagement?"

A hint of mischief breaks over her features, reminding me of her villainous expression twelve years ago, before she explained the definition of rat torture.

She fans her hand to her cool patchwork couch. "Have a seat. I made some lemonade."

"Sure," I say, surprised she's willing to serve me anything. Knowing Larkin, she probably poisoned my cup.

I set down my toolbox and head to her couch, looking

forward to getting off my feet. I love the physical aspect of my job. Being outside and active keeps my mental health in check, but some days it feels like I've been hit by a truck.

I sigh as I lower down, but the second my ass hits the cushions, the couch drops. I hit the floor. My knees shoot up to my chin. I think my nuts have lodged into my stomach.

"What the fuck?" I growl as I attempt to get up, but the angle is awkward and I don't want to ruin what's left of this deathtrap disguised as a couch. Giving up, I slant Larkin a dark look. "So, you *are* trying to kill me?"

She slaps her hand over her mouth, her eyes so bright with amusement I can't even be pissed at her prank. "Maybe just a little," she says through her fingers.

"Whatever." I try to sprawl out and look relaxed. I must resemble a contorted circus freak. "I'll just stay here for a while. It's actually comfortable."

She snorts, then doubles over laughing, losing it so hard, I can't help but laugh too. The couch frame is digging into uncomfortable places. My hips are screaming at me to stand, but I don't remember the last time I laughed like this, stupidly, no holds barred.

When a sharp pain jabs at my ribs, I wince. "Help me out of here before I break in half."

Larkin collects herself enough to come over and hold out her hand. I grasp it and debate yanking her in here with me, but she wouldn't want me to flirt with her like that. Using her leverage, I extricate myself from the couch prison, but it's not an easy journey up.

I stumble, catching myself with my hands on her hips, and I don't move.

Touching her feels too damn good, as does the way I hover over her just enough. She tilts her head up. If I didn't know better, I'd say she was breathing harder and staring at my lips.

I should release her. Go back to discussing lunch and our fake engagement. "You read my letter," I repeat instead.

She nods, but her forehead creases.

"Are you mad I wrote it?"

She dips her head down. "I don't know."

I can deal with indecision. *I don't know* is a hell of a lot better than the intensity of her hatred. "You don't have to know. I only wrote it so you'd see yourself the way I see you. So you'd understand you were never a conquest or a joke to me. Going forward, we'll just work on helping your brother, okay? And fixing this couch, which I'm guessing is why my tools are here."

She doesn't pull back or lift her face. Concerned, I fit my fingers under her chin and tilt her head up. "I'm sorry if I made things worse."

"It's not that."

"What, then?"

She blinks up at me. Tears are shining in her eyes. "I've been unsettled since I read it, for a number of reasons. Some of which I've started working through, but..."

I search her face. "But?"

She frowns deeply, like she's untangling complicated thoughts. "It's been so easy to hate you all these years. To believe you were fucking with me and didn't answer the call because you didn't care. I'm still mad about the call, but I understand your actions better. But if I can't put some of the blame on you, then..." She blows out a shaky breath. "Then everything that happened was *my* fault."

"*Nothing* that happened was your fault."

She pulls back from me and jabs at her chest. "I chose to date Derek. I chose to grab my stuff that night by myself. I trashed his house, which is why he knew I was nearby. I'm the one who called Hunter to help me and stayed silent in the aftermath. He told me not to tell the cops I was there, but I shouldn't have listened. I should've been honest instead of being a selfish coward. And Hunter isn't doing well emotionally," she goes on, her voice cracking. "Last time I was at Langmore, he told me not to visit him again. So, yeah, all of this is my fault, and if he doesn't get released, I'm terrified about how hard it'll hit him."

"Fuck, sweetheart." I crush her to my chest. Try to absorb the pain she carries all by herself. I didn't know Hunter was refusing her visits or that she trashed Derek's house after she left my truck. I have so many questions about that night—what Derek did to her, how badly she was hurt, as though I need to know just how awful it was so I can suffer alongside her.

Right now, that's not what she needs.

I smooth my hand down her back. "The only person to blame for that night is Derek. You were young and hurt and lashing out, as was your right. Everything else was a domino effect of bad consequences."

She trembles, sagging into me. I kiss the top of her head. Get a bit lost in how good she smells—sweet and a little citrusy, like that glass of lemonade she offered.

Eventually, she sniffles and rubs her face into my shirt. "I still don't know if I can forgive you for not answering my call."

"I don't expect it." Even if hearing the truth hurts.

"But I hate you less," she adds on a soft exhale. "And for the record, I never cry."

"Then that's something else you can hate me for—making you cry."

"And for getting me stuck in a fake engagement."

"True. We should add another line to your Kill Jake list—Death by Couch Entrapment."

This next sniffle sounds mildly amused. "Consider it added."

I ease her back and run my thumbs under her eyes, catching the moisture before it falls. "I won't tell anyone about these tears if you warn me about any other booby traps in this place."

She wrinkles her nose. "Always an angle with you."

"Not really. I'm an open book."

She glances at my letter on her kitchen counter. Her next swallow seems to drag on forever. She looks about to speak, but her expression evens out. She steps farther away from me, and her attention snags on my chest. "My snot is on your shirt. How's that for a warning?"

I look down. And, yeah. There's a big wet splotch on my T-shirt. The perfect opportunity to lighten the mood. I palm the back of Larkin's neck and say gently, "Seems you need a taste of your own medicine."

I press her face into my shirt, making sure to get the snotty splotch all over her face until she's shrieking and laughing and shoving at me.

"What the hell was that?" she says, wiping at her face.

"Retribution."

"Okay. It's on." She gleams in a concerning way. "You've been warned."

"Larkin," I say sternly.

"*Jake.*"

"There's no need to retaliate."

"Oh, there definitely is. As for the couch, can you fix it? I bought it last week, knowing it was in rough shape, but I couldn't pass up the price or the style."

"If you pour me a glass of lemonade, I'll fix it for you."

"So, you *are* blackmailing me now." She goes to the kitchen and pulls out a pitcher, casting me a saucy look. "I guess those town rumors weren't so far off."

"Lemonade just sounds too perfect right now." My stomach rumbles. Food probably wouldn't be bad either. Maybe my appetite is coming back.

She frowns at my midsection. "Did you eat lunch?"

I wave her off. "I'm fine. Would just love a cold drink."

She hesitates, then pours me a cup. I gulp it down, sighing at how refreshing it is. "Fuck, that's good."

She licks her lips like she can taste the tangy sweetness. "It's nothing fancy. Just from a can."

"Still appreciated."

I have no clue what's running through her mind, but she's watching me a lot. Assessing me, maybe. She clears her throat. "Now that I've been blackmailed by you, you need to fix my couch before you head back to work."

I dip my head. "I'm nothing if not an honest blackmailer."

I walk into her living room and remove the couch cushions, checking out the old frame. I tip the piece of furniture on its side, confirming my suspicions. "I need to add a metal mending plate to strengthen the frame." I speak as I lower the couch back down, but the old piece is heavy. I strain my arms to make sure it doesn't scratch the floor. "Won't take long, but I'll have to come back with the materials. Is next Tuesday okay?"

When it's down, I turn and check why Larkin hasn't replied.

She's staring at my arms with her jaw slightly unhinged, and my muscles tighten.

I've never had issues attracting women. My body is cut from my job and working out, but I've never had someone's interest shoot through me like a shot of Patrón.

I cock an eyebrow at her. "You seem distracted."

She snaps her mouth closed. "I'm not distracted."

"What day did I ask if I can come back to fix the couch?"

Pink sears her cheeks. "The day that ends in a Y."

I chuckle. "Tuesday. And you're welcome to watch me work. It might be hot enough to remove my T-shirt too."

"I don't think that would be appropriate."

"Aren't we engaged?"

"*Fake* engaged."

I wink at her, enjoying how flustered she is. Hell, if I worked near Larkin wearing less clothes, I'd be flustered enough to send my hammer flying. "I need to head back to work soon, but we haven't discussed more of our backstory."

"Right, yeah." She gives her head a small shake. "We'll work on that Tuesday when you're back?"

I nod, unsure why we keep getting distracted by other conversations, instead of the reason we're hanging out. "At least Dallas Humphrey saw me coming in here. More people will talk about us and the engagement."

"Excellent point. And…" She pauses, looking almost bashful. "I could maybe meet you at that community farm this Sunday since we're making that the site of our meet-cute. As long as I don't have to be at the Barrel early."

I'm not sure why the idea of her working at the farm with me makes me want to grin, but I keep my face in check. "If you can make it, that would be great. It's actually a carnival day, with games in the morning and farming work in the afternoon. And I'll come here next Tuesday at lunchtime for the couch. You start your shift at midafternoon on Tuesdays, right?"

She lifts her chin. "Is this you 'noticing what you notice' around this small town?"

"It is," I say, not caring to mention I get details about her work from Callahan—how the renovations were going, if the reopening is still a success, which shifts she works, so I can try to avoid her when she's there. Although I may show up more often now that we're "engaged."

Our new reality will take some getting used to, as will seeing Larkin at the community farm, if she shows up. I debate mentioning that tomorrow's carnival day includes a dunk tank, where we volunteers will take turns sitting on the dreaded "dunk" seat. But the last thing I need is Larkin getting ideas about adding Drown Jake in Front of Families to her Kill Jake list.

CHAPTER
Sixteen

Jake

I wake up with a gasp, my heart pounding a mile a minute. I glance around my bedroom, take a moment to orient myself. Finally realize I'm not standing on top of a bottomless pit, reaching for Larkin, who's clinging to the side, desperately trying to reach me...before she falls.

Fuck. I scrub my hand down my face and blow out a rough breath. That's the fourth nightmare in the past two weeks, and they suck each time. Two were of Larkin, one was of Callahan drowning, and one was Desmond locked inside a room I couldn't breach. Each one leaves me feeling jittery for a while.

Good thing I have the farm's carnival today.

By the time I'm showered and dressed, I feel less on edge. The drive to the farm calms me more. I play my music loud and enjoy the rolling hills I pass.

The farm is already busy when I arrive. Some attendees are regular volunteers. Some are newcomers we're hoping to get involved in the program, either physically on the farm or through donations. The more people, the better.

I wave to a cluster of folks I know, stopping to chat with Frank, who coaches Windfall High's football team. I watch the pumpkin-seed toss and cheer for the little kids lined up in front of their small baskets. Most tossed seeds end up on the grass, but little Henry lands two in his basket, and the spectators go wild.

"He's a natural," I call to his parents, who volunteer here most Sundays.

His mother, Mayumi, gives me a bland look. "Just think about how great this will look on his résumé one day—excels at tossing seeds into things. He'll probably get a scholarship."

I chuckle, loving her sarcasm.

Feeling relaxed and happier, I scan the area for blond braids and blue-green eyes. Larkin hoped to be here by now, unless she decided spending this much time together would be painful for her. Or she rethought my letter and hates that I keep bringing up our past, despises that she's stuck in this fake relationship with me.

Trying to curb my disappointment, I watch the banjo player a moment, then stroll past a few other games and makeshift booths—buttermilk chalk pictures being drawn by attendees, kids racing one another to dress up as scarecrows, a craft table where participants play a version of Mr. Potato Head with pumpkins instead of plastic potatoes.

Everyone is having a good time, but I spot the farm owner, Phoebe, on her own by the pumpkin patch, wiping her eyes. She bought this land with her wife, Jane, and is always upbeat and motivating. I've never seen her lose her temper or seem down.

Concerned, I make my way over to her. "Everything all right?"

"Oh, Jake. Yeah." She shakes herself and wipes her eyes again. "I'm just upset about this outfit."

She points at her overalls and the red bandanna around her neck—the stereotypical farmer costume she chose for her turn as a dunk-tank victim. Considering she was a finance guru in New York prior to starting this nonprofit farm, wearing designer suits and high heels, I'm sure the overalls are an eyesore for her, but she's not being honest.

I cup her shoulder and dip my head. On closer inspection, her brown skin looks a bit sallow, with darker smudges under her eyes. "I'm a good listener," I say, letting her know I'm here for her.

Her shoulders drop, along with the rest of her posture. "My mother passed away this week. I'm trying to stay upbeat for the event, but it's tough."

"Phoebe." I pull her into a hug, hating how sad she sounds. Phoebe's mother had her when she was older and lived a long, full life, but the end is always tough. "I'm so sorry."

"Thank you. We knew it was coming, but it's still hard."

"That's to be expected. Hopefully the festival this morning and working the farm later will help distract you."

"It will. And your hugs help too. Except..." She stiffens and steps out of my arms.

I frown at her. "Except what?"

She glances around my shoulder and nods at something I can't see. "*Except*, I heard you got engaged recently, and based on the dirty look I'm getting, I think your fiancée is here and doesn't like seeing your arms around another woman."

Heart beating faster, I turn, and yeah—Larkin is here, and she doesn't look happy. Abruptly, she swivels, like she wasn't just watching Phoebe and me hugging. She marches toward a group of adults and kids playing Pin the Tail on the Donkey, standing so stiff I'm worried her joints might crack.

"If you need to unload at any time," I tell Phoebe, "find me, yeah?"

"I will, as long as you go smooth things out with your mystery woman and promise to introduce me later."

I nod and head toward Larkin, my pulse tapping as fast as the banjo tune being strummed. I stop behind her, wanting to pull her back into my chest. I settle for placing my hands lightly on her hips. "You made it," I say by her ear.

She shrugs a shoulder. "Said I would."

"How was the drive?"

"Fine."

"What time do you have to be in at work?"

"Whenever."

I'm no expert on women. I've barely dated the past twelve years and haven't come close to being in a relationship. Still, based on Larkin's ramrod-straight posture and her clipped one-word answers to my questions, I'd guess Phoebe was right about Larkin's jealousy.

A chuff of happiness fills me, which isn't good. Larkin affects me too damn much, and I don't seem to have the willpower to keep my emotional distance.

I flex my hands on her hips and press my lips closer to her ear. "The woman I was hugging is the co-owner of the farm. She's married and just lost her mother, in case you were wondering why I was hugging her."

"I wasn't wondering," Larkin says, but her body softens, swaying slightly into me.

Sure, she wasn't. "We should sign up for the three-legged race," I suggest, tired of overthinking everything with Larkin. All I want is a day of fun.

"Or we could play a round of this." She points to the game of Pin the Tail on the Donkey. "But instead of trying to pin the tail on the donkey picture, I try to nail-gun the tail to your ass."

I bark out a laugh. "You've obviously been thinking a lot about my ass."

"In a 'kicking it' sort of way."

"Come," I say, taking her hand. "Phoebe wants to meet you, and I did actually sign us up for the three-legged race."

The second I introduce the two women, Phoebe pulls Larkin into a hug and whispers something to her I can't hear. Larkin blushes and ducks her head.

"Where's your ring?" Phoebe asks, taking Larkin's hand.

"Being sized," I say quickly and immediately feel guilty. I don't like lying to Phoebe about who Larkin is to me, but Larkin is my priority. Which means the ring issue will need to be addressed.

I'm about to lead Larkin away, saving her from more uncomfortable "fiancé" questions, but a kid smacks into my legs.

I look down at the little girl suctioned to my thigh and smile. Gabriela helps out some Sundays with her father and also takes part in Lennon's hiking program. She's the definition of cute, with an adorable lisp and a button nose. Today, her face is painted like a tiger.

I try halfheartedly to shake her off my leg. "How did this worm get on my jeans?"

She giggles. "I'm not a worm, Mr. Jake."

"Are you a snake?"

She hugs me tighter and makes the cutest darn growl. "I'm a tiger."

"I wonder if this tiger flies." I pick her up and swing her through the air in circles. She squeals and kicks her legs, having a blast. Chuckling, I deposit her back on the ground and point her toward her parents. "Go growl at your mom and dad."

She tears off, and I check for Larkin. Phoebe has left, but Larkin is watching me with a strange expression on her face. "You all good?" I ask.

A soft pink decorates her cheeks. She takes my hand and

gives it a squeeze. "Perfect. Lead me to this race, where I plan to trip you and shove your face in the grass."

I grin. "That's not how the race works."

"Because they're not playing it right."

"Because most people don't make kill lists in their spare time."

She shrugs. "Those people are boring."

She's probably right.

We spend the rest of the morning bantering and playing silly games. She does trip me in the three-legged race, at which point, Gabriela shows up and attacks me with her tiger claws until I'm laughing so hard, I nearly bust a rib.

I try to coax Larkin to volunteer herself as a dunk-tank victim. She flat-out refuses, but she's first in line when I'm called to participate. She doesn't sink me, thank God, but when Phoebe lands her ball on target and I splash into the water, Larkin cheers the loudest. I peel off my wet shirt afterward, not minding one bit how hot and bothered she looks.

"I like her," Phoebe tells me when I return in a fresh change of clothes. "She's fun."

"Yeah," is all I say, breathing through the too-tight feeling in my chest.

At the barbecue lunch, I don't put much food on my plate. My appetite has still been off lately, but I like watching Larkin shovel potato salad into her mouth and moan appreciatively.

She nudges my foot under the table. "You're not hungry?"

It should be a simple question, but with me, it's not. "Not really."

"We've been running around all morning. How could you not be hungry?"

I run my thumb along the edge of my paper plate and shrug. "I don't eat well when I'm stressed."

She cocks her head, assessing me. "Why are you stressed at a fun farm carnival?"

There's no way I'm explaining that being with her like this makes me a bit anxious—my real feelings getting mixed up in our fake charade, or that our complicated past has me in a continued state of discomfort. Or that I've been having nightmares about her and my brothers.

"It's not the carnival that has my stomach uneasy," I say, keeping things vague.

"Oh." She doesn't say more, but she stares at me so hard, I glance back down at my plate.

Thankfully, she doesn't push.

After cleaning up from lunch, we work in the fields and greenhouse. We tend to the fall lettuces, the green beans, the various pumpkins and squash. I love this part of being at the farm, having my hands in the earth. Growing good food. Helping the larger community.

As the day wears on, I glance at Larkin. She's talking to Gabriela's mother and helping the little girl pick beans. Contentment spreads through me at the sight. She seems like she's had fun today. I've certainly had a blast with her, but she's probably just a good actress, putting on a show for the crowd. She won't give me a second thought when she leaves here.

Wish I could say the same.

Reminding myself that my only job is to support Larkin and this engagement ruse, I think back to Phoebe's ring question. Our story still has holes we need to fill. Larkin should have a ring by now. Getting it sized would only take so long.

I have an idea for a ring that would suit Larkin and her style, but for some unfathomable reason, my nerves riot even worse. A stupid reaction, when there's nothing real about my relationship with Larkin. She'll probably hate whatever ring I choose anyway.

CHAPTER
Seventeen

Jake

Tuesday at noon, I knock on Larkin's door, ready to fix her couch as we discussed. She doesn't answer right away. As I wait, I study the lighting fixture attached to her exterior wall. There's no bulb inside and no other lights out here. This area of Windfall might be safe, but Larkin often works late. I don't like the idea of her fumbling around for her keys at night.

I alter my grip on my supplies, getting a better look at the fixture, and an object digs into my thigh. *The ring.* Something else that has me uneasy. Not sure what I was thinking, buying a ring without discussing it with Larkin first.

Footsteps indicate she's on her way. The door pulls open, and she sasses out her hip. "You're late."

"I thought I was on time."

"Not for lunch, you aren't. Get in here."

I follow her, trying to remember if I forgot she told me we were having lunch. I put my tools and supplies on the floor, waiting as she busies herself in the small kitchen. She fusses with a casual platter of deli meats, cut veggies, hummus, and cheese, then she cuts thick slices of a delicious-looking grain bread and puts them on a plate.

"I wasn't sure what you liked," she says, surveying the food. "I also have minestrone soup and tuna."

What she has is enough food for eight people. "Why'd you make all this?"

She shrugs a shoulder and uselessly adjusts the platter again. "I don't like that you're not eating well."

My throat suddenly feels tight.

It's just food. A simple lunch she made for me. My underfed stomach seems to think she's offering her heart and soul. "The platter is perfect. I don't need anything else. And assuming you poisoned everything on there, I'd hate for all that arsenic to go to waste."

Her lips twitch. "Excellent. And don't worry about wasting the arsenic. I bought it in bulk. There're also cookies from Delilah's shop—figured you need more calories to maintain all that." She gestures at my body and blushes.

"All what?" I ask, remembering how tuned in to my body she was when I moved her couch last time. I also really like seeing her blush. A hint of innocence added to her sharp wit.

She raises an eyebrow. "Don't play dumb, Jake. You know your muscles have their own zip codes."

I cross my arms over my chest, making sure said muscles pop. "I wasn't aware you noticed my physique."

"I'm not blind. And stop doing that."

I flex my biceps harder. "Doing what?"

She lets out a cute growl, picks up a carrot, and tosses it at me.

Laughing, I catch it one-handed. "I appreciate the food more than you know. This looks great."

"Based on the noises your stomach was making last week, and your meager lunch at the farm, I figured you needed to be force-fed." We sit on stools at her counter. Instead of helping herself to the food, she angles toward me. "Are you stressed and not eating well because of the fake engagement?"

If only it were that simple. "Partly."

She huffs. "Care to elaborate?"

Not really, but shutting her out doesn't feel right. "The engagement thing is stressful, but it's also because of our past. But it's no big deal," I add quickly. My regrets are mine to shoulder. She has enough to deal with. "The eating thing started during WITSEC. When I got overwhelmed or extra-stressed, I'd lose my appetite. But this lunch looks good enough to pull me out of the pattern."

"Okay," she says, sounding kind of distant. When I wait for her to start eating first, she elbows my side. "Shovel something into your mouth before I do it for you."

Says the woman who probably has Death by Starvation on her Kill Jake list. "Yes, ma'am."

We don't grab separate plates. We share the platter, snacking as we talk about my bad eating habits when stressed and how much she moved around before settling back in Windfall, never feeling like she quite belonged. She tells me about her youngest brother, who works in New York doing a consulting job he enjoys.

"I'm so proud of my brothers," I say, taking a big bite of bread topped with butter and salami. Feels like I haven't eaten in a year. "They've all pulled themselves together. They have careers they enjoy and women they love. Never thought I'd see them this settled and happy."

"I'm sure you had a lot to do with that."

I make a noncommittal sound. "It wasn't a choice. I'm the oldest. Someone needed to be strong. Pick them up when witness protection and our father knocked them down."

She drags her finger along the edge of the counter. "Who picked you up?"

"Taking care of them was my purpose. That's what kept me sane."

"But you didn't eat well during that time, probably had other stress-related habits that weren't healthy."

"Is that why you're feeding me?" I face her more fully. "You want to keep me healthy?"

"Of course." She shifts on her chair too, her knees landing between my spread thighs. "I prefer my murder victims to have enough stamina to fight back."

I laugh—a common occurrence around Larkin. I also feel overwhelmed.

I never expected anything with her to be light or easy, but our day at the farm and our biting banter from day one has been fun. I don't think I've enjoyed a woman's company this much since... well, a long time. The urge to flirt with her is strong. To press my hands to her thighs, lean forward, drop a kiss by her ear. This quiet comfort is upping my attraction to her in a more emotional way, and Cal's warning pokes at my brain.

If you pretend to be engaged to Larkin and get closer with her, you'll get hurt.

She stands to clean, but I touch her arm. "I've got this."

She hesitates but nods, her gaze laser focused on me as I move around her kitchen, washing up.

"Our meet-cute story is solid now," I say when her attention gets intense. We keep forgetting to talk about the reason we're spending time together. "Everyone at the farm loved you, and volunteers aren't regular enough to know if they missed a day when you showed up and we met. Even Phoebe misses the odd Sunday."

Her smile is a bit distant but light. "Everyone there is so nice, especially Phoebe. She has a soft spot for you."

"I saw her whispering something to you when you met."

Larkin's eyes twinkle with mischief. "She suggested that I should get you to wear better deodorant."

I bark out a laugh. "I call bullshit."

She laughs with me but doesn't tell me what Phoebe actually said.

I wash our dishes, stealing looks at her over my shoulder. "Are you still surprised I don't spend my Sundays murdering puppies?"

"I never thought you murdered puppies. I assumed you worked in a secret lab, experimenting on baby pandas to develop an airborne disease that would wipe out humanity."

I chuckle under my breath. "That's my Saturday gig."

She glances at a spot on the counter. My letter is still there, but in a different position. Like she maybe read it again since last week. "I've spent a lot of years turning you into a villain. Changing that perception isn't easy."

I put the last dish down and lean my elbows on her counter, getting so close to her face, I could almost rub my nose against hers. "You don't have to change how you see me. We just have to know each other well enough to fool your ex. I was thinking my proposal might have happened at a garage sale. Does that work for you?"

Her eyebrows drop into sharp slashes. "How do you know I love garage sales?"

"Your decor in here. It's funky and eclectic—the kinds of secondhand furniture a person takes the time to find at garage sales or antique stores. I'd wager you enjoy the search as much as the purchase."

"You're disturbingly observant."

I shrug. "Only with things that interest me. I love your stuff, by the way. This place has tons of personality."

She picks up a stray pen and flips it through her fingers. "Hunter used to take me to garage sales. We couldn't afford much, but I'd get so excited about finding something special. A diamond in the dirt, he'd say."

"And pieces that might end up in a junkyard get a second chance."

"Exactly," she says, sitting straighter. "We've become a throwaway culture. When something breaks, we buy a replacement. We don't care about our possessions enough to fix them."

"It's a problem," I agree. "That's actually part of why I built that bookcase for Delilah's shop. I saw something online and thought it was a great idea. A chance for people to share and reuse. Swap one of their books for another, without them landing in the trash."

She rolls the pen in her hand faster. "What do you think of—" She stops abruptly and stares at the counter.

"What do I think of what?" I prod.

She drags her teeth over that thick bottom lip of hers. The movement mesmerizes me for a moment, until she says, "It's nothing."

"I won't fix your couch until you tell me."

"So, we're back to blackmail?"

I smirk. "It was either that or I unleash the mutant pandas in your home until you cave."

Her laugh is sharp but bright, then she studies me with a shy expression. "What do you think of us hosting a fix-it club at the bar? One day a month, maybe? We'd need to recruit people with fixing skills—sewing, electronics, woodworking. I'd pay them in dinner and drinks, and people could bring their broken items to be fixed, or they can learn how to fix stuff themselves with guidance."

"I fucking love the idea." Especially her use of *us* and *we*. Although that was likely just a slip of her tongue. "I could help on the woodworking end of things, but without payment in food and drinks."

"That part isn't up for discussion. You deserve compensation."

"Helping in the community is compensation enough."

She blinks at me for a few prolonged beats. "You feel you have something to prove, don't you? To show people you're not like your father?"

I never thought long enough to pick apart my reasons for volunteering at Phoebe's farm or for helping Delilah with the bookshelf in her shop. I study Larkin more closely, amazed once more how quickly she makes sense of me. Sees things I don't dig deep enough to notice myself. Maybe it's because we're more similar than I realized.

"I fucking despise my father," I say. Words I rarely say aloud. My family doesn't need to deal with my anger. "There isn't a redeeming thing about that man. I hate that any part of him is part of me."

She raises her hand, like she's a pupil in class. "I'm a member of the same awesome club. I was lucky enough to have a father who sold drugs to an underage kid, and that kid overdosed and now has brain damage."

"Xavier Tully," I murmur, remembering that horrible event.

I was young at the time, but the story raced around Windfall. There wasn't enough evidence to pin Otto Briggs with charges. He didn't get arrested for stealing cars from Malcolm Boyd's body shop either. I never forgot the outrage, though. He and his two sons were vilified. The boys were tormented at school. Xavier's family moved to the city to give their unwell son better care. Otto moved away with Hunter and his other son. Not to save them the harassment. To find other places to earn cash off misery, likely.

Otto may be gone, but Windfall is a town that remembers.

I understand why Larkin's wary of people discovering their connection. She exudes confidence and sass, but being linked to a degenerate lowlife eats at you. Knowing my father damaged businesses and livelihoods with his money laundering infuriates me. That history probably *is* why I help out the community as much as I do. Anything to prove I'm better than the man who destroyed lives.

"Can we earn badges in this club of ours?" I ask.

A puff of amused air escapes her. "How about every time we hear our respective fathers mentioned in town, and we don't go ape shit, we get a special patch?"

If I earned a penny every time that happened, I'd be rich. "Count me in. Also…" I dip my hand into my pocket, feeling around for the ring I bought. She'll probably hate it. She might get frustrated all over again that this fake-engagement thing needs to happen. Every time we see each other, the topic barely comes up. She must be avoiding it, and here I am shoving the situation in her face.

Swallowing thickly, I pull out the ring and place it on the counter.

Larkin inhales sharply. "What's that?"

Yeah, she's pissed. Not sure why I thought this was a good idea. I went to three antique stores in surrounding towns before choosing this ring. The central yellow stone is set in what looks like a flower, the sides detailed with tiny leaves and filigree. There's a slight chip in the band, but I liked that. Imperfect beauty. A ring that has endured.

"Figured we needed a ring to go with our story, so we can stop getting flustered with people like Phoebe. Assuming you preferred interesting secondhand stuff, I thought this was something you'd like or choose for yourself. But I'm obviously wrong," I add, when she barely moves. I'm not sure she's breathing. "I'll take it back. Grab something simpler you'd like better. Your fiancé should know you well enough to know what you like."

I reach for the ring, but she snatches it up. "No."

"No?"

"I like it."

"You're sure? Because it's no big deal to take it back."

"Ask again, and the arsenic is happening."

There's no fighting the smile pushing at my cheeks. "There's a date on the inside too—1910. The shop owner said it was a couple's wedding date, but he didn't know anything about them."

Larkin examines the ring, running her fingers over the stone and the inner inscription. "It's perfect," she says quietly. "To fool Drew," she adds.

"To fool Drew," I agree. A fact I need to remember, instead of wishing I could sink to my knee, slip this ring on her finger for real. Ridiculous, considering how little time we've spent together, most of it volatile. There's just always been something about Larkin. Or maybe it's me—how long I've kept my desires and dreams on hold, putting my family first.

I suddenly feel like I want everything I've been denied. Love. Connection. A person to share my worries with—and my bed.

She slides the ring on and blinks rapidly. "Drew never understood my love of secondhand stuff. He hated going to garage sales. Made me feel silly for liking them."

"Just another reason for me to hate him." My tone is angrier than warranted. Annoyance that anyone didn't treat Larkin with kindness and respect has that effect on me. "I'll get to the couch now. Uphold my end of the blackmailing."

I sit on one of her dining room chairs and dig into my toolbox. The chair wobbles under my weight. I peer below me and see folded papers propped under one leg.

"The chair came wonky like that," she says. "The papers do the trick. If you need anything while you work, I'll just be reading."

I grunt, feeling irritated. The chair legs should be level. And there's a lightbulb in the hanging antique fixture that needs changing. The outside light is definitely not safe. She's likely too tired from her long shifts at work to tackle mundane house tasks.

Focusing on the issue at hand, I work on her couch. The few

times I glance over at Larkin, who's sitting on one of the non-wobbly dining room chairs, her book is on the table and she's staring at the ring. Thankfully, the size fits her well. She's tracing the tiny leaves like they're precious, and I swear I can feel that soft drag of her fingers down my sternum.

CHAPTER
Eighteen

LARKIN

On Thursday, I'm at home, still stuck in a ring trance. The number of comments at work the past two nights got so intense, I almost removed Jake's engagement ring. But this is why he got me the ring. Our cover story. Convincing the town we're in love, so we can convince Drew I wasn't lying to him.

The fact that it's the absolute perfect ring I would choose myself is inconsequential. The number of times I've caught myself smiling over remembered banter with Jake is irrelevant.

Yes, Jake and I connect as easily as we did the fateful night he drove me home. We have way more in common than I'd ever have thought. He's actually funny and thoughtful, and I find myself worrying over whether he's eating enough or taking proper care of himself, along with wondering what his thick body looks like under those worn T-shirts and Henleys.

All unwelcome fixations.

If Hunter knew I was having sexy thoughts about the guy I've shit-talked and blamed for everything from the beginning, he'd do worse than ask me to stop visiting him in jail. My brother would never speak to me again.

Yet, here I am, staring at the damn ring, picturing Jake fussing over options in an antique store, *caring* what he chose.

A knock at my front door has me tearing my gaze from the pretty band around my finger. I'm not expecting anyone, unless the owner of this property, Audell, is here to discuss the outdoor lighting he's planning to fix.

I open my door to find the man behind the pretty ring. "Isn't today the day you experiment on pandas and plan world domination?"

A crooked smile breaks through his scruffy beard, and my belly decides it's a merry-go-round.

"That's Saturdays." He nods to my dining area. "I'm here for the chair and that lightbulb."

"We didn't discuss you fixing that stuff."

"Didn't need to be discussed." He walks in, brushing past me like he owns the place.

I stare at the spot he vacated, piecing through Jake's motivation. Is he here to hammer out more of our backstory while he hammers my chair? Is he here because he was thinking about me as much as I've been thinking of him? Or, more likely, is he simply being the nice guy he appears to be?

I step outside my front door, taking a deep breath.

Everything was simpler when I hated Jake and believed he was responsible for Derek's death and Hunter's incarceration. When I didn't have sweet women like Phoebe whispering to me that Jake was one of the nicest men she'd ever met and that I was so lucky to have him. It was certainly easier when he didn't do annoying things like swing Gabriela into the air at the farm, a huge grin on his face, causing my womb to clench.

My agitated attention snags on the exterior light fixture Audell planned to fix. There's a bulb in it, but there shouldn't be a bulb in the glass shade. Audell needed an electrician to come by first.

I turn and march up to Jake, who's on his knees beside my flipped chair. "Did you put a bulb in the outside fixture?"

"I did," he says without glancing at me.

"Well, you need to take it out. There's a faulty wire that has to be fixed before a bulb is put in."

He removes a screw from the chair leg and tucks it into his pocket. Slowly, he stands, like some kind of mythical god stretching out his massive body. I should hate how the thick cut of his muscles makes my skin tingle. I should despise the way he stands close and hovers over me, blocking out everything in this room except for his handsome features and soulful dark eyes.

Should being the operative word.

"I spoke to Audell already," he says in that sincere way he speaks. Deep voice, with a slight rasp I feel down to my toes. "I fixed the wire before putting in the bulb."

"Why?"

"Because it was broken."

"No, Jake. *Why?* Why are you here to fix my chair leg? Why are you talking to my landlord without asking me? Why are you here right now?" And why the heck am I so damn frazzled? My emotions are all over the place today.

A line sinks between his brows. He doesn't answer.

Which leaves one explanation. "If this is guilt, I'll save you the effort. You're forgiven."

He startles. "What?"

"For the night we met. I understand why you wanted me out of your truck and didn't answer my call. I know you weren't trying to use me. You'll always be intertwined in those horrible events, but you're not to blame, so you don't have to kill yourself trying to do things for me, like making amends through favors, or whatever this is." I don't say again that everything is my fault. There's no need to point out the obvious.

Jake frowns at the floor. His Adam's apple drags down his strong neck. "I appreciate that you understand. Means more than you know, but that's not why I'm here."

"Then why?"

He lifts his attention, and I'm not prepared for the intensity of his gaze. "You don't want to know."

"Don't tell me what I do and don't want."

"Trust me, Larkin. You don't want my honesty, and I don't want to lie to you. I'll never lie to you again."

"Then stop being so cryptic and tell me why you're here."

"Because I can't stop thinking about you," he growls. "Because the idea of you being unsafe in any way upsets me, and that broken light outside was unsafe. Thinking of you wobbling on that chair, or straining your eyes because you're missing a bulb in here, frustrates the hell out of me. I know I'm not supposed to care about you this intensely. I know you don't want a repeat of that kiss from the town square. All I ask is that you let me make sure your home is comfortable and safe."

He's breathing hard, eyeing my mouth like I'm the tastiest thing he's ever seen.

Heat flashes through my core, turning everything sensitive and achy, while my brain goes on the fritz.

The memory of our kiss is still alive and well, circling on repeat most hours. The ring he gave me feels like a brand on my finger. In one visit to my home, he understood my design aesthetic and the type of engagement ring I'd love. The gifts Drew bought me were always trendy and new. But Jake and I— there's something different there. We have fun together. We tease each other mercilessly, but I think we both enjoy being scrappy.

Then there's that brutally honest letter.

I'm sorry I kissed you so intensely yesterday. I've been dreaming about doing that for twelve years.

You're smart and gorgeous and witty as hell.

I thought Jake's description of his attraction to me in the

letter was maybe surface. I was a challenge. A woman he never conquered. Except that's not what he's claiming now, and I don't know what to do with that information. Jake's not just handsome and sexy. He's kind and intuitive. No one has ever made me feel this safe and cared for, and we're not even dating. At least, not for real. But everything with us is so complicated.

"Can I ask you for a favor?" I say, choosing diversion over responding to his shocking confession. I still haven't retaliated to his stunt of shoving my face in his snotty shirt. Pranking Jake is easier than dealing with my messy feelings.

He rubs his bearded jaw, assessing me. "Ask me anything, but know I'll blackmail you in return."

I even like the idea of him blackmailing me. "It's actually a favor for Jolene and me—helping us with our booth at the Dog and Pony Show this weekend."

He folds his arms over his broad chest, one eyebrow cocked. "Does this have something to do with me covering your face in snot?"

And there goes my surprise attack. "Are you able to read my mind?"

"Not even fucking close," he says, his tone resigned. "And your motivation doesn't matter. Whatever you need, I'm all in."

"I thought I was going to be blackmailed?"

He rolls his tongue over his front teeth. "Do you want to be blackmailed?"

"Yes," I say, not letting my brain overthink my reply. I want him to ask for something from me. Take instead of this constant giving.

"Okay." Those dark eyes of his roam my face, like he can sense something has changed in my Jake-addled brain. Carefully, he reaches up and brushes loose hairs off my face. "Next time I try to kiss you, I need to know if it's real or fake for you."

My brain stutters on *next time*. I want that next time to be *now*, when I shouldn't want his lips anywhere near mine. "When should I expect this kiss?"

"When the time is right."

"And how will I show you if it's real or fake?"

He drags in a big breath and slowly lets it out. "An ass-grab will do."

My laugh startles me. "So, if I grab your ass, you know it's real for me?"

"Yep." He winks and steps back, creating space between us that I hate. I like joking with Jake. Flirting and having fun.

A glance down shows a hefty bulge behind his fly. Proof this bit of noncontact interaction turned him on too, and I become very aware of Jake Bower. My saliva evaporates. The heat behind my navel intensifies. With the size of his muscular body, I imagined all of Jake was well proportioned. I wasn't wrong. His denim jeans don't show details, but they show enough.

If he follows through on his threat and kisses me again, I'm not sure it's his ass I'll grab.

"Fine," I say, needing a bit of an upper hand with Jake. More equilibrium. And I love a good prank. "Consider yourself doing me a favor at the Dog and Pony Show. I promise you'll have fun."

While being embarrassed in public.

CHAPTER
Nineteen

Jake

"I'm not having fun," I say, glaring at Larkin. "Not even a little."

She doesn't bother trying to hide her amusement. "But you look so fun."

"Fucking hell," I mutter, tugging at the dog costume she brought for me. My pinched face pokes out from a hole below the cocker spaniel's plush head. The rest of me is stuffed into this furry onesie, with a tail hanging off my ass, upping my humiliation.

I'm pretty sure she purposely ordered a size too small.

"Watch your language," she says on a laugh. "This is a family event."

"Then maybe you should've bought something that doesn't show every inch of my body." I point a furry paw toward my crotch.

Pink steals across her cheeks. I'd be pleased my body has an effect on her, even in this outfit, except thinking about Larkin turned on isn't helping the downtown situation in this ridiculous costume.

I avert my attention from her, attempting to think about non-sexy things as I watch townsfolk enter the fairgrounds.

Kids are already running ahead of their parents, aiming for the funnel cake booth and the Tilt-A-Whirl. Puking will definitely happen at some point. Puppy yoga, which is apparently yoga where puppies walk all over you, is being held on the other side of the large field. Pony rides are offered by the rodeo rings. Dog agility contests will be hosted, along with dog-grooming lessons and pony-pulling races. A local pottery studio is letting townsfolk paint premade ceramic dogs and ponies, and businesses like Larkin and Jo's fill the booths between the events.

All I have to do is uphold my end of our agreement for a few hours.

"I'm done at lunch," I tell her. "Not a second past noon."

She shoves a stack of flyers at my chest. "I accept your terms. Smile pretty for the festivalgoers and pass out these sheets, so they know where to find our booth."

Her attention strays downward, to the too-tight fabric attempting to contain my dick, which is highly attuned to this woman. Her teeth sink into her bottom lip, then she fans her face with her hand.

Maybe this asinine costume has it perks.

"Your cheeks seem a little blotchy," I say, leaning closer. "Are you allergic to dogs? Should I go find an EpiPen? Or do you need something else to alleviate that hot flash hitting you?"

Her answering stare is bland. "The only dog I'm allergic to is the one I'm talking to, who's about to be shoved into a crate for annoying me."

"So you're into dominance with furries? Is that your kink?"

Her nostrils flare as she opens her mouth, probably to yell at me in that feisty way of hers, but Mrs. Jackson waves at us with a knowing look. Right. We're engaged. Larkin notices the attention and wraps her arm around my waist, cuddling in close. Innocent enough, but a rush of desire makes this onesie painfully tight. I jerk away from her.

"What the hell?" she whispers. "Did you forget everyone thinks we're betrothed? We need to sell our story."

I shove the flyers in front of my crotch and focus on the grass, imagining all the dog shit that'll have to be cleaned up today. "Just stay over there for a sec," I say, sounding way more strangled than I'd like.

Amusement breaks over her face. "Are things getting snug down there?" she asks, stepping closer.

I give her a warning look, but I'm dressed in a onesie with a dog's face on my head. All she does is laugh.

"This isn't funny, Larkin."

"Oh, it definitely is. I'm just surprised you have so little control over your body."

My nostrils flare on a low growl. "Normally, control isn't an issue. But it's always been different with you, because, for some reason I've never understood, this goes beyond simple attraction for me. If you touch me in any way, I might bust a hole through this stupid suit. So please do me the kindness of keeping your distance. I don't need to get arrested for indecent exposure."

"Wow." She touches her clavicle and seems to be having trouble swallowing. The ring I gave her catches the light, and another rush of heat spreads through my body. Not a blast of lust this time. Something softer. She shudders out a breath. "That was…a lot."

"Yeah, well, everything with you is a lot. Which would be fine, if I wasn't wearing this fucking outfit." Or if I wasn't overwhelmed by seeing that ring on her finger.

We stare at each other, both of us breathing faster, and one thing is very clear to me.

I want this woman.

There's no controlling how worked up I get around her, how

badly I want to kiss her again, lick into her mouth, show the world she's truly mine. Test if she shocks me by grabbing my ass or keeps her hands safe, telling me we'll never be more than fake engaged. That prospect has me leaning away, not closer.

"Larkin!" a deep voice calls from behind me. Definitely Callahan, and my desire for her deflates faster than a punctured balloon. "What did you need to see all of us about?" he asks.

All of us? A muscle by my eye twitches. "Please tell me you didn't invite my brothers to witness my mortification."

She presses her lips flat, but a laugh squeaks out. "I didn't?"

This goddamn woman. "I was planning to let this be your last prank. Be a good sport and move on. Now I have no choice but to come up with something horrendously awful to embarrass you on this level."

Her face is red from suppressed laughter. Her attention shifts over my shoulder, where my brothers have no doubt gathered.

Attempting to ready myself for their reaction, I slowly turn.

And the assholes lose it.

Four dickheads, who will never let me live this moment down, are laughing so hard they're wheezing. Even Desmond can't control himself. He's half leaning on Callahan's shoulder, one arm around his stomach, as he has a conniption at my expense.

"Are you all happy?" I demand.

"Not yet," Lennon says on a snort. Eyes damp from laughing, he pulls out his phone and snaps a series of shots. "Now I'm happy. And if Larkin has a leash, I'll take you for a walk later."

E elbows Lennon. "We should take him to visit Avett. He might need his anal glands expressed." The two morons guffaw.

"Or at least get him neutered," Callahan adds, getting in on the ribbing. "Wouldn't want him humping every leg he sees."

I try to flip them my middle finger. All they can see is my raised paw.

Desmond's full-teeth grin, from the guy who only shows his

teeth when snarling, has me wanting to punch his neck. "This made my fucking year," he tells Larkin and holds up his hand for a high five.

Normally, Larkin shoots my brothers down with witty jabs. Today, she high-fives Desmond and shares smiles with the rest of these idiots.

"You're definitely paying for this," I tell her, except there's no censure in my tone. I should be furious right now, but Larkin's amusement has me feeling twisted up. Like I'd do anything to be partly responsible for her happiness. Even deal with my obnoxious brothers.

She gives a cocky shrug. "Do your worst."

I don't know what comes over me then. Maybe it's the twinkle in her eye that's so damn cute. Or seeing her laughing with my brothers, who mean the world to me. Or this unquenchable thirst to claim Larkin temporarily muddles my brain.

Whatever madness propels me, I haul her in for a kiss.

CHAPTER
Twenty

LARKIN

Jake's demanding lips are on mine, and I'm not sure how or why this happened. Last thing I remember is *laughing* with his brothers—an oddity in itself—basking in Jake's humiliation. Now I'm as stiff as he was the day I kissed him by the fountain.

He doesn't abate. One of his plush-covered hands is on my neck, angling my face. And my traitorous body *melts*. I kiss him back, slow and deep, our gentle passes mingled with small groans. We're not getting dirty and devouring each other this time. This is gentler. Deeper. More intimate, like he really is my fiancé, our bodies snug and hearts tapping out the same devoted tune.

Catcalls come from his brothers, bringing me back to reality.

Maybe I shouldn't have invited them.

"Careful," Lennon says, amused. "He pees when he gets excited."

Jake and I both laugh, but we don't pull apart.

I don't know what kind of voodoo this is. I never *laugh* while kissing men, and I've always been intensely private about relationships. Never openly affectionate. A side effect of being considered a slut in high school, likely, courtesy of the Grade A asshole Ian Parks.

He'd broken up with his girlfriend, Stella Bohen, the day prior. I'd been crushing on him from afar for months, going to his football games and watching him at his locker. He'd see me in the halls and would smile at me or wink, building my crush into a full-blown obsession.

Then he invited me to a party. He wasn't subtle about his intentions. He had me in an upstairs bedroom before I finished my first drink. The night was consensual, but the zing and flutters I expected weren't there. He tried to have sex with me, and I said no. He didn't push, but he wasn't pleased.

Then he spread rumors that I seduced him and we *did* actually have sex.

The town, of course, ate up the gossip and spat it out even worse. People said we'd been hooking up for a while, while he was with Stella. They claimed I was the reason he dumped her. Ian never once defended me or told the truth. His friends would hum porno music as they passed me in the hallway, and the prick would laugh. Girls ostracized and antagonized me, going so far as to paint the word SLUT on my locker.

I became intensely private after that. Struggled making friends. Made horrible choices, like dating Derek, because I didn't think I deserved better. And when things with Derek got scary, I didn't have anyone close to confide in. Until that night with Jake.

I still don't share the way normal people do. Jolene is my best friend, and there's so much I keep from her. Jake is different. He knows me, warts and all, and we're laughing while kissing, putting on a show for the whole town, and I'm not freaking out or pulling back. I'm not worried he's using me or trying to embarrass me in public. He worries *after* me, fixes stuff around my place without being asked. He blatantly admitted he's into me beyond attraction.

The more I've thought about his letter and him not answering my call when I was in trouble, the less anger I've felt. We were young and both made horrible, knee-jerk decisions. Jake shouldn't have let fear of his emotions stop him from answering my call, but he also had a ton going on emotionally that night—turmoil over Jolene, worry over his parents. *I* shouldn't have trashed Derek's home, a worse action with more obvious consequences.

There's no undoing those choices, but the ones I make now also have the potential to alter my life.

Jake gave me a direct challenge—grab his ass to show him if our next kiss is real or for show. *Real*, my mind chants, but I lock up. I disengage our lips, needing a moment to breathe, recalibrate.

He rubs the back of my neck in slow strokes, presses a tender kiss to my ear. "It's okay," he says quietly. "I wasn't expecting you to feel the same."

The half smile he gives me is disappointed, though. His shoulders fall and his brow furrows. Crushed—that's how he looks. And my heart is racing so fast I'm dizzy. Regrets start to build, a tumbling mess of what-ifs. *What if I ignore my feelings and miss out on something surprising and fun and meaningful that could change my life for the better?*

He starts to pull away, but I yank him back and slam my hand on his ass.

The abrupt move draws more laughs and hoots from his brothers.

Jake isn't laughing. He gazes down at me with so much intensity, I shiver. "Are you fucking with me?" he asks.

"Do you think I *want* my hand on your ass when you're wearing this stupid outfit?"

Asinine suit or not, I feel how thick his length is against my stomach. "You're the one who put me in this stupid outfit."

"You're the one who kissed me while wearing it."

A wicked grin cuts across his strong features. "So, furries *do* get you hot?"

"Unless you want me to step back and reveal just how turned on you are, I suggest playing nice."

Emotion blows through his dark eyes. "I don't want nice with you, Larkin. I want real."

I'm not sure how he knows blunt honesty is my kryptonite. More things we have in common, I guess. Both of us drawn to the rawness of life. Must be what happens when you live through hell.

Too bad the sincerity of the sentiment is spoken with his face poking out of a cocker-spaniel suit.

I turn to his brothers, while barricading Jake's crotch. "I'm done with you all now. You can move along."

Lennon folds his arms over his chest. "And miss the part when Jake gets arrested for public indecency and has to have his mug shot taken wearing a onesie? I think not."

"Okay," I say sweetly. "But if you linger, I'll hang a sign in the bar that says Call Lennon a Hipster and You Get a Free Drink."

Fear flits across his face. "You wouldn't."

"Try me."

He glares at the rest of his brothers, pointing a finger at each of them. "If you'd all quit calling me a hipster, shit like this wouldn't happen."

E shrugs. "What's the fun in that?"

Lennon directs his angry pointing at Jake. "He has a fucking beard now. Why aren't you calling Jake a hipster too?"

"That also wouldn't be fun," Des says.

"My fucking family," Lennon grumbles as he storms away.

"One of you definitely needs to make some kind of hipster

sign for the bar," I say, already picturing Lennon's indignant fury.

Callahan gestures to E. "Let the artist do it. It's time I head to your booth and help Jolene. Appreciate the laugh, though."

E and Desmond depart too. With no Bowers around, I turn and glance down at Jake's lower half. "Seems you're more in control."

"As long as you keep your distance, yeah." He pulls at the plush suit and scratches under his doggy hood, then yanks the headpiece off and shakes out his hair. "Does this mean I can take you out now? On a proper date?"

Reality quickly sobers me. Grabbing Jake's ass in public was a whole lot easier than dealing with the complexity of our situation.

"I'd like that a lot, but I need to speak with my brother first. I've talked a lot of shit about you to Hunter, told him you were playing me that night and that you're a big part of the reason he's been in jail. I know everything you wrote in your letter is true. I can forgive you for everything that happened, but he's not your biggest fan." To put it mildly. "I won't lie to him about my life, so he'll have to know if we're actually dating. If he gets mad to the point of cutting me out of his life, which is kind of how he's dealing with his anger these days, I'm not sure we can take this any further, no matter how I feel."

He nods and blows out a breath. "I understand."

I ache to kiss him again, feel his hard body against mine without that ridiculous suit in the way. Unfortunately, we have ten tons of baggage between us.

I'll have to ask Hunter's attorney to help me. Jesse can hopefully convince my brother to accept a call since he's no longer keen on visits. The prospect already has me nervous. Hunter might not believe Jake is different from the man I've hated all these years. He hasn't experienced Jake's sincerity and humor, his kindness and generosity.

I'm still shocked by Jake's true personality. Not long ago, the idea of talking to him made me want to poke my eyes out. Now I'm worried he'll never be more than my fake fiancé.

"I respect how much you care about your relationship with Hunter," Jake says gently. "Whatever you decide, I'll still help with Drew and his wedding. I'll play whatever role you need me to play. I won't deny that I want a hell of a lot more than friendship with you, but I won't push. All I ask is that you're honest with me."

Exactly why this man is chipping away at my defenses. "Same goes for you."

He lifts his dog hood back on, his expression flat. "I honestly hate this fucking outfit and am cursing you internally for thinking up this level of torture."

I tip my head back and laugh. "I'm evil like that."

"And kind of cute."

He winks at me and leaves to hand out flyers for our booth. I debate telling him I've also volunteered his services to clean up dog shit during the afternoon but decide to let him enjoy the surprise.

CHAPTER
Twenty~One

LARKIN

I curl into my couch and stare at my phone while spinning my engagement ring in circles. Not that the ring is actually mine. Or real. I mean, the ring itself is real, obviously, but the sentiment behind it is as phony as a three-dollar bill. Jake will have to resell it after this ruse, and I have no clue why I'm fixating on counterfeit bills and this phony, *really* pretty ring when I'm waiting on my brother to call.

Jesse spoke with Hunter yesterday. He said my brother still seemed down and refused to hope he was getting out early. Jesse thinks Hunter is smart to expect the worst. Better that than facing the harsh blow of being denied release. Jesse's probably right, but seeing Hunter this despondent is torture.

My phone rings, and a rush of nerves fills me.

I'm suddenly not sure organizing this call was smart. I shouldn't be discussing Jake with Hunter. Bringing up the past will upset him and is purely selfish on my part. I don't deserve happiness when he lives in a hell I created.

On the third ring, I snap up my phone, quickly agreeing to accept the prison call.

"Hey," Hunter says, sounding like he's chewing on gravel.

My throat tightens. "I'm so glad you called."

He grunts. "What's up?"

He's being abrupt and cold. I'm definitely not mentioning Jake. "Just wanted to check in and see how you are. I hate not visiting you."

"It's better this way, Larkin. But Jesse made it sound more important than that."

Before this call, dating Jake seemed hugely important. If I let myself think about *not* having more time with him—an actual date, more jokes and laughs and sincere talks—I feel bereft. Like I've lost someone close to me. But I can shut down those emotions and stay platonic friends with Jake. Hunter deserves all my focus. At least, until he's released.

"Whatever Jesse said, he's probably just worried about you," I say. "Like I am—worried about how you're coping with the Parole Commission news and everything. Not that I expect you to be okay. There's nothing okay about any of this. It's okay not to be okay."

Unless you're me, babbling like a lying teenager.

He makes a rough sound. "What happened?"

"Nothing happened."

"You spew lots of words when you're nervous or upset, and there's definite word vomit going on. So, I'll ask again, what happened that has you rattled? I'm short on time here. Other inmates need the phone."

The fact that he knows me this well has me shrinking in on myself. I used to know him inside and out too. When he liked a girl, he'd blush something fierce. When he'd look at a bridge or a skyscraper, I could practically see his mind pulling apart the mathematics behind the materials, so I'd ask him—my brother, the future engineer—how he'd design the structure differently.

I'd push him to think in big, creative strokes. He'd come alive while talking about sustainable infrastructure and new software programs, using words I'd barely understand.

Now he talks about inmates and phone privileges, and I never know the right thing to say. One wrong word can have him closing off from me.

Quelling all thoughts of why I orchestrated this call, I say, "It's nothing. I just wanted to hear your voice."

This grunt doesn't sound pleased. "I thought we didn't lie to each other, Runt."

He's right. We don't lie to each other or evade and placate, as per our ongoing pact.

The day we made the agreement, he was furious with how the cops and press were twisting his story—strangers painting a man guilty by his name alone. He looked at me across the prison table, his cuffed hands curled into fists, and said, "I need honesty from you, Runt. Whatever happens with this trial and my case, I need to know someone has my back. That means unadulterated truth from you, no matter how shit it is."

If I honor that request now, I have to tell him about Jake. And Drew. And my plans to convince my ex to look favorably on Hunter's case.

I grip my phone, wishing I could see into the future—how upset Hunter will be by each piece of that story, if telling him will drive a larger wedge between us. In the end, it's not my choice to make. He dropped the honesty card. I have to comply.

"My ex Drew came to the Barrel House on the grand reopening," I say.

"The prick psychiatrist who liked analyzing you to make himself feel superior?"

Maybe I was too honest when discussing him with Hunter. "That's the one. And I, of course, let my awkward flag fly, word vomit and all. Got flustered and wound up telling him I had a fiancé, like I had to prove I could be in a committed relationship."

"You don't have to prove shit to that guy."

"Theoretically, I agree. Emotionally, I had a break with reality or something. And a...*man* I knew was at the bar when it happened." Someone I thought I hated but turns out is sweet and caring and wants to take me on a date...if Hunter doesn't blow a gasket. "He noticed me fumbling with Drew," I go on, sounding shakier. "He stepped in and said he was the fiancé I was lying about, and then Drew told me he was getting married too and invited us to attend his wedding. So now, we have to go together."

The sordid story sounds more ridiculous each time I say it aloud.

"Just tell Drew you can't make it. And who is this mystery guy who agreed to that sham?"

Because I'm the talker of the two of us when I visit Hunter— aka word-vomiter who overshares—he knows the ins and outs of my love life, including the moment I told Drew about my past and how intense things got afterward. The overanalyzing. How pitied and broken I wound up feeling.

Hunter was vocal at the time. He blatantly told me he didn't like the guy. Said I was stubborn and looking for acceptance in the wrong place—our honesty pact hitting hard. Hurt bloomed at the moment, and I reacted rashly. I defended Drew, falling prey to the mansplainer's negative reinforcement, believing I loved him and we were simply having a rough spell.

In the end, Hunter was right. I sought Drew's approval to feel more loved and less damaged. To feel like I belonged somewhere, even if that place was tearing me down. And Drew wasn't much better. As far as I'm concerned, his emotional baggage was just as heavy. He treated me the way his father treated him—passive-aggressive comments, stepping on other people to feel taller.

I stayed in that toxic relationship longer than I should have. A pattern with me, apparently. Now Hunter wants the name of the fake fiancé I'm falling for, as well as the reason why we have to attend Drew's wedding.

Best to start with the lesser of the two evils.

"Drew is on the Parole Commission. That's why I have to attend his wedding. He'll have input on any decisions made, and I plan to convince him you deserve to be released. I'm still reeling from it all—seeing him out of the blue like that. But I'm not looking this gift horse in the mouth. As far as I'm concerned, luck is finally on our side."

Silence answers me. Harsher breaths, then a quiet "Fucking asshole" hisses through the line.

"Why does this make Drew an asshole?"

"This isn't luck, Larkin. There's no coincidence here. Drew is conniving and manipulative. When you were with him, he fucked with your head for kicks. He knew exactly what he was doing showing up at your bar, so no. You won't be attending his wedding with a real or a fake fiancé."

Unease slips down my spine. Jake was wary of Drew's motivations too. He wasn't as angry and forceful on the subject, but neither he nor Hunter trusts my ex. I wholeheartedly agree that he's a manipulating dick. I just don't see how inviting me to his wedding benefits him. Maybe he's changed and wants to show me how much *he's* matured.

Either way, his motivation doesn't matter. Not when Hunter's life is in the balance.

"Since we don't lie to each other," I say, "I won't agree to your demand and then do the opposite. I'm telling you now, *honestly*, that I'm going to Drew's wedding. And I'm going to make it very clear to him, through some horrible sucking up, that you never should've been locked up in the first place."

"Except he knows my story, Larkin. He knows *your* story. A

credible psychiatrist would state conflicting interests and recuse themselves from the case. Has he done that?"

"I don't know. I don't even know if your file has crossed his desk yet. Either way, I'm doing this." If Drew has an ulterior motive, I might be able to use that against him. Quid pro quo. Find out what he's after. Forcefully suggest he help Hunter if I help him.

Hunter clacks his teeth. Usually a sign he's giving up fighting me. "You didn't answer the other part. Who's the fake fiancé who's supporting this farce?"

Right. *That.* I brace myself, readying for Hunter to blow up at me. At least, as much as he can on a prison phone.

"Jake Bower," I say quietly. "And before you freak out, I've gotten to know him recently, and he's nothing like I thought. I was sure he ditched me that night and didn't answer my call because he was playing me and didn't give a shit. That's not the case. And his family has been through hell since then. He's become so kind and thoughtful, and I think I might really like him. At least, I want to give him a chance. Go out with him and see if we click, beyond the fake-fiancé stuff. If you're okay with that," I add.

Hunter doesn't make a sound. He's so silent I worry he's hung up or maybe he's covering the phone so I can't hear him swearing a blue streak.

"If you think he's changed," he says evenly, "if you understand his choices that night and don't blame him any longer, then I'm fine with you two going out."

I'm so shocked, I nearly drop my phone. "Really?"

"On one condition," he adds firmly.

"Okay…"

Muttering comes from Hunter's end, like an inmate is demanding the phone. "Back the fuck off," Hunter says to someone, then his full volume returns. "Jake has to come see me at the jail."

Nope. I don't like this option at all. "Why?"

"Because I want him to know he has to treat you right or he deals with me, and I have to go. If you want my blessing, Jake comes here alone. And I still don't like this Drew stunt. Don't let your guard down around him."

He hangs up. I'm equal parts agitated and relieved.

I'm glad I was honest with Hunter and he didn't cut me permanently out of his life. He wasn't happy about Drew and my plan to suck up to him, but I'm still moving full steam ahead on that end. Whatever Drew's motivations, I'm no longer the fragile bird he helped manifest, desperate for affection. I'm strong and independent and can handle him.

The real surprise is Hunter not freaking out about Jake. He actually listened to me. He must have heard the truth of my affection for this man who has somehow snuck into my heart. Hunter will no doubt posture with Jake, lay down the older-brother law. That's his right, considering our history. I just have to convince Jake to visit my brother in jail. Then we can finally see how deep this connection between us runs.

CHAPTER
Twenty-Two

Jake

Working with a wet saw is turning into a messy affair, but the Huertas want a tile floor for their screened-in porch, and I aim to please my clients. Cal and I borrowed the saw from fellow contractor Lemarcus Palmer for a few days, allowing us to cut the tile we need for the project.

Fortunately, we aren't paying for the use of his equipment. Unfortunately, the water, which flows while the saw rotates to prevent the blade from overheating and smoking, is spurting out at unexpected angles. The tiles may be cutting properly, but my T-shirt is half drenched.

"You should wear that dog costume," Cal says when I take a break. He shuts off the stereo and joins me by the saw. "The fur might repel water."

"Fuck you." I flip him the finger.

He chuckles. "I'm just glad Larkin excels at putting you in your place. And that you two seem closer," he adds. "The letter did the trick?"

"It helped, yeah. We've also spent more time together—at the farm, and we've hung out while I did stuff around her place." Having a blast together and sharing intense talks. Perfect dates, if this were a normal relationship, but guys in normal relationships don't have nightmares about being unable to save the woman he's falling for. "It's all freaking me out a bit, to be honest."

He cocks his head. "What is?"

Cal hasn't prodded about Larkin since I told him about our history. I imagine he's been dealing with his own remorse on the matter. He gets quiet and in his own head when he's introspective. I certainly haven't brought her up. I'm not used to leaning on my brothers. I'm the one who stares at them until they get annoyed or worn down enough to open up.

I take a breath and glance around the neighborhood. A few neighbors are on their front porches. All women, by the looks of things, drinking cold drinks in small groups. Book clubs, maybe. Or just friends getting together to chat.

Ms. Osorio flutters her fingers at me.

I offer a distracted wave and face my brother. "It's freaking me out how quickly I'm falling for Larkin."

"Okay." Cal nods thoughtfully. "Except it's not really quick."

"How do you figure that?"

"She's been on your mind for twelve years. With that kind of buildup, things either fizzle fast, because the real thing doesn't live up to the fantasy. Or, in this case, it's better, and you fall like a meteor."

I certainly feel like a meteor, hurtling through space when I think of Larkin's hand on my ass at the Dog and Pony Show. My heart damn near exploded at the contact, a combination of shock and relief hitting me. I never expected her to have feelings for me too. *Real* feelings. For her to want me as much as I want her.

Unfortunately, the euphoria of her admission didn't last long.

"I'm still really affected by our past. I think I can move past it, but Larkin said she needs to speak with her brother before things go further with us. Ask for his blessing, because of our messed-up history." I drag my hand through my damp hair. "Haven't heard from her since."

"Doesn't mean the news is bad."

"What else could it mean?"

"Maybe he said yes, but she needs to decide whether she really wants to date you."

I glare at him. "How is that better?"

"You won't have a convicted murderer out to kill you."

This is why I don't confide in my family. "Helpful, Cal. Really fucking helpful. And we need to get back to work."

I dip my head and fire up the wet saw, wincing when the water pelts my chest again. I have no doubt Lemarcus chose not to warn me about the erratic spray. We were on the football team together in high school. I was the quarterback and captain. He was the center. If he showed up hungover to practice, I'd make him do laps and would bet with the other players how long it would take for him to puke. Good times had by all, but I wouldn't be surprised if he showed up with a beer to laugh at me while I work.

Cal turns the stereo back on. James Brown blasts, singing about being a sex machine. The funky beat and provocative lyrics have me conjuring images I should ignore. But I can't.

I picture Larkin under me while it plays. I imagine her moving to the rhythm, biting my shoulder when I glide my fingers down her belly, through her delicate curls. Feel how fucking wet she is. I bet she's a biter. Feisty and responsive. The perfect amount of demanding when in bed.

I move to the song, can't control the small rolls of my hips as the fantasy takes shape, but this damn shirt is even more drenched and suctioned to me. Frustrated, I peel it off, tossing it on the ground as I shake out my damp hair.

When I look up, I freeze.

Larkin is staring at me from the end of the driveway. She's wearing jeans and a cropped T-shirt that shows a hint of her flat stomach, the braids over her shoulders unbearably cute. Her often challenge-filled eyes are intense and molten, drawing torturous lines over my body.

I turn off the saw and strut toward her with hungry strides, wanting my hands on her, until I remember we have unfinished business. I can't tell if she's here for good news or bad. I don't know if she talked to her brother yet. If she did, he might be happy she's happy and gave us his blessing. Or maybe she's here to warn me I once again have a hit out on my head.

Not able to read her for shit, I stop a foot away. "This is a surprise."

Her eyes lock on my bare chest. "Did you get a role in the traveling *Magic Mike* show?"

"The what show?"

"*Magic Mike*." When I shrug, she gestures at my general self. "It's a strip show, Jake. Hunky guys dress up like cops and cowboys and construction workers and do things like douse themselves in water while sexy music plays and they rip off their pants. This whole situation is one big lady boner."

I full-on snort. "Lady boner?"

She flings out her arm, pointing across the street. "Have you not noticed your audience? You're seconds away from women shoving dollar bills down your briefs."

Frowning, I glance at the porch ladies with new eyes. Two different homes have small gatherings out front, all with chairs facing the street. I assumed they were watching townsfolk walk by as they discussed books or yarn or whatever it is groups of ladies discuss.

According to Larkin, they're watching Cal and me.

I narrow my eyes at them.

"You're doing excellent work," Ms. Osorio calls. "Especially with the water machine."

Nods move through the group, along with some whispers. One woman fans her face and mimes fainting, earning tittering laughs from the others.

Yep, they're ogling us.

"Honest to God," Cal says, marching to the stereo and yanking out the plug. "I will not have this town gossiping about the stripping they think I do. Not again." He points an accusing finger at me. "You need to wear clothing at all times when working. No exception."

I try not to laugh, but it's no use. I remember the stripping rumors Cal started earlier this year. Something about him taking off his sweaty shirt when renovating with his buddy.

I give a halfhearted shrug. "The saw is a mess. The water was spraying everywhere, and my T-shirt got drenched. What was I supposed to do?"

He huffs. "Wear the wet shirt, obviously."

"Bad call," Larkin says. "The suctioned shirt was just as hot, being all clingy on those beefy muscles."

I can't help the puff of my ego. First, she compares me to hunky strippers. Now, she's talking about my *beefy* muscles. If I didn't know better, I'd say the call with her brother went well.

"Should I put the wet shirt back on?" I ask, testing her flirting boundaries.

"Yes," she says, eyes sparkling.

Cal huffs and raises his phone. "Sandra texted me. Townsfolk are already calling us the Hustlers of Elm Street." He tries to scowl at us, but a Callahan glare looks more like polite disregard.

Not that I care right now. Larkin *definitely* has good news to share.

Callahan casts a wary glance at the porch ladies and waves. "We weren't stripping," he calls to them. "The water from the saw was malfunctioning, and the music sounded sexier than intended. But no clothes were removed for money."

"The shirt did leave his body," one of the women points out —Wanda Canning, age eighty-plus. "And he gets paid to work."

Cal opens his mouth and closes it. He jabs his finger at my chest. "Clothes on at all times from now on, no exceptions."

He marches off toward the far side of the screened-in porch, grumbling as he goes.

"You definitely need to wear tear-away Velcro pants next week," Larkin says, grinning at his back. "His head might actually explode."

I chuckle. "And *I'm* the one who experiments on baby pandas and plans world domination?" I tsk and tug on one of her braids. "Aside from watching me strip, is there another reason you stopped by?"

"As a matter of fact, there is."

She tucks her hands into her front pockets, but they don't go in too far. Her ring rests on the pocket lip, and I can't help the happy dip in my stomach at the sight. I like seeing that ring on her finger. I'll like it even better when I kiss my way down her arm and hand and finger and every other inch of her. "Your talk with your brother went well?"

She nibbles her lip. "Mostly. Talking to him is always rough, but I told him about everything—Drew, the wedding. How things have changed with you."

"And?" I ask, sensing hesitation and…desire. Her attention keeps falling to my chest and abs in a way that has my jeans feeling tight.

She gives her head a small shake and smiles bashfully, when nothing about Larkin is bashful. "He said if I trust you, he's okay with us dating."

My heart fucking thunders. "And do you trust me?"

"I feel pretty overwhelmed by all of this, but yes. After hating you for a lot of years, somehow, I trust you now."

Thank fucking God. "Well, in case you're wondering, I trust you too." And will hopefully quit having bad dreams about her one day soon. I brush my knuckles down her cheek. "I really want to kiss you now."

Her attention flits behind her, to the ladies gabbing on their porches. "We have an audience."

I shrug, not caring one bit. I lean down and kiss her softly. Linger just long enough to dredge a happy sigh from us both. "When can I take you out?"

Her eyes slowly flutter open. "I might have forgotten to mention a caveat to the dating."

"Okay," I say, waiting on her, unsure why she's suddenly hesitant.

She rocks on her heels. "My brother wants to meet you, which means you'd have to visit him in jail."

"He...*what*?"

"Hunter wants to talk to you, so if you want to take me out, you have to go to Langmore and see him."

Yep, that sounded as terrifyingly horrible the second time.

I may not have left Larkin in the lurch twelve years ago or dismissed her call because I was playing games with her, but those actions had consequences. Malicious intent or not, I'm a big part of the reason Hunter is in jail. The guy must want to rip my head from my body.

"But he said he's fine with us dating? Didn't seem pissed off?"

"Hunter always seems pissed off these days, but we don't lie to each other—it's our thing, like a pact we made. If he said he's okay with us going out, then he is. He's just overprotective and wants to do some male posturing, to make sure you treat me right."

"I would," I say, dropping my voice and catching her eye. "I'd always treat you right, Larkin. Better than right. Like a fucking queen, even without a scary older brother breathing down my neck. You deserve a man who falls to his knees for you."

She sucks in a sharp breath. "That was intense."

"You make me feel intense, but I'm just being honest. The question is if you believe me."

She hesitates a beat, then her face softens. "I do. I trust that you won't hurt me."

Words I never dreamed I'd hear from this woman. "Good," I say gruffly.

"But you'll go see Hunter?" she pushes. "I know it's a bit over the top and old-fashioned, wanting my brother's approval. He's just so important to me, and I want him to feel like he's part of my life, especially because he can't be physically. And—"

"Hey." I slip my hand around hers, lacing our fingers together. "If it's important to you, it's important to me. Of course I'll go."

She releases a rush of breath. "Thank you."

"I'm a bit slammed with work. Was planning on putting in some hours this weekend, and I don't know how visiting works. Any chance I can go next Thursday?"

"Shouldn't be a problem. Drew's surprise party for his fiancée is that night, but you'll be back in time for that."

I nod, trying to get my head around it all. Facing Hunter. Drew's party, which has me uneasy. I still don't trust that guy. Also, next Thursday is ten days away. No way I can wait that long for Larkin. Not with how hard my heart is pumping.

I dip my head and brush my nose against hers. "If meeting Hunter is just a formality, and he already said he's okay with me taking you out, there's no harm in going out before then, right? Tomorrow, if that works for you."

A pretty blush dusts her cheeks. "I don't work late on Wednesdays, but Hunter seemed to want to talk to you first."

"Nothing he says will change how I feel, sweetheart. He said he's good with us hanging out, and I'm feeling pretty fucking impatient to get you alone. Unless you don't feel the same."

She worries her lip, then presses her hand to my chest,

drawing a torturous path from between my pecs, over each bump of my abs, ending at the waistband of my jeans. *Fuck.*

"Depends what you have planned," she says, flirty as hell.

This woman will be the death of me. "I can set up the wet saw outside your place and give you a proper show since you seem to be into male strippers."

"And take you away from your rapt audience?" She walks backward slowly, adding a sway to her hips. "I value my life too much to mess with those ladies. Wanda might knock me out with her rolling pin and steal you away. But I'm not sure you ever need to wear a shirt again. Half naked looks good on you. Also…" She fiddles with the end of her left braid. "I'd love to go out tomorrow."

I almost give a victory whoop. "I'll swing by the bar and grab you."

The excitement on her face nearly undoes me, and I grin too damn wide.

CHAPTER
Twenty-Three

Larkin

I'm holding Jake's hand. In his truck. No one is here to see us. We're not putting on a show to sell our fake engagement. The butterflies in my stomach certainly aren't playing around. They're dipping and diving as Jake rubs his thumb along the outer edge of my hand. Tiny strokes that feel like heaven.

"You good?" he asks, stealing a glance at me.

"I don't think I've ever been this nervous but excited for a date."

A crooked smile tilts the corner of his beautiful mouth. "Me too."

"Really?"

He pulls up our linked hands and kisses my fingers. Right over the ring he gave me. "I've never felt this way with a woman before. Not even close."

Jake Bower sure knows how to serve up my romance catnip, that honesty of his knocking me for a dizzying loop. I'm used to games from men—controlling assholes who get off on pushing me down. Derek, physically. Drew, mentally. Others in between them who played emotional games, keeping their feelings on lockdown or not contacting me for days.

Everything with Jake seems…too easy. Natural in this organic way that scares me. But I'm done questioning how I feel. I want to sink into this night with him. Believe in happily ever afters. Not worry about Drew or Hunter's release for a spell.

"Where are we going?" I ask.

He shoots me a tender look. "My boat. There's a cove I love. Peaceful and pretty. Thought it would be nice to have you all to myself. I hope that's okay," he adds, sounding a bit nervous.

"More than okay. I don't think I told you, but I loved the boat and being on the water, even though that outing didn't end well. And I loved that you named the boat after your mom."

A distant look crosses his face. "No clue how that woman is so strong. We'd all have been a mess without her. And glad you like the boat. It's my haven in a way—a place where I can escape and be on my own."

"You never take your brothers out?"

"They've all seen it and been out for a spin, but they know it's my refuge."

"But you're taking me there."

He scrapes his teeth over his bottom lip. "Guess I feel comfortable enough with you to have you in that special space." The way he says this, with his tone deep and heartfelt, hits me in the heart.

The instinct to pull away hits briefly. Slam up my walls. Stop myself before I fall harder and get hurt. My usual pattern with men. But with Jake, everything feels different. I feel considered and safe, understood in a way that just feels *good*.

I send up a silent prayer that he really is different. That we're different together.

Lord knows I don't have the willpower to resist his charms. "Pretty and peaceful sounds perfect," I say.

An hour later, we're anchored in his favorite cove as the water gently laps at the boat. Colorful fallen leaves blanket the rocky shoreline. Those still clinging to branches—yellows, oranges, and reds—are caught in the last rays of today's sun. The air is fresh and invigorating, the quiet profound, and I understand why Jake loves coming here so much.

Country music plays softly from his phone. He lays out a blanket on the boat deck and opens the basket he brought. Working methodically, he pulls out one item at a time.

Gin coolers, which he knows I like.

Lemon pomegranate bars, which he also knows I like.

Then Tupperware containers of homemade foods.

"I made potato salad with bacon and avocado," he says matter-of-factly, as though he's unaware he made my favorite potato salad recipe. He proceeds to point to each dish, shocking me more as he goes. "Grilled chicken with peach and pepper sauce. Marinated mushrooms. Lemon olives. And we have strawberry mousse for dessert, to go with the lemon pomegranate bars."

"Jake."

"Yeah?" He looks up at me, uncertainty in his rich brown eyes.

"These are all my favorite foods and recipes. I'm guessing this isn't a coincidence?"

He rubs the back of his neck. "I can't guarantee they're as good as how you make them, but yeah—I spoke with Jolene and found out what you like. Wanted to make tonight special for you."

"But I don't want tonight to be all about *me*. It's about us."

He frowns at our spread of food, picks at a loose piece of rattan from the wicker basket. "Jolene was my only serious relationship. That was twelve years ago, but I've realized a lot about myself since then and have talked with Jo about where the two of us went wrong."

He plants his foot beside my hip and rests his elbow on his knee, freeing his hand to play with my hair. "I was pretty self-absorbed back then. Didn't consider Jolene's interests when we were together. I did what I wanted, and she went along with my wishes—because of her own insecurities, which was upsetting to learn about in the aftermath. But two years with Jo, and I barely knew her. I didn't try to understand the woman she was or what drove her. This thing with you and me…"

His gaze roams my face like he's trying to memorize each feature. "I want to know who you are, Larkin—what you want, what you like. I want to earn your smiles every time I'm with you." He shrugs. "I just like seeing you happy, sweetheart. It's as simple as that for me."

My heart drums as fast as the new song coming from Jake's phone. There's nothing simple about his admission. He's become so incredibly thoughtful, honest and openly emotional. I'm not sure how he's still single now. I'm not sure how I got lucky enough to draw his attention.

Feeling overwhelmed in a good way, I eye the spread he laid out. "I can't believe you cooked all of this."

"My kitchen is a fucking disaster right now, and it took two tries with the peach and pepper sauce. I forgot the first round on the stove."

And modest to boot. "I love it all."

"You haven't tried anything yet."

"I love it all," I say again and kiss his lips, pressing hard enough to show him how happy I am, and maybe to feel the gentle roughness of his beard. "Thank you so much."

A masculine sound of pleasure moves through him. He gestures to our picnic. "Let's eat."

We don't just eat, though. We talk. About…everything. We laugh about Callahan's conniption over those stripping rumors. We discuss the Barrel House's success and the stress that comes with growing and running a bar. He tells me about the trials and tribulations of the construction business he built with Cal, which is booked for the next six months. We share Windfall stories, both of us surprised that this town drew us back into its fold, even though it held dark memories.

"There's something about this place," he says, chewing on a lemony olive. "People can be invasive, which annoys me at times, but there's a comfort here I can't quite describe."

There certainly is. "No matter where I lived—New York, Philadelphia, Raleigh—nothing gave me this sense of home."

"Yeah," he says more quietly. "For a while there, I didn't think I'd ever see this place again."

He describes his horrible time during WITSEC in more detail. What his brothers went through and how worried he was about his family. "I felt so disconnected from people," he says, tracing lazy patterns on my arm. "And I was really fucking angry, but I couldn't let on just how bad I was with my family. So, I turned that anger into action and focused on them."

"Always wanting to protect the people you care about."

"Trying more than succeeding at times." His tone darkens, likely tainted by the suspicions he never shared about his father before their lives got turned upside down. History that can't be changed.

"They're lucky to have you, Jake. And you're lucky to have them and your mom. I only speak with my mom on holidays and birthdays, like it's an obligation."

"It's her loss," he says roughly. "Anyone who knows you knows how amazing you are."

I duck my head, embarrassed by the compliment. "Thank you. But I have Julian, even though he's in New York. And Hunter," I add more quietly. "But the awful thing that eats at me sometimes is that I think I'm more like my mother than I realized." Truth I've never shared aloud.

He leans back and flicks on a switch. Fairy lights wink on along the edges of the boat. Romantic and perfect as he sets the music to something softer with a backbeat. "I find that hard to believe," he finally says.

"She always chased toxic men. Some of them were just cruel with her, others weren't great with Julian and me. But the day one of them made an advance on me, I left and never looked back. I got a job and found a place with two bedrooms, and Julian basically lived with me until he went to college. But historically, I've done that too—dated men who are bad for me on so many levels."

He tenses and seems to hold his breath. "Am I lumped into that group?"

I run my fingers over his thick scruff, loving the rough-soft feel. "I don't think so. At least, not anymore."

But I piece through my childhood, meeting Otto Briggs and being told he was my dad. I was scared of his gnarled features and aggressive tattoos. He'd call my mother. She'd bring me to his house, where he'd use her for sex, then he'd kick us out afterward. Still, a vulnerable part of me craved his affection.

"Drew loved telling me I had Daddy issues," I say. "He'd suggest I had bad examples of what constitutes affection from both of my parents, not that he's one to talk with his domineering father."

"Prick," Jake mutters.

An accurate description. "Hunter changed my understanding of what family was when I was younger—the unconditional acceptance that comes with an older brother who truly cares and watches over you—but I think part of me is still that little girl, wondering what she has to do to make her father love her. So, I chose assholes I thought I could change, the way I wanted to change my dad. But there's nothing I want to change about you."

"Larkin." Jake moves our plates to the side and slides forward until his outer thigh presses against mine. "If a guy can't see how special and smart you are on their own, they don't deserve you. You're successful, confident, and stunning. As pissed as I am that men haven't treated you right on any level, I'm glad none of them was worthy enough to lock you down, because I'm really fucking into you."

God, this man.

I kiss him, unable to handle any distance between us. I grip his neck and straddle his lap, locking my legs and arms around him. Because...*how?* How did I ever think Jake was like all the other assholes? How did I stay so angry at him for so long?

"I'm sorry," I say as I come up for air.

He has one arm around my back, his other hand sunk into my hair. "What for?"

"For believing you were cruel. Nothing about you is cruel."

"Please don't apologize for that. You had every right to hate me. You still do, but I won't belabor that point, because I'm falling too hard here. Just know that I'll never fully forgive myself for not answering your call. That's a shame I'll always carry."

I nod, understanding him better. Jake holds himself to a higher standard. He was the stand-in father who looked after his family with single-minded determination. The eldest brother who had to set an example. The man who wants to be nothing like the father who destroyed his family.

"How about I help you carry that shame?" I say, pulling him back toward me.

His breath is shaky on this kiss, his hands more insistent. Like he's both overwhelmed and horny as hell. *Feeling is mutual.*

Our lips slant and part, moving deeper, sending flutters through my abdomen. The warm slide of his tongue pulls a throaty moan from me, and I lose my composure. I writhe on him, desperate for more—to know the fullness of this sweet man inside my body and heart. He's hard as steel between my thighs, his rough thrusts showing just how much he wants me too.

I fumble with his Henley, shoving it up his broad chest. "This needs to get out of the way."

Instead of complying, he stills my hands. "Nothing has to happen tonight. We can take this slow. I'm dying to be with you, but that's not why I brought you here. Spending time with you is a fucking gift."

I exhale on a smile. "That means more than you know, but I want this, Jake. I want *you*."

"You're sure?"

"Definitely sure."

His chest swells deeply, emphasizing the thickness of his pecs. "Then I'd really like to remove your shirt, if you don't mind."

I nod, awed by his gentleness and care. He can't hide how turned on he is, not with the way his fly strains, but I know he'd stop in an instant if asked.

Working slowly, he lifts the hem of my light-blue sweater, guiding it up and over my head. His jaw sharpens as his hooded eyes devour the pink lace encasing my breasts. "Do you know how fucking gorgeous you are?"

For some reason, shyness has me dipping my head. "Still a charmer."

"Just honest."

The cooler air kisses my exposed skin. I shiver and reach for him. "I thought we agreed you'd wear less clothing around me."

"Not a tough ask." He tosses his shirt onto the deck, his grin utterly wolfish.

I shiver for an altogether different reason and crook my finger, beckoning him closer. "I'd like to inspect those muscles, if you don't mind."

I need to run my tongue over the deep grove between his thick pecs, over those defined abs, feel that smattering of dark chest hair against my cheek, nip those angled hip bones.

Honestly, Jake's body should be a World Heritage site.

His brown eyes darken to midnight, but he says, "I'll join you in a sec."

He disappears into his boat's small cabin, then reappears with a fleece blanket and a pillow. Working quickly, he clears away the rest of the food, lays the fleece over the picnic blanket, and pulls back a corner. "Get in here."

"You're demanding."

"I don't like seeing you cold."

"Charming *and* chivalrous."

"And you're stubborn, but I'll offer you a trade."

"More blackmail?"

"If that's what it takes." He gestures to the plush blanket and pillow. "If you get in here, I'll strip before joining you."

I rush to the makeshift bed so quickly, Jake laughs. God, I love that sound. How much fun we have together, even after intense talks.

"Your turn," I say with a wink.

His crooked smile is all kinds of sexy, as is the hint of color on his upper cheeks. Jake is embarrassed to strip for me, but he complies. He removes his boots and socks, then rolls his hips to the song's deep bass. He flips the button on his jeans, each movement slow and sensual, including the downward drag of his fly. And that knowing smirk? Those huge muscles of his? The way he does that sexy body roll?

I'm dangerously close to coming too soon. "Since when can you dance like this?"

"Since I practiced in my room so I wouldn't embarrass myself at prom."

That image is just too much. "Please tell me one of your brothers caught you in the act."

"Not a fucking chance." His next hip swivel comes with a pelvic thrust.

I whistle with my fingers and give a few catcalls that probably have the wildlife running scared.

He tips his head back, laughing. "You're making me work for this, Feisty."

"Is that my nickname?"

"It suits you."

I think it's Jake that suits me. A fact becoming clearer by the second.

Smoldering at me—seriously, the guy is total *Magic Mike* material—he grabs hold of his jeans and shoves them down past his ass.

I forget how to blink.

He's still in tight briefs, but the *size* of him, how hard and thick he is? My imagination did not do him justice. I whistle again, egging him on. He kicks off his jeans and struts toward me in his briefs but doesn't try to get under the blanket.

"You still want me in there?" he asks, his voice strained.

"I want you naked first." To see all of him, then feel every inch of that hard body sliding against mine.

Need blows through his hungry eyes, but he doesn't push down his briefs. He rakes his hand through my hair, dragging his nails along my scalp. "I want you to know you're the one in control here, Larkin. I've never wanted anyone the way I want you, but what does or doesn't happen tonight is in your court. My briefs can stay on. If you just want my hands or mouth on you, consider it my fucking pleasure, and I wouldn't need anything else. Whatever you want, it's yours."

Emotion scrapes at my throat. "I've never met a guy like you before."

"Extremely handsome and incredibly brilliant?"

My laugh is watery. "That, along with caring and thoughtful and kind." I skim my fingers around his waistband. He lets out a gravelly moan as goose bumps spread down his thick thighs.

Something about that sound and his visible reaction to me does me in. I go from turned on to nearing orgasm. I've never experienced this connection with another man. This level of desire, the way my core contracts, like it feels desperately empty and needs him—*only him*—to ease the ache.

With my focus on his rapt face, I stretch the band of his briefs and pull them over the sharp jut of his erection. He hisses out a breath, and my mouth goes dry.

He's as magnificent as expected, but I don't touch his impressive length. I slip his underwear all the way off, drag my hands up his powerful legs, loving the feel of the soft hairs curling over his calves and muscled thighs.

"You're so fucking beautiful," he rasps, playing with my hair. "So fucking stunning on your knees like that, your hands on me. I swear—"

I lick a path up the underside of his cock, stealing whatever words were about to fall from his mouth.

He grunts. His thigh muscles contract. I take his balls in one hand and his length in my other—so hard, yet smooth; a striking contrast, like the man himself—and I swirl my tongue around his tip.

"Larkin." God, I love hearing my name in that deep growl. The way his hands grip my hair and give a slight tug. "You're fucking killing me here. Nothing has ever felt this good."

I suck harder, get lost in the moment. Jake and me alone on this boat, in the open air, the salt-tinged taste of him on my tongue and his guttural noises. I've never enjoyed giving head this much. Feeling ownership of a man's pleasure.

I move my mouth over him and take him deeper.

"Fuck. *Fuck.* Gotta stop." He pulls out of my mouth and squeezes the base of his cock. The sight of him like that, panting and touching himself, is beyond sexy.

Next thing I know, he's pulling me under the fleece with him, kissing my mouth, then my jaw and neck, working off my clothes until there's nothing but our naked bodies tucked together.

"Fuck, you're stunning." He's unrelenting as he explores my

body—thorough with every lick and kiss—eventually disappearing under the blanket. I squirm and sigh. His teeth and beard graze my ribs, his huge hands charting every inch of my skin, like I'm undiscovered land, being mapped for the first time. "I'll never have enough of you," he says against my hip.

My heart seems to trip over itself.

I'm not sure why that comment has me suddenly feeling vulnerable. Never having enough implies wanting more. Exactly what I want too, but my head starts spinning. Wanting more also means there's a possibility of less. Of losing Jake. Of him getting to know me better and deciding I'm too closed off or too snarky or too much work.

His mouth pauses on my hip. Then he's moving up, his heavy body weighing me down. He plants his forearms on either side of my head. "What's wrong?"

"Nothing."

"Don't lie to me, Larkin. Not like this. Not when we're both getting in deeper."

His hard length is pressed to my stomach, but he's not moving his body. His gorgeous face is utterly focused on me. Tenderly, he brushes his nose against mine. "What's bothering you, sweetheart?"

"Feeling this much for you, I think." This man is so tuned in to me, he read my body language and knew my mind had hit a speed bump. And he stopped. He checked in to make sure I'm okay. He is such a *good* man. And I'm not sure I measure up. "I think I'm worried that when you get to know me better, you won't like me as much."

"Not fucking possible."

"Anything is possible."

The way the fairy lights shine, the rugged maleness of his face is cast in sharp relief—deep concentration on me or his own thoughts. "You're right," he says quietly. "There's no predicting the future. But I know a lot about you. I've lived with you in the back of my mind for over a decade, and you're all I think about these days. Any relationship is a risk, but I'm ready and willing to risk my heart on you. Do you feel the same?"

The niggle of insecurity is still there, but only one answer is possible. "Yes."

This kiss is harder as he slides his body off mine and lines up with my side. He hooks his foot over my ankle, spreading my legs apart, then slides his fingers through my wetness. "Fuck." His gravelly grunt turns me liquid. "Look at you, so wet and ready for me."

He applies pressure to my clit, and I nearly fly off the boat.

"Jake." That's all I can say. His name, as my nerve endings spark and quiver. All I am is sensation. Tiny lightning strikes of pleasure. He moves his mouth to my breasts, greedily sucking as his fingers work their magic, and my hips buck.

"I'm close," I say, pulling his mouth back to mine.

He cradles me close, never losing his rhythm, kissing me with hungry noises that push me over the edge. I come with his breath in my mouth, his other arm latched around me, and my heart in the sky.

"More," I say, boneless but desperate to feel him moving inside me.

"More," he agrees and grabs a condom from his jeans.

CHAPTER
Twenty-Four

Jake

If this is a dream, I'll kill the person who wakes me. Larkin's face is beautifully flushed, painted with the aftershocks of pleasure. I'm between her thighs, about to be welcomed into her body.

Swear to God, never thought I'd be this lucky.

I shift my hips forward, the head of my sheathed cock nudging her entrance. "Jesus," I murmur, already overwhelmed. It feels like I've wanted Larkin forever. I don't deserve the trust shining in her eyes. Lord knows I'm too weak to deny myself. Still selfish at my core.

Utterly focused on her, I push inside an inch.

Her nostrils flare. "More."

"More," I agree again. All of her is what I want. More picnics on my boat. Or wherever she wants. On a garbage heap for all I care, as long as we get to talk and joke and enjoy each other's company. I want that ring on her finger to be fucking real.

I push in slowly, addicted to each shift in her expression, the pinch of her brow as I penetrate her body, the softening when her inner walls ease up, allowing me in farther. I can't get over how fucking *good* I feel when I'm with Larkin, just talking and hanging out.

Joining our bodies takes our connection to a whole other level.

The wet heat of her grip has my balls already full and tight. My ass is flexed, my body tensed. Pleasure twists at the base of my spine, but I hold it together. I drag out slightly and ease back in, a bit deeper each time. But Larkin doesn't want slow. She grabs my ass as she cants her hips, forcing us flush.

I drop my head forward and growl. I can hardly handle how full my heart feels. "Never felt like this. Too fucking good."

She wiggles. "Don't stop."

I kiss her, unable to speak. I just need to feel her. How well we move together, matching each other's rhythms, like we've done this dance a thousand times before. I pinch her nipples. Feel like a king when she gasps and bites her lip. Her pussy squeezes my length, and I nearly blow my load. But I don't want this to end. I drag through her tight entrance, finding the spots and angles that make her breath quicken and body jerk.

There. Right fucking there.

She claws at my ass, bites my shoulder. Hugs her knees into my sides and meets me stroke for stroke. She's wild, just like I imagined she'd be. But vulnerable too, her eyes damp with emotion as we make love on the deck of my boat, touching and kissing with urgency.

I feel it when she's close. How fucking hard her pussy tugs and tightens. I grit my teeth, hold out as long as I can. When she cries out and her inner walls flutter, I am fucking gone. I come so hard my pulse thunders, like I'm a caged animal finally released.

Slowly, my breathing regulates. I roll us together, until I'm on my back but still inside her, my arms firm bands around her body. "You good?"

"I don't know what year it is or if my head is attached to my body, but…yes?"

I chuckle and lock my leg over hers, refusing to lose this connection. I want to make love to her again. Every day, over and over. Maybe even share the wonder of making a kid together one day. Watch her belly grow. Build a family with this amazing woman.

Fuck, am I in deep.

I kiss her soft and slow. Press my forehead to hers, definitely keeping those thoughts to myself. "You're amazing."

"I think we were amazing together."

"I'll second that. I also don't want to move, but we should get cleaned up."

She nods, watching as I deal with the condom and grab a cloth for her. I dampen it in the lake and slip back under the covers, kissing her while I tend to her body.

Afterward, I settle facing her, both of us resting our heads on the pillow I brought.

She runs her fingers over my scruffy jaw. "When do I get to see you again?"

"You're seeing me right now."

"That's not soon enough."

I laugh. "I like how you think."

"I'd love to see you tomorrow night," she says quietly, "if you don't mind waiting up for me until I finish my shift."

"I was already planning on spending my evening at the Barrel, hanging out at the bar while you work, if that's cool. So I'd say the odds are high I'll stay until you're finished."

Odds are even higher I'll do that every night until I have to meet with Hunter in nine days. Make sure we're solid enough that anything he says won't ruin the best thing to ever happen to me.

CHAPTER
Twenty-Five

LARKIN

"Is he going to spend all night staring at you?" Jolene asks with a bump to my hip.

I sneak a look at Jake. He came to the Barrel as promised. He's been camped at the bar since he got here, nursing his beer, his attention mostly locked on me, except the times he's been busy on his phone. The way he's watching me right now, his brown hair askew and dark eyes molten, has me needing to stick my face in an ice bucket.

"It's pretty sweet, right?" I say as I grab a cucumber garnish for tonight's special tequila cocktail, only to realize I actually grabbed a piece of pineapple. Yep, my brain is sex scrambled.

"Sweet in a horny way," Jolene jokes. "Is this all a show for the fake-engagement thing?"

Jo and I haven't had time for personal chatting tonight. The bar's been steady, only winding down recently, but there was no avoiding her questions forever.

"It's not fake anymore," I say, grabbing a cucumber strip and threading it onto a metal pick. "Things feel pretty real and pretty amazing." The second Jake walked in here, my heart did an excited palpitation I've never felt. "But are you sure this isn't weird for you? I know you said you're okay with us dating, but seeing us together is different."

"Weird?" She scoffs. "If you recall, I'm the woman who's living with Jake's brother. I've got the weird quota on lockdown. I'm just glad you two worked out whatever drama had you hating him for so long. You seem really happy."

So happy I'm nervous it'll all blow up.

I steal another look at Jake. He's watching me, the corner of his lips curved into a sexy half smile. His rapt attention messes with my internal temperature again, but I manage to put the correct garnish on the right drink this time.

"Everything about Jake is surprising," I tell Jo. "In a good way."

She gives a cute clap. "Now I get to say I set you two up."

She can say whatever she wants as long as I don't lose my best friend.

"Are you two ladies talking about me?" Jake calls from down the bar.

"Only about your disturbing furries fetish," I quip back.

He shakes his head, grinning. "Pretty sure you're the one who grabbed my ass."

"And you're the one who kissed me."

"Do you blame me, with those lips of yours?"

"I could say the same about your tight ass."

Jolene snorts. "You two are adorable." She gives me a light shove and drops her voice. "Go hang out with him, and leave early if you want. If any other drink orders come in, I'll cover."

"You sure?"

"Definitely. Plus, if you two fall in love, I'll feel less guilty about how gooey I get every time Callahan walks in."

If you two fall in love. A fizzy feeling bubbles through me—

effervescence I prefer not to analyze. I'm not in love with Jake. We're just…really into each other. Connected in a way I can't fully explain, the same way I'm drawn to him right now, hating the distance between us, but this can't be love. Not this fast.

I saunter toward him, adding an extra sway to my step.

Once in front of him, I lean my elbows on the bar. "Hope your night hasn't been too boring."

He mirrors my pose—elbows on the wood bar, our lips dangerously close. "There's nothing boring about being near you, Feisty."

"I barely had time to talk to you."

He shrugs a shoulder. "I'm happier near you. And I was being productive."

"By distracting me with your hotness?"

He chuckles, looking more shy than cocky. "I was planning our fix-it club. Was thinking we could start it with a food drive. Work with the farm volunteers since we don't grow food in the winter, and the food drive might get more people to sign up as volunteers for the summer. The bigger we make the event, the more of an impact the club will have."

His passion for charity work and this project has a seriously strong impact on me. "I love the idea, and I know Jo will support it. Maybe we can find a radio station to sponsor us, help spread the word."

He nods, tapping his fingers on the bar. "We could play up that angle by highlighting old radios. Classics that someone from the club helps fix. We can showcase them and other retro items, auction them off to raise money. Make people think salvaging old stuff is cool."

"I think your clever mind is pretty cool."

He brushes loose hairs off my face. "The feeling is mutual."

"You think *your* mind is cool too? That's pretty egotistical, Jake."

He shakes his head, laughing. "Always busting my balls."

"Or fondling them," I add, loving the way his cheeks pink above his scruffy beard. "On a more serious note—is it okay if we work on this after Drew's wedding, when things are less stressful?"

He takes my hand, stroking his thumb over my ring. "Of course. And if me being here while you work distracts you or makes you uncomfortable, just say the word. I won't come."

"No," I say quickly. "I like it."

"Yeah?"

I nod. "It's hard not kissing you right now, but—"

His lips land on mine. It's not a deep kiss, but there's no missing his quiet groan and the hungry nip of his teeth. "Sorry," he says roughly. "Been wanting to do that since I walked in."

My eyes slowly flutter open. "Took you long enough."

His crooked smile adds more heat to my cheeks. "I can wait while you clean up. Take you home after, assuming you walked here?"

"I did, but Jo said she'd clean up for me. We can go now."

Except we barely make it to Jake's truck.

The second the bar doors close behind us, he has me against the building, one hand in my hair, his other on my breast, our lips locked and tongues busy as I pant out a moan.

"I thought about you all day," he says, his mouth moving to my neck. I knock back my head, giving him better access. "Couldn't wait to see you," he goes on. "Not sure what you're doing to me."

"The same thing you're doing to me." I grip his muscled back, dig my fingers into the groove of his spine. "But we shouldn't do this here. Respectable bar owner and all."

His next kiss is biting, then he yanks himself away and takes my hand. He walks so briskly to his truck I have to jog to keep up. He doesn't talk when we're inside. He looks kind of mad, but in a fierce, too-turned-on way.

I press my thighs together, fired up from the entire night—

Jake showing up at the bar, just to be close to me. The flutters he constantly inspires. How easy it was talking to him on his boat. No posturing or worrying about saying the right thing. Just real emotion.

And wild attraction.

If I don't have him inside me soon, I might combust.

A few blocks away from his place, on a dark section of street, he yanks his truck to the side of the road. "Can't wait," he says, clicking off his seat belt. "Get the fuck over here now."

He pushes his seat back as I fumble with my seat belt and climb over his lap. "You read my mind."

He palms the soft cotton of my yellow sundress, bunching it up at my hip. "Did you wear this flirty dress for me? You knew I'd want easy access to that sweet pussy of yours?"

A hot pulse grips my core. "God, that was hot."

His smirk is all pirate. "You like a little dirty talk, Feisty? That gets you going?"

"With you, it definitely does."

He growls his approval and grinds me down on his lap. His rough jeans rub against the thin cotton of my underwear, the ridge of his cock hitting me *just right*. He swallows my moan with a filthy kiss. Nips at my lower lip and pushes his hand into the front of my underwear.

"Look at you, fucking drenched for me. So wet and tight. All I could think about today was filling you up. Driving into you, remembering how hard you came on my cock last night."

My internal muscles spasm with desire. When men have talked dirty to me in the past, I felt more like a prop for their pleasure. With Jake, it's like his growled words are meant for *my* pleasure. So he can watch how hot he makes *me*.

"I need you in me, Jake. *Now*," I add in case my panted words weren't clear.

I shove back on his lap, the two of us working on his jeans until they're pushed down past his ass. His engorged cock springs free, and we don't waste time. I've never been this impatient to be joined with a man, to feel him moving inside me.

Looking as frenzied as I feel, he tears open a condom, sheathes himself, then pushes my underwear aside and impales me on his erection. The intense stroke hurts at first but quickly turns delicious.

We pause a beat, breaths ragged, eyes blown wide.

The cords along his neck strain, his upper cheeks flushed with color. "I'm so fucking wrecked for you," he grinds out.

All I can think is *yes*. This mix of desire and desperation is exhilarating, the hard slam of my heart almost painful, all these overwhelming feelings taking me for a ride I can't control.

We start to move—hard, needy, *wild*. We get lost in the moment and each other. *I'm* lost in how utterly safe I feel with Jake, the two of us going for broke and fogging up his windows as we fall apart together.

CHAPTER
Twenty-Six

Jake

I lie in bed, naked and euphoric, my hands clasped behind my head as I wait for Larkin to join me back in the sheets. I don't have to wait long. She makes her way out of the bathroom, so damn sexy in nothing but those braids, and my spent cock twitches. Not sure how that's possible after the amount of sex we've had the past eight days, including two rounds tonight, but that's how things seem to go with us.

She gives my body a thorough once-over. "You look like a Greek god lying there, waiting to be fed grapes by his mistress."

She picks up my briefs from the floor and flings them at me.

I catch them with one hand. "If I have you, I don't need a mistress."

"Sweet-talker," she says as she slips one of my T-shirts over her head. "I bet you say that to all the girls."

"You know there are no other girls. And I fucking love seeing you in my clothes." Especially when my T-shirt barely covers her ass.

She hops on the bed as I pull on my briefs, the two of us cuddling together the way we've done all week.

We never discussed sleeping over. It just happened naturally, this need to fall asleep in each other's arms. Aside from the messed-up way this relationship started, everything between us has felt organic. We had a fun ice cream date this week, sitting on my truck bed, licking our cones and enjoying the mountain views while we chatted about music and movies. When she's working, I hang out at the bar, then take her home to her place or mine. We make love and talk until our eyes are too heavy, eventually waking up tucked together, my arm fastened around her waist.

I didn't know relationships could be this easy.

"You want anything?" I ask. "Water? Ice cream? I got the mango flavor you like."

"Just you," she says with a kiss.

I trace my finger down the dusting of freckles on her nose, then touch the scar beside it. "How did you get this?"

"My father."

Fury punches through my happy high. "He hit you?"

"Not exactly. It was one of our last visits before he cut my mother out of his life completely. He was drinking and angry at my mom about something—probably for asking him for child support. Anyway, he smashed his beer bottle on the counter and turned really fast. I was behind him and caught the edge of the bottle with my face."

"Jesus." I press a kiss to the scar, my blood hovering at an angry boil. "I hope he apologized."

Her laugh holds no humor. "He told me to suck it up, while my mother fawned over him, apologizing for whatever made *him* mad. Hunter was the one who guided me to the bathroom and took care of me. He told me the scar would be badass."

"He was right." I run my knuckles down her cheek. "I'm really thankful you had him growing up."

"Me too."

Like with our other sleepovers, we haven't discussed tomorrow's planned visit with Hunter, beyond Larkin explaining the prison rules. We know it's happening. We seem to have a silent agreement not to worry about it since Larkin believes the talk is a formality. Older brother protectiveness, which I support.

We're both happy existing in the moment, but hearing about her parents' carelessness with her has me thinking about Larkin's other hardships. The details I don't know about her life.

The one night she specifically asked me not to mention.

Too often, thoughts of what she went through filter into my mind, and I imagine the worst. I feel suffocated by the unknown. Blank spots that are big and dark enough to block out all the goodness between us. I've still heeded her rule. I haven't pushed for more information, but that request was made before sleepovers and dinners and hours talking about everything and nothing. Not broaching the subject now feels wrong.

I move us so we're eye level, sharing a pillow. "I want to ask you something, but I'm worried you'll get upset."

She catches my hand and kisses my palm. "You can ask me anything."

Tentatively, I forge ahead. "I know you told me not to ask, but I want to know what happened that night with Derek. I'm not sure why I can't let it go, but I wake up some nights with these awful images scaring the shit out of me." I give my head a rough shake, try to dislodge the imagined scene of Larkin falling, unable to catch my reaching hand. "If you say no now, I won't ask again. I swear. I just can't seem to let that part of our past go."

She goes quiet, her troubled frown seeming distant. Like she's not seeing me any longer, only ghastly images that haunt her. And *fuck*, I am an asshole. There's a reason Larkin asked me to avoid this topic. Yet, here I go, picking at her wounds because *I* need closure.

"I'm sorry," I say in a whispered rush. "Forget I asked. I have no right to—"

"No," she says, cutting me off. Her fierce eyes flick up to my face. "I want to tell you. That part of our history is a constant presence for me too. If we don't discuss it, it might hurt us down the road. I don't want it to become this big, unspoken thing between us."

At least we're on the same page about that.

As far as I can tell, I'm already halfway in love with Larkin. Or maybe all the way. I've never felt this consumed with a woman. When she's happy, I'm happy. When she's upset, I want to raze the world for her. Or fix things around her home to make her comfortable.

I want to cook her favorite foods. Strip for her, even though I felt like a fool that night. I enjoy sitting at her bar just for the privilege of being in her presence. Whenever we make love, I picture us building a family together one day, and the idea grips me with such ferocity, my heart damn near explodes.

Still, our history is far from simple.

My shame hasn't gone away—disgust with myself over my choices, no matter how often Callahan tells me I'd have answered Larkin's call if I'd actually thought she was in trouble. Nothing will change the twelve years Hunter has spent in jail. And there's this fear of the unknown—what truly happened to Larkin that night.

"Stop whenever you want," I say, gathering her hands in mine.

"I will."

"And I…" *Love you*, I nearly say. The words won't push past the thickness in my throat. "I'm here for you. This won't change how I feel."

She nods and holds my hands tighter. "I was obviously angry

when you left me on the side of the road. I thought you'd been playing games with me, working me to see if I'd hook up with you."

"You believe me, though, right? You know I'd never do that to you, or any woman."

She kisses me softly and rubs our noses together. An intimacy we both seem to like. "I believe you now, but I had no clue then. And I was pissed off. Decided I could only rely on myself, so I went to Derek's on my own to get my passport and clothes—one of those 'I am woman, hear me roar' moments. But I trashed his place while I was there, which I think I mentioned to you already."

"You did, yeah."

Her frown deepens. "I honestly don't know what came over me. I mean, I obviously wasn't thinking straight. If I'd just left with my passport and bag, he wouldn't have known I'd been there. At least, not until the next day or whenever he saw my stuff missing. I was just so mad at...everything. You, Derek, men in general for thinking women were possessions they could use or hurt on a whim."

Her cheekbones sharpen with the brutal memory, and my stomach pitches. Hearing my name associated with Derek's is a blow.

"Were you in the house when he turned up?" I ask in a harsh whisper.

She shakes her head. "I was down the street a bit. I'd hidden behind a tree, worried if I stepped out, he'd see me. That was when I called you." She pauses on an extended blink. We both know what happened then. "When you didn't pick up," she goes on, "I called Hunter. He was already in his car and luckily didn't take long to find me. Although maybe that's the unlucky part."

Her next swallow has my throat feeling raw. "Derek was drunk and furious. After he saw the mess I'd made of his place, he came tearing out looking for me. And I freaked out—took off running. But he spotted me and caught me as I was scaling the fence into the junkyard."

Pain lances through my chest, and I realize I'm not breathing. I force air into my lungs and attempt to keep my face calm. "Hunter wasn't there yet?"

"I'm not exactly sure when he got there." She blinks, and a tear slips down her cheek. "I remember Derek grabbing my ankle and yanking me down. I remember the fury on his face and the pressure of his hands on my neck, how weak I felt. No matter how hard I tried to kick or punch, he was just too strong. Then things get a bit hazy."

Jesus Christ. I pull her into my chest. Kiss the top of her head, then each of her closed eyes. I kiss the tears on her cheeks, the tender line of her neck where that asshole nearly stole her life. "I'm so fucking sorry, Larkin. So, so sorry."

Swear to God, if Derek weren't already dead, I'd hunt him down and kill him ten times over.

She shudders out a shaky breath. Slowly, she relaxes and wipes her cheeks. "The next thing I remember is Hunter holding me, telling me everything was okay. But I saw Derek on the grass with a bloody gash on his head. And I knew—I knew nothing would be okay. And Hunter wouldn't let me tell them I was at the scene. He sent me away, warned me the cops wouldn't treat me fairly. He said he'd deal with them, but it all got so fucked up."

She sniffles, looking both angry and sad. "Derek owed Hunter money from a motorcycle build they'd done together, and the prosecution latched on to that. Said Hunter went to collect his cash and killed Derek when he couldn't pay. And I never once said a thing to protect my brother. He asked me to stay quiet, and I did. I listened, because I was a coward."

I cup her cheeks and look her in the eye. "He was right, Larkin. They would have dragged you down too. Told some bullshit story that you worked with Hunter, assumed you were lying under oath to protect him. They would've learned you trashed Derek's place, maybe thought you were looking for hidden money. You could've been arrested and convicted too."

She stays quiet and seems to bite down on her cheek. "Maybe. Not that it matters now. Hunter is still in jail, and he's been far from a model inmate. He's caused fights and spent time in solitary. They might need space in the prison, but my gut tells me they won't grant his early release, unless I convince Drew to press for it."

"Unless *we* can convince him," I say. Tomorrow is the party at the Barrel, followed by the wedding weekend. I'm more determined than ever to help Hunter. "We'll make sure Drew sees the positive environment Hunter will be in when he's released. If he understands that, he'll have to be more open-minded about his case. And you're so fucking brave—picking yourself up after everything you've been through."

She runs her fingers through my chest hair. "I was messed up for a long while. Had really bad nightmares and would wake up in cold sweats, pawing at my neck, sure someone's hands were squeezing out my last breath."

I can relate to hellish nightmares. I'm just glad I've never woken Larkin up when I jerk awake. "You don't seem to have bad dreams now. Not that I've seen, at least."

"I haven't had any for a long time," she says, laying her head on my chest. "When it got bad, I started taking self-defense classes. And I found a free support group in a church basement. I only went because it was anonymous and no one knew me, but it really helped. With the PTSD, at least. Not so much with the guilt."

I stroke her hair gently. "You have nothing to feel guilty about. Derek is the asshole who hurt you."

"And I'm the one who dated him, when Hunter warned me the guy was bad news. I trashed Derek's place, and I didn't come forward to tell the cops my story. I've rebuilt my confidence and don't live with fear. I know I'm not responsible for Derek's abuse. What he did was on him, but I made my own horrible choices along the way."

"I guess we both have that in common," I say, understanding her all too well.

She creates space between us and palms my neck. "You asked me to tell you what happened, and I'm glad I did. But you have to promise me you won't beat yourself up over this. You didn't know I was in trouble. You were going through your own stuff that night, struggling with your relationship with Jolene, all that worry over your father's lies."

My muscles flex involuntarily. I don't like talking about that shit with my father. I wish Larkin didn't know I chose silence over watching out for my family and royally fucked them over. I wish I'd made a million different choices back then. "What I was dealing with was nothing in the face of an abusive man coming after you."

"But you didn't know."

I should have known. I should've seen my father for who he truly was. I should've had the courage to answer Larkin's call. I hoped knowing the truth of what she went through would give me closure, release me from this unrelenting guilt and the occasional nightmares. I'm not sure it will, but that's probably my lot in life.

CHAPTER
Twenty-Seven

Jake

Considering the criminals my father associated with, it's shocking that this is my first time in a prison. The experience is as unpleasant as one would expect. Procedures are strict and abrupt. *Sign this. Put your personal items in here. Walk through the metal detector. Wait until you're called. No raised voices once inside, and no physical contact.*

I follow the rules and sit on a hard plastic chair, waiting to be called into the actual visiting room. The gray walls feel oppressive, even out here. Other visitors are solemn on their seats, looking bleak in the fluorescent lights. I wore a tucked-in button-down shirt today, made sure my jeans didn't have holes. Respect for Hunter in one of the few ways that can be shown.

I pass the next few minutes being decidedly less respectful to Larkin's brother.

I replay the past ten days I've spent with his sister—that night on my boat and every night since. Larkin in my bed. On my floor. On *her* floor. Her chair. Over the side of the couch I fixed. The two of us insatiable for each other, with talks and fun dates in between.

Now I'm meeting her brother.

When the door to the visiting area is finally opened, I'm overheating. I stand and wipe my damp palms down my jeans. *Be honest*, I tell myself. Hunter already told Larkin he's okay with us dating, and he appreciates honesty. He demands it from Larkin and offers the same in return. No matter how hard he comes down on me, honesty will get me through.

I step into the stark room and take a seat at one of the beige tables. I bounce my heel as we wait, my attention darting around skittishly.

Then the gate at the far end slides open.

Nothing happens at first. A few seconds later, a parade of inmates appears, shuffling into the room and finding their people.

During WITSEC, when I read every article I could about Hunter's trial, I saw pictures of him—long, sandy hair, intense eyes like Larkin's, but the rest of him was hard and intimidating, with his slightly crooked nose and thickset jaw. I remember a birthmark by his left eye and frown lines by his mouth. I imagine those lines are etched deeper now.

I study the subdued men filing in and spot Hunter easily. Yeah, those creases by his puckered mouth are deep, the bunch of his huge shoulders adding a dangerous air to the large man.

When his attention slides my way, I nod.

He lumbers over, his focus on me absolute. He sits and rests his massive forearms on the table but doesn't say a word.

I tug at the neck of my button-down, feeling a trickle of sweat glide down my back. "Thanks for seeing me."

"Don't fucking thank me." His voice is pitched low, his arms tense, like he's trying to refrain from punching me. "You don't need to speak. You only need to listen."

He can say whatever the hell he wants. Now that he's closer, I see more than an intimidating inmate. His cheeks are hollowed, and his skin is pale. His eyes are hard but sad, like he's witnessed too much and is on the verge of giving up, and I'm part of the reason he's in here.

Head bowed, I wait for him to go on.

He slides closer. "You will stay the fuck away from my sister."

My heart rate kicks up, and I squint at him, wondering if he's messing with me—trying to scare me before demanding I treat Larkin with kindness *or else*. But I sense no posturing.

Those murderous eyes are dead serious.

Bewildered, I attempt to keep my voice level. "You told Larkin you wouldn't mind if we dated."

"What did I say about you speaking?"

I should listen. Shut the fuck up and lower my head again. Do whatever he asks, but I picture Larkin and me making love, our intense talks. How fucking in love I am with her, even if I haven't said the words, and my sense evaporates. "I'll speak, because I care too much about Larkin to take a back seat to this conversation."

Hunter glares at me. His grunt isn't kind, but he doesn't tell me to fuck off.

"As far as I know," I say carefully, "you and Larkin don't lie to each other. So why would you tell her you're okay with us dating when you're clearly not?"

If I understand his motivation, I can think my way through this. Figure out how to make him see me differently. Coax him to put Larkin's feelings ahead of his animosity.

He torques his neck until it cracks. "Larkin is the only true family I have. She was the only person who encouraged my academics growing up. She'd check in on me, make sure I was studying for my night classes. She'd come to me when she was sad or upset, because she trusted me implicitly. I could've gone down some dark paths at times, but when the choices were there, I'd picture Larkin—her trust, her unconditional love—and I'd choose right. I chose to be a better man for *her*. I'm not saying I'm a fucking saint. I killed a man and live with the consequences of my actions every day. But I'd protect Larkin with my last dying breath, which is why I lied to her on the phone."

I agree with protecting Larkin, but that's not what this horrible discussion is about. "I'd never hurt your sister. Never in a million years. I know I should've answered her call that awful night. I won't make excuses for that choice and the consequences. There are none that are adequate. But I'm a different guy now. I'd do anything for Larkin."

He silences me with a hiss. "Tigers don't change their stripes, Bower. Larkin told me plenty over the years—that you had a girlfriend that night and still planned to hook up with her, then ditched her on the side of the road when you lost your nerve. Whatever you've told her since is clearly bullshit, so fuck off with your innocent act. You gave her your number and told her to call you if she was in trouble. She called. You didn't answer. That's all I need to know about you."

I drop my head, barely able to swallow. "I swear to God, I wasn't playing games with Larkin that night. I was only trying to drive her home, then we got to talking and I felt things for her I didn't expect. *Real* feelings, and it freaked me out. That's why I dropped her off, why I didn't answer her call."

He sneers at me, looking like he wants to slice my jugular. "Save that bullshit for someone who hasn't spent twelve years in jail because you didn't show up for a woman in trouble. I may have torn into Derek with that pipe, but I was only there because you weren't."

My fight leaves me. There's no point defending myself. Everything he said is true.

"My sister is stubborn and prideful," he goes on. "I told her Derek was trouble, but she dated him anyway. That Drew guy was a piece of work from the start. He fucked with her head, and I saw the damage it was doing. He broke down the one person in my life I would die for. I *saw* her insecurities taking hold and told her to ditch him, but she hung on tighter. Tried to prove me wrong, or prove herself right. Whatever her reasons, that's her nature—to swim against the stream, but the stream always wins.

"So, yeah, I lied to her. Told her I didn't care if she dated you, because I'm not prepared to watch her do the opposite of what's healthy for her again and get hurt. She's too damn good for you. She's too damn good for *me*, but she's all I fucking have. So you won't say a word to her about this talk. You'll tell her I gave you shit and threatened to hurt you if you hurt her, but that I'm okay with you two dating. Then you'll make it clear you're not into her. I don't care how you do it, but you won't date my sister or lay a fucking hand on her. And the second this stupid fake-fiancé sham is done, which you'll sell like your life depends on it, you'll never talk to her again."

A cavern widens inside me, deep and dark and endless. I knew today would be tough. I figured Hunter would give me hell and make me feel like shit, while threatening me like he suggested—if I hurt Larkin, he hurts me. But that's exactly what he's asking me to do—hurt his sister. "I get that you don't believe my feelings are genuine. With our history, it's no surprise. But you don't know what you're asking."

"I know exactly what I'm asking."

"I'm in *love* with her, man. And yeah, I probably don't deserve her, but I promise I'll work my ass off to be worthy of your sister, because she's fucking amazing—smart and funny and sweet. And I swear to God, I'd never hurt her. Never again. But pushing her away will do just that, because I'm pretty sure she loves me too."

"Exactly my point." He glares at me like I'm gum on his shoe. "She only has feelings for you because she's always been drawn to the wrong guys."

The insult is a blow. Larkin told me about her pattern with men, her attraction to unhealthy relationships. Everything with us is different, though…isn't it? I can't be misreading our intense connection, and I would never mistreat her or bring her harm.

Or is our history itself damaging?

Dating me might always remind her of the worst night of her life. Being with Larkin has certainly brought my old panic dreams back to life.

Hunter lifts his chin and works his jaw, looking down at me through slitted eyes. "I know your type, Jake. Chasing tail because it's a challenge. And I'm fucking done watching my sister get hurt, not being able to do shit for her while trapped in here. But I can help her now."

"What you're doing," I say, trying to keep my voice even, "is being another controlling man in her life, which isn't what Larkin needs."

Deeper frown lines sink between his brows. "No, it's not like that with us. I'm doing what's *right* for her. She's too sweet. She wants to see the best in people. But I see what she can't. Losing you now will hurt her less than if she gets in deeper and you inevitably break her heart."

I scrub my hand over my mouth, searching for a solution, but there's no winning here. Hunter won't budge. He's seen Larkin's worst moments and has been locked in prison, unable to help her. That kind of impotency must eat at a man, make him look for control in irrational ways. And his insult about Larkin's draw to unhealthy relationships is playing on repeat in my head.

She may have shared her trauma with me last night, but we both admitted how guilty we still feel. With our complicated history, that deep-seated remorse might develop roots. Grow bigger. Cause rifts over time. Without me in her life, she might meet someone better for her. A man who isn't tangled up in the worst night of her life.

Or I'm wrong, and we'll both feel broken beyond repair.

"I'm stuck in here," Hunter says, talking over my suffocating thoughts. "I can't make you do what I say, but you're partly responsible for the way my life turned out. A big fucking part. The least you owe me is the respect of not dating my sister—and not fucking up my relationship with her in the process. Or are you too narcissistic to manage that?"

My stomach roils.

I have no rebuttal. This man lives in hell partly because of me, and here I am dating his sister. Kissing her and spoiling her, like we're a normal couple falling for each other, making love nightly, no cares in the world. Which leaves me between a rock and a devastating place.

I'm not sure I can do as he asks, but I'm not sure I can live with myself if I *don't*.

"Okay," I say, the word barely scraping past my throat. It's the only answer he deserves, and the only one I can muster in the moment. The rest, I'll have to figure out when Hunter isn't glaring at me. "I'll make it clear to Larkin there's no future for us, and I won't tell her what you said."

He grunts and leaves the table.

I don't budge. Numbness spreads through my limbs.

Eventually, I get up and drag my ass back to my truck. I replay the conversation, wondering if I could've done or said something else for a different outcome. Shown Hunter my intentions with Larkin are forthright. But there's no changing my involvement in Hunter's incarceration.

Driving to Windfall is a hazy blur. My history with him billows around me, freshly detonated, fogging up my head. And the more I think about Larkin's history with men, the more I worry loving each other is more toxic than healthy.

I need more time to think, but Drew's party at the Barrel House is tonight. I'll barely have enough time to get home, get changed, and show up at the bar, where I'll have to play the role of doting fiancé, while a hurricane of emotion rages through me.

CHAPTER
Twenty-Eight

LARKIN

Hosting Drew's special event is as aggravating as expected. The first thing he says when he walks into the Barrel is, "We need to add another couple of vegan appetizers. Natalia is off meat this week."

I nearly knee the asshole in his nuts.

"This week" indicates he could have given us a heads-up sooner that his fiancée's diet had changed, but no. Drew loves feeling important and tossing his last name around. He would complain at most restaurants we dined at. Tell them the food was cold or the meat was overcooked, expecting supplication and a partial credit, even though he could afford the food. He just liked being the king who snapped his fingers and the world fell at his feet.

Which is exactly what happens now.

I smile sweetly and say, "No problem," then run to the kitchen in a panic and beg Emmanuel to concoct last-minute hors d'oeuvres.

The stoic chef he is, he nods sharply and says, "On it."

Now Drew is in front of me again, introducing Natalia with a smug look on his face.

"Meet the love of my life," he says, clutching her to his side. "She's the most brilliant, kind, beautiful woman I've ever known."

Natalia blushes, and I somehow refrain from punching Drew in the dick. Could that comment have been any ruder to me? It's like he's trying to push my buttons.

But I will not react.

My plan is to be the hostess with the mostest tonight. Effusive kindness. I will bend over backward to make his evening a success. This weekend, at his wedding, I'll appeal to his ego and tell him he changed my life for the better. I'm a success in love and business because of him! Then, when he's sufficiently buttered up, I'll mention Hunter's case and suss out if he's aware of the upcoming evaluation. I'll gauge his reaction and supplicate as needed.

"So lovely to meet you, Natalia," I say as I shake her hand, trying to exude calm confidence. She *is* absolutely stunning, with a sweep of thick, dark hair and green eyes. I hope Drew has at least figured out how to be kind and caring with her. "I'm very happy for you two."

"Thank you." She leans her head on Drew's chest. "And thanks for letting us rent the bar. It's such an amazing space. I've had my eye on it for a while."

I squint at her. "Really? I thought you booked another place that got canceled?"

She glances around the busy room, almost with a hint of longing. "I have some not so nice memories of the Barrel, which is why we didn't book here first. But this is great in the end. I really do love the space."

I don't recognize Natalia. Her bad memories must be from before I moved back to town and bought in to Jo's business.

Drew kisses her cheek and strokes her hair. "All things work out as they should, love."

"I know," she says, sounding a bit defeated. "Anyway"—her attention swings to me—"thank you for letting us book last minute. It's so nice seeing exes that are still friends. Especially when things didn't end the way you wanted." Her sympathetic look and concerned tone have me inwardly seething.

Drew definitely told her *he* broke up with *me*. Who knows what other stories he concocted, and I'm in no position to call him on his lies. "Like Drew said," I force out through a clenched-teeth smile, "everything worked out as it should."

Drew's hair is gelled, his suit neatly pressed. Outwardly, he is utterly poised. Except for the calculating gleam in his eyes. "Your fiancé isn't here yet. More role-playing games tonight? Or are you two having issues?"

"We're *amazing*, thank you." Effusiveness has nothing on me. "He just had an appointment this afternoon and is running a bit late."

Later than expected, but the "we're amazing" part is the only real thing I've said to Drew tonight, even though *amazing* doesn't begin to cover my feelings for Jake Bower.

The need to have Jake here with me now is staggering. An anchor to tether me through this mess with Drew. I want his arm around my back, reminding me some things in life are steady, which is still shocking. I don't know how Jake became my rock, and I don't really care. I've never felt happier than I have the past week.

A halo of curls catches my eye. If I didn't know better, I'd say that perm belongs to Sandra, but Sandra wouldn't have been on Drew's guest list.

"Excuse me," I say and head for her, but she's already heading for me.

"Jake is on his way," she says in that clipped way of hers. "It did not go well."

"What didn't go well?"

"His visit with your brother."

I freeze. "You know who my brother is?"

She looks at me like I'm one Skittle shy of a full bag. "Of course."

"Since when?"

"Since your reappearance in this town caused a stir. There isn't much I don't know about the Bowers and the people in their lives."

If she's known that long and gossip hasn't spread, at least I don't have to worry about rumors getting out. Sandra keeps her intel close to her chest. I also don't bother asking how she knows Jake was meeting Hunter. She's probably linked to every underground spy cell in the country. "How *not well* did Jake's visit go?"

"Prepare to do damage control. Also, keep an eye on Natalia. I'm surprised she chose your bar for her event." Sandra spins on her heel and leaves.

I stare at the closed door, baffled. Sandra must also know why Natalia has bad memories associated with the Barrel. I debate running after her to ask what's up, but the door swings back open and Jake steps in, looking devastatingly handsome in his slacks and blue button-down, the cuffs of the shirt rolled up to his elbows.

He has great forearms. And hands. And lips. And eyebrows.

Yep. I've fallen hard for this man, and I'm slightly worried after Sandra's warning.

He scans the chatting patrons and staff passing around appetizers. Nods to Jolene, who's helping out to save money on staffing tonight. The second his eyes land on me, his brow creases.

That tense expression is definitely not good.

I hate that we have to be in public right now, putting on a show for Drew. All I want is to curl into Jake's arms, remind him how good we are together, and make sure Hunter didn't say something too damaging.

"Seems your man made the time to join us," Drew says, back in my space with Natalia in tow. His proximity is unnerving, as is his interest in my relationship.

Jake's attention slides to Drew. He seems to shake himself and marches stiffly our way. "Sorry I'm late."

I step into his side and rub a circle on his back. "Did everything go okay?"

"Fine," he says stiffly. Not fine, judging by the tension in his body. "I'm just glad to be here to congratulate the happy couple." He nods to Drew and Natalia and slips his arm loosely around my waist. "It was kind of you to invite us to the wedding."

"Couldn't pass up the chance," Drew says, his grin wolfish. "I had to get to know the man who won Larkin's heart."

Darkness streaks across Jake's features but disappears quickly. He grips my hip tighter. "She's the one who owns mine."

There's an ominous tone to Jake's voice that freaks me out. His talk with Hunter definitely messed with his head. "If you'll excuse us a moment," I say sweetly to Drew, "I need Jake's help with something in my office."

I bow as I step back, which is absolutely ridiculous. Being around Drew turns my awkwardness to high. I take Jake's hand and lead him to the office I share with Jolene.

The second the door closes, I spin around and press my hands to his chest. "What happened?"

He heaves out a breath and focuses on the floor. "We should talk about this later."

"Later implies something bad, Jake. Which means later isn't happening. What did Hunter say?"

"Nothing. I just realized some stuff when the reality of his situation hit home."

"What stuff?"

He rubs the back of his neck. "Can we please talk about this later? We need to be out there buttering up Drew, who still seems like a prick, by the way."

"He's definitely a prick. And no—we can't talk about this later. Not if you want me to be in any kind of headspace to deal with that shitshow out there."

Jake passes his hand over his mouth, seeming at war with himself. Quietly, he says, "I think we should put on the brakes with us."

"What?" I must have heard him wrong.

The past ten days, Jake has been as into us as me, showing up at the bar every night, waiting for my shifts to end, kissing me desperately before we made it to his truck, making love to me with fierce tenderness and sometimes wild abandon, telling me he's never felt this way about anyone before. "Hunter said something to you."

He gives a twitchy shrug. "Nothing unexpected. Just warned me not to hurt you."

"You're lying."

He paces and yanks at the back of his hair. "Please don't ask me to discuss this. The decision was mine to make."

"If I can't ask you, you can sure as hell bet I'll ask Hunter. Or I'll ask Sandra, who seems to know every fucking thing in this town."

His puff of air holds a hint of amusement. "If she warned you I left the prison in rough shape, it's because she knows a guard there."

"I don't care who Sandra knows. I know *you*, Jake. This isn't what you want. So, I'll ask again, what did Hunter say to you?"

He marches toward the wall, paces while flexing his hands, then he slams his palm into the wood. His back ripples with frustration. "Please don't ask. I gave your brother my word."

Yep. Hunter will be getting an earful from me. There's only

one explanation for Jake's behavior. Hunter didn't just warn Jake not to hurt me. My brother lied to me, told me he was okay with us dating, and told Jake I was off-limits.

I approach him cautiously and place my hand on his back. His coiled muscles jump then relax. "Hunter doesn't get to decide what happens in my life. I thought I needed his approval before we dated, but the past ten days have changed that for me. I want you, Jake. I choose *you*. Losing you now will absolutely devastate me, and I don't believe this is what you want either. So you need to look at me and tell me what you *do* want. Not what Hunter demanded."

Slowly, he spins to face me, and...God. The torture in his dark eyes has my stomach dropping to my toes.

"I..." He trails off, clearly struggling. His chest heaves. "My head is a mess. Today threw me for a complete loop. I need time to sort through it all, but I know we have the wedding this weekend. So I'll be there for you, Larkin. I'll show up for you and do whatever is necessary to prove to Drew we're solid, while you convince him to go easy on Hunter's case. I might need a break after that. I honestly don't know right now. All I ask is that you don't come down on Hunter or push him away. I gave him my word I wouldn't tell you what he said. You're all he has, and he doesn't want to lose you."

Funny way my brother has of showing he cares by destroying my love life.

He's always been opinionated about the men I've dated. Not that I blame him, with my track record. But this? Scaring Jake so badly he's spiraling, considering ending us? I'm furious with Hunter, but I'm also sad. I *am* all he has, and he's in no mental state to have a fight with the only person in his corner.

"I won't tell him. *Yet*," I add, crossing my arms. A barrier to protect myself. "Not because you made a promise to him. I'm not okay with him trying to manipulate my life like this and will have to bring it up eventually, but I'm too worried about his mental health right now to tell him how pissed I am." I blink, forcing the moisture in my eyes to stay put. "As far as you and I are concerned, if you need space to think, then I guess we're on a temporary break. But we're currently *fake* engaged until at least Sunday. If you can act the part, so can I. We'll revisit this conversation next week."

After I figure out how to show Jake there's no other option but the two of us ending up together. "Think you can handle that?" I ask.

"Yeah," he says, hoarse, rubbing his sternum like he has a wicked case of heartburn.

CHAPTER
Twenty~Nine

Larkin

By the time Drew's event is over, my positivity hovers at zero. The handful of times I interacted with Drew, he was patronizing. He doted on his fiancée, at least. Never left her side and seemed genuinely into her. Tomorrow, at the lodge outside of town, I'll need to be more proactive and directly mention Hunter's case. I'll also need to fortify myself to handle this whole Jake mess.

He's one of the last stragglers, being the kind man he is, helping my servers clear the tables.

I walk over and touch his shoulder. He flinches and moves out of touching distance. Forget fortification. I need to build a moat around my emotions and prepare for the worst.

"Thanks for helping, but the staff have everything under control, and you've had a long day." I leave the comment open-ended, hoping he asks me to leave with him or says he'll wait for me. We'll go home together afterward, to his place or mine, the way we have every night since our boat date.

A furrow sinks between his brows. "Probably best if I get

some rest before the weekend. I'll pick you up tomorrow at two?"

I deflate. "Sure."

His jaw knots. The tendons along his neck strain. He looks as though he's about to speak, but he dips his head and turns, leaving without another word.

I stare at the closed bar door as an upswell of hurt rises. Is this what I get for being happy? For letting my guard down and opening up my heart?

I want to regret getting to know Jake, making myself vulnerable with him, but...I don't. *I can't.* Giving up on us doesn't feel right. And judging by the physical pain lancing through my chest, I think the worst might have happened—I've somehow fallen in love with this man I used to despise.

My throat burns. The backs of my eyes sting.

"Larkin?" Jolene appears beside me, watching me with concern. "Did something happen with Jake?"

I try to find my usual armor, shake off the sting of Jake's distance and the fear that I've lost the best man I've ever known. I try *so* hard, but my chin trembles. I cover my mouth and curve away from Jo.

"I'm not usually this messy," I say more to myself than to her. At least, I didn't used to be.

For most of my life, I've relied on myself. When I fell, I picked myself back up. Self-defense classes. Group therapy. Helping raise my youngest brother. Saving to buy in to this business and making it a success through hard work and determination.

Me. I did all that, with no help from anyone. But I look at Jo, and my sadness builds along with the memories Jake and I have started to create, all of it rising to a crescendo I can't control. "I'm not sure we'll work out," I say as a tear slips out.

God, I never used to cry like this. At least, not since I was young and stupid.

I dash at my face, but Jo has her hand on my arm and is ushering me to our office. The second we're inside, she pulls me into a hug and doesn't let go. I sink into her, my adrenaline from tonight seeping out as I slow my breaths.

When I'm somewhat calmer, she leads me to the sofa, where we both sit.

"What happened?" she asks, her voice full of compassion.

I don't know where to start. There's so much Jo doesn't know. Details I've been too scared to share, but skirting subjects with her is exhausting—picking and choosing what to say. Jolene is my closest friend. I've been there for her through her physical and emotional setbacks. I'm pretty sure she'd support me too, but will she be mad she's business partners with Otto Briggs's daughter? That I've kept this information from her for so long?

For better or for worse, keeping these secrets is getting too hard. I want to be a better friend. More open and honest, and that starts with the tough stuff.

"When I was younger," I say, taking a fortifying breath, "I was in an abusive relationship."

Jo startles and presses her hand over her heart, but she doesn't interrupt. She listens while I tell her about Derek. The party where I drank too much. Jake driving me home. Our instant connection. How safe I felt with him. Our almost-kiss. The devastation that followed, including who I am. Who Hunter is. Our father. Where Hunter has spent the last twelve years, and Drew's involvement in his case.

Finally, I tell her about Jake's visit to the prison, and why I'm blubbering all over her. "I love him, but I'm not sure it's enough. There's so much baggage between us."

"I don't know what to say." Jo takes my hand, like holding it fiercely will protect me from my memories. "I can't imagine how terrifying that night was. And Hunter? To be in jail all this time, just because he saved you." She shakes her head, tears shimmering in her eyes.

"Yeah," I say on a sad sigh. I'm exhausted from telling my story again, emotionally, physically. But also relieved to have it out in the open. "I'm sorry I didn't tell you sooner. I felt so badly about my involvement with Jake that night, even though you said you weren't mad about it. And you should've known who your business partner is—what could happen if the town finds out. So if you want to buy me out now, I understand. I wouldn't blame you at all. I broke your trust and put your aunt's legacy at risk."

"At risk?" Jolene's incredulous expression matches her tone. "Larkin, you're the reason this bar is thriving. I had one foot out the door when you offered to buy in to the Barrel. *You* brought new life to my aunt's business and to me. The only way you're getting out of this partnership is if you're six feet under."

My laugh is watery. "You're not mad?"

"I'm furious that Derek hurt you and that the courts were unfair to Hunter, but I'm not upset with you. I wish you'd told me sooner about your father, only so you wouldn't have spent all this time stressing over it, but you obviously had your reasons."

None of them are good enough in the face of Jo's understanding, but the biggest one is still an issue. "If people learn I'm related to Otto Briggs, it'll probably affect our business."

"Fuck that," Jo says, not skipping a beat. "Let this town talk. You're smart and kind and have improved Windfall by helping give them a welcoming bar where they can have fun and unwind. Anyone who says otherwise can screw off."

I pull her into another hug, less snotty and snivelly this time. "I love you."

"The feeling is mutual. But there's still the issue of Jake's visit with Hunter that needs dealing with. I actually think I have something that could help." Her eyes twinkle as she releases me. She walks to our shared desk, opens a lower drawer. Rummages around until she pops up with what looks like a computer printout. "You need to seduce him."

I raise an eyebrow. "We've had sex plenty." Mind-blowing, earth-shattering, angels-singing sex. "Seduction isn't the issue."

Jo stands in front of me, like she's doing a high school presentation. "Remember when I was in love with Cal and was stuck living with him and wasn't sure if he felt the same, and you told me to test my hypothesis by flirting with him?"

"Sure, but how does that help me convince Jake to ignore my brother and be with me? You know him. The man's entire identity is built on doing the right thing. If he thinks pushing me away is the most honorable choice, that's where he'll lean."

I don't mention that Jake had suspicions about his father's lies and never told his brothers. It's not my secret to share, but there's no doubt that choice impacted the man he's become. He thinks he failed his family. He believes he failed me and Hunter the night I went to Derek's home. Past trauma that intense shapes a person. I mean, I took seven months to tell Jolene about my father and my history with Jake. Flirting won't sway Jake an inch.

Jo flips the page she's holding and fans her hand below the bolded title.

I stutter out a laugh. "You have got to be kidding."

"Not even a little."

I read the title again: **7 Steps to Seducing Your Best Friend.**

"First," I say, "you're my best friend. Jake is the runner-up. Second, I told you, seduction won't make a dent in Jake's armor. The man is determined when he makes up his mind." Like how he pushed into my home and life, repairing furniture, planning a fix-it club with me, cooking my favorite foods, making love like he was trying to win a freaking medal. "The way he left here tonight, I'm pretty sure he'll keep his physical distance from me, unless we're in public and have to put on an 'engaged' show. And why do you even have that printout?"

"Before I told you about my Cal crush, I was a tad desperate and looked up ways to seduce him." She leans down and puts the paper on her knee, talking while she writes something on the sheet. "This came up on a website, and the ideas weren't half bad. I was too much of a wimp to do any of them, but things are different with Jake and you. You *know* he's into you. Emotional seduction is the key with him."

She swivels back and hands me the paper. Part of the title is crossed out and rewritten, pulling another laugh from me.

7 Steps to Seducing Your ~~Best Friend~~ Fake Fiancé

"You're ridiculous," I say, but I read the listed points.

1. Try a new hairstyle or outfit to make him see you in a different light.
2. Do something new together that puts you in close proximity.
3. Make him jealous without going too far.
4. Tell him your deepest fantasies to fill his head with images of you.
5. Use touch to communicate your true emotion.
6. Leave him wanting more by giving him a tease of intimacy and walking away.
7. Be vulnerable to earn his trust.

"I don't know," I say slowly, unsure how some of this applies to Jake and me. She also didn't see his face when he said he needed time apart to think. "Jake is pretty tormented by whatever my brother said. I'll feel bad for making it worse."

"If he puts a physical boundary between you, which is what I'm pretty sure he'll do, you're right—these suggestions will be painful for him. But you said it yourself: Jake sets his moral bar unachievably high. He's his own worst enemy right now. He's hurting himself and you for some imagined line he's drawn in the sand, as if that will erase the mistakes he made in the past, when all any of this will do is hurt you both."

She's right. He's being a stubborn bull and not a rational one. If I accept his choice and back down, I'll probably hurt him more than if I push back.

I read the list again, with more of an open mind this time.

A new hairstyle to surprise him would be fun, and being in close proximity isn't tough at a wedding. There will likely be music and a dance floor. I wouldn't want to push too hard on the "make him jealous" angle, but seeing me casually with another man might stoke his possessiveness. Fantasies and tender touches are certainly no hardship.

Being vulnerable with him would be hard, but I can handle riling us both up physically and walking away if it means we'll have a future together.

Unfortunately, I'd need to do all this while convincing Drew to go easy on Hunter's case.

I take Jo's printout and pull her into a hug. "Thank you for this. And the pep talk. And for not being mad I kept my father's name from you."

She rubs my back, then holds me at arm's length. "Without you, I'd still be dreading going into work most days, too scared to change anything about the bar, positive I'd fail. Now I love this place and can't imagine doing anything else. Who your father is doesn't change that."

"I'm so glad we run this place together." I couldn't have a better business partner or friend. This place has become part of both our identities, filling us with pride and purpose, but Jake is a part of me too. In a short time, he's become a vital organ I didn't know I needed.

I breathe through another round of nerves. "If this doesn't sway Jake, I'm not sure how I'll cope."

"Jake's in a rough place, but he'll see the light. You'll show him exactly what he's missing, and he'll make the right choice, which is you."

Or I'll fall more in love with him and will be devastated when he decides his moral compass doesn't point in my direction.

CHAPTER
Thirty

Larkin

I follow Jake down the hallway of this historic hotel, focusing on the charming decor, not the near silence of our twenty-five-minute drive and how unsettled I feel.

According to the research I did to suss out the environment for this painful weekend, I learned that the sprawling structure of Longleaf Inn was built in 1878. The exterior retained its original stone walls and black shutters, a large portion of which is covered in crawling ivy. The current owners did a massive renovation fifteen years ago, updating the rooms and adding intimate cottages on the treed property.

Jake and I are staying at the original inn, where we may or may not talk to each other. Hard to say with how this day is going.

At least the patterned rugs and nostalgic wall sconces we pass make my inner garage-sale hunter happy. "I love the old feel of the place. I'm glad they didn't modernize everything."

"Yeah," Jake says absent-mindedly, not glancing at me or his surroundings.

I refrain from groaning.

His behavior indicates he's still completely in his head, probably obsessing over his visit with Hunter. I wasn't sure how committed I was to Jolene's seduction steps. The whole thing felt kind of ridiculous. With how distant Jake's been, I'd cluck like a chicken while hopping on one leg if it would help him move past his consuming guilt.

"Looks like we're here," I say too loudly. Awkward for the win.

Jake pulls out our keycard from his pocket, but it doesn't work the first time. Thinking of the list, which is tucked into my purse, I place my hand on his back—*Use touch to communicate your true emotion.* I lean toward his ear, making sure my breath hits the spot that usually makes him moan. "I can try, if you want."

He finally does make a sound. Not quite a moan. More of a pained whine. "I've got it," he murmurs.

A second later, he opens the door and marches to the far side of the room, angling away from me. If I didn't know Jake was attracted to me, I'd be offended. But his current behavior can't erase how insatiable we've been the past couple of weeks or his unchecked admissions while thrusting deep inside me. *I'll never have enough of you.*

Based on that evidence, my closeness a second ago has his body in turmoil. I'll take that as a step in the right direction.

The room is another point in my favor. The four-poster bed and lush sheets add a sexy hit to the subdued decor. Cream walls. Patterned maroon carpet. A gas fireplace on the far wall.

"Not too shabby," I say, leaving my bag and strolling to the bed. I run my hand up one of the wood posts. "I've never slept in one of these."

Another sound comes from Jake. This one plaintive. "I'll sleep on the floor."

"Why would you sleep on the floor?"

He gestures between us. "We're not doing...*this* right now."

"Doing what?" I say, playing dumb. As much as I hate this limbo between us, his struggle to use basic words is highly amusing.

He points an accusing finger at the bed. "We're not doing anything in there."

"Like...sleeping?" I give the bed an exaggerated perusal. "We're not allowed to *sleep* on the plushest bed I've ever seen?"

His bearded jaw looks ready to snap. "You know exactly what I mean, Larkin. Only one thing happens when you and I are in reaching distance of each other."

The best sex of my life is what happens, but he's not getting off that easy. "I'm really in the dark. You'll have to spell it out for me."

"Sex," he hiss-whispers, like saying the word any louder will cause our clothes to spontaneously vanish. "I'm trying really hard to heed your brother's wishes while I figure out the right thing to do moving forward. Sharing a bed won't help the situation."

Most of the time, Jake's chivalrous nature is unbearably attractive. Right now, it's irksome. "We're both adults, and that bed is huge. Based on how you've been acting today, I doubt you'll have any issues staying away from me."

His brows dive into a deep furrow. He rubs aggressively at the back of his hair. "Fine. I'll stay in the bed."

Another point for me, but I'm not done with him yet.

Focusing on step four of Jo's printout—*Tell him your deepest fantasies to fill his head with images of you*—I fondle the wood post some more. "I've actually never stayed in a fancy hotel like this."

Jake drops his bag and leans on the dresser. "Drew never took you away?"

"We were together for, like, a year and a half, but it was a busy time for him, workwise. And I bartended on weekends. We also never did romantic things like that, which says a lot about our relationship." Along with the fact that it was toxic on a million levels. "Most other guys I dated didn't last long enough to start vacationing together, but I always wondered…" I trail off, hoping Jake follows my breadcrumb trail.

He clears his throat. "Wondered what?"

Bingo. "It's nothing."

He studies me in that intent way of his, those dark eyes warm but penetrating. "It's clearly not nothing. Tell me."

Nerves flutter through my stomach. Yes, I'm trying to break down Jake's walls. I want him to suffer a teeny, tiny bit. I need to *show* him what he's missing by keeping his distance, but this is a real fantasy I've never voiced.

I focus on my hand, on how smooth the post feels under my touch. "I may never have been to a fancy hotel, but I'd look up places online sometimes. Imagine going to a pretty spa or a gorgeous inn like this, and if they had pictures of this type of bed, I'd stop on those pages." Tentatively, I lift my attention to Jake. "I'd picture myself tied up to the bed."

Jake's next swallow drags so slowly, I'm not sure his Adam's apple is actually moving. The veins on his forearms and neck protrude, and his hands curl into fists.

He's as wound up as I hoped.

"I've never asked for that from a man," I go on. "I've never trusted anyone enough to give them that much control, but something about it excites me—the idea of letting go and focusing on nothing but my pleasure. The intimacy of that kind of trust." I shrug a shoulder. "I know you won't tie me up and have your way with me this weekend. I guess I still feel safe enough to share my secrets with you."

Either the lighting is playing tricks on me, or beads of moisture have gathered on Jake's forehead. His neck is definitely mottled red. There's no hiding the thick line stretching the fly of his jeans. Time to let him marinate in his turmoil for a bit.

"Sorry for oversharing, and I have to go. Spa appointment soon," I say as I head for the door. I also need to find Drew, finally discuss Hunter with him. "No need to wait for me," I add. "You should go for a walk, enjoy the property. Meet me at tonight's cocktail party later."

The place where I'll surprise him with my new haircut. Step one—*Try a new hairstyle or outfit to make him see you in a different light.*

He doesn't say a word, just watches me like a caged panther who hasn't eaten for weeks.

The second I slip out the door, a bang carries from the room, followed by a growled, "Jesus fucking Christ."

CHAPTER
Thirty~One

LARKIN

I spot Drew by the inn's expansive gardens. He's with Natalia and a photographer, who's snapping photos of the couple against a backdrop of orange marigolds and purple asters. The couple really does seem in love. Their expressions are relaxed and happy as they gaze at each other.

I linger, unsure if I should speak with Drew another time. Badgering him this soon might annoy him. He could get angry I'm attempting to interfere with his job, but waiting won't change that aspect. Best to hurry this along.

Natalia says something to Drew. She kisses his cheek and leads the photographer around the far side of a cute stone house. Drew watches them a moment, a small smile on his face, then he turns and spots me.

Taking that as my cue, I wave and join him, attempting to quell my unease. "Did you make a deal with the devil to get this blue sky?"

He doesn't glance at our gorgeous surroundings. He's utterly fixated on me in a way that has the fine hairs on my neck rising. "I only do deals I can't lose," he says.

Okay, then. "Thanks again for inviting Jake and me. We're thrilled to celebrate with you."

The only way to describe his smirk is *devious*. "You don't have to pretend you want to be here."

I freeze. "Excuse me?"

"I'm not stupid, Larkin. I know being here pains you. There's no need to fake emotions with me."

If he knows I don't want to be here, then why the hell did he extend the invitation? And why does he look smug, like a master of ceremonies watching a rehearsed show being performed?

"None of this was a coincidence, was it?" I ask, taking a step back. Jake worried Drew had an ulterior motive for inviting me to his wedding. As did Hunter. Nothing made sense at the time. Nothing still does, but there's no denying Drew's conniving expression. "You know Hunter's case is coming up for review, don't you? You knew exactly whose bar you walked into on our opening night."

He gives a small bow. "Excellent deduction skills."

Unease spills down my spine as I sift through any reason for him to orchestrate this series of events. I come up empty. "Why?"

He tugs at the cuff of his sport jacket and checks his watch. "Part curiosity—wondering how you'd act. I've always been fascinated by human behavior, especially when confronted with one's past."

"So, I'm a scientific study to you?"

He shrugs, and part of me buckles. Of all the people to confide in, why did I have to choose Drew? I was just so… untethered back then. So alone. Julian was off living his best life in New York. My mother had long since been out of my life. I wasn't living as close to Hunter and couldn't visit him in jail as often, and I'd moved around so much I didn't have close friends.

Then Drew came into my life. A customer at the bar where I worked. He asked me questions, listened intently. When I turned down his offer of a date, he pulled out all the stops to win me over: buying me expensive gifts, leaving me sweet notes at work. There's no doubt his persistence worked its magic. Feeling wanted is a heady cocktail. I think I was also so desperate to feel connected—to belong with someone—that I ignored any red flags his personality waved.

Until his questions were used to overpower me emotionally.

Until his passive-aggressive comments sabotaged my self-confidence.

Until I was strong enough to finally tell him to fuck off.

And here I am again, letting this asshole make me feel damaged.

Well, fuck that.

I know my worth now. Jake has shown me how kind and caring a real man can be, even when keeping his distance from me now. But I can't lash out at Drew. He knows I have to stand here and take whatever bullshit he doles out.

"I thought you were lying about your fiancé at first," he goes on. "I was curious how far you'd push the ruse, but there's no denying your relationship. Not with the way he looks at you."

Hearing him confirm Jake's feelings vindicates me for a moment. If a trained psychiatrist sees Jake's affection, surely Jake and I will find our way around this latest obstacle. But Jake isn't why I was invited to this wedding.

There's more going on here than Drew observing me like I'm some kind of lab rat. "If you invited me *partly* out of curiosity, what's the other part? Why am I actually here?"

He runs his hand along the side of his gelled hair. "I have something I want to give Natalia for our wedding. A special present. Turns out, you can help me with that. Since I can help you with something near and dear to your heart, figured we could do an exchange."

"As in *blackmail*?"

"No need to use harsh terms. We'd just be two old friends doing each other favors."

I almost laugh, thinking about all the blackmailing jokes Jake and I have been slinging, but Drew hasn't cracked a smile. This guy actually plans to barter for Hunter's life.

Anger blows through me, followed swiftly by hope. I don't know what I have that Drew could possibly want this badly, besides bartending lessons, but I'd sell him my limbs if it means saving Hunter another three years in jail.

"May as well spit it out." I'm well past pleasantries. If he needs me, my attitude toward him doesn't matter. "No point beating around the bush."

He checks his watch again. "Unfortunately, I have to meet with the florist. I'll find you when I have more time."

He struts off, leaving me standing there like an idiot. And I *fume*. I'm furious at him for turning Hunter's life into a game. I'm sick that I need Drew to ensure my brother's release. At least I have cards in this game. I just don't know what they are yet.

I close my eyes and draw in a deep breath. I have no choice but to wait. Drew will reveal his hand soon, but the urge to gain control is strong. Drew. Jake. They both have the power to alter my life, and this sense of impotency is infuriating.

With Jake, I at least know why he's keeping his distance. And I know it's killing him.

Tackling the rest of that seduction list will help me gain more control. I've already enacted step four—*Tell him your deepest fantasies to fill his head with images of you*. Five has been played with—*Use touch to communicate your true emotion*—but I can do better with that one. Most of the other steps can also be implemented tonight: dancing with him to put us in close proximity, lightly flirting with a man to make him jealous, and leaving him wanting more.

Most important, though, is step one: my new hairstyle.

I turn and stride toward the spa at the opposite end of this sprawling property. My hair appointment is in ten minutes. I was planning highlights and adding layers. A change, but nothing dramatic. Suddenly, I'm craving a massive heaping of drama.

When Jake and I were together and on the same page, I felt sexy and confident. Feminine, yet powerful. The best version of myself.

What better way to regain control than through a shocking transformation?

CHAPTER
Thirty-Two

Jake

I am a fucking mess. It's late afternoon. As per Larkin's suggestion, I'm walking through the inn's property before tonight's cocktail party. An attempt to calm down after picturing her poster-bed fantasy on repeat. I'm in my clothes for the event —slacks and a button-down that feel suffocating. Or maybe that's the way it feels to be on the same planet as Larkin without having her in my arms.

The early evening weather is perfect, sunny but not too hot. I pass through gardens and a forest trail I'm sure are pretty. I barely notice a leaf or flower.

I've gone from fantasizing about Larkin to replaying my visit with Hunter and the hatred in his eyes as he laid down his law.

She only has feelings for you because she's always been drawn to the wrong guys.

You gave her your number and told her to call you if she was in trouble. She called. You didn't answer. That's all I need to know about you.

The least you owe me is the respect of not dating my sister.

I breach the woods and drag my hand down my face. I can't rebut one of Hunter's points, but not being with Larkin the past two days has been torture. For both of us, I'm pretty sure. And I haven't done a damn thing about it.

I barely slept last night. Woke up in a cold sweat—another nightmare taking control of my mind. Desmond this time, drunk and belligerent the way he was for a solid portion of WITSEC. He was getting into a car, about to drive away, and I didn't take his keys or tell him to stop. I watched as he drove and plowed into an oncoming car, and my legs couldn't move. Sirens blared, and I screamed myself raw, then I finally ran to him, but he wasn't in the mangled wreck.

Hunter was in there, bleeding out.

I've been in a state of emotional paralysis ever since I woke up.

Clacking my molars together, I march toward the main building. Larkin will be at the party soon. I need to get my head right and be there for her.

When I walk into the event room, I don't see Larkin, but the vaulted ceilings are at least airy. Long cream curtains are pulled back, letting in sunlight. I bet Larkin loves this place—the history in the old stone walls and vintage paintings. I wish we could truly be here together. A real couple, strolling through the room, discussing the paintings and enjoying the gardens visible through the windows, then using that four-poster bed the way she described.

But every time I think about apologizing and telling her I was wrong to let her brother decide our fate, my lungs constrict.

"Have you been chopping wood?" a girl beside me asks, sounding condescending.

I cut a glance to my right and do a double take. *Shit.*

Normally, I'd be fine talking to a young girl who brokered conversation with me, but I know this mini tyrant. Olivia assists my brother Desmond on his hikes and generally drives him batty, although it's clear she's his favorite of his outdoor programs. Lord knows why. She's around thirteen. A small Black girl who looks innocent enough in her bright-pink pants, yellow top, and cute stack of braided bracelets on her wrist.

She's also too damn clever and loves sassing anyone with the last name Bower.

"I have not been chopping wood," I tell her, examining the room for an escape route. She wouldn't follow me to the bar, would she?

I turn and aim that way.

Two steps toward my much-needed glass of bourbon, Olivia catches up to me. "You look like you've been chopping wood," she says.

I don't reply. Nothing good will come from egging her on. I make it to the bar and wave to the bartender, hoping he hurries the fuck up.

"If a man chops wood for an hour," she goes on, staring at my profile so hard I start to sweat, "their testosterone levels increase by forty-eight percent. And when testosterone increases in men, they have greater levels of aggression and uncontrollable emotions, among other effects. You look like your emotions are *way* far out of your control."

This is why Olivia is to be avoided at all costs.

I look down at her and attempt to exude a calm façade. "My emotions are just fine."

"Tell that to your tortured eyes."

"My eyes are also *just fine*."

"What can I get you two?" the bartender asks, smiling at Olivia and me.

"I'll have a martini neat," Oliva says.

I muffle a laugh. Unnerving intelligence and nosiness aside, maybe I get why Des has fun with this kid. "She'll have a soda. I'll have a double bourbon on the rocks."

"Way to steal my fun," Olivia mutters. She crosses her arms and leans her back into the bar. "If you weren't chopping wood, I assume your emotional mess is due to a girl."

"Definitely not a girl." Does she think I'm asinine enough to admit my weakness to her?

I'm about to invent a reason for my tortured eyes—the dog I don't have died, I've just learned I have a rare blood disorder, I ate a little kid for lunch and have indigestion—but a woman catches my eye, something about her height and stance strangely familiar.

I can't see her face, but I squint at her shapely legs accentuated by a pair of mile-high heels, the swell of her hips in her formfitting green dress that dips dangerously low in the back, the sensual line of her neck. She's talking to a man with tattoos visible below his cuffed sleeves, laughing with him. If I didn't know better, I'd say that body belongs to Larkin, but this woman has wavy, shoulder-length dark hair cut in what's probably considered a special style, but I'd just call sexy as hell.

Maybe Larkin has a relative I don't know about.

The man leans into her ear and whispers to her. Her angle changes, and I damn near storm over there and punch the guy in the neck.

When did Larkin change her hair? And why the fuck is she flirting with a random guy when I'm right here?

Olivia snickers. "Wanna tell me again how your tortured eyes aren't because of a girl?"

"It's a complicated situation," I grind out.

She stares at me blandly. "Did you know fifty percent of human DNA is shared with a banana?"

I glare down at her. "What?"

"You're fifty-percent banana. How complicated can this situation really be?"

Ignoring Olivia's invasiveness, I attempt to quit glaring at the guy with Larkin, but it's an uphill battle. Is this what it's going to be like back at home? Windfall is the size of a bird's nest. I already run into her around town a ton. If I keep my word to Hunter and stay away from his sister, I'll have to see her with other men, flirting, smiling, laughing, touching an asshole's arm, like she's doing right now.

"She's not playing the field," Olivia says. "If that's what has your head about to explode."

The bartender returns with our drinks. Olivia tries to grab my bourbon, but I give her a hard stare and snatch it up. I should ditch this kid. Step outside and take a breather, but I'm sliding down a very slippery slope toward my fist meeting that tattooed man's face.

A large swallow of bourbon later, I jut my chin toward the most stunning woman I've ever known, who isn't even glancing around the room for me. "Do you not see her over there, flipping her new haircut in that guy's face?"

An ache I've never known grabs hold of my chest and squeezes.

Olivia points at a petite Black woman, who's talking animatedly with a bearded man. "That's my mother. She's been speed dating since my father screwed her over, but this new guy is sticking."

"And?" I ask, unsure why I think this barely teen can fix my abysmal love life. No one is supposed to know Larkin and I are having issues while at this event. I just feel so...fucked up. Unable to talk to Larkin about the shame eating at me, how badly I want to do the right thing for Hunter, but that I'm not sure what he's asking is actually *right*. I don't fully understand why I'm not storming over there to crush my mouth to hers, showing that man she's very much taken.

And...Jesus *fuck*. His hand is heading toward the bare skin on her back.

"When women want a man who's being cagey," Olivia drawls, "which is clearly you and that murder face you have going on right now, they sometimes revert to jealousy games. She doesn't want that dude. His eyebrows are way out of control. She just wants you to know how crap it'll feel to see her with another guy."

If that's accurate, mission accomplished.

Olivia takes her soda and walks off to torment someone else. Or maybe to give them a PowerPoint presentation on evolutionary psychology.

I should stay where I am, not encroach on Larkin when I'm still too muddled to have a proper conversation with her about us. But Drew could walk in at any moment, right? If he sees her flirting with a stranger, he might clue in to our ruse. Larkin's plan to soften Drew toward Hunter will be a bust. Yep. Going over there is doing a kindness for Larkin.

I knock back the rest of my bourbon, wince as liquid fire burns down my throat, then march over to Larkin just as the tattooed asshole reaches up to touch her goddamn hair.

I don't go for subtle. I latch my arm around her waist and pull her against me. She makes a surprised sound, then relaxes into my side.

"Did you do something different with your hair, Feisty?"

She tips her face up to me, and damn. This new look is *fire* on her. "I'm surprised you noticed."

"I notice everything about you."

"Such a charmer." She eyes my lips, like she wants a taste of me.

I'm dying to have my mouth on her, but playing fiancé is one thing. Kissing Larkin is a whole other emotional land mine I'm not prepared to detonate right now.

A throat clears. "I assume this is the lucky betrothed?"

Larkin settles her hand on my stomach and addresses the man I assumed was hitting on her. "It is. Jake, this is Anthony. He works with Drew's wife, and his husband did my hair today."

Relief rushes through me, so forcefully I need to close my eyes for a beat. She wasn't flirting. She wasn't moving on from me. More concerning is how utterly wrecked I was over the imagined possibility.

Swallowing roughly, I nod to Anthony. "Your husband did great work. I didn't think Larkin could get more beautiful, but..." I take in her new look. Her blue-green eyes are intense against the darker hair. The wavy strands frame her face, the smattering of freckles on her nose even sexier like this. "You're breathtaking," I say more quietly.

Color blooms on her cheeks. "Thank you." She presses her hand harder into my back the way she does when I'm on top of her and moving deep. "You clean up pretty well yourself."

Anthony fans his face. "Excuse me while I go take a cold shower." He touches Larkin's arm and flicks his head toward me. "This one might need a moment alone with you."

He leaves, but I don't loosen my arm from Larkin's back. I do move my hand, though. I let the tips of my fingers trail down her exposed spine.

She shivers on a sigh. "Do you?"

"Do I what?"

"Need a moment alone with me."

Yes. I need a lifetime of moments with Larkin, but the disgust on Hunter's face still hovers at the back of my mind, as do imagined images of the night Larkin was attacked: Larkin scrambling up a fence, scared and desperate. Derek yanking her down, his hands on her neck. The terror and desperation she must have felt, then Hunter smashing that pipe into Derek's head to save his sister's life. All because I didn't answer her call.

Feeling shaky, I remove my hand from Larkin's back. "We need to stay here, make sure Drew sees us together."

She sighs as her shoulders curve forward. "Right. This is all for Drew."

The man in question walks in, and Larkin goes from hunched

to ramrod straight. She watches him and his fiancée mingle, her eyes narrowed, like he's a spider slowly creeping along the wall.

"You okay?" I ask.

She cuts me a hard look. "No, on many levels."

I scratch my beard, glancing away from her gorgeous face and the mistakes I'm probably making. Why is it so hard to get my shit together?

A band is playing now. Hors d'oeuvres are being passed around. I keep my focus on the happy guests chatting and drinking, trying to control my erratic pulse, only to spot Olivia. She's standing on her own, watching me with unnerving intensity. She gives her head a disappointed shake, then holds up her phone like she's snapping my picture.

I don't have the mental energy to figure out what she's doing. Probably writing a Wikipedia page titled: Selfish Men Who Ruin Their Own Lives.

I try to think of something to say to Larkin. Words to lighten the mood since I can't muster anything more meaningful. All my turmoil does is sap my ability to converse and act normal.

Drew and Natalia are standing nearby. His attention settles on Larkin a moment, his lips hitched in what appears to be a challenging smirk. There's certainly no missing the tension in Larkin's body as she wraps her arms around her waist, like she's holding herself together.

I dip my head toward her. "Did something happen with Drew this afternoon?"

She nibbles the inside of her lip, seems about to speak, but she glances at me...or maybe at the space I've left between us. "It's nothing I can't handle."

"Then something *did* happen."

"Pretty sure it's none of your concern."

"I'm here with you, aren't I? You asked me to help you with Drew, and I want to help."

"You're not here with me, Jake. You're in your own head."

Dammit. She's not wrong, but even if I could order my thoughts, this isn't the time or place to talk through my turmoil. "I'm sorry. You're right. I didn't sleep much last night and have been struggling to focus. Not that my sleep is an excuse for my behavior. I'll try to do better. But if Drew is making you uncomfortable, I want to know."

Compassion softens her face. She fits her hand into mine and gives it a tender squeeze. "Thank you, but like I said, I can handle Drew. And I'm sorry for being so frustrated with you. I know how intense Hunter can be, especially lately. I respect that you need time to sort through your emotions. But can we just try to have fun tonight, maybe? Forget about Drew and our past and just be *us*. Even if it's only as friends."

There's nothing friendly about my feelings for Larkin, but I nod. "Fun sounds good. Platonic fun," I add, reinforcing her point. Anything more might short-circuit my already haywire brain.

She searches my face. I'm not sure what she sees, but the slightest curve tilts her lips up. "Platonic, because you don't want to be with me?"

"Do you really have to ask that?"

"Apparently."

If I had tortured eyes before, they must be agonized now. "Because I want to be with you too much, but I also want to do the right thing. Getting deeper right now could end with us both hurting more."

She shrugs, but the move is lighter. "If that's the case, we'll keep things PG-13. I promise not to grab your ass like I did at the Dog and Pony Show."

She winks at me. Goddamn winks, like I'm not holding myself back from devouring her. There's a sparkle in her eyes too—unbearably attractive and worrying. I'm pretty sure there was challenge in that ass-grab quip.

The band plays a slow song with a sultry beat. Larkin glances at the stage, then back at me. "Since we're having fun, we may as well dance together."

She takes my arm before I can form a reply. Being pressed against Larkin as music plays may not be R-rated, but my body only has one reaction to her—on fire.

CHAPTER
Thirty~Three

LARKIN

Being in Jake's arms again has me turning liquid. It's been less than two days since we've kissed, but I swear it's been an eternity. I press my face into his neck. Feel his shudder when I run my nose up the side. We don't talk, but we don't need to. I sink into the moment, quit thinking and worrying. I let myself enjoy the feel of this strong man hugging me close.

Until I catch sight of Drew.

He's dancing on the opposite side of the dance floor with Natalia. He doesn't move half as well as Jake, but he kisses her temple and sways a bit. When they do a quarter turn, his focus lands on me. Like when he walked into the room tonight, he smirks.

I wish I could spit in his eye.

There's a reason he didn't lay out all his cards earlier. He knows he has the upper hand with me and is enjoying every second of it. Such an utter dick.

Jake slows and follows my line of sight. He doesn't ask again what happened with Drew, which I appreciate. He tightens his hold on me, making me feel safe, and another piece of my heart finds its way into his hands.

I turn my face into his chest, block out Drew and the other guests. Whatever song the band is playing is basically sex in instrument form. Seductive bass. Tight guitar. A raspy voice singing about hot nights and smooth skin. Jake may still be at war with himself over our relationship, or over his past mistakes. His body, however, isn't confused. There's no mistaking the bulge thickening against my stomach, the harsher pulls of his breath.

And I will not feel badly for orchestrating this dance.

We're too good together to leave us to chance. We're too good *for* each other. And he was clearly jealous of my talking with Anthony.

I lean into the moment, show him how well we move together. Chests pressed tight. Hips in sync. His thigh nudges between mine as we do a slow grind that drives me wild, but I need more. I tip up my face, let my nose drag under his strong jaw and into his beard. I tilt my hips just enough to put pressure on the thick line of his cock.

He grunts out a muffled curse.

"Too much?" I ask, even though I should enjoy his reaction. As per my seven-step seduction plan, I'm supposed to push his buttons, work him up, then leave him in a frenzied state, wanting more.

His nonverbal answer is to hold me tighter, his hand splayed possessively on my bare back, and my eyes burn.

I love you, I want to whisper. *So, so much.*

I want this man so intensely I'm nearly in tears over him on a dance floor at an asshole's pre-wedding party. But this isn't the place to confess how hard I've fallen for him. There's no way I'll make myself that vulnerable when he's on the fence about us.

At least he doesn't let me go.

One song bleeds into two. The third gets more upbeat. We keep dancing, not as close, but touching at all times. His hand is on my hip. Mine are on the wall of his chest. We still don't talk, but holy hell, can this man *move*. He hits every beat, his expression severe but sexy—slashed cheekbones, molten brown eyes, coiled muscles that know how to groove.

I should step away right now. Leave him wanting like the article suggested. But I can't. I'm not that strong. I stop in the middle of the song and cup his scruffy cheeks, hating how my hands tremble. He grips my wrists, his focus on my mouth absolute.

Yes, my mind chants. *Take what's yours.*

I close my eyes and tilt my head, waiting to feel his lips on mine, but nothing happens.

"Why do you have to be so perfect?" he asks, his voice strangled.

Slowly, I open my eyes and feel wrecked all over again. The only way to describe Jake's expression is devastated. "Why are you fighting this so hard? We're amazing together, Jake. *We're* perfect."

He opens his mouth, probably to list another reason why we can't be together, but he freezes and frowns. Instantly, he steps back and digs his phone from his pocket.

His expression turns from tortured to worried. "Desmond is here—outside. Something must be wrong. Sorry," he adds distractedly. "I'll be back soon."

He takes off, leaving me standing there alone. A feeling I should get used to. This stupid list isn't working. The mistakes from Jake's past have too strong of a hold on him and his conscience. All I'm doing is getting in deeper, when I should be shoring up my defenses and protecting my heart.

CHAPTER
Thirty-Four

Jake

I rush outside, my heart hammering in my throat. It's dark out, the area sparsely lit by the lights outside the inn. I don't see Des right away and start prowling through the parking lot.

He wouldn't show up at a wedding twenty-five minutes outside of Windfall unless something bad happened. Really fucking bad. Our father could have gotten involved with the cartel again. Or he did something to hurt Mom—wrote a sequel to the tell-all biography that will drag her through hell for the millionth time. Or something happened to one of our brothers. A car accident. A freak heart attack. Or…Jesus.

What if Mom had a stroke?

By the time I spot Des resting his ass on his truck's bumper with Sadie tucked under his arm, I'm nearing hyperventilation.

"What happened?" I have no clue how I sound so firm and normal. I'm a second from breaking down.

Des slides his attention to me, but he doesn't speak. That's when I notice more people huddled a short distance from his truck, talking quietly to one another. Callahan and Jolene. Lennon and Maggie. My fucking *mother* is here too. But I don't see E or Delilah.

No. Please God, *no*.

"E?" I ask, my frantic gaze darting over each of them. I don't sound firm or normal this time. My voice is shredded.

Just then, E's truck pulls into the lot. The second I confirm he's driving and Delilah's in the passenger seat, a rush of breath leaves my lungs. "What the hell is going on?"

"Olivia texted me," Desmond says.

I blink at him, unsure what Olivia has to do with my entire family turning up here.

Except...

That terrifying girl *did* take a picture of me earlier, while I struggled to talk with Larkin, when all I wanted to do was claim the woman who owns my fucking heart.

Not good.

The only reason Olivia would have texted Des would be to inform him of how messed-up I am. Which means this isn't a family emergency. This is a family intervention.

"I'm not sure what Olivia said, but that girl needs a time-out and some boundaries. There's nothing wrong with me, so you can all get in your trucks and go home." Avoiding my mother's scrutiny, I glare at each of my brothers, including E when he joins the group.

Desmond looks at his phone. "Olivia said, and I quote, 'Jake is a bigger mess than you were with Sadie. He's gonna hurt her. And himself. It's not pretty.'"

Goddamn that kid. I spin on my heel to head back inside. Olivia will be receiving a stern talking-to from me. Next time I see her, she'll also be getting the silent treatment.

Two steps away from my family, I hear, "Jake."

Mom's voice locks me in place. That's all it takes—my name spoken softly by her, and I'm turning back around.

Chelsea Bower looks more rested than I've seen her in ages. No dark circles cradle her eyes. Her gray-streaked brown hair is longer and loose. She's tanned from working in her garden and going for walks with her friends. She's flourished since moving back to Windfall, even making awful quilts again with her quilting group, but there's no missing the concern bracketing her mouth.

"Callahan brought us up to speed on what happened with Larkin and Hunter before WITSEC," she says. "And Jolene told us about Larkin's ex and why you're here. We know about Larkin's past and what she went through that awful night, and we're all worried about you, Jake. We know how hard you're still being on yourself about the incident."

I scowl at Cal. "Consider that the last time I ever confide in you. And you"—I give Jo a stern look—"I doubt Larkin will be happy you broke her trust."

She bites her lip but doesn't back down. "I'm doing what's right for both of you."

Cal gives me a sad smile. "If I was struggling, you'd do the same."

"You *did* do the same," Jolene adds.

I glare at her. "No, I fucking didn't."

She raises an eyebrow. "When Cal used Sandra to sell my building and have my business evicted, because he was worried I only kept the Barrel out of guilt—"

"Meddler." Lennon half coughs out the word through his hand.

Cal hangs his head.

Jolene shoots Lennon an unimpressed look. "Says the guy who forcefully suggested I move in to Cal's apartment when mine flooded."

"Are you upset about the outcome of that maneuver?"

Jolene beams up at Cal and takes his hand. "I am not."

Cal kisses the top of her head.

Maggie wraps her arm around Lennon and covers his mouth with her hand. "Y'all can continue now. I have him silenced." Except she yelps and scowls at her palm, then wipes it on Lennon's shirt. "Gross."

We all laugh, a coping mechanism I'm thankful for. No matter how messed up we are, my family knows how to lighten the mood.

"As I was saying," Jolene goes on, "you found me the night I ran out of Cal's home and told me about the secret things he did for me while you were all in Houston. You knew he didn't want me to know about that stuff, but you told me anyway. Why was that?"

I sigh and slump. "Because I hated seeing Cal so sad and knew you two were meant to be together."

"That's why we're here," E says, holding Delilah close. "We hate seeing you so sad. We know you and Larkin are the real deal."

"You don't understand." I shake my head while tearing at the back of my hair. "I visited her brother in jail. He told me to stay away from her and said some stuff that hit home. Made me promise I'd do what's best for Larkin."

"Staying away from Larkin is the opposite of what's best for her." Jolene sounds annoyed with me now. "Since when do you let someone else dictate your life?"

"Since I ruined his!" I drop my arms to my sides, breathing hard. "It's not even about Hunter. Not fully. Yeah, Larkin and I have serious feelings for each other, but eventually what I did will get between us. She'll resent me. I'll always be a reminder of what she went through—of what Hunter's still going through. Ending it now will be easier on her."

"No, it won't," Des says, terse. "It's easier on you."

"You think this awful feeling"—I jab at my chest and the unrelenting pain I can't shake—"is easier for *me*?"

He sucks his teeth. "Yep."

Sadie elbows his ribs. "Be nice."

"That was nice," he says with a kiss to her temple.

"Worst intervention in the history of interventions," I mutter. "I think we're done here."

But Delilah says, "He's right. I did the same thing with E."

Her quiet voice silences the rest of us. We know what happened when E vanished on her into witness protection, the emotional hell she went through and the physical repercussions.

"I didn't tell E what happened to me, because I thought he'd be better off not knowing. Then when I did tell him, I broke up with him, thinking the same thing as you—that he'd resent me down the road or we'd always remind each other of that awful time. But I was wrong, Jake." She presses her head under E's chin. "We're stronger together. We have hard days. Memories come back, but we talk through it and lean on each other, because we're a team. Larkin is your team."

I close my eyes and rub my forehead. She doesn't have to tell me Larkin is my person. I know how perfect we are together, dancing, talking, joking, making love so intensely I damn near black out. I want nothing more than to be Larkin's team, but they don't understand.

"I don't deserve her," I force out. "Not with the things I've done. I'll ruin it all eventually."

"Jake." Mom's hand is on my back, rubbing a soothing circle. "Something else is going on with you. We're your family, and we're worried. *I'm* worried. Why won't you let yourself be happy?"

"Because I don't deserve her," I repeat, breathing harder, glaring at the asphalt under my shoes.

"What happened with Hunter and Derek wasn't your fault," Mom says, not letting this slide. "You can't keep blaming yourself."

"I sure as hell can." My furious gaze flies up as my heart races. Everyone's frowning at me, looking confused and concerned. I don't want their worry. "I've done unforgivable things."

Mom blinks. There's no missing the moisture gathering in her eyes. "What is this, Jake? Tell us what's really going on. You're scaring me."

Jesus. Is this what I'm doing now? Scaring my mother and making her cry?

More self-reproach packs into my lungs, but what if saying this thing I've never said hurts them more? What if I lose the people I need most?

A lump rises in my throat, along with words I've kept buried for twelve years. Keeping them down is only doing damage. "I knew Dad was lying," I say, the words sounding choked.

Mom rears back, squinting at me. "What do you mean?"

I swallow and broaden my stance. I deserve every shot I'm about to take. "A couple months before the US Marshals turned up, I knew Dad had been lying."

"Lying about what, exactly?" Desmond is the exploder of the family. The one who punches and yells and disappeared on benders when he was at his worst. Right now, he sounds like the dangerous calm before a storm.

And I get it. Of all of us, he lost the most when our father ruined our lives. He put off proposing to Sadie. Since they weren't engaged, she couldn't come into witness protection with us. She didn't know why we left or where we went.

She couldn't contact Des when she discovered she was pregnant.

Desmond thought our father was solely to blame for the ten years he lost with his son, Max. I'm about to add myself to that unforgivable list.

I face my family, feeling like I've already lost them. "I caught Dad lying to Mom about traveling for work. I thought he was having an affair but never said anything to him or anyone. At the time, I thought I kept quiet because I wanted to find more proof first, make sure my suspicions were right, but that's not why I didn't tell you. I was going through my own shit, cared more about my life than everyone else's. Dealing with Dad seemed like a hassle, so I didn't do shit. And you all paid the price."

Desmond's resting I-hate-the-world face turns darker. A vein in his forehead bulges. He separates himself from Sadie and balls his hands into fists, looking like he wants to punch me. He spins around instead and jams his palms against his truck.

Sadie rushes over and cradles his back.

All I can do is sink. Internally, there's a landslide I can't control, a rush of helplessness and self-hatred that crashes so hard and fast, my knees nearly buckle.

Cal is in front of me, his huge hands clamped on my shoulders. "You didn't do this, Jake. Our father is the only one responsible for what happened to us."

I shake my head vehemently. "If I paid more attention, if I fucking *did something*, I might have figured out what he was up to. We would've had time to do damage control before we left. We wouldn't have vanished without everyone understanding why."

"And they all would've been in danger." The tender words come from Mom. "We left the way we did because it was safest for everyone, including the people we left behind."

I shake my head again. "You don't know that, and Sadie would have been with us. Des would have proposed."

"No, I wouldn't have." Des turns then, his expression still hard, but I can't tell if it's his usual glower or if he's plotting my murder. He runs his hand through Sadie's hair and cups the back of her neck. "I loved you so much, Sprite. Enough that I wouldn't have put you in danger—for any reason. Especially not for my own selfish need for you. So, no, if I'd known we had a cartel after us and were about to be tossed in witness protection, I wouldn't have proposed. I'd have ended things with you and left without a word. Anything to keep you safe. To make sure you had a full life, even if it was without me."

"Oh, Des." Sadie pulls his head down for a tender kiss. "I love you so much."

He presses his forehead to hers. "You're not mad about what I said?"

"Mad you loved me enough that you'd hurt yourself? No. But the way you stack the dishwasher is a different story. That definitely upsets me."

They share a smile that has the pressure on my chest lifting slightly.

Until Des turns his thick-lashed eyes on me. "Fuck you and this what-if bullshit. You didn't know Dad was laundering money. You didn't have a crystal ball to see into our future. You were a twenty-five-year-old guy getting by the way we all did, making mistakes and thinking about ourselves first. Thankfully, we've grown the fuck up since then. Trial by fire and all that, and you're the reason the rest of us are halfway sane. So, quit focusing on the few bad choices you made, and remember the ten million good ones. You deserve to be as happy as the rest of us."

Without thinking, I storm over to Des and pull him into a rough hug. Hold him so damn tight as I blink out a tear and try not to bawl on his massive shoulder. "I'm so fucking sorry, man."

"So am I. Wish I'd known you were struggling with this sooner."

He pounds my back, and more arms come around us. A crush of Bowers offering support in this messed-up life of ours. Maybe my nightmares are more bundled up in all of this than just my history with Larkin—feeling like I let my family down, manifesting as dreams where I can't save the people I love. Whatever the source, I breathe easier than I have in ages.

Eventually, we part, all of us discreetly wiping at our eyes.

Lennon smirks and lifts his phone. "In case anyone wants a copy, I recorded Desmond's speech. Posterity to commemorate the most consecutive words he's spoken since WITSEC."

Des snarls at him, whips out his phone, and snaps a photo of Lennon. "That's in case you want to remember what you look like before I rearrange your face."

Cal steps between them and makes a joke I don't listen to while the others laugh and rag on one another. My head is too overloaded to pay attention. I'm five steps ahead, figuring out how to undo the mess I've made of my life.

Mom comes over and brushes hair off my forehead like she used to do when I was a kid. "What are you going to do about Larkin?"

"What I should've done after meeting with Hunter." Quit beating myself up for past mistakes, imagined or real. Tell her no one will get in the way of our relationship, especially me. "I love her, Ma."

"Then go tell her. And if you're still struggling afterward, talk to me. Or your brothers. Or a counselor. Do whatever you need to make peace and live your best life."

"I will." I should also thank Olivia for texting Des, but fuck that. Olivia is best avoided at all costs. The only person I need to see right now is the woman who has a list of ways to murder me.

CHAPTER
Thirty-Five

LARKIN

I check my phone again and frown. Still no word from Jake. I've been a wallflower since he left. A fixture next to a landscape painting against this old stone wall. I've debated returning to our room and going to sleep, maybe take one of those cold-medication pills I keep in my toiletry bag. Pass out so I don't have to deal with the pain of lying next to a man I love but can't have.

As appealing as that option is, I don't like the way Jake tore of out here. Desmond wouldn't turn up unless something was wrong. I still care about Jake too much to take off without making sure he's okay. A feeling I'm guessing I won't shake for a long while, judging by the jump of my heart every time someone walks into the room.

I pull my phone from my purse again, debate calling Jake.

"Seems your fiancé left you in the lurch." Drew's smarmy voice has my gag reflex kicking in. "Maybe my first guess was right and you two are playing engaged for my benefit."

I return my cell to my purse and give him my blandest face. "Jake had a family emergency he's dealing with."

"That's unfortunate."

"It is."

"He's been gone a while, and you keep checking your phone. It's not very considerate of him to leave you worried like this."

Damn him for being so observant. "I'm sure he has his reasons."

Drew *humphs*, and I bristle. When we were together, he used to make that sound a lot, especially after I confided in him about my past. He'd ask if I visited Hunter in jail out of guilt. I'd say no, that I loved him and worried about him, and he'd *humph*. He'd ask if Derek was like my father, suggesting that was why I dated him. *Daddy issues.* I'd reply with an irritated *I don't know*, because I didn't, and he'd *humph*.

I understand now that I was a curiosity to him. A subject to observe. Or he was projecting his daddy issues onto me. Whatever his motivations, I'm so done with his air of superiority.

Yes, I have issues. Yes, I've done work over the years to better understand myself and my choices. Do I still have miles of self-improvement work to do? Sure. But who doesn't? Everyone gets help at the pace that suits them, and this asshole has no right to judge me.

"We need to have a word in private," I tell him, already on the move. I don't check that he's following me. Curiosity will no doubt string him along. I march toward a separate conference room with outdoor access.

When I'm far enough inside, I spin around and cross my arms. "I'm not staying for the wedding tomorrow. You clearly need something from me. Spit it out now, so we can get on with your blackmailing."

"Again with that crass word."

"Do you prefer extortion?"

His lips pinch. "Natalia has been planning to open a brewpub for some time."

Relief has my nerves unwinding. She must need business advice. I don't know why Drew would come to me instead of paying an adviser. He certainly has the cash. But if helping her means Hunter gets out of jail, I'll lick her manicured feet. "I can help her with whatever she needs—supplier names, promotional ideas, staffing insights. If you push to have Hunter released, I'll do whatever she wants."

"Wonderful to hear, because what she wants is the Barrel."

I almost swallow my tongue. "Come again?"

Drew dusts a piece of lint off his arm. "As I'm sure you know, the owner of your building wanted to sell it earlier this year. Natalia had been looking for the right space and loved the idea of opening near her hometown, which isn't too far from Windfall. When she saw the Barrel House, she fell in love, and we were told the current tenants didn't have a lease and could be evicted. So, we offered to buy the real estate with the expectation that Natalia would open her brewpub in the location. Then the deal got ripped away from us, and Natalia was devastated."

His assessing gaze sharpens into a gleam. "Imagine my surprise when I did some research and discovered *you* had bought in to the Barrel with your friend, and that your brother now owns the building."

Trepidation slowly slithers around my neck. Callahan was the catalyst that set that stupid scheme in motion, not Jo's landlord. He was convinced Jolene hated the bar but was too beholden to her late aunt to leave the business. But all Jo needed was me. Someone to share the burden of broken equipment and staffing issues. A partner who could help implement changes, plan for growth. Jo is amazing with people and ideas. I'm great with big-picture changes and numbers and promotion. We are a dynamic team, and I'd never, in a million years, screw over my best friend.

"I'm not sure what you think I can do here. I'm only a part owner. And my brother owns the building, not me."

Drew shrugs. "I guess it depends how important Hunter is to you. You could convince your brother to sell us the building. You could then accidentally not pay me your rent so that I can evict you. A simple error, and Jolene never has to be the wiser. It's really not that hard."

"Are you fucking serious? Hunter has been in jail for twelve years because he *saved my life*. You know he didn't hit Derek with that pipe because he was owed money. You know he was only there because I called him to come. How could you even think of punishing him so your wife could open a fucking pub?"

His slow blink brims with condescension. "When you truly love someone, you want to give them the world."

No. Drew was born with a silver spoon in his mouth and a tycoon for a father. He's simply used to getting whatever he wants, by any means necessary.

My pulse pounds in my temples. My hands shake. This must be why Natalia said the Barrel held bad memories. She was upset she'd lost her chance to take over the space. I grip my purse tighter and try to think, but there's no way out of this without ruining someone's life—Jolene's, Hunter's, mine.

I need time to plan. Figure out how to turn the tables on Drew, if that's even possible. "I'll think about it," I say and head for the door.

He grabs my upper arm. "No."

I glare at him. "Get your hands off me."

He grips me tighter. Painfully tight. "You'll decide now. Tomorrow is my wedding, and I plan to tell Natalia about her special gift."

CHAPTER
Thirty-Six

Jake

Larkin isn't here. The band is loud, playing a version of "Stand by Me" that has half the room singing along. I scan the dance floor, the bar, the clusters of chatting guests rimming the room, my gut sinking with each passing second. Of course Larkin left. She probably went up to our room. Or she got herself a different room. Or she plans to sleep outside, far away from me.

It's going to take more than an apology to set things right with us. I'll wear that damn furry onesie daily, if that's what it takes.

"You look more desperate than tortured now." Olivia meanders up to me, full of lordliness, like she's the duchess of these lands.

"Shouldn't you be pestering your mother? My life is none of your business."

"Actually, it is. Des knew my mom and I would be here tonight. He told me to watch out for you."

Of course he did. "I've got things under control now."

"Does that mean you know Larkin's ex was making her uncomfortable and they disappeared into the conference room, where they've been for"—she checks her phone—"five minutes and thirty-seven seconds?"

I don't thank Olivia for that intel or ask for more details. I shove past a group of laughing guests and beeline for the door in question, anger building with each step. There's something up with that guy. His superior looks and haughty attitude are more than posturing. He reeks of deceit, the kind someone exudes when they have a plan in play.

One step into the conference room, I see red. More specifically, Drew's goddamn hand holding Larkin's arm aggressively.

She tries to yank away, saying, "Okay. Fine. You can have what you want. Just let me go already."

Not okay or fine.

I rush the asshole, my arm pulled back, and punch him square in the face.

Blood gushes from his nose. He goes down.

Ignoring Drew's groan, I spin and reach for Larkin, checking over every inch of her. "Are you hurt? Did he hurt you?"

She shoves me back, fury in her eyes. "What the fuck did you just do?"

"What did *I* do?" Not nearly enough, as far as I'm concerned. "He had his hands on you, Larkin."

"And he was about to leave. Drew and I have an agreement."

A ball of dread hardens in my stomach. "What kind of agreement?"

"Absolutely none now." Drew slowly pulls himself to his feet. He has a white handkerchief pressed to his bloody nose and murder in his eyes. "Consider the deal off."

"Drew, no." Larkin holds up her palms, like the move will stop this guy from being a creep. "I'm so sorry. *Jake* is sorry. It was a misunderstanding."

Drew scoffs. "You're clearly still attracted to controlling, aggressive men, which is why you weren't happy with me. You didn't know what to do with a healthy relationship."

"A *healthy* relationship?" Larkin's cold tone could douse a wildfire. "If you think stomping on my self-confidence to make yourself feel superior was healthy, someone should revoke your psychiatric license."

Drew curls his lip. "And you should—"

"Shut the fuck up," I say, cutting him off. I'm done giving this prick airtime. "The only one being aggressive with her was *you*."

He shrugs. "It's the only language Larkin and her family know."

I curl my hand into another fist. It's like he *wants* to swallow his teeth.

Larkin jumps in front of me, her hands still up in supplication. "Please, Drew. None of this was Hunter's fault. He shouldn't be punished for our mistakes. If the bar is what you want, it's yours."

A vein in my head throbs. "What the fuck does that mean?"

She shoots me a lethal look.

Drew laughs. "Like I said, deal's off."

"If you don't handle Hunter's case fairly," Larkin says, her voice injected with more iron, "I'll lodge a complaint with the Parole Commission. I'll tell them you were biased and hurt Hunter to get at me."

Drew smirks from behind the bloody handkerchief. "Will you also mention you were there the night Derek was killed? If not, I could tell them you recently shared that tidbit while drunk at your bar. If it's your word against that of a successful psychiatrist, I wonder who they'll believe? They might consider reopening the case. Maybe decide Otto Briggs's other kid should be behind bars too."

She freezes. "You wouldn't."

"Don't give me a reason to. And I suggest you get off the property before I have someone throw you out."

He walks out the far door that leads to the outside grounds, his head held high, like he's the winner here, but I don't know what sick game he's been playing with Larkin. All I know is the woman I love looks like she's been punched in the gut.

She plants her palms on the conference table and drops her head forward. "Fuck."

I flex the hand I used to punch Drew and approach her slowly. "Larkin, sweetheart. What the hell just happened?"

She swivels, and I take a step back. Her eyes are red and watery, infused with fury. "You knew I needed to work Drew. You knew we were here so I could convince him to go easy on Hunter. Then you barge in here, have no clue what's going on, and punch the guy in the face."

"He had his hands on you. There is no world in which I'm okay with that."

"The only thing that's not okay is the fact that Hunter is going to spend another three years in jail. *Three years*, Jake. He's already a shadow of the man he was. This will kill the rest of him."

Goddamn it.

I pace, jamming my hand through my hair as I picture Hunter in jail, how beaten down and drawn he seemed under his anger. Yeah, this might be the last straw that breaks him.

"What was the deal?" I ask, breathing harder.

She may have forgiven me for not answering her call. She no longer blames me for Hunter's arrest, but she'll blame me for this, as she should. All I did when I stormed in here was react. I didn't think for a goddamn second.

She rubs her brow. "Remember when Cal thought Jolene hated the bar and found a buyer who could evict her because of her lack of lease?"

"Yeah," I say slowly.

"Drew's future wife is the person who wanted to buy the building and open a brewpub. Now he wants to give it to her as his wedding gift. He said he'd recommend Hunter's release *if* I convince my brother to sell him the bar and then default on rent so they can evict us."

"You can't give him your fucking bar."

"I know that."

"But you told him he could have what he wanted."

"To buy myself time! Right now, it's just words. Drew's father was a self-made man who earned his fortune by viciously overtaking companies by any means necessary. Drew may not have joined his father's business, but he has the same God complex. He takes what he wants because he feels entitled. He likes the challenge of acquiring something out of reach. Me, at the time. The bar now, which I only learned right before you came barreling in here. So I agreed to his demands to give myself time to figure this out and change Drew's mind or find a way to turn the tables on him."

She glares at me, her chin trembling.

I resume pacing. Try to think through this mess. I don't get far, not with how angry and upset I am, and how little sleep I've had. Larkin was right to temporarily agree to Drew's outrageous demands. Currently, I'm not rational enough to think my way out of a paper bag.

"We still have time," I say, my voice coming out rough. "We'll figure this out. Let's get out of here and get some sleep, then regroup tomorrow. We'll get through this together."

"Together?" She gestures from me to her. "There is no *together*, Jake. You made that perfectly clear before this weekend, and when you came storming in here to fuck everything up. You never intended to give us a real chance. You're still too selfish to put someone else's feelings before your own. The only help I need from you is for you to stay away from me."

She pulls off her engagement ring, drops it on the table, and rushes out of the room.

"Fuck." I kick the closest chair to me, barely refraining from punching the wall with my already-sore hand.

I want to run after Larkin, finally tell her I love her. Apologize for pushing her away and beg her to put that ring back on, but now's not the time. Not like this, after I fucked everything up. But no way in hell will I let her deal with Drew on her own.

I put the ring in my pocket, pull out my phone, and dial.

Callahan answers swiftly. "Do you need us to come back? We're still driving and can turn around."

"I don't need you here," I say, so damn thankful for my brothers—asking Olivia to spy on me, turning up for an intervention, willing to come wherever and whenever they're needed. "What I need is help with a delicate situation."

"Cal doesn't meddle anymore," Jolene says through their Bluetooth speaker.

"Unless asked," he says over her. "It's not interfering if it's requested."

"Since you're partly to blame," I say, "it's more of a you-owe-me situation. Actually, it's Larkin you owe." I explain about Drew's blackmailing, the brewpub his wife wants to open, thanks to Cal's meddling, making it clear Larkin had no intention of actually screwing Jolene over.

"Of course she wouldn't do that," Jo says. "Larkin would never hurt me or sell the bar. But I'm pretty darn furious at her asshole ex."

"I think I broke his nose, if that helps."

"Barely," Jolene mumbles. "But what can we do? He said the deal's off. From the sounds of things, he wants to hurt Larkin through Hunter."

I flex my hand, furious with myself and with Drew. "Based on Larkin's description of him, I'd bet this isn't the first time he's blackmailed someone to get what he wants, or at least colored outside the lines legally."

Cal and Jolene are quiet, all of us parsing through this disaster.

Then Callahan says, "This calls for Sandra. If there's dirt on Drew, she'll find it."

I nod, feeling the first bit of hope since I barged into this room. Cal may have cut ties with Sandra when he vowed to quit trying to control the outcome of our lives, but his former spy has proved her skills over the years—keeping tabs on our brothers when they returned to town before us, alerting Cal to trouble with Jolene and others he cared about. Odds are high that Drew has skeletons in his closet. We just have to find them.

"Don't tell Larkin yet," I say. "I don't want to get her hopes up only to let her down. And thanks for being there for me."

"Thanks for asking for help," Cal says. "We're here for you, always."

A support system I should've leaned on years ago.

I hang up and trudge upstairs, not surprised to find Larkin's belongings gone and a note on the dresser.

I got an Uber to take me home.

I'm thankful she let me know she's getting home safe, but I already miss her. I can't imagine spending a lifetime without kissing her again. I hate that our last days together were spent with me fighting our undeniable connection.

I am such a fucking moron.

Sandra might be able to help us get at Drew, but she can't help me fix what I broke with Larkin. I look at the pretty room, that four-poster bed.

I know you won't tie me up and have your way with me this weekend. I guess I still feel safe enough to share my secrets with you.

A knot forms in my throat.

Larkin shared her fantasies with me, because she trusted me. She could picture losing control with *me*—a man she openly loved, even if she never said the words. There's no other interpretation of her admission. And I ruined everything.

Furious with myself all over again, I toss her note in the wastebasket, but my attention snags on a crumpled piece of paper beside it. I pick it up and unfurl the page, frowning at the odd title.

7 Steps to Seducing Your ~~Best Friend~~ Fake Fiancé

I read the listed points, my confusion turning to understanding as I go.

1. Try a new hairstyle or outfit to make him see you in a different light.
2. Do something new together that puts you in close proximity.
3. Make him jealous without going too far.
4. Tell him your deepest fantasies to fill his head with images of you.
5. Use touch to communicate your true emotion.
6. Leave him wanting more by giving him a tease of intimacy and walking away.
7. Be vulnerable to earn his trust.

I have no idea when Larkin printed this list, but I'd wager it was after I told her I wanted to take a break and before we left for this shitshow of a weekend. The first five points have checkmarks next to them—the new hair tonight, dragging me onto the dance floor, chatting with her hairstylist's husband in plain view of me, touching me at every chance, driving me wild with her shared fantasy.

I'd bet my family intervention got in the way of points six and seven, but the rest? Her wanting me so badly she thought this list would help win me over?

Fuck, do I love her. So much my chest feels like it's in pieces.

I need to plan my apology better. Not just blurt my feelings and hope she opens her heart back up. She was willing to fight for me, and I need to do the same. Not just tell her. Show her. Finish her list. At least, step seven. I have no intention of working Larkin up and leaving her wanting, but I can be vulnerable with her. True honesty for the first time, after Sandra comes through with her end of this plan.

If Sandra can't find dirt on Drew and Hunter spends another three years in jail, there will be no mending what I broke.

CHAPTER
Thirty-Seven

L<small>ARKIN</small>

I stare through my car's windshield, unable to move. I've been to Langmore Penitentiary more times than I can count. Twelve years of visits. Weekly when I lived close enough. More sporadic when I was away. I'd send letters during those years, making sure Hunter knew he had someone who thought about him and loved him. Now I have to tell him he needs to spend another three years in this hellhole.

I rub my eyes. They feel gritty from the past nine days of little sleep and my raw emotions.

I spoke to Jesse the day after that debacle with Drew, but our lawyer warned me lodging a complaint against Drew could do more damage than good. It would be my word against Drew's, as Drew had threatened. The courts would never side with the daughter of Otto Briggs.

I confided in Jolene about Jake and Drew and his threats regarding the bar. She didn't seem as shocked as I'd imagined and said she'd think on how she could help. So far, she's had as much luck as me. Namely, none.

Sighing through my building headache, I get out of my car and lock the door. I check the handle as usual…and freeze. The handle doesn't creak the way it does when I tug on it. The tension is snug, not loose.

Jake, I think in a rush.

There's no other explanation. No one else would anonymously fix my car handle, and something behind my ribs twists. Why does he have to be so sweet? Why does my past keep ruining the good things in my life?

My phone rings, cutting through my pity party. I catch Jolene's name on the screen and answer quickly. "Hey," I say, trying to sound like I'm halfway together.

"What's wrong? You sound off."

I guess I can't hide anything from my best friend. "Hunter. Jake. Take your pick." My messed-up life.

"Well, I have news on both fronts."

My spine straightens. "What kind of news?"

"First, promise you won't be mad."

"If you're about to tell me we have a way to shut Drew up and free Hunter, I won't care if you sold my soul to the devil."

She pauses a moment. "We didn't go that far, and I don't have concrete news yet, but I've known things this week I haven't told you."

"Considering I hid my family history from you for almost a year, let's call us even."

"Okay," she says, sounding more relaxed. "It's about Jake."

My low-grade headache gives a deeper twinge. I'm still angry at Jake for punching Drew, but in the aftermath of that adrenaline-filled night, I understand he was only protecting me. I'm glad he was there. I felt unsafe with Drew, but Jake hasn't once fought for my heart. He hasn't told me he loved me or put his heart on the line. His last concrete words about our relationship were that he wanted us to take time apart.

His continued silence since then has left me wrung out and sad. Especially since everything in my home reminds me of him —the couch he fixed, where we had sex, the chair he fixed, on which we also had sex, along with every other flat surface in my place. He's in the light that glows with warmth when I come home late, ensuring my safety. He's in my heart every time I take a breath and it contracts painfully.

Now he's in my freaking car door handle.

"What about him?" I ask Jo cautiously.

"Jake called Cal and me from the wedding. He was upset, desperate to help you any way he could. So, we hired Sandra, who used to work for Cal, and she found dirt on Drew—a bribe he paid to a permit officer. I don't know the details, but Jake is waiting for her to send him evidence, so he can confront Drew and force him to recommend Hunter for release."

My mind whirs as I struggle to digest all this news. "Did you just say Jake is planning to reverse-blackmail Drew to get Hunter out of jail?"

"That about sums it up."

"Why isn't Jake telling me himself? And why didn't anyone tell me this was going on? Not that I'm mad," I add. *Beyond thankful* is a more accurate description of my current feelings.

"Jake didn't want to get your hopes up, and I agreed. We weren't sure we'd find dirt on Drew or that it would be enough to sway him. Sandra did find something, but she's taking longer than expected to pass along the evidence, which is why I'm calling now. We didn't want you going into Langmore and giving Hunter unnecessary bad news.

"As for Jake not being the one to tell you"—her tone gentles the way it does when she gives me advice—"I think he's worried you'll think it's a stunt to win you back, when he's just trying to undo the damage he caused. He's planning to blackmail Drew because it's the right thing to do in a weird way, but he knows he has to work harder to re-earn your trust."

I squeeze my eyes shut and send up a silent prayer that Jake's stunt works. "Do you think Sandra's evidence will be enough to manipulate Drew?"

"Like I said, I don't know all the details, but Jake feels confident."

Hunter, nearly free. Jake, scheming to help my brother. My head is even more jumbled than before. "I can't believe Jake's been planning all this. I assumed he was relieved we broke up and would steer clear of me."

"Oh, honey." Her words sound like a warm hug. "Remember how torn up Cal was when I very temporarily broke up with him?"

"Yeah." I didn't see Cal during that time, but I heard he almost started a brawl with Jake at his mother's welcome-home party. All because he was devastated over losing Jo.

"Jake is even worse," she says. "I hope you give him a chance to prove how much he cares about you."

"I miss him so much," I say on a shaky breath, strangely nervous. Ever since Jake visited Hunter and pushed me away, I've wanted him to fight for me, but Jolene's admission has me feeling suddenly anxious. "I think about him constantly, but I was cruel at the wedding. I called him selfish and tossed his ring on the table. He might not be as forgiving as you think, and I think I'm maybe a bit of a hot mess."

"Aren't we all?"

"But what if I hurt Jake again down the line? Lash out at him instead of having a reasonable conversation? I think I yelled at him because it was easier hurting him than accepting that Hunter might stay in prison. Like, I still blame myself for everything my brother's been through, even though, logically, I know it's not all my fault."

"You probably will," Jo says kindly.

"I will what?"

"Lash out at Jake and have fights. Relationships aren't perfect, and you two have an intense history, but some people are worth fighting for. They're worth fighting *with*. Is Jake that person for you?"

This answer comes without a second thought. "He is."

"Then take a breath and trust yourself. Trust that Jake will find his way too and fight for you. And I have no doubt Sandra will come through with the evidence we need."

Life has never been that kind to me, but I cling to Jo's positivity and hope she's right.

CHAPTER
Thirty-Eight

Jake

I'm still a fucking wreck. I haven't seen or spoken with Larkin in nine days. My sleeping is still shit. I can't quit thinking about her. Missing her. Wishing she was pressed against my chest as we talked about our days. I live with a constant scratch in my throat and hollow in my stomach. If I didn't know I loved her before, I sure as shit do now.

And I will not fail her.

I've been sitting in my truck for fifteen minutes, checking my phone constantly for the intel Sandra promised to send.

Still nothing, and I curse. Time is not on my side.

Thanks to Jolene, I know Larkin arranged a visit with her brother today. Larkin probably begged and pleaded for him to agree to the meeting, so she could tell him he has to endure another three years in prison. Her visit starts at 12:30 p.m., but she goes in early to walk through the metal detector and get patted down. That only leaves me about ten minutes to undo the damage I caused, *if* Sandra gets the evidence against Drew she was hoping to find.

Two minutes before I punch my windshield, my phone pings.

> Sandra: Sent you screenshots in an email.

I quickly tap on my email icon and open her attachment. *Fuck yes.*

> Me: Thank you.

> Sandra: If you Bowers would quit making messes of your lives, you wouldn't need me.

She's right about that. Partly.

> Me: We'd still need you. You're an honorary Bower now.

I don't get a reply, but the second I leave my truck, my phone pings again.

> Sandra: Your family is the only real family I've ever had.

> Sandra: And don't you dare mess up the blackmailing.

Touched by her admission, I jog to Drew's Porsche, feeling more in control. He's at his first day of work after returning from his honeymoon. Based on his office hours and Sandra's sleuthing, he heads out for lunch every day at noon.

I pace by his Porsche and check the time on my phone. He's four minutes late, which isn't good. Just as I'm about to bust through the back entrance and into his office, the slick asshole appears. He walks down the stairs and nods to a man he must know. They smile at each other and talk briefly, then Drew's on the move again, the corner of his lips lifted, clueless to the fact that he's about to have a very uncomfortable conversation.

He fishes his keys from his pocket, looks at his posh car...and jerks to a stop.

"We have security in the building," he says. His face is tanned from his Jamaican honeymoon, but there's no missing the slight paling of his skin. Or the bruises still there from his broken nose.

I step toward him, enjoying how he flinches. "No need for security. This won't take long."

His posture shifts from stiff to aloof. "Word of warning—the second you're not useful to Larkin, she'll drop you and move on. Fighting her battles for her won't change her nature."

"Her nature is to be thoughtful and kind and hardworking, so I'm happy it won't change. And I'm glad you haven't changed much over the years either. It wasn't tough to learn that you bribed city officials when building your fancy house in the suburbs. That was a lot of money given to a permit officer to jump the line and have them sign off on more square footage than the lot limit allowed." All done so he could have the largest home on the block.

He snaps his jaw shut, and his nostrils flare. "So you claim."

"I also have proof of a money trail." I flip my phone toward him and show him the screenshot. I don't know how Sandra hacked into computer systems for this evidence. Woman is nothing if not resourceful.

Drew's answering glower barely covers the fear in his eyes.

I grin really fucking wide. "Unless you want the cops slapping you in cuffs while I video the moment, I suggest you do everything in your power to have Hunter released on parole."

His eyes darken. "Larkin won't stay with you."

"Not why I'm doing this." The only thing that matters at the moment is getting her brother out of jail.

"Whatever," Drew says, acting like he suddenly doesn't give a shit about Larkin or the dirt I have on him. I don't buy it. Drew Carrington probably has access to ruthless lawyers who'd get him off this charge, but reputation is too important to snobs like him to risk the scandal. "I'll be thrilled to be done with Hunter and his whole degenerate family," Drew goes on. "Consider him free. Now get out of my way."

I want to punch the air or punch him. I settle on copying his condescending smirk. "If you ever contact Larkin again or show up in Windfall, you'll have to deal with me, and you'll be begging for just a broken nose."

I strut away from him, pulse revving.

Putting Drew in his place felt good. Fixing this problem for Larkin was the most important thing I needed to accomplish, but I plan to fight tooth and nail for her too. Prove we're meant to be.

Taking a deep breath, I pull out my phone to text her.

CHAPTER
Thirty-Nine

L ARKIN

I clutch my phone, pacing a frantic line beside my car. Jake should have messaged by now. He knows the prison keeps strict visiting hours, and I can't cancel on Hunter. If I don't show up for his visit, he'll be upset and worried about me. If I do go in, I'll have to be honest and tell him about Jake and the potential blackmail, give him hope that might be dashed.

A startling buzz has me nearly dropping my cell.

My belly riots at the sight of Jake's name, but now is not the time to focus on me.

Forcing a swallow, I tap on his text.

> Jake: It's done. You don't have to worry about Drew anymore. He'll be recommending Hunter for release.

I drop to a crouch, covering my eyes as a wave of emotion flows through me. My hands shake. My whole body trembles. I never thought this day would come.

When I'm a bit more under control, I wipe my cheeks and stand, then reply to Jake.

> Me: I can't thank you enough.

> Jake: I don't need your thanks. I did what needed to be done. And I'm sorry I didn't call you myself to fill you in. Thought it was better for Jo to do it. I know talking to me would be tough with all you have going on. I wanted you to stay focused on seeing Hunter.

There Jake goes again, being unbearably thoughtful.

> Me: You're right, and I appreciate it.

His dots bounce and stop. Bounce and stop, like he's nervous and overwhelmed too. Like he maybe misses me as much as I miss him, as Jolene said.

> Jake: Can you meet me when you're done? I'll text you where and won't take much of your time.

Part of me wants to call him. Hash out why he pushed me away, why he's working so hard to help me now. Confronting Drew could have backfired on him. Drew is conniving enough to sabotage Jake's business, ruin his reputation somehow. But Jake didn't hesitate to help me.

I can't be sure what all this means. I'm scared to put too much hope in Jake's actions, think about a future with this man I love, only to be disappointed. I could call him now and clear this up, but he's right about my mental headspace. Seeing Hunter always takes an emotional toll on me. If Jake is only trying to do the right thing for his head, not his heart, I won't be able to hold it together for Hunter.

My reply to Jake is simple, even if my emotions are anything but.

> Me: OK. I'll meet you after.

I inflate my lungs fully and slowly let the air hiss out, along with a portion of the dread I've been holding. For the first time in twelve years, I have good news for Hunter.

————

Hunter files into the visiting room but avoids my eyes.

Convincing him to see me again was easier than expected. If I had to guess, I'd say he feels guilty that he threatened Jake and interfered with my life. Or maybe he's lonely. He's definitely more haggard-looking, more vacancy in his deep-set eyes.

He folds himself onto his seat and keeps his hands on his lap. He focuses on my hair. "Dark suits you."

"Thanks. You, on the other hand, look like crap."

The smallest smile tilts his lips. "Good to see you too."

Hunter always liked that I didn't treat him with kid gloves in here, but my concern is real. About him and our relationship. "Is it *actually* good to see me?"

He blows out a breath and rubs his brow. "If you're here to give me shit about Jake, just know that what I did was for you—to protect you from a selfish guy who only cares about himself. He would've shown his true colors sooner or later, and I'm tired of being stuck in here, unable to protect you."

If he weren't locked in here, I'd give him hell for overstepping. Instead, I aim for a calm but forceful tone. "I'm an adult now, Hunter. I have to learn from my own mistakes. *And*," I add when he looks about to dig his grave deeper, "you *are* in here. Which means you haven't had the chance to get to know Jake, outside of the hate I used to spew about him. You don't know he's gone out of his way to make sure my rental house is safe. You don't know he does things like fix parts of my car without even telling me. You don't know he punched Drew when he was getting rough with me, or that Drew was trying to blackmail me, using your future to get something he wants. And you don't know Jake risked his reputation to turn the tables on Drew and ensure your early release."

Hunter blinks, barely reacting to my word vomit. I, on the other hand, am breathing way too fast, wishing so hard I could reach under the table and grab Hunter's hand, give it a reassuring squeeze.

He looks utterly stunned.

"Hunter?" I say softly. "Are you okay?"

His next blink is faster. His huge chest swells. "How sure are you I'll get out?"

"Ninety percent? According to Jesse, the space situation here is pretty dire. If the psychiatric eval is strong, they should overlook your previous behavior."

He closes his eyes, his jaw looking like a steel trap.

Sensing he needs a moment of quiet, I glance around the room. A woman around my age is sitting across from a prisoner who shares her features. His sister, if I had to guess. She looks unbearably sad, and I instantly feel for her. Living inside these bleak walls is hell. Living outside of them, knowing your family is suffering in here, isn't fun either.

Tentatively, I revert my attention to Hunter. The veins on his arms stand out under his taupe T-shirt, like his hands below the table are squeezed into fists. "I'm so fucking scared to hope," he whispers.

"I know. I'm scared too. But from what I understand, Drew doesn't have much choice but to push for your release now."

His dark eyes flick up to me. "What was he blackmailing you with?"

"The bar. It's a long story that started before I bought in, but his new wife wanted the location for a brewpub. He thought I'd convince Julian to sell him the building in trade for your release, and that I'd default on rent so he could evict us without Jolene knowing."

A thundercloud blows across his face. "That fucking piece of shit."

"Understatement."

"And he was rough with you?"

I wave off his worry, even though there was nothing okay about Drew's actions that night. "He just grabbed my arm, but Jake showed up and got things under control."

"Fuck." Hunter drops his head and runs his hands over his shaved scalp. When he looks back up, something in his eyes looks vulnerable, younger. "I'm sorry you got in the middle of this."

"I'm not. We got exactly what we needed from Drew."

He nods and rolls his jaw. "Jake told you what I said to him, then?"

"No. He told me not to ask him. He said he made a promise to you, but the way he acted after his visit here wasn't hard to interpret. He pushed me away, Hunter. He broke my heart to do what he thought was the right thing, but it wasn't. Not for him and certainly not for me. I'm not sure Jake and I can repair our relationship, but I'm willing to try with him. I'd love your blessing where he's concerned. Your opinion means the world to me, but I don't need your approval. No matter what you think, I'm following my heart with him."

He watches me carefully. "Do you trust him with *my* heart?"

I startle. "What does your heart have to do with this?"

"That's what you are to me, Runt. My goddamn heart. You're the only reason I've survived this place—your visits, you reminding me again and again there's goodness in this world. If he breaks your heart, he breaks mine. So do you trust him with *my* fucking heart?"

Just when I thought my brother had hardened too much in here. I lean forward and soften my eyes, hoping he feels the hug I want to give him. "I trust Jake with both our hearts."

A bigger smile softens his harsh jaw. "Then he has my blessing. But I'll still fucking kill him if he hurts you."

I let out a watery laugh. "Of course you will."

CHAPTER
Forty

LARKIN

I drive to the address Jake texted me, unsure why I'm on a sparsely inhabited street at the edge of town. Properties are larger out here. Instead of colorful Victorian homes, the houses are smaller, some in disrepair, others outdated but well tended. My GPS tells me to stop in front of a red-brick bungalow that's seen better days.

Weeds poke through the driveway. Chunks of brick are missing, and the trees on the unkempt lawn look sickly. Jake's truck is parked out front. I don't see him, but the second I step out of my car, the house door opens and he appears in the frame.

I haven't seen him in nine days—an eternity in a town the size of Windfall—but it feels more like nine years. There are darker smudges under his eyes, like he hasn't been sleeping much, and his brown hair is tousled as though he's been running his fingers through it. He's wearing his usual uniform of worn jeans and a Henley that clings to his thick arms.

An involuntary sigh escapes me.

He approaches me with long strides and an intent expression I can't decipher.

He stops a foot from me, swallowing hard. "Thanks for coming."

"I can't believe you blackmailed Drew."

A small smile tilts his lips. "It was easier than expected since I had all that experience blackmailing you."

I laugh, but there isn't much heart in it. Not when my actual heart is hovering close to my throat. "I assume he didn't go down without a fight."

"He actually didn't push back much. He cared more about his reputation than hurting you."

"Sounds on-brand."

He gnaws at his lower lip as his eyes gently roam around my face. "It's over now. Drew won't bother you again, and he'll make sure Hunter gets out. I'm just sorry about what he put you through."

"*I'm* sorry I got so mad at you for punching him. It was just a lot at once, and I was reeling over his threats. Worried about Hunter and—"

"Larkin?" he says quietly, cutting off my babbling.

I try to locate saliva. "Yeah?"

"Please don't apologize. I don't regret hitting Drew, but I regret how it happened. I could've simply gotten between you two, asked questions before reacting. It was wrong of me to go off like that."

I nod, fighting the urge to wrap my arms around him and breathe him in. To feel safe and protected in his embrace.

"How's Hunter?" he asks.

"Better by the end of our visit. If he doesn't get released, it'll be rough, but we're both feeling optimistic, thanks to you."

His wide shoulders relax. "I'm glad."

Silence settles between us. When it drags on, I gesture to the house. "Who lives here?"

He rocks on his heels, then holds out his hand. "Mind coming inside for a sec?"

"Sure," I say, even though he avoided the question. "But if your brothers are in there with booby traps and stuff, you're all banned from the bar."

His crooked smile sets my belly spinning. "Noted, and my brothers are nowhere near here."

I take his hand, and he lets out a breathy grunt. *Feeling is mutual.*

Inside, there's no furniture. The living area is small and walled in, with a brick fireplace at the side. Drywall is cracked in places. The ceiling has watermarks in the middle. "If this place is haunted," I say, "you also get banned from the bar."

His eyes glint with humor. "Not haunted."

"Infested with zombies?"

"Only in the attic."

Still jittery about where we stand, my jokes dry up. "Why are we here, Jake?"

I'm not sure if he hears the bigger question in my words. *Are we okay? Are you finally ready to open your heart?*

Instead of replying, he leads me into the old kitchen, complete with khaki-green appliances, but he still doesn't speak. There's one chair in the adjoining dining room. Unlike everything else in here, this chair is old in an appealing way. The frame is red and covered with painted flowers. The worn seat is woven with rattan. It's not in tip-top shape, but it has so much personality, I already feel proprietary toward it.

"Please sit," Jake says, his voice less sure.

Confused by all of this, I sit as requested.

Jake rubs his hands down his jeans, then he tugs at the back of his hair the way he does when he's overthinking.

Then he drops to one knee.

"Um," I say. Because what the fuck is happening right now?

He takes my shaking hand. His palm is damp and his eyes

are so earnest, so vulnerable and open, all I can do is sit here and try not to melt into the floor.

"We're here," he says in that deep voice of his, "because I'm so goddamn in love with you, Larkin Gray."

I suck in a sharp breath. "You are?"

He shrugs, like he's helpless to control his emotions. "Have been for a while, but you were right. I've been all in my head about my past—guilt over not answering your call, anger over my inaction with my father. Every day for the past twelve years, I've existed under all this pressure, believing I let my family down, feeling responsible for their pain. So, I ignored mine. I busted my ass to keep my brothers afloat, and it's all just catching up with me now."

He inhales and lets out a long breath. "I also think I'm scared. Terrified of what I feel for you, of wanting something this good, because I know what it's like to lose everything. And honestly, the thought of getting in deeper, loving you even more and…"

He rubs his chest, like his heart hurts.

I grab both his hands with mine, still shocked Jake is on his knee, peeling back his complicated layers. If he's kneeling for the reason I think he is, I'm about to be a certifiable mess. But I wait patiently, sensing he needs to get his feelings out.

"Hunter's demand to break up with you," he goes on, "gave me an excuse to run away from the pain I've ignored. Away from you and these huge feelings. You were ready to risk everything on me, and I pushed you away. But I don't want to run anymore. I want you, Larkin. I want you forever."

Releasing one of my hands, he pulls my fake engagement ring from his pocket. The one he picked out for me at an antique store—central yellow stone set in a white-gold flower, the sides detailed with tiny leaves and filigree. The perfect ring from the perfect man.

His hand trembles as he holds it out. "Larkin Gray, I love you now and want to love you for the rest of my days. Will you marry me?"

Tears slide down my cheeks, unbidden. The happiest tears I've ever shed. "Are you sure? This feels so fast."

He wipes my cheek with his thumb. "I'm sure, sweetheart. I've lived a stalled life for twelve years and don't want to waste another second without you. Maybe this is fast. Maybe I'm being impulsive, but I can't deny how you make me feel, and how shit I felt without you the past week. I want to live in the moment for a change, and I want to do that with you. But if you want to go slower, I can do slower. If you need space, I'll give you space. I'll do whatever you want. But please don't turn your back on us yet."

"Yes," I say quickly. I don't need to think when my heart is pumping with this much joy. I felt a special connection with Jake twelve years ago. He's earned my trust a million times over since we've come back into each other's lives. "Yes, I'll marry you," I specify and wrap my arms around his neck.

He lifts me up, swings me around, and crushes me to him. He buries his face in my neck, holding me tight. I feel moisture against my skin. *His* happy tears.

"I love you," I whisper.

He hugs me closer. "Say it again."

I laugh. "I love you, Jake Bower, and I can't wait to be your wife."

"Wife," he murmurs, like it's the best word he's ever heard. Slowly he lowers me down his chest. He wipes his eyes and holds the ring back out. "I can get you a new one if you want. This one might be tainted with thoughts of Drew and us faking a relationship, but—"

I snatch the ring from him. "Don't you dare return it. This is mine."

His crooked smile reappears. "Yes, ma'am."

"But tell me again how shit you felt without me the past week and a half."

He sits on the lone chair and pulls me into his lap. He kisses me long and slow, then brushes his nose against mine. "I was a disaster without you, baby. Couldn't sleep. Barely ate. Only left my apartment to work."

"I hate that you were sad."

"No, you don't. You love that I missed you so much I couldn't function."

I nuzzle my head under his chin and kiss his chest. "Maybe a little. I was in rough shape too."

He noses my head, breathes me in. "I'm maybe a bit happy to hear that too. But I never want us to feel that pain again. I also have something else of yours." He adjusts so he can reach into his back pocket and hands me a folded piece of paper.

I frown. "What's this?"

"Something you started and I finished."

"Okay…" I say, completely in the dark. Curiosity piqued, I unfold the crumply page and stutter out a laugh. "Oh my God. Where did you find this?"

My stupid fake-fiancé seduction list.

"You tried to toss it out at the inn, but your wastebasket aim sucked and it landed beside it. Imagine my surprise when I realized you'd been trying to seduce me—telling me that hot fantasy, cutting and coloring your hair, which I fucking love. But you didn't finish the last two points. Figured it was my job to seduce you now, except we won't be doing point six. I have no intention of working you up and leaving you wanting."

"You better not," I say, kissing him while pressing the note to my heart. He certainly fulfilled point seven with flair—*Be vulnerable to earn his trust.* Or, in this case, *hers.* "I won't always be easy," I tell him, offering the same vulnerability. The insecurities I rarely share. "I'm not always good at saying what I feel, and I'm scared I'll fuck this up somehow."

He runs the backs of his knuckles down my cheek. "And I'm scared my feelings of self-loathing will come back, but if they do, I promise to talk to you about it. And I promise to always be patient with you."

We kiss again. And again, sighing as we cuddle in close. "You didn't answer me about this house before," I say, placing our seduction list safely on the floor. "Who owns it?"

"That depends."

I pull back to look at him. "Depends on what?"

"How much you like it." When I raise my eyebrow, he glances around the old room. "I know it's in rough shape, but the property is great and the price is low. It backs onto a forest and a ravine. And the bones are good. I could renovate it, preserve some of the good stuff, like the fireplace and the old brick, and we'd add modern touches. We could design it together, build our dream home, starting with this chair I found at a garage sale and thought you'd love. But only if you like the idea."

"Like it?" I move so I'm straddling him on the chair, all of me wrapped around this sweet man. There's no missing the hard line of his thickening cock. "I love it. I want it for our future, but I have a stipulation. Two, actually."

His grin looks half amused and half horny. "You're blackmailing *me* now?"

I swivel my hips, and his eyelids fall heavy. "I am."

"Hit me with your best shot."

I brush my lips lightly over his and lean back. "We make extra rooms for our future kids."

Emotion blows through his dark eyes. "I'd really like that."

I don't know when my biological clock started ticking. Probably one minute ago, or maybe the day I read Jake's apology letter and realized I'd gotten him all wrong.

He rubs my hip bones with his thumbs. "What's number two on this blackmail list of yours?"

I nip his ear. "You fuck me on this floor right now."

He grunts and plunges a hand into my hair, holding me down as he rocks his pelvis and claims my mouth in a bruising kiss. *Yes, please.* We're a mess of tongues and teeth and desperate noises as we peel off clothes and tumble together, naked, onto the old wood floor.

I'll never tire of how good his skin feels sliding against mine or the perfect roughness of his beard, but I pull back. "Have you been tested?"

His forehead creases, like he's not sure what I'm asking, then I feel his thighs flex against mine. "I've never been with someone bare. But, yeah, I've been tested."

"I've been tested too, and I'm on the pill. We don't have to rush the kids thing. I just really want you inside me with nothing between us, if you're okay not using a condom."

He swallows hard. "More than okay. And ditch the pills if you want. Even thinking about having a baby with you..." His nostrils flare. "I fucking want that, Larkin. I want a family with you. So fucking much."

I kiss him with everything I have, rubbing myself all over him like the desperate woman I am. *Kids. With Jake Bower.* Wonders will never cease.

Impatient now, he rolls to his back and positions me over his jutting erection, looking almost angry in his need. The second I sink down, we both curse. His hands are brands on my hips, his mouth hot and hungry on my sensitive breasts. My heart has never beat so hard, all for the man under me and the future we'll have together. And God, we're so in sync. Our movements are frantic, the wet sounds our bodies making obscene, but he matches my rhythm.

I change my angle, my clit hitting his pelvis *just so.* I gasp. "Your cock is magic."

"Is that why you're marrying me?"

"That, and because you fixed my car door handle."

He chuckles, then tugs me down and kisses me breathless. He grinds me harder against his pubic bone, rubbing me exactly where I need it. "Come on my cock, baby. Milk me dry. Need to watch you fall apart."

A few more rolls of my hips later, light explodes behind my eyes and my pelvis jerks. When Jake's face comes into view, the possessiveness in his expression has more aftershocks shaking me. He grips my hips tighter. Lifts me slightly and thrusts up into me in merciless strokes. The veins on his neck distend, his length growing bigger and harder inside me.

He comes on a shouted "Fuck!" his head tilted back and eyes closed, like he's never felt anything this good.

"Goddamn, woman." Sweat sheens his upper lip and forehead.

I kiss both spots and fall forward onto him. "I can't believe you're going to be my husband."

He squeezes my ass. "If we keep making love like that, I might not make it to that day."

"Death by good sex?"

"Nah," he says, dropping soft kisses all over my face. "Death by being too damn happy."

Epilogue

FOUR MONTHS LATER

Jake

"How about this?" Larkin asks from behind me. I turn to find her pointing at an old record player. She moves the arm, showing that the hinge is loose. "It's not a radio, but it's music-related and playing records is hip again."

"It's perfect, as is your timing. We should get back to the bar."

We gather the last of our garage-sale finds, including the two silk ties in my hand. "To tie you up later," I murmur in her ear, loving the slash of red on her cheeks.

We don't do bondage play often, but I can sense when Larkin needs to lose control for a night and let me lead. Her fantasy come to life.

"I'll consider letting you have your way with me if you do me a favor and grab the reusable bag I left in your truck. We'll need it for some of the smaller stuff." She nibbles her lip as she says this, as though she's unsure or nervous.

"You okay?"

She waves me off. "Absolutely perfect. Couldn't be better. Better than the best."

There's nothing good about a babbling Larkin, but I don't push. Tonight is our first fix-it event to launch our monthly club. We have radio sponsors and have found experts willing to donate their time to promote repairs over trashing and rebuying items. She's worried people won't turn up, even though I have no doubt they will. But I sense more going on with her—she's been acting off for a couple of days. Maybe she's worried about Hunter being there. His social skills haven't exactly been plentiful since he's been out.

I kiss Larkin softly, hope she feels my undying support, then I pass her the ties and jog to the truck for the bag as requested.

When I return, she still seems distracted. We pay for our finds, load up the truck, and head for the Barrel. She's quiet on the drive. Her attention stays on her window as she bounces her knee and smooths her hand down the front of her long-sleeve blouse repeatedly.

"Hunter will be fine," I say as I park in the lot.

"I know," she says quietly, but she presses her hand to her stomach like she feels ill.

"If anyone is unkind to him in any way, I'll show them the door."

She nods, and I hate how distracted she seems. I've only had to play bouncer once since Hunter's release. Tired of hiding her history, Larkin told a few townsfolk that she's Hunter's sister, and who their father is, knowing word would spread. She finally stood up for her brother, explaining that he'd hit Derek to save her. She braced herself for disbelief and a decline in business.

What she got was support.

People told her they were impressed with how she'd

overcome her past. She was invited to an ongoing support group for abused women. Windfall pulled around her and proved this town understood that kids aren't responsible for their parents' mistakes.

But when loudmouth Candace Sinclair sat near me at the Barrel and told her friends Jolene should fire Larkin before she follows in her father's footsteps and starts selling drugs through the bar, I walked over and said, "We don't abide slander in this establishment. If you can't speak nicely of the owners, you'll need to find another place to hang out."

She huffed and stormed out. No one has been openly rude since.

Larkin rolls her head toward me. Her hair is longer than when she chopped it to seduce me, but she's kept it dark, making her eyes pop. Right now, they look bright with unshed emotion. "I love you so much," she whispers.

Worried now, I palm her cheeks. "Something else is going on here, sweetheart. What's upsetting you?"

"I just need a minute in the truck on my own, if that's okay."

No part of me is okay leaving Larkin when she's struggling emotionally, but I nod. "I'll be inside. Text if you need me." I search her face, trying to read her mind. "I love you more every fucking day. You know that, right?"

"I do." She gives me a watery smile that has me second-guessing my easy agreement to leave her alone.

Larkin isn't always great at speaking up when she's upset. She's used to keeping her feelings under wraps, but we both see therapists now. I'm learning to accept the choices I made when I was younger, and my nightmares have stopped. I also have better emotional tools. I've learned to give Larkin time when she gets quiet. Just enough so she doesn't overthink her worries to a damaging point.

Eventually, I prod and she explains what's troubling her— worry over Hunter reintegrating into society, concern over a staffing issue at the bar, a silly disagreement with me over our renovation plans.

I love those moments the most, I think. Larkin sitting with me on our couch, unburdening herself. Both of us talking openly with each other, ready to listen and support, or compromise if the situation calls for it.

The past couple of days, though, she's been particularly quiet. Whatever she's struggling with feels big.

Doing as I promised, I force myself into the Barrel and take a deep breath. Hunter is talking with the host broadcasting the event, nodding and pointing to the radio he fixed for us. They're getting ready for his interview, likely. I watch him a moment, glad he seems relaxed. He doesn't smile easily and is a bit paranoid at times, like he has to watch his back, but he's been showing progress too, even talking about going back to school.

I glance back at the door, wondering again what has Larkin acting off. I come up blank. Leaving her to her thoughts might have been a bad call. She might need a pep talk, or something else is upsetting her that she hasn't mentioned, a possibility I don't like one bit.

We've been so solid together since we got married last month. An impromptu event with our families at Lennon's farm. Happiest fucking day of my life. And we've been amazing since then—intimate candlelight dinners at home, picnic dates lying in the grass, popcorn movie nights, annoying evenings where my brothers insist on family gatherings and I have to deal with them telling Larkin embarrassing stories about me.

Could I have done something to upset her since then?

"What's up with you?" Hunter is standing near me, frowning. "And where's Larkin?"

I scratch the side of my neck, fighting the urge to race back to her. "She's in the truck. Needed a moment to herself."

His face darkens. "Because you pissed her off and now she's upset?"

To say Hunter has been slow to come around to me is a bit of an understatement. In front of Larkin, he's cordial and nice enough. Alone, he has me on a tight leash.

The first night we had him over, he took me aside and said, "I appreciate what you did for me, but you haven't earned my trust yet. Fuck with Larkin, and you fuck with me."

He doesn't have to threaten me to make sure I treat Larkin right. She's the most important thing in my life, and she's keeping something from me. "We didn't fight. She's been off for a couple days. Withdrawn and quiet. I usually give her space, but I don't know. This feels different."

The grooves on his brow deepen. "I'll speak with her." He takes a step toward the door but swivels back. "This fix-it thing wasn't a bad idea."

He struts away, and I allow myself a small grin. Maybe Hunter won't hate me one day...unless I actually *did* do something to upset Larkin and am too dense to even know what it was.

———

Larkin

I run my fingers over the extra purchase I made at the garage sale, unsure why I'm so addled. I should have told Jake what I was buying. I mean, I bought it for *him*—my surprise to tell him our lives are about to change. All I can manage to do is to stare out the windshield.

A knock on my window makes me jump. I turn, and Hunter is there, looking like a thundercloud.

Sighing, I gesture to the driver's side and wait for him to get in.

"Whatever he did," he says, his voice low and menacing, "I

will make him pay, starting by shaving off his eyebrows while he sleeps."

I shouldn't laugh. Hunter's overprotectiveness is totally overboard, but it's kind of entertaining watching Jake squirm. And I don't hate having family love me this much.

Instead of saying anything, I take the baby rattle from my garage-sale bag and hold it out to Hunter.

"Why do you have... Oh," he says, his eyes growing wide. He takes the rattle, looking nervous to hold it. "Are you?" He juts his chin to my stomach.

I bite my lip and nod. "Took the test two days ago."

"And you haven't told Jake?"

"I don't know why." I press my hand to my belly. I can't feel the baby, but I feel completely different. Totally freaked out, when this is exactly what I wanted. "Why am I so scared?" I whisper.

"Are you worried Jake won't be happy?"

I shake my head. "He's all over the idea of having a family. He'll be absolutely thrilled."

Hunter shakes the rattle and stares at the used toy a moment, a small smile tilting his lips, then he passes it back to me. "I need to head inside. We'll talk later."

Abruptly, he leaves the truck.

If anyone else blew me off after the news I just shared, I'd be upset. But Hunter's been different since returning home. Big emotion seems to freeze him at times. He doesn't speak as much. He's slow to show he cares, but that small smile told me all I need to know about how he feels. He'll be a great uncle.

My car door is suddenly yanked open, and Jake is there, his worried eyes darting over me. "What's wrong?"

I shove the rattle under my thigh. "Nothing."

He does another thorough check of my face. "Hunter came storming into the bar and told me you needed to see me, looking like he wanted to punch my face."

"He always looks like he wants to punch your face."

"This glare was extra vicious. Sweetheart..." He cups the edges of my jaw and tilts up my face. "I'm getting really worried here. Did I do something wrong?"

"No!" I clutch his wrists and shake my head. "You do everything right."

"Then what has you acting so distant? Talk to me."

Unsure why I'm falling apart over amazing news, I wiggle from his grip and retrieve the rattle. Slowly, I hold it out to him.

He blinks at the toy, then tilts his head. I see it the second realization hits—the faster expansion of his broad chest, the sheen glossing his warm eyes. "Does this mean what I think it means?"

I nod. "You're gonna be a dad."

"Jesus Christ." He pulls me from the truck and hugs me so hard it's tough to breathe. Then he's kissing me, deep and thorough, while holding me protectively against him. "We're gonna have a baby," he says with his lips against my temple, sounding awed.

"We are."

He pulls back just enough to force eye contact. "But you've been distant the past couple of days. I assume that's how long you've known." His next swallow is a slow drag. "Are you not happy about this?"

"No, no." I kiss him softly. "I'm thrilled. The second I found out, I nearly ran to your worksite to tell you, but then...I don't know. I think I got really scared."

"About what?"

"I don't know," I say again, pressing my face into his chest.

He breathes more evenly and runs his hand soothingly down my back. "You'll be a great mother," he says quietly. "We won't repeat our parents' mistakes. We aren't them. We're stronger together. We'll give this child all the love and support they need to succeed in life."

This is why I love Jake so much. Sometimes, he understands me better than I understand myself. "How can you be so sure?"

"Because." He kisses the top of my head, then my temple, then my wet eyes, my cheeks, my lips. "We're unstoppable together. We make each other better, and we know how shit a parent can be. We *know*, and we'll work our asses off to do better."

"Okay," I say, feeling more excited than nervous now. "We're having a baby," I add, like I didn't already ruin the big reveal.

His grin melts my heart. "We're having a baby."

He kisses me again, a little filthier this time, and my body lights up. We share a moan as I grab his narrow hips, trying to figure out how quickly we can get to my office and get naked.

A teasing whistle pierces the air.

"Last I checked, this is a family-friendly event," someone calls. The chiding comment sounded like E.

Staying tucked into Jake's side, I face his brother. Make that *brothers* plural. His whole family is making their way over, including the women in their lives. "What are you all doing here?" I ask.

"Better question," Lennon says. "Why was Jake attempting to remove your tonsils with his tongue in plain view of an inappropriate audience?" He gestures to Desmond and Sadie's son, Max.

Max rolls his eyes. "Dad kisses Mom like that all the time."

Des shrugs. "Guilty as charged."

Sadie laughs, her cheeks pink. "We get excited to see each other when I've been away for a while."

Des grunts and wraps his arm around his fiancée. They had to delay their wedding due to Sadie's travel schedule working for the art gallery in Arizona, but they don't seem to mind. Saying their vows won't change how madly they love each other.

Delilah is standing awkwardly, holding a large board of some kind behind her back. She angles it away from us and smiles. "We came to help you set up for your fix-it event, but my obnoxious boyfriend couldn't resist coming over here to heckle you first."

E scoffs. "I'm not obnoxious, babe. Lennon's the obnoxious one. I'm the funny one."

Lennon flips him the finger. "You're the uncoordinated one."

Maggie steps between them with her hands on her hips. "If you want to fight it out, I'll set up a Jell-O wrestling ring in the town square and charge admittance. Actually…" Her green eyes glint with mischief. "That could be a great town event—shirtless Bowers would bring in a *huge* crowd."

"No damn way." Cal shakes his head and crosses his arms. "I do not remove my clothes for any reason in this town. Goddamn stripping rumors," he mumbles.

Jolene laughs. "He still has PTSD from the time they thought he was having a threesome with—"

"Enough from you," Cal says, playfully covering her mouth with his hand.

She punches lightly at him, as everyone gets in on the jokes. Everyone but Jake and me. We lock eyes, and I give him a nod, knowing what he's silently asking.

Puffing up his chest like a man who has conquered Rome, he says loudly, "Larkin and I are having a baby."

His family freezes. Just a moment, before bedlam ensues— whoops, hugs, a few *oh my God*s from the women, and huge smiles all around.

"So damn happy for you," Callahan says, pulling me into my fourth Bower hug. These men are good huggers. "Thanks for making my brother the happiest he's ever been."

"Not a hardship."

Jolene wiggles her way between us and takes over hugging duty. "I'm gonna be the best aunt and spoil your kid rotten."

"I'm counting on it. And you'll be on speed dial for when I'm freaking out and worried I'm doing everything wrong."

"I'm counting on *that*."

I spot Hunter by the doors, watching our little celebration from a safe distance. He catches my eye and presses his hand over his heart. I smile at him. He smiles back, and the stress of the past two days evaporates.

Our child won't just have Jake and me. Our baby will have this whole family and Hunter. My younger brother will visit from New York. An entire team of support, who will rally if we ever need them.

"To celebrate this momentous news," Delilah announces, looking a bit red-faced, like she's holding in a laugh, "E and I have something we'd like to donate to the bar."

I squint at them. "You just heard this news a second ago."

"We brought the gift to kick off the fix-it club, but it's more of a general celebration token. A way to entertain customers who frequent your fine establishment." She shares an amused glance with E.

With a shit-eating grin that makes me uneasy, E nods to her. Slowly, she flips the sign around for us to read.

If you call Lennon Bower a hipster,
you get entered into our
"free beer every day for a month" contest.

We all crack up.

Except Lennon, who's glaring at E and Delilah. "You fucking assholes," he mutters and lunges for the sign.

Jake grabs it from Delilah and holds it away from Lennon. "Best gift you could've gotten me," he tells Delilah on a laugh.

Cal gives E a thumbs-up. "I'll donate to the beer fund."

Even Desmond is grinning. "I'll send notices around town and pack the place."

Lennon growls and reaches for the sign again, but Jake passes it to Cal, who passes it to Desmond, who flicks his middle finger at Lennon, and I have to clutch my stomach I'm laughing so hard.

Yep, our kid will have the best family in the world.

———

Thank you for reading Jake and Larkin's story!
I hope you loved your time with them and all the Bower boys as much as me.

If you want to revisit the quaint town of Windfall, make sure you check out the prequel to this series: *This Can't Be Goodbye*.

———

And if you're already missing the Bower boys, don't fret. You're cordially invited to Desmond and Sadie's wedding! To attend, join my newsletter and you'll receive all my bonus content.

Also by Kelly Siskind

Bower Boys Series:

This Can't Be Goodbye

50 Ways to Win Back Your Lover

10 Signs You Need to Grovel

6 Clues Your Nemesis Loves You

4 Hints You Love Your Best Friend

7 Steps to Seducing Your Fake Fiancé

One Wild Wish Series:

He's Going Down

Off-Limits Crush

36 Hour Date

Showmen Series:

New Orleans Rush

Don't Go Stealing My Heart

The Beat Match

The Knockout Rule

Over the Top Series:

My Perfect Mistake, A Fine Mess, Hooked on Trouble

Stand-Alone: Chasing Crazy

Visit Kelly's website and join her newsletter for great giveaways and never miss an update! www.kellysiskind.com

About the Author

Kelly Siskind lives in charming northern Ontario. When she's not out hiking or skiing, you can find her, notepad in hand, scribbling down one of the many plot bunnies bouncing around in her head. She loves singing while driving, looks awful in yellow, and is known for spilling wine at parties.

For giveaways, free bonus scenes, and early peeks at new work, join Kelly's newsletter: www.kellysiskind.com

If you like to laugh and chat about books, join Kelly in her Facebook group, KELLY'S GANG.

And connect with her on X and Instagram (@kellysiskind) or on Facebook and TikTok (@authorkellysiskind).

Printed in the USA
CPSIA information can be obtained
at www.ICGtesting.com
LVHW051508080224
771185LV00052B/1286